An April To Remember

by

Lauri Robinson

An April To Remember

Contact Information: info@thewildrosepress.com

Cover Art by *Nicola Martinez*

The Wild Rose Press
PO Box 708
Adams Basin, NY 14410-0706
Visit us at www.thewildrosepress.com

Publishing History
First American Rose Edition, 2008
Print ISBN: 1-60154-456-1

Published in the United States of America

Dedication

This book is dedicated to my three sons:
Justin-for your guidance
Dallas-for your inspiration
Cody-for your zeal
May you never change!
Love,
Mom

April 1865
New Orleans, Louisiana

Chapter One

April Simonson was madder than a wet hornet in a jar. Twin tails of the pink, silk ribbon stitched to the wide-brimmed, flower-trimmed hat, slapped the back of her neck as she stepped onto the brick street. Teeth clinched, she crossed the busy road. The heels of her new, brown boots echoed a steady beat, drowning some of the nearby shouts and squeals.

She tugged the hat low on her forehead. For once the appalling filth and stench of the lower New Orleans streets didn't overwhelm her senses. She ignored the sweltering humidity, sour smells, and crowded boardwalks. But the woeful stares made her flinch. They had tugged at her soul since arriving in the port city seven days ago.

Sprinkled amongst the hustle and bustle, tiny orphan eyes, filled with fear and hunger, and wicked-looking older ones, dark with anger and deprivation, stared about. The little ones hit the hardest. They brought back memories. Hunger and loneliness had a way of lingering over the years.

Chin up, April avoided the eyes and made a beeline for the building in the center of the block. She bit her lower lip. When she got her hands on that no good scoundrel she'd skin him alive. As long as breath filled her lungs, she wouldn't permit her niece to become the victim of a man's obsession.

Children should be loved and protected, not abused and forgotten.

She straightened her shoulders, and after one last hat check, proceeded onto the boardwalk in front of the Golden Girl. Without a pause in stride, she pushed the doublewide, swinging doors open and strode into the tavern.

The stench of stale cigars and whiskey filled the air. She blocked the smell with three fingers, took a deep breath, and scanned the sinister area. Squinting didn't help. Outlandish gold paint covered the walls, ceiling, and every piece of wood, and did little to lighten the area.

Blinking away the darkness, she focused on the saloon's occupants. Her gaze touched on twenty or so sets of eyes—none familiar. But, in the far corner, blond hair curled over the high collar of a stylish, brown, suit coat. Grasping the yards of white seersucker material flowing from her waist, she hitched her skirt and held it out of the way of grungy looking men, tables that desperately needed to be wiped, and rickety built chairs.

His back was to her. Disguising her nervousness, she let the sweet element of surprise twist the corners of her mouth into a wicked smile.

The rest of the table's occupants were a blur as she clasped the collar of the evening jacket. Her fingernails scrapped skin. She dug deeper, giving the fabric a hard yank.

"What do you think you're doing?"

Willie dropped the cards to claw at his throat. She gave the collar another jerk. His hat toppled to the floor as he turned to gape at his attacker. His face flashed fear before recognition.

"Get up!" Right now she'd give her last hat for a willow switch.

Willie slipped his fingers inside his collar and gulped for air. The beet red glow on his face returned to a pale pink as his body relaxed beneath her fingers.

With her free hand, she grabbed a handful of light-colored hair and pulled. "Now!"

Wooden chair legs scraped against the floor as he rose. His gaze flashed between her and the haphazard pile of money lying on the table.

"I'm winning," he whispered.

"I don't care!" Luckily he was only a few inches taller than her five and a quarter foot height, or she wouldn't have been able to give his hair another sharp tug.

"We do," a deep voice growled from the table. Gray smoke swirled around the red-tipped cigar stub sticking out from yellow teeth. Between the smoke and the folded brim of his hat, she couldn't see the gambler's face but felt a menacing stare.

"This game is over." April glared from the man with the shadowed eyes to the rest of the gamblers around the table. "Gentlemen." She spoke the last word with disgust. No gambler could ever be called a gentleman. Their father had proven that, before he'd gambled away his own life and left them destitute.

The muscles in her neck tightened. Like a bee to pollen her gaze bounced back to the man directly across the table. His flawless appearance and attire was inconsistent with the other occupants of the tavern. Her cheeks tingled as one brow lifted into a perfect arch, and a glint of humor crossed his clean-shaven face.

April pulled her gaze from the neatly dressed man as the one with the cigar spoke again, "Come on now, honey, he's got a lot of our money. We need a chance to win it back."

"If you haven't won it back in the past eighteen hours, that's your problem, not mine." She glanced at Willie and tipped her head to the table. "Pick it up."

Her brother gathered the bills and coins with both hands. After stuffing the money into his hip pockets, he stretched an arm to the floor to pick up his hat.

April eased the grasp on his hair a touch, allowing him to gather the headwear.

With a broad smile and a bad impression of a southern accent, Willie said, "Gentlemen, please excuse me, it is time for me to leave. But I will return this evening, and look forward to playing with you again."

She gave his hair another hard yank, a few roots let go beneath her palm. "No, you won't." She forced his body to turn, and using both her hold on his collar and the solid clutch of hair, pushed him to the door.

She blinked against the bright sunlight as the dimness of the saloon was left behind. A shiver trickled down her spine, bravado slipping away. April exhaled and let go of Willie's hair. She released the collar of his evening jacket and thumped the back of his head.

"Hey!" He rubbed the spot then planted his hat over the curls.

Clammy sweat tickled the back of her neck. She dug her fingernails into his jacket sleeve and tugged him into the busy street. They weaved to and fro, around and between the odd assortment of wagons, coaches, and horses. Once safely on the opposite boardwalk, she set a quick pace, leading the way to their hotel.

"That wasn't necessary," Willie grumbled.

April grimaced. "Yes, it was. We are scheduled to board the steamer at noon. It's almost ten now."

Willie rubbed a hand over his mouth. "Well, about that, Sis. I've been thinking, maybe you and Suzie should go on ahead without me."

She stopped and thrust her hands onto her hips.

"Don't! Don't say another word. I'm so mad at you right now—your suggestion almost sounds good."

Willie opened his mouth.

"Don't say another word!" One finger shook as it pointed toward the hotel. "Go!"

He lowered his head and with sluggish footsteps started walking.

April took a deep breath and counted to ten before following. Guilt at the way she treated her younger brother made her throat burn. If only he would learn. Grow up and act his age. Accept his responsibilities. Become the man she knew he could be. Couldn't he remember how bad it had been? Did he really want that for his daughter?

She rubbed her temples. Now wasn't the time for a walk down memory lane. A lump formed in her throat. For her and Willie it had been nightmare lane.

They strolled past several businesses. An assortment of citizens meandered in and out. All ages and sizes, as different as night and day, blended together like ingredients in a pot of stew. A man stumbled. April paused while he retrieved something from the ground. The building he'd exited was a large, lavish one, covered with decorative sculptures, brass, and huge panes of glass. Gold letters neatly painted *Union National Bank* across the door.

"Willie," she said.

He kept walking.

"Willie!"

He turned and gave a 'what now?' look.

She held out a hand. "Give me the money you won."

"What?" His hands shot to his pockets. "Why?"

"We have to exchange those southern bills." She stepped closer and whispered, "The war is over. By the time we get home, they won't be worth the paper they're printed on."

"What?" Willie shook his head. "A dollar's a dollar no matter where we are."

"Believe me I know what I'm talking about." She pulled him toward the brick wall of the bank building. "Others talked about it when word of Lee's surrender hit the steamer on my way down here. Now that President Lincoln has been shot, who knows what's going to happen to this country." She held out her hand. "Give me the bills. I'll exchange them for gold."

"Sis." Willie rolled his eyes. "Just because Lincoln died doesn't mean our money isn't any good. I think you've been living around those northern sympathizers too long."

"Oh, you damn men are all alike." The heel of her left boot smacked the ground. She wanted to box his ears again, but the street held too many onlookers.

"April, watch your mouth," Willie whispered with a huff.

"Just give me the money." She wiggled her fingers. "Now."

Willie shook his head. "No, I might need it."

"Your *daughter* needs it. Have you forgotten that?"

With a long sigh, he dug into his pockets and began to hand over wadded bills.

April straightened each curled piece of paper, sorting them by denominations. A large portion was shinplasters, the paper coins Congress designed and issued due to the lack of metal for coins. The shinplasters or fractional currency was backed by the government and would hold its worth. Whereas the currency the Confederacy had issued was backed by cotton, their gamble on winning the war. The highly colorful bills of the South would soon have little value.

She glanced at her brother and decided not to mention the insightful knowledge all the years working at the bank for Mr. Green had provided.

Willie handed her the last bill. "Thank you." She neatly stuffed them into her satchel. "Stay here, I'll be right back." April turned to enter the glass doors, over her shoulder she added, "I'll be watching out the window."

He rolled his eyes then leaned back against the building.

Moments later, extremely satisfied, April exited the bank and waved an invitation for Willie to join her stroll to the hotel. The banker fell under feminine charm and eagerly gave her the full amount for each and every bill. The lace-trimmed satchel she clutched with both hands was packed full.

"I'll be needing that back," Willie said as his steps fell in line with hers.

"I'll give you what I think you need, when I think you need it."

"Sis—"

"Willie, that's enough!" She took a deep breath. "I suspect you've squandered an adequate amount of money the last four years."

Willie's mouth opened and closed like a fish out of water. She glared at him. His lips slapped shut, and he turned to walk up the boardwalk.

They continued on in silence. April pressed a hand to her stomach where the sinking feeling of regret rolled. The two of them had always been close. She'd missed him so much the past few years, but having to pull him away from a gambling table had sorely frazzled her nerves.

His gaze never wandered her way as he held the elaborate lobby door of the downtown hotel open, nor as he stomped up the wide staircase to the second floor.

She hitched her skirt out of the way of her boots and followed. He had no idea how worried she'd been, waiting up for him all night.

"You can pay the chamber maid I hired to watch Suzie with the bills you have in your breast pocket," she said when they reached the top.

The creak of a door drew both of their gazes to the end of the hall before Willie had a chance to answer. His three-year-old daughter poked her head out and let out a squeal, "Daddy!"

The door flew wide open. Suzie's little legs leaped forward and scrambled across the carpet. Curls of blond hair bobbed, fluttering around a face glowing with happiness. Sparkling, blue taffeta flailed in her wake.

April's heart lurched as the little bundle of sweetness leaped into Willie's wide-spread arms.

"There's my baby girl." His hands wrapped around Suzie's waist. He lifted her high in the air then covered her rosy cheeks with kisses.

Suzie's giggles grew louder. April pressed the heel of her hand against the sting in her eye. When would Willie realize he already had more than any amount of gambling could give him?

An hour later, a bellboy, dressed in a bright red uniform with corded gold fringes hanging off his thin shoulders, stowed their luggage onto the back of a coach. The fancy rig would take them to the dock where they'd board the *Sultana* and start their voyage home. April smiled her thanks as the boy aided her climb into the carriage. She sat down on the plush leather and let out a sigh, ready and anxious to leave the war-torn south behind.

****

Jerek Brinkley leaned against the stone wall and withdrew a match from his pocket to swipe over the bricks. He touched the flame to the end of his cigarillo and puffed until the tip glowed. With a flip of his wrist, he extinguished the blaze and let the spent match tumble to the ground as a trio excited the hotel.

The man, woman, and little girl paraded into the waiting coach. He almost felt sorry for Willie Simonson. It appeared the older sister was well on her way to reforming the lad. Poor sap, he had the makings of a good gambler.

Harnesses creaked and wheels groaned as the shod horses clip-clopped the rented livery into traffic. Jerek eased from the wall and strolled over to an awestruck bellboy.

"Pretty lady." He took a long draw on his smoke.

"Huh? Oh yes." The boy, who looked no more than fifteen or so, let out a long sigh. "That she is, Mr. Brinkley."

"Miss Simonson wasn't it?" Jerek asked.

"Yeah, Miss April. Did ya know her?" The bellhop's gaze never wavered from the matching team and carriage rolling away.

"No, I can't say I did." Jerek threw the half-smoked cigarillo on the ground then crushed it with his boot. Why hadn't he noticed her at the hotel? Had he become so used to the environment he no longer noticed new faces? Naw, she must be a recent arrival to New Orleans. A woman that exquisite, he would have noticed. Lucky for him, it wasn't too late.

"I'm gonna miss her." The boy sighed again as the vehicle turned onto a side street then disappeared.

"You say that like she's not coming back." Jerek glanced toward the corner that had swallowed the carriage. Front Street twisted its way around tall stone buildings and smaller wooden structures before it ended at the waterfront.

"She's not." The bellboy turned to walk back into the hotel.

Jerek grasped a thin arm. "Where's she going?"

"They're heading home, back to Minnesota." The boy shook his head and sighed again. "Boarding the *Sultana* at noon."

"They are?"

"Yup."

Jerek lifted the watch fob to draw the timepiece from his pocket. After snapping the lid closed he withdrew several bills from his breast pocket and flashed them before the boy's glassy eyes. "Would you have my luggage sent to the *Sultana*? And settle my room charges. Keep the rest for your trouble."

"Yes, Mr. Brinkley, thank you!"

A backward wave while walking down the street acknowledged the boy's reply. It was time to move on—had been a while since he'd been up the river. Some riverboat gambling sounded fun. He might even stop by a few old stomping grounds.

Besides, the South was in real turmoil. Lee's surrender at Appomattox earlier this month had caused quite a stir, and yesterday, the news that President Lincoln had been shot five days later hit New Orleans like an out of control wildfire. It was too soon to know if the event would send the whole country into upheaval and reignite the war. Might be interesting, and safer, to see how the Union States reacted to it all.

Getting to know Miss April Simonson would be an added bonus. The vision of how she flew into the gambling house this morning brought a smile to his face. Her large, pristine-white hat, covered with pink flowers, bows, and feathers, had caught most everyone's attention. Those who didn't notice the hat certainly noticed the woman wearing it. The white gown, decorated with a belt of pink flowers around a tiny waist made her look like a runaway bride in search of her bridegroom.

Jerek sighed. Every detail lingered in that area just behind his eyelids. The bodice of the dress fit her like a glove. Tiny buttons, adorned with flower petals, made a delightful row up her torso, and pulled the material over firm, full breasts. The low neckline allowed just enough cleavage to draw a man's attention, and the trim line of her neck beckoned a man's lips to have a taste. Her petal mouth, even though it held a frown during most of her visit, was pert, and those rosy lips begged to be kissed. A button nose sat in the middle of high cheekbones, cradling eyes as blue as the Louisiana sky. Long, straight cut bangs, the color of wheat in July, stuck out from beneath the hat to catch on the upward curls of darker tipped lashes.

He'd never been so drawn to a face. Interested in seeing it again, he'd excused himself from the table as she pushed poor Willie out of the Golden Girl.

April Simonson had been madder than a wet hen. The whack she'd given Willie on the street curb made it clear. She'd probably be even madder if she knew how easily Jerek had persuaded her brother to explain who she was after she slipped into the bank, and he, very nonchalantly, approached Willie Simonson.

With a nervous twitch in his cheek, Willie had explained she was his older sister, and another question or two clarified her bank mission. Jerek, extremely thankful she wasn't the other man's wife, had slipped into the crowd before she exited the building.

Encouraged by the information Willie provided and enticed by the woman's knowledge, Jerek copied her activities. Now gold coins and Union bills filled his pockets. Besides being remarkably pleasant to look at, April Simonson appeared to be a very smart woman.

The hustle and bustle of the wharf grew thick as his jaunt continued. Brick buildings gave way to large, wooden warehouses and the smell of dead fish, dirty water, and rotten cargo intensified. The buzz of insects filled his ears, and the air grew heavier with moisture. People of every shape, size, age, color, and sex mingled about, some selling wares, others begging. A loud hiss floated above the other sounds as one of the many steamers moored along the shore released pressure from her boilers.

Jerek waited for a carriage to roll by before he crossed the street and noticed his carpetbag balanced in the luggage rack. When the wagon stopped, he claimed the bag, tipped the driver, and then made his way over to the floating dock beside one of the long steamers. Bright red letters flashed the name *Sultana* across her wide side wheel. The large rudders stood motionless as crew carried cargo up the thick planks.

The river was high. Muddy water churned mere inches beneath massive dock pilings and slapped the side of the boat. Jerek stepped onto the solid plank and examined the white paint covering the rest of the ship. Small, dark spaces showed where weather and wear had flecked it off the rails. He lifted his gaze to the upper decks.

Like a king overseeing his kingdom, Captain James Cass Mason stood at the bow on the main deck. Rays of sunshine glistened off the brass buttons of the navy blue jacket decorating his tall, lean frame. Jerek closed one eye against the glitter and waved.

The captain squinted then smiled and raised a hand in recognition.

Ah, yes, it's good to have friends in high places. Satisfaction lightened his steps and with a smile tugging at his lips, Jerek tightened his hold on the luggage bag swinging to and fro near his knee.

The boat was fairly new, no more than a couple of years old, but she'd been well used. One of the regulars that made runs from St. Louis to New

Orleans and back again, hauling cargo—namely sugar and cattle—as well as Army personnel up and down the Mississippi River. The *Sultana* was a solid, big boat with a crew of eighty or so, and one Jerek had traveled on before. Her maiden voyage brought him to New Orleans, and J.C., the captain and part owner, was a good, knowledgeable river man.

Passengers mingled about the decks above, families, river men, and a few smartly dressed gamblers. A bouquet of pink petals, sprouting a long ostrich feather, caught his eye on the hurricane deck. Whistling a tune, Jerek hopped off the dock and onto the planked ramp. It was going to be a good trip, a mighty good trip.

The ship appeared to have plenty of open passenger space, and even if she didn't, he had a silver tongue. There was no reason to worry about securing his last minute passage. What he needed to know was which cabin April Simonson had booked. A neighboring one would be ideal. Jerek pushed back his shoulders. He wouldn't settle for less.

Captain J.C. Mason met him as his feet topped the landing. "Jerek, it's good to see you."

Jerek took the proffered hand in a firm shake. "J.C., how have you been?"

"Busy, these are some busy times. You joining us for the trip north?" J.C. glanced to the carpetbag.

"Yes, thought I'd head up river for a bit. See how things are settling there." Jerek nodded to several smartly-dressed soldiers walking past.

The Captain maneuvered a path to a more secluded space. "Unbelievable isn't it? Lee surrendering? Never thought that would happen."

"Nor the shooting of the President. Last I heard they still haven't found the guy." Jerek rocked on his heals.

J.C. shook his head, and then asked, "Where are you headed?"

"North." Jerek shrugged. "Not really sure." He set his bag on the floor. "Can I see what cabins are still available?"

Captain Mason nodded and waved for the first mate to join them. Shorter and wider than the Captain, Bill Rowberry flashed a welcoming smile. Jerek shook his hand, "Hi, Bill."

"Brinkley, haven't seen you for awhile. You joining us this trip?" His gaze floated to the passenger roster in his hand.

"Hoping you have space for one more," Jerek said with a light chuckle.

Bill shot a quizzical look to Mason. The captain gave a slight nod.

Jerek lifted an eyebrow, but didn't comment on the exchange. "Can I see what's still available?"

Bill ran a hand over the ledger list. "We normally don't show others our passenger assignments."

"I know, and I usually wouldn't ask, was just wondering what's open. Thought a quick glance would be easier than you reading it all aloud." Jerek, feigning indifference, pulled a box of the best cigarillos this side of New York from his pocket then offered the contents to the other two.

Each man took one. The first mate handed the list to Jerek while withdrawing a small box from his pocket. Bill struck a match on his pant leg, lit Captain Mason's cigarillo, then ignited his own.

Jerek scanned the cabin listing. W. Simonson was neatly penned beside eleven and twelve. "I'll take cabin number ten." He handed the booklet back.

Rowberry glanced at the list. "Sorry, that one's already reserved."

Jerek nodded. "But have they boarded yet?"

"Not yet." Bill shook his head.

"Then assign them to a different cabin. I'll pay

extra. I want to be as far away from those hissing boilers as possible." Jerek slipped a hand into his pocket. "They tend to keep me awake at night." He handed the first mate several bills.

The man once again looked for approval from his supervisor. With a slight nod it was given. Jerek held his sigh of relief.

"I'll have some boxed meals sent down to your cabin as well," Bill said as he counted the money.

"That won't be necessary, I'll eat in the galley," Jerek answered.

Mason cleared his throat. "We won't be serving much out of the galley, Jerek. We'll be picking up several passengers at our stop in Vicksburg and won't be able to accommodate all of them with full galley meals. In preparation, we made cabin boxed meals available for those who care to purchase them."

Jerek rubbed his chin. "How many passengers you plan on picking up?"

With a wave, J.C. dismissed his first mate and turned to walk toward the high rail of the main deck.

Jerek followed.

"I wouldn't tell this to many." The captain braced both hands on the wood.

His gaze was reminiscent of the awestruck bell boy's. Jerek rested a hand on one of the tall pillars supporting the rail and waited for J.C. to say more.

"The war has been tough on all of us, Jerek, me included. I'm finding myself in dire straights." His chin lowered then glided back and forth like a dog-tired horse. "Everything depends on a successful trip this round. You may have heard the Army is shelling out five dollars a head, ten for officers, to any steamer hauling paroled prisoners home. I plan on picking up several in Vicksburg. When I drop them off in Cairo, well, as I said, I'll get five bucks a head."

Jerek hadn't heard, but wasn't surprised. He slipped one hand into his pocket and fidgeted with a few coins. "How much of a kick back do you have to pay?"

Captain Mason's cheeks puffed as he let out a long breath. "A dollar fifteen a head, or two thirty, accordingly."

Jerek let out a low whistle. "Pretty steep kick back."

"Yeah, but I've been promised a full load."

"What's a full load?"

"A few hundred or so."

A rumble of apprehension rolled across Jerek's stomach. He arched his spine. "You're comfortable with this idea?"

Mason ran his hand along the painted railing. "Yeah, got a good ship here, she's in top shape." He patted the wood. "And I got a good crew banking her."

Jerek laid a hand on the rail. The boat was solid and could carry a large load. The tinkle of a woman's laughter filtered down, drawing his gaze to the deck above. With a boat full of soldiers, Miss April Simpson might need a tall, dark stranger to come to her rescue. "All right then," he slapped the Captain on the back, "let's stoke the fires and pull the lines."

Chapter Two

The wind on the hurricane deck was strong enough to uproot April's hat. She wasn't willing to take that chance and tugged on Willie's arm. "Let's go have a look around the main deck."

He scooped his daughter into his arms and winked at April before he took her elbow. She returned his knowing smile, glad they'd left their dispute at the hotel.

Several men carrying a large, wooden crate with a couple of long poles blocked their passage. The crate swayed and joggled as the men struggled to maneuver it. They twisted and shifted positions while lugging the jostling structure up the stairs.

As the crate cleared the landing, April gasped. "Good Lord! There's a beast in there!"

A crewman gave her a wide smile. "It's not a beast, Ma'am, it's a gator. He's our mascot."

A long snout and huge teeth snapped at the wooden slates. Grey-green hide filled the entire box. "Land sakes, he must be ten feet long! You can't have him on this boat!" she insisted.

"Why not?" the man asked.

Goosebumps popped on her arms. "Well, b-because it's not safe."

The man let out a chuckle. "Don't worry, honey, he's not going anywhere."

April folded her arms across her chest and glared at the sailor.

The alligator whipped about. A lump covered tail slipped out between two slats, and a large hiss came from the other end of the cage. The men struggled to hold onto the long poles stretching through the wooden bars as the crate began to jostle again.

Wood creaked and moaned. She scurried past the men to the steps. "We'll see what the captain has to say about this."

"Sis...Sis!" Willie caught up with her. "Don't go making a fuss now. It's safely caged and won't bother anyone."

The sailor above laughed. "Tell the captain he's a man-eater."

She jutted out her chin and continued to stomp down the stairs. Men were such filthy creatures—every last one of them. Through clenched teeth, she hissed a breath and focused on the layout of the main deck. The huge boilers and water paddles were in the middle of the boat. The captain would most likely be near them.

With one hand holding her floppy hat in place, she stepped off the stairs.

Willie caught her arm over the hand rail as she turned toward the big wheel. "April, please don't cause a scene."

"Cause a scene?" She never did such things....well, only when necessary. Her mouth opened.

The pleading look in Willie's eyes hit her like cold water. Her lips closed.

He made a grimace that caused creases to form on his forehead, and shook his head. "We aren't eight-and-ten- years-old any longer."

She tugged the front of her hat down. His face brightened, that crooked little smile, the one he'd mastered at birth, touched her heart.

Willie lightly pinched her cheek. "I'm twenty-one and you're twenty-three, time for you to treat me like a grown man and act like a grown woman."

She stopped shy of touching his rosy cheek. "What's that suppose to mean?"

"Now, don't get flustered. You know what I'm talking about." Willie paused and gave her time to think before he continued, "The man said the gator was their mascot. That means the captain already knows about it, and you talking to him, isn't going to change anything."

April took a deep breath. Willie's face held a please-understand look. His deep blue eyes shimmered down at her, and a twitch of his old smile pulled at the corners of his mouth.

He was right. They were no longer children. He was a grown man, a very handsome man. Just as she'd always known he'd be. And, she had to admit he was right on the account of her causing a scene. As a young girl, she'd been extremely good at it—a consequence of her upbringing. She ran a hand over Suzie's little arm. They now had a second chance.

"I'm sorry," she whispered.

Willie wrapped his free arm around her and squeezed. "I know."

Suzie laid her head on his other shoulder. April pressed a hand on the child's back. "I missed you so much these past few years," she confessed.

"I missed you too, Sissy." His finger gave a playful tug on the front brim of her hat.

She giggled, straightened the head covering, and flashed him a wide smile. A tingle colder than ice in January ran up her spine.

"Willie!" She pointed over his shoulder. "That man, talking with the captain, he was one of the men playing poker this morning." Fear or anger, at times she confused the two, rumbled across her chest. "Is he looking for you?" Her forehead felt damp. "Do you owe him money?"

Willie started to turn his head.

She grabbed his cheek. "Don't look. He might see you."

He chuckled and twisted toward the men. "That's Jerek Brinkley. No, he's not looking for me. And no, I don't owe him money."

Mr. Brinkley's eyes found hers. She swung her head about, letting his gaze fall on the side of her face, and pretended to take in the scene of the deck.

The surroundings did catch her attention. Several women stood near the railing. Every one of them openly ogled Mr. Brinkley's tall form and overly, fine-looking face. April let out a huff of air reinforced in her belief—women were stupid when it came to a handsome man. Just as stupid and foolish as men were when it came to gambling.

Refusing to let her wandering eyes touch on the man, she turned to Willie. "Is he a riverboat gambler?" Out of the corner of her eye, the man separated himself from the captain to walk toward them. She grabbed her brother's arm. "Come on. Let's go to our cabin."

"But our cabin is that way." He pointed in the direction of the man.

April pulled his arm and rounded the corner. Several life vests hung on the wall separating the walkway from the paddle wheels. She pointed at them. "We are going this way so you can get three of those to put in our cabins."

Willie stopped to pull three of the belts from their hooks. "Trust me, Sis, this little bit of cork on a rope isn't going to keep you afloat, not with all the gold you've sewn into your petticoat."

"Willie!" She took the vests from his hand. "Shush! Someone might hear you." Without a backwards glance to the man trailing them, she hurried along the walkway to the far side, where they walked along the side rail to the alley near the bow that held their cabins. The man followed. The shiver running up her spine confirmed the fact.

They stopped beside their cabins. He stopped behind them. A chill made her shoulders shiver. Willie fumbled with the keys in his hand. She tapped one toe. *Hurry up, open the door. If you so much as say hi—*

Willie greeted the man.

Damn him! Checking her hat to make sure it covered her forehead, she turned around after her brother said her name in introduction.

Her gaze swept upwards. His face was a good foot above hers. Last spring while working in the yard, she'd looked up to see a huge hornets nest hanging over her head. That's exactly how she felt now. Saliva stuck to the lump in her throat.

Mr. Brinkley touched the brim of a round bowler with the tips of two fingers. The hat, tipped to one side, was perched on his head like a drunken bird on a branch. Waves of dark brown hair flowed from beneath the cockeyed rim. "Miss Simonson, it's a pleasure."

Thank goodness he didn't talk with an irritating drawl like most of the men she'd met lately. And at least he was clean and knew how to dress. His pants and jacket were the color of a newborn fawn, and the material looked just as soft. A shirt, black as the sky at midnight, was beneath the waist length jacket, and a black silk tie, embroidered with silver stitches, looped beneath the collar tips. He was by far the most attractive man she'd ever seen.

"Sis?"

"Um, what?" She tore her gaze from the man to look at her brother. Why did her palms feel sticky?

"Mr. Brinkley asked if you enjoyed your time in New Orleans," Willie explained as he pulled the key from her cabin.

"Oh." Her face grew warm, and blood pulsed in her neck. She unclenched her fingers to wipe her sweaty palm over her skirt then turned to her door. "Yes, fine thank you. Please, excuse me." Hinges creaked as she rushed into the room and slammed the door. The life vests fell to the floor. She leaned against the wood and pressed both hands to her chest. Good heavens, the man frightened her. Only fear made her heart race this way. Mr. Brinkley had absolutely no manners, stalking them like that.

A thump sounded as the woman disappeared into her room. At second glance, she was even more exquisite than he remembered. Jerek repositioned his stance and looked at her brother.

Willie glanced at the door. "She's a little skittish around men she doesn't know."

"That's hard to believe after this morning." Jerek crossed his arms over his chest.

"Yes, well that was just because she was mad at me. She has quite a temper when riled." Willie's gaze went to Jerek's bag. "Where are you headed?"

Jerek wanted to talk about the woman, not his travels. He uncrossed his arms. "St. Louis for sure, maybe further, no real plans." The roster had informed him the Simonson's were going as far as Cairo, where they would board another steamer to take them further north. Over his shoulder, he pointed to the cabin behind him, the one straight across from hers. "I'm in cabin ten."

"We're in eleven and twelve. This is my daughter, Suzie." Willie tickled the chin of the little girl he held in his arms.

Blonde curls and sparkling blue eyes were identical to her aunt's. "Hello Suzie," Jerek said.

Suzie buried her face in Willie's neck. He rubbed her back. "She's a little shy."

"Is your wife..." Jerek let his words float

questionably.

"Dead," Willie finished. His eyes grew dim while his hold on his daughter increased.

"I'm sorry. I-I didn't know." Jerek felt tongue tied.

"She died in January. The fever." Willie's lids blinked several times.

The man's pain showed on his face. Lost for words, Jerek rubbed the toe of his boot over the planked floor.

"That's why April came down to New Orleans. To convince me it was time to go home. Don't know if it's the right thing or not, but I owe her," Willie sighed.

"You owe her?" Jerek asked.

Willie's gaze wandered somewhere beyond Jerek's shoulder. "Yeah, our Ma died when I was little, and our Pa, well, he passed away when I was ten. But even before that, he wasn't around much. April raised me and introduced me to Suzanne, my wife." Willie's hand patted his daughter's back. "Four years ago, when we married, her parents sent us to Europe to stay with family, to keep me out of the war and save Suzanne from becoming a war widow. She became ill last winter. After she died, Suzie and I came back to the states."

Jerek unfolded his arms then refolded them again.

Willie blinked several times, as if coming back to the present. "Forgive me, Mr. Brinkley, I usually don't wear my life on my sleeve, nor blurt it out to everyone. I guess the notion of going back to Minnesota hasn't settled."

"Think nothing of it, Mr. Simonson. I am sorry for your loss." Jerek looked from the man to the door beside them. The number eleven engraved on the small brass plate nailed to the center of the solid wood reminded him of his past. How many of those had he nailed on in his life? More than he cared to remember. "May I ask one question?"

"Certainly."

"Where did you live? You and your sister, after your father died, with relatives? An orphanage?"

"No, there were no relatives. The town folks tried to send us to the children's home in St. Paul, but April refused to let it happen. She was only twelve, and somehow wrangled a job out of the town banker. She made enough money to keep the taxes paid on the small house Pa had on the edge of town and food on the table. I still owe her for all she did. Alfred Green, the banker is—was Suzanne's uncle. Her parents sent her to live with him when the war broke out."

It was clear Willie's mind reflected on his deceased wife. Jerek found his conjured up images as to what a twelve-year-old girl could do to earn money. A deep scowl pulled on his brows.

"Excuse us, Mr. Brinkley, but I think it's time for someone's afternoon nap." Willie hoisted his daughter higher on his hip as Suzie let out a large yawn.

"Forgive me for detaining you." Jerek smiled at the child. "Mr. Simonson would you, Suzie, and your sister of course, join me for supper this evening?"

"It's my understanding all meals will be eaten in our cabins," Willie said.

"Once we arrive in Vicksburg, yes. Prior to that the galley will be serving," Jerek answered.

"Then yes, I accept." His gaze bounced off door number eleven before he added, "For all of us."

"Splendid, I'll see you later. Have a good nap, Suzie." Jerek winked at the little girl then turned to enter his cabin.

The small room hosted few amenities. Nothing like the cabins of the upper deck, the ones he usually stayed in. The cot, square table, and side chair left little space. Jerek flipped his hat on the table and loosened his tie. He crossed the room and pulled open the small window. Confined by the upper deck, air didn't flow in, however sound did. He leaned closer.

"It's not safe, I tell you!"

"Those boilers were tested less than a month ago. They're perfectly fine." Jerek recognized Mason's voice. He lowered one knee to the bed below, but stalled the motion when the frame creaked.

"No they aren't, there's a bulge in one. It needs to be repaired."

"There's no time, I tell you," the Captain insisted.

"I refuse to sail on her as she is."

"Then take your leave. I've plenty of crew. One less won't hamper us."

"If that's how you feel, Captain, I wish you a safe trip."

"And I wish you luck in finding new employment." Departing heels clicked on the deck floor.

Jerek pushed away from the wall and exited the cabin. He rushed to the end of the walkway and stopped the shipmate.

"How bad is the bulge?"

The mate glanced around.

Fine fuzz sparsely littered the man's chin. The tiny hairs along with a tall, gangly frame made Jerek judge the mate's age below twenty. "How bad is the bulge?" he repeated.

"It's not too bad, but with the load he expects to carry, these boilers are going to be under a lot of work. I'd board a different steamer if I were you." The man pulled his arm out of Jerek's grasp then hurried down the walkway.

The mate turned to climb the stairs. A few minutes later, carrying a small pouch, he descended and walked toward the landing plank. Could a simple deck hand know the condition of the boilers, or had the young man gotten a taste of the port city and didn't want to leave? It wasn't unusual. Boats often lost crew at departure time.

Jerek moved to the rail and watched the man stroll off the dock and up the beach. He drew a cigarillo from his breast pocket. When the sailor became lost within the waterfront crowd, he pitched the butt over the rail and headed toward the boiler room.

****

The boat swayed. Awakened from her short nap, April stretched and rose to her knees. The small window beside the bed, sandwiched between the other decks, didn't provide a view. After fluffing her skirt, she settled the floppy hat on her head.

The door squeaked as it cracked open to reveal an empty hall. With a sigh of relief, she scurried out.

Her tap on Willie's door went unanswered. She checked the knob, it twisted beneath her fingers, and the door slid open. Willie and Suzie were snuggled on the bed, sound asleep. Quietly, April pulled the door shut, glanced about, then walked down the companionway to the railing.

Below, shipmates pulled long, thick ropes over the bottom rail. The lengthy, massive riggings slid into coils like a large bull snake. She shivered and looked toward the New Orleans's wharf. People flocked the shore, but only a few waved as the *Sultana* pulled clear of the dock area. Soon the boat would turn about and begin puffing up the Mississippi.

April took a deep breath and gagged. The wet, heavy air clung to her nostrils. She shuddered. Dirt, stale fish, and remnants of the coal smoke billowing from the boiler stacks. Absolutely nothing like the pleasant, fresh aroma of standing on the shore of one of the fresh water lakes back home.

Home. She smiled and placed her elbows on the rail. Willie wasn't going to recognize their little house. In the years since he left, she'd repaired and repainted every board. The house sparkled white, like when Mama was alive. Now it also sported a matching picket fence enclosing the tiny front yard. It was a good, solid house and would be a fine place to raise Suzie.

April lifted her face to the breeze. Willie could get a job, a respectable job; one Suzie could be proud of and hold her tiny head high as she walked down the street. Other children wouldn't spit and chant behind her back. She checked the position of her hat.

Suzie would be happy to tell others her papa's name, and she'd anxiously await his arrival each evening. Her niece would always have plenty to eat, and have nice, clean clothes that fit. When her feet grew, she'd get new shoes—immediately, she'd never wear ones with the toes cut out.

A deep sigh flowed over her lips. But would any of that make the little house a home? Would she, April Simonson, ever feel safe, happy, and content? Isn't that what home was supposed to feel like?

The wind grew stronger. She clutched the hat brim, securing it from being lifted off her forehead and the deep, ugly scar above her brows. A loud, steam-filled hiss filled the air. Black smoke bellowed from the tall smoke stacks. The *Sultana's* horn let out three long blasts. Echoes of water slapping off the wide rudders of the deep wheel intensified as the sirens faded. Waves started to hit the side of the boat.

She pushed a finger under her cap and ran the tip along the revolting mark spread from temple to temple. Unlike the loud signal the scar never faded. If anything the tight, thick skin darkened and grew more offensive. Each day, for over eleven years, the disfiguring reminder of her childhood had bounced back from the mirror.

Time had eased her fear, but not the memory of how Tom Hix plowed into the little house, looking for her father. He'd wanted the money owed to him—another gambling debt.

April squeezed her eyes shut. She had shuttled Willie into the bedroom and closed the door. Determined to guard and protect him with her life. Tom didn't listen when she said their father wasn't home. He stomped through the house, overturning furniture as he searched for anything of value. His burly arms shoved her away from the bedroom door. Fearful he'd hurt Willie, she'd leaped onto his back, scratching and hitting with all her might. Huge hands had grabbed her waist, pulled her from his body like an old shirt, and flung her across the room.

She'd never forget flying through the air. The way her arms and legs flailed as she sailed over the table. Landing on the big, cast iron stove had hurt, but the thud had been nothing compared to the excruciating pain of skin melting against hot iron. She wrapped both hands around the ships rail. Chips of paint dug into her palms.

Willie said she'd been unconscious for five days. She couldn't confirm nor deny it, but did remember waking to his little face streaked with tears. The mean-spirited Mrs. White stood on the other side of the room and announced the same night she'd been hurt their father had been rolled and murdered in the alley behind the local tavern, supposedly just after leaving as the evening's big winner. The woman had come to take her and Willie to the home for unwanted children in St. Paul.

April arched at the shiver sliding up her back. Mama had made her promise she'd always take care of Willie. With all the grit a twelve-year-old could muster, she'd crawled out of the bed then sent Mrs.

White on her way with words and actions she'd learned from her father.

"Miss Simonson?"

Torn from the past, she blinked several times before turning around. *Him again!* She held the groan in her throat and braced trembling hands on her hips.

"I apologize, I didn't mean to startle you," Mr. Brinkley said.

"You didn't startle me," she lied. "You interrupted me."

His tall frame cast a shadow on the deck floor. The elongated silhouette fell across her feet. Her toes curled, and a heavy thickness formed in her throat. Except for her and Mr. Brinkley, the deck was empty. Men could do anything they wanted and get away with it. Tom Hix still roamed the streets back home—living liked he'd never harmed anyone.

"Forgive me then for interrupting you. I was unaware you were busy."

People lined the shoreline behind her, but they were too far away to offer any help. She prayed her voice wouldn't tremble. "If you must know, I was saying good-bye to New Orleans." She turned toward the walkway. "Please excuse me, I must return to my cabin."

"No, please don't leave on my account." He touched her forearm, right above the wrist.

His fingertips were hotter than a pressing iron. The sting made her stumble backwards. An acidic taste filled her mouth. "Kindly remove your hand, *sir*."

He pulled his hand away. "I'm sorry if I upset you."

Without acknowledging his apology, she turned and ran into her cabin. Shaky fingers fumbled with the sliding lock. After the latch caught, she twisted around and flopped onto the bed. Cold sweat trickled over her body, and painful heartbeats thumped against the inner wall of her chest.

It was several minutes before her fingers were capable of pulling the long hat needle from the back of her head. With a hard tug she removed the garment, tossed it onto the table, and laid her head on the pillow. She lifted legs that felt like dead weight onto the cot and closed her eyes. One hand patted at the pain behind her breastbone.

The man was appalling, simply atrocious. All gamblers were, whether well-dressed and striking, or filthy and garish. One eye opened to look at the flesh of her forearm. She rubbed the area. How could a woman, any woman want one of them to touch her? Why would any woman in their right mind want to marry a man who was already married to a deck of cards? That was a part of life she would never understand. Nor ever participate in.

****

Jerek took one step then stopped. Racing heels clicked on the floor faster than a woodpecker's beak on a dead oak. Real fear distorted her lovely face. What had caused it? The billowing white dress barely slowed before it disappeared into her cabin.

Confusion and concern made him send a fleeting glance around. The deck was vacant, and the high rail should have relinquished fear of falling into the muddy, rolling water.

He rubbed his thumb over the four fingers that had brushed her wrist. Her skin had been chilly; almost ice cold, and a great contrast to the heat of the southern, spring afternoon.

In the thirty years he'd been alive, he'd never been so intrigued and drawn to a woman. This overwhelming sense of wanting to be near April Simonson was captivating and mysterious at the same time. Or was it she who was captivating and mysterious?

He leaned back against the rail. Either way, he was going to find out. There wasn't anything better to do, and what harm could come of it? It wasn't as if he was going to marry her. Jerek fumbled for a cigarillo.

If he was the marrying kind, he would have gotten hitched prior to the war, before he started traveling across the battle torn south. And before the night he'd found his fiancée and his brother in the hayloft of her father's barn.

Jerek tossed the unlit smoke over the edge of the boat and pulled out his watch. Tucking the timepiece back into his pocket, and leaving the past in the past, he walked toward the galley to reserve seats at the captain's table for himself and the Simonson's.

A whistling tune blew across his lips. Seducing Miss April Simonson was going to be a challenge. Throw in a little mystery and the reward became all the sweeter. His fingers ran over the door of cabin number eleven before he turned the corner. First he'd have to get in her good graces. After making the reservations, a quick exploration of the ship might give him an idea of how to bring a smile to those pert, pink lips.

****

Early that evening, April flipped around to give her brother an icy stare. "But I don't want to have supper with that man." She settled her hands on her hips. "You know how I feel about gamblers."

Willie shook his head. "Sis, how many times do I have to tell you? What happened last night was a one-time thing. I knew it was my last night in New Orleans, probably forever, and wanted to experience the nightlife. It was no more than a friendly game of cards. Mr. Brinkley only joined the game an hour or so before you arrived."

"Those men didn't seem too friendly to me." She

took the hat he lifted off the table.

"For the two months we've been here, Suzie and I spent our time sight seeing when it was safe. When it wasn't we stayed in the hotel room. It wasn't until you arrived and could stay with her that I even thought about venturing out at night. I'm sorry. I don't know what more to say. I wish you'd believe me. Your philosophy of gamblers and instructions of not participating in the activity were well learned over the years." He tapped at his temple. "They are permanently embedded in my mind. In the last four years I've rarely played a game."

He sounded honest and sincere. She ran her fingers over the rim of her hat then checked the stitches securing the flowers.

"Mr. Brinkley simply invited us to dine with him. After we pick up the soldiers in Vicksburg, we won't be able to leave our cabin much. Please can we enjoy the freedom while we have it?" Willie set Suzie on the bed and adjusted the little bonnet covering her blond curls. A smile covered his face. "Suzie, tell Auntie to put her hat on so we can go eat."

The little girl glanced up. Her tiny nose wrinkled and her smile showed miniature, snow white teeth.

April reached over and brushed a finger over the tot's nose. Suzie let out a silly snigger. It made her want to giggle. Turning to the mirror, April settled the hat low on her crown then pinned it to the bun at the nape of her neck. "What do you mean we won't be able to leave our cabin?"

"The *Sultana* will be transporting a load of Union soldiers from Andersonville to Cairo, and I don't want you or Suzie mingling about once they board," Willie answered.

"What's Andersonville?" She fluffed her bangs, poked a few stray hairs behind her ears, and pulled the rim lower.

"A Confederate prison, I've heard it's one of the worst. In February, the whole camp flooded. The prisoners spent over a week standing in chest deep water. Or was that Cahaba?" He shook his head. "More men have died in those two prison camps than on any battle field. They haven't been treated as humans, and I don't know how they'll behave once they're released."

Her stomach churned. "Why didn't anyone do something about it?"

"Sis, the country was at war, and prison camps are a part of war. The North has some unscrupulous prisons too." He fluttered a hand. "But the war is over now."

"I'll never understand it," she sighed. Not the war *or* her brother, he never wanted to talk about unpleasant topics.

Willie picked up his daughter and opened the door of her cabin. "Come on, we're to join him at the Captain's table."

She rolled her eyes. Of course he'd sit at the captain's table. Anyone as arrogant as Mr. Brinkley would insist on such a position. She pressed a finger into her chin. If only there was a way to bring the gambler down a notch or two. With Willie at her side she'd have protection.

Willie stopped her stroll into the hall with pressure on her elbow. "April, promise me you'll be nice."

Her chin dropped. Had he read her mind?

He waited for her answer.

"Fine, I promise." With a sideways glance she asked, "How did you become so genteel?"

"Oh, I had a very good teacher. My older sister insisted on proper manners at all times." He looked at the ceiling. "Even though she rarely uses them."

She tapped a toe. "William Simonson, I will not tolerate such offensive—"

"See what I mean?" With a wink and a smile that touched his eyes, he grasped her elbow and pulled her down the walkway.

He did have a way of making her see the silliness of her actions. She held a chuckle, and in silent companionship walked beside him. Now that he was back, she'd never be alone. If it made him happy, she'd behave.

The galley was on the same deck as their cabin, but near the stern. Empty tables sat amongst those surrounded by people, making her once again question why they had to dine with such riffraff as Mr. Brinkley. She refused to let her gaze wander to the captain's table as they walked through the room and discovered there were a large number of women and children on the boat, twenty-nine, to be exact, including her family.

Willie's elbow tapped at her ribs and brought her gaze about. Two other people sat with the Captain and Mr. Brinkley at the round table. She held her gasp. The woman sitting next to a dapperly dressed older man was one she'd witnessed gawking at the gambler earlier.

The woman had a head full of dark, lengthy curls that bounced about as her red lips let out a lilting laugh. Acid rose to the back of April's throat, and her stomach churned at the sound. It was going to be a long evening. Captain Mason rose to introduce her and Willie to Mr. Randall Hanson and his wife, Abigail.

Mr. Hanson, as well as the gambler, stood and shook hands with Willie, while Abigail Hanson remained seated. However, she raised her hand then cocked her wrist. Was her brother supposed to shake it or kiss it? How could some women be so forward? April pressed her hands to her sides, and when Captain Mason made her introduction, she simply tipped her head to the men and woman.

Willie pulled a chair out and nodded at her. She scowled. The chair was next to Mr. Brinkley. The gambler's grin displayed prize-white, perfectly formed teeth and grated her nerves. She gave him a fake smile then separated her chair as much as possible from his.

Willie pulled out the chair on her other side. A waiter appeared with a narrow, wooden box and placed it on the seat. She had to scoot her chair back toward Mr. Brinkley to make room for the edges of the box. With a bright smile Suzie wiggled her rump on the box and placed her feet on the chair seat.

The gambler eased his chair closer. She ignored him and pulled her niece's adapted chair up to the table.

Beneath his breath he tsked. April rolled her eyes to the ceiling. Tsked! Of all things, men do not tsk. Gamblers are truly insufferable.

The waiter returned with a thick, clumpy soup. The first spoonful hit her stomach like a glob of old bread pudding. As the other courses arrived the conversation around the table pondered on the war. She cut the food on Suzie's plate into bite-sized pieces. How could one man think he knew so much? His silky voice droned on and on. It was more irritating than a buzzing flock of mosquitoes.

Sickened, she laid her utensils across the top of her half-full plate. Abigail Hanson's irksome little laugh was just as bad. The woman hung on every word Mr. Brinkley said and openly batted her eyes at him.

By the time the desert plates were removed, she wanted to throw up. Mrs. Hanson wasn't nearly as attractive as she believed herself to be. Her teeth were as bucked as a mule's, and her high pitched voice sounded like a meowing kitten.

"Twitter brain," she mumbled beneath her breath.

"Excuse me, Miss Simonson?" Mr. Brinkley leaned an ear her way.

She shot a smile around the table then let an unimpressed gaze land on his cheerful face. "Nothing."

He leaned closer. His chin almost touched her shoulder. "Did you call someone a twitter brain?"

How foul could one man be? "No," she hissed for his ears only.

"Funny, I could swear that's what I heard."

She pressed her napkin to her lips. "Maybe you have an ear wax problem."

His full belly laugh drew the attention of everyone at the table. Passengers at other tables glanced toward them as well. She used the napkin to hide the blood rushing to her face. A great urge to grab and yank a handful of the thick, brown hair haloing his head made her fingers twitch.

Randall Hanson pulled a pack of cards from his pocket. "Gentlemen, could I interest any of you in a friendly game of cards while our wonderful meal settles."

"Oh, yes, do my dear." Abigail patted her husband's arm, but her gaze was on Mr. Brinkley. "I love watching a good game of cards."

This could be her chance. April bit at the smile forming on her lips. It had been a while since she'd handled a deck, but the art of counting cards wasn't easily forgotten. The ache in her stomach disappeared. She pulled the sleeves of her dress from their fashionable elbow placement down to her wrists and flexed her fingers under the table. She would show the gambler how just ill-fated cards where. It wouldn't hurt to remind Willie either.

The men accepted the invitation, minus Willie. April shot a glance his way. He read her mind—knew she wanted to pull a trick out of her sleeve.

Willie narrowed his eyes and shook his head.

She widened hers and nodded, silently encouraging him to agree.

"No," he mouthed.

"Yes," she silently insisted in return.

His shoulders drooped. He turned to the men. "One quick one, Suzie may get restless."

She couldn't hide the smile that lifted the corners of her lips. When she was done, both Mr. Brinkley and her brother would think twice before sitting down at a gaming table again.

"Oh, that reminds me." Jerek Brinkley reached into his breast pocket. "Here Suzie, look what I found for you. Miss Simonson, would you please give this to Miss Suzie?" He held out a small, life-like pony, carved from a piece of cedar. The familiar scent filled her nostrils as he waved the piece in front of her face.

"Little girls play with dolls, not horses, Mr. Brinkley." She laced her fingers together and laid them on her lap.

"April!" Willie admonished. His hand reached over to take the toy as he continued, "Suzie likes horses and can play with one if she wishes."

The stare her brother gave her was not one of humor. A sincere smile covered his face after it left hers. "Thank you, Mr. Brinkley." He handed the toy to his daughter. "Suzie, tell Mr. Brinkley thank you for the pony."

"Tank you, Misser Bink," Suzie replied as she grasped the toy with both hands.

The table chuckled at the sweet voice of the child, and April returned Mr. Brinkley's self-righteous smile with a half smile, half sneer.

"You must have got that from Jake Houston, Jerek," Captain Mason remarked, "that man can carve anything. He spins those little toys out two at a time."

"Yes, I did. I ran into him up on the hurricane

deck earlier. Perhaps tomorrow I'll see if he can carve a doll." He lifted a brow as his eyes turned to her.

Irritated, she ignored him and flashed a smile at Mr. Hanson. "What are you men going to play?"

"How about a game of draw?" Randall Hanson asked.

Each man tossed a coin into the middle of the table while Mr. Hanson shuffled and dealt out the cards. She didn't watch the game—she studied the cards. Her fingers drummed, one at a time, against the seersucker material of her skirt.

Captain Mason dealt the next game. She tapped a toe on the floor. The first two men knew how to shuffle, but not with precision.

Abigail Hanson made a comment as Mr. Brinkley took the deck. The sound of the woman's catlike voice made her cringe, but her gaze never left the cards. She bit on her bottom lip and under the table, twisted her wrists.

Captain Mason claimed the win, and she dried her palms by rubbing them along her skirt.

"Could I deal a round?" she asked.

"Of course," said Captain Mason.

"Sure," said Randall Hanson.

As she took the cards her brother's hand came down on top of hers. Trapping them against the table, Willie's voice emitted a demanding, "No!"

Chapter Three

Scowling, April tried to pull the cards from Willie's grasp. He'd already agreed, why was he refusing now? "Willie..."

He shook his head.

She sent a reassuring smile to the other men and Abigail. "They all said I could."

"Let her deal, Simonson," Brinkley said.

Willie scrunched up his face like he was in pain and pulled his hand away. "Fine, but there will be no bets on this hand."

"Willie!" she protested.

He looked her way. She read the warning in his eyes as he insisted, "No bets."

"Fine, no bets," she agreed. The money didn't matter. It wasn't needed to prove a man should never count on cards being friendly. She set the cards on the table, and cracked her knuckles before picking the deck up again. "Same game," and with a satisfied grin at Mr. Brinkley, she added, "gentlemen."

The cards were warm and moved across each other with perfect ease. She juggled them from hand to hand. The final few barely fell into place before she flipped them upside down and passed them to the other hand. With showmanship and flair she'd practiced since childhood, April began to seriously shuffle the cards. They flew to and fro, over and under, and in between each other with quick accuracy.

Perfectly, the deck made a large arch then fluttered together as she shifted them through her fingers. Next, the small rectangles formed a long staircase high into the air before she slowly drew the cards from one palm with the fingers of her other hand.

She had them! Gazes full of amazement and astonishment followed her quick movements. As the cards floated into her palm, she flipped them into a wide fan and waved it in front of her face.

The next few tricks were more for her to learn where each card was, than entertain the crowd. Holding the deck in one hand, and careful so know one could tell what she did, she concentrated on the numbers as her fingers quickly flipped each card side to side. After the last card, she switched hands and counted again, this time swiftly flipping them end over end.

Confident every card was exactly where she wanted it she set the deck on the table and looked at Mr. Brinkley. "Would you care to cut the deck?"

"My pleasure," he said and split the stack in two, then set the bottom half on top.

She scooped up the deck and with a flick of her wrist let each card spin across the table like a smooth-flying bird before landing facedown in front of each player.

Suzie's hands clapped together as the final card fell from the air with a snap.

"Very impressive, Miss Simonson," Captain Mason said with a wide smile.

"I've never seen anything like it," Abigail Hanson admitted.

"Quite right, my dear, amazing," Randall Hanson agreed.

Mr. Brinkley had both brows raised, and Willie, with a finger pressed between his brows, shook his head.

"Oh, my." She pasted on a sad frown.

"What?" Abigail asked.

Hosting a frown was difficult when your heart sang like a meadowlark. She hoped her sigh was believable. "Gentlemen, I'm afraid, I'm going to have to re-deal."

"Why?" Mr. Hanson asked.

She shook her head. "There's not a full deck here."

"Yes, there is, it's mine, I should know," Randall Hanson insisted.

"Oh, there was a full deck, before the last dealer stuck the ace of spades up his sleeve." She gave Mr. Brinkley an accusing look.

Willie moaned.

"Miss Simonson, I assure you, I do not have a card up my sleeve, an ace or any other card," Mr. Brinkley said. He held up his arms then pushed his cuffs to his elbows.

"You don't?" she asked.

"No, I don't." That perfectly arched brow appeared again. She hadn't noticed how brown his eyes were. They reminded her of morning coffee—deep and rich brown.

April blinked away the mental image then shook one finger in front of his nose. "Tsk, tsk," she mocked. Reaching over and twisting her wrist so no one else could see she let a card slip from the lacy cuff of her sleeve. Silently it dropped into his breast pocket. When the bottom of the card hit the base of the pocket, she grasped the top with a finger and thumb.

Pinching her lips together, she pulled the card out for all to see. "That's because it's here in your breast pocket." She flipped the ace of spades onto the table and sent the man a 'shame on you look'. "Mr. Brinkley, you've been caught cheating."

Satisfaction faded as laughter rolled across the table. Her chin dropped. Why weren't they shouting at the man? Wasn't cheating at cards inexcusable? She frowned and glanced around. Merriment filled everyone's faces—except Willie's.

Her brother's face was red. Was it anger or embarrassment?

"Oh, Miss Simonson, that was wonderful!" Abigail Hanson clapped her hands. "I've never seen a magician before, can you do other tricks? Show us some more."

"That was very clever, Miss Simonson." Jerek Brinkley picked up the card and examined it. "And now we know why your brother wouldn't let us bet against you."

Her stomach sank. She'd done nothing but gave them all a show to enjoy. She glanced around the table again. No one believed he'd cheated. No one had learned a lesson. Other than her—the exhibition proved gambling was a fickle activity. Her shoulders drooped.

"Yes, Miss Simonson, show us some more," Captain Mason encouraged.

The bogus smile she tried to provide was harder to muster than the frown had been. Gathering up the deck, she reshuffled, and asked, "What's your favorite hand, Captain Mason?"

"A full house, my dear, aces over kings."

She nodded, loosened her hold so she could feel each card, then one after the other flipped five cards. Face up and in a perfect row, three aces and two kings fell onto the table in front of the captain.

"Remarkable!" Captain Mason touched the cards.

"And yours, Mr. Hanson?" she asked.

"Royal flush."

April counted as her fingers secretly searched. Unnoticed, she pulled cards from the top, bottom, and center of the deck. In a straight row, one at a time and face up, ace through ten, all spades, landed in front of the man.

Bored, she waited for the ooh's and ahh's to pause before asking, "Mrs. Hanson, what is your favorite card?"

"Oh, my," Abigail fluttered her lashes, "I don't know, I've never thought of it, but my favorite number is seven."

"My favorite card is the queen of hearts," Jerek Brinkley leaned his head toward her.

Her neck muscles tightened against the way his husky voice tingled her spine. With a false smile, she tossed four sevens one on top of the other in front of the woman. Skipping her brother she looked at her niece. "I think three's are in order for Miss Suzie, since she is three years old."

"Yes! Free!" Suzie squealed as four three's landed beside her pony.

"I'll take the jack of hearts, jack of clubs, a ten of diamonds, an eight of spades and, let's see, a two of clubs," Willie said with an imitation smile.

She rolled her eyes and while her fingers found each card she let the queen of hearts float into her sleeve. Undaunted, she met her brother's challenge with five quick flicks of her wrist. The table filled with clapping as the two of clubs landed on top of the others in a neat pile. April laid the rest of the cards on the table in front of her. The last flick of her wrist was unnoticed as her hands fell to her lap.

"What about me, Miss Simonson?" Jerek Brinkley asked.

With the tip of her toe, she slid the card across the floor. "Oh, I believe if you look under your left boot, Mr. Brinkley, you'll find your queen of hearts."

He pushed his chair back and others stood to see

over the table as he lifted his foot. Face up, the smiling queen appeared. Jerek Brinkley leaned down to pick up the card. As he stretched back in his chair, he ran a finger over the top edge.

April blinked, trying not to look at him, but it was like catching a glimpse of a spectacular sunset, one that made her want to stare in awe.

His gaze met hers and with a sultry voice he declared, "I'd prefer she were in my breast pocket, where I could keep her close to my heart."

A feline moan floated across the table. She turned in time to watch Abigail Hanson pretend to collapse in her chair with her hands pressed between her breasts.

Randall Hansen laughed and as the others joined in, April pushed her chair away from the table. Hiding her trembling hands in her skirt, she said, "Captain Mason, thank you, it's been a most pleasurable evening, but now if you will excuse us, it's time for Suzie to be put to bed."

Willie rose. "I believe my sister is right, it was a pleasure to meet you." He shook hands with the Hansons, and then nodded to the other two men. "Good-night Captain, Brinkley." Lifting his daughter into his arms, he took hold of April's elbow.

Once they reached the hall, his hold tightened, and he pulled her to the corner. "Are you trying to get us kicked off this boat?"

She opened her mouth to protest, but Willie asked another question before she had a chance to speak.

"Have you forgotten the *Sultana* is one of the few ships taking passengers right now? Do you want us to be stranded in some little river town for weeks, waiting and hoping to secure passage on another ship?"

"No, I—" she started.

"You what? What is this all about? Why have

you taken such a dislike to Mr. Brinkley?"

"I-I don't know." She ran a hand over the queasiness of her stomach. "The man is appalling!"

"Why? What did he do?" He pointed toward the galley. "You'd never met him before today. And trying to accuse him of cheating? That's a dangerous game, Sis. One you don't want to get into." Willie grabbed her shoulder. "Promise you'll never pull that little stunt again."

Evening had grown into night. A million little dots, twinkling like miniature fireflies in the dark sky, reflected off the water flowing behind the boat. Why did she dislike him? Why did she dislike all men? She didn't know. Years ago she'd decided she hated men and never questioned why. Maybe because she'd never met one who was kind and cared what she thought. That wasn't true, Willie was kind, so was her boss Mr. Green. Captain Mason didn't raise her ire, neither had the bellhop at the hotel.

Willie put a finger under her chin and forced her to meet his gaze. "Promise me, April."

"What?" She tilted her head, trying to jog her memory.

"Promise me you won't pull that little stunt again," he repeated.

That's right, the card tricks. "I promise," she said with a wave of her hand. After one last look at the star-filled sky, she turned to walk down the passageway.

She scratched at her neck. Was it because Jerek Brinkley was like Tom Hix and her father—obsessed with gambling? He wasn't impolite. Nor was he crude and uncouth like some of the men she met on her trip downriver. She touched the area of her cheek his warm breath had floated over when she called Abigail Hansen a twitter brain.

A smile lifted the corners of her mouth and sent warmth all the way to her toes. He had a lovely smile, and his memorizing eyes made something flutter in the lowest pit of her stomach. She placed a hand over the low, flat area between her hips. The sensation was odd, almost like a hunger pang, one that didn't hurt.

Lost in thought, she would have walked past her cabin had Willie not brought her to a halt. He unlocked the door, waited as she lit the lamp beside the bed then bade her a good night.

Turning in the doorway, he pointed to the latch. "Secure your door with the latch. You don't want to be searching for the key if there's an emergency in the middle of the night."

She nodded and murmured, "G-good night," then shut the door and hooked the latch. After pulling the curtain over the tiny window, she caught a reflection in the small mirror on the back of the door. Her hands flew to the rim of her hat. Not once during the evening had she checked to be sure it wasn't askew. Turning her head from side to side, she sighed with relief. The floppy brim still covered the scar.

Pinching the hat pin, she pulled it out and with the other hand lifted the garment from her head. Not wanting to see the blemish, she turned, settled the hat on the table and proceeded to remove her dress. She lifted her carpet bag onto the narrow cot, certainly not large enough for two, and pulled out a nightgown.

Her mind wondered back to Mr. Brinkley. What compelled people to marry? *Love?* She loved Willie and Suzie with all her heart, but they were born for her to love. She pressed a hand to her chest. How could someone fall in love with a stranger, someone they'd never known?

It was inconceivable. She slipped on the gown and pulled the combs from her hair. When Suzanne came to live with her uncle, Willie had become obsessed and shortly after they met, they decided to marry. She'd protested, but in a matter of weeks Willie and Suzanne were wed and off to Europe.

They'd written several times over the years, and when Willie's letter arrived from New Orleans, she'd been extremely saddened by the news of Suzanne's death. Knowing her brother needed her had sent fears of being in public aside. She boarded a southbound steamer, determined to bring him back to Minnesota. And then she met Suzie. The little girl was the most precious thing, and they quickly bonded.

At first, she didn't know how to behave around the child. She rarely interacted with people, except Mr. Green and occasionally his wife, Deana. Each morning, as the sun made its debut, she hurried up the street to the bank building to hide herself in the small back room, and recompose the business Mr. Green had completed the day before.

The poor man's eyesight continued to disintegrate with each passing year. She did hope Mrs. Green would be able to keep up while she was gone.

Leaving after work was a bit more difficult, but her fears were usually unfounded. It was rare anyone stopped her to talk on the way home. The whole town knew to stay clear of April Simonson, *the spinster*.

Moisture slipped from one eye. She wiped it away then twisted and thumped the pillow. She had a fine life, just how she wanted it. Friends or acquaintances might be nice, but she didn't have time for them, especially now that Willie and Suzie were back.

She twisted again, this time to lie on her side and draw her knees up. The trip down and her stay in New Orleans had allowed opportunities for her to become a mite more gregarious. Meeting new people was exciting. Her gaze went to the cabin door.

Except when it came to the odious Mr. Brinkley! The man was absolutely appalling. The way he walked, straight backed, head held high, as if he owned the world. And his voice was so annoying, slow and smooth, almost like he was singing a tune. Then there was that stupid way he smiled all the time...

The image of his smooth shaven face, smiling down at her, floated across her mind. She closed her eyes and sighed. He was very handsome, and kind. Why *did* she dislike him? Another tear slipped out. Maybe it wasn't that she disliked him, but feared someone so fine looking would surely realize how ugly her scarred face was.

****

Jerek lay on the tiny cot. The top of his head hit the wall and his feet hung over the bottom edge. Why hadn't he asked for a first class cabin? He snorted. Because he wanted to be near the card-wielding woman across the hall; April Simonson had more than a card up her sleeve. She was also more of a challenge than he first thought. Didn't matter—he was up to it. A little practice on Abigail Hanson had proven his prowess before April and Willie arrived at the table. In a matter of seconds, even with a husband at her side, he'd had Abigail eating out of his hand. The homely woman had been what he needed to test his skill and make sure he hadn't grown rusty.

He rolled to his side and pulled his feet onto the mattress. Twinkling lights filtered in through the small window. One of the tiny illuminations flashed brightly then burnt out as it shot across the night sky. If he were still a child, he might have made a wish. Instead, he flopped to his back and thought of having a warm body snuggled next to him watching the light show. A smile filtered across his face. Before they reached St. Louis, April Simonson would be nestled to his side, and he'd be exploring a great many more delights than shooting stars.

****

Jerek waited. It shouldn't be much longer. The sun crept higher into the sky. Red and gold rays danced off the tips of placid waves. His fingers tapped a rhythm on the deck rail. The heavy, salt-filled air of New Orleans lightened with each mile the ship chugged north. Several varieties of birds, busy with a late morning feeding, filled the bushes and long grasses growing along the banks of the river. Beyond the vegetation, hills dotted with trees and fields of green rose to merge with a sky of brilliant blue, the same blue as the eyes of the queen of hearts.

A door opened and closed. He smiled. She was finally exiting her tiny cabin. He started to count to ten, not wanting to appear too anxious; at five he turned around. "Good morning, Miss Simonson."

The familiar, flower-topped hat perched on her gold hair didn't even flutter as she turned to glance his way. Her eyes rolled, and her chest puffed like a roused grouse. "Good morning, Mr. Brinkley." Her tone wasn't friendly as she lifted her skirt an inch or so above the toes of brown boots and scurried to her brother's door.

Jerek wiped the smile from the corners of his mouth before he left the rail at the end of the alley. Walking toward her, he pointed up. "Willie and Suzie are on the hurricane deck, looking at the alligator."

The section of her face not hidden by the floppy hat scrunched into a worried frown. "Good heavens, why would they do that?" She puffed again and gave her head a dainty shake. "Willie just doesn't have any sense." Making it obvious she didn't want the material to brush against him, she gathered her ruffled skirt aside and tried to squeeze between him and the wall. "Excuse me, I must go get Suzie."

"Why?" He stepped closer, blocking her exit. How could a woman grow lovelier overnight?

A red blush grew on cheeks as flawless as those on a porcelain doll. "Because she's just a small child, he has no business showing her that monster." She pivoted to take the long route to the upper deck.

Jerek sidestepped then quickly caught up with her quick pace. "He's her father, and she wanted to see it." They arrived at the corner. A short distance down the walkway a large pile of cargo filled the deck.

Daggers flew from blue eyes as they settled on him. With a huff, she turned to go back the other way. "Willie isn't much more than a child himself. He has no business raising one."

Jerek strolled beside her, hands firmly thrust in his pockets. Cupping her elbow in assistance would be the gentleman thing to do, but Miss April Simonson would not appreciate his touch—yet. "He seems to be doing a fine job. I can tell how much he adores his daughter, and likewise for her."

"Yes, well, he doesn't always think before he acts." Her little chin pointed forward so far the hat on her head tilted back. Flower petals bounced about and the ostrich feather stuck straight out like the tail of a galloping horse.

"Must be a family trait."

Her stride increased. "Mr. Brinkley, is there a reason you are trying to irritate me this morning?"

His long legs had no problem keeping up. "Am I irritating you? I do apologize, Miss Simonson, I was just making conversation." They arrived at the other end of the walkway, turned the corner and came to an abrupt halt. Another large pile of crates covered this side of the deck.

"What on earth!" Her hands landed on her hips.

The stance was adorable. Jerek rubbed his chin

and shrugged his shoulders. "Guess they're transferring from hull to hull." He walked to the edge of the ship. "They must have thought everyone was already up and about." Placing a hand on one of the two chairs he'd positioned earlier near the rail, he said, "Here, have a seat. When the crew clears it out of the way, I'll escort you up top."

She stood on her tiptoes, trying to look over the crates then looked over her shoulder. He could almost see little wheels turning as she contemplated her options. His heart thudded when she stepped back to gaze down the alleyway to her cabin door.

"It shouldn't take long," he added.

Her eyelids closed.

Jerek held his breath. Should he try and persuade her? Assure her he was safe, wouldn't hurt or cause her any harm. No, no, she had to decide on her own. "Suzie will be fine, Willie won't let any harm come to her."

Her sideways glance looked him up and down before she moved to the chair. "I suspect your right."

Locked air exhaled from his lungs, and a warm smile filled his face.

"I would have thought you'd be up on the Texas deck with the rest of the gamblers." Her tone had a sharp edge to it. He held the chair steady while she sat. Petite hands smoothed the folds of her dress neatly across her lap.

Jerek rubbed his hands together and settled into the other chair. "Naw, not this morning, the game last night was enough for me."

"That was hardly a game." The water seemed to hold her gaze for a moment. "I hear there's quite a high stakes match going on up there. Full of officers and riverboat gamblers."

He shrugged his shoulders. "I heard as much."

She turned to look him square in the face. "Are you trying to say you aren't a gambler?"

Her eyes were so blue they almost took his breath away. "Oh, I dabble in it now and again," Jerek said. "But sometimes it's not the challenge I'm looking for."

Tufts of bangs, poking out from beneath the hat, caught on the dark tipped lashes every now and again. Behind the golden strands, a furrow formed. "It's not?"

"No, it's not," he said. It was obvious she didn't like gamblers. Yet, she was quite a dealer. How had she learned such a trade? "So tell me, why isn't a pretty thing like you married?"

"Mr. Brinkley, how dare you ask such a personal question?" A light blush covered her cheeks.

Hiding his nerves with a chuckle, he said, "I was just curious." Damn, where had the question come from? Sure he wanted to know, but hadn't planned on being so blunt.

"Well, if you must know, I've been much too busy to worry about marriage."

"Really? I thought maybe you weren't the marrying kind."

"What do you mean?" she asked.

"Like me, I'm not the marrying kind."

"You're not?"

He scratched the back of his head. "No, I guess I'm not. Never quite figured out what people see in it."

"Me neither, why last night I was just thinking..." she stopped herself.

"About me?" he asked.

"No! How dare you ask that!" she huffed.

"Because I was thinking about you," he answered.

"You were?"

Was his silver tongue tarnished? He sounded like a schoolboy. Parts of him felt like one. His hand brushed against hers. "Yes, I was."

Their eyes met. Confusion, disbelief, and yes, wonder. He had her wondering. That was a good sign. He let his fingers trail along the back of her hand, while holding her gaze.

"W-what were you thinking about?" Her voice was barely a whisper.

He wanted her more than a soldier wanted boots. The jolt in his groin area hit like a bucket of cold water. Back off Brinkley, you need to take it slow. Letting out a deep sigh, he turned her hand over. "How these hands could be so quick. Those were some fancy card tricks last night."

"Oh." Her gaze went to their hands.

"Where did you learn to count cards like that?"

She looked out over the water and sighed, "Watching my father."

Winning her trust would take time. Instead of caressing the hand in his, he cradled it, let the small knuckles press against his palm, and waited for her to continue.

A few silent moments slipped by before she spoke, "When we were little, after our mother died, Dad would take us with him to the card games. Willie and I would sit in the back of the room on a blanket and play with an old deck, sometimes all night. When we got older, he'd leave us at the house, and since it was what we'd always done, we'd sit on our bed and play cards." Her shoulders slightly rose then fell. "It just kind of happened. One day I knew the exact placement of every card. I created tricks to entertain Willie."

His fingers applied a small amount of pressure. "How did you and Willie live? I mean money wise. Did your father leave an inheritance when he died?"

"No, there was no inheritance, other than the house. The state was ready to take it for the taxes owed. I went to the bank," a small laugh fluttered out, "I thought you just went in and if you needed it, the bank gave you money. As it turned out, Mr. Green, the banker, had a hard time seeing the small numbers in his ledger, so he hired me to decipher them. After he learned how easy numbers were for me, he gave me more duties. I still work for him." The side of her face lifted with a smile.

"Didn't you or Willie go to school?"

"Yes, we both did."

"Well, how did you work and go to school at the same time?"

"I worked every day after school and on Saturdays." Her shoulders floated up and down, as if it was no consequence.

He massaged her hand. "It must have been a relief for you when Willie married Suzanne."

She would have pulled away if the hold had been less. "Excuse me?" A puckered frown marred her face.

"When Willie married, you didn't have to worry about him any longer."

"Of course, I stilled worried about him, and I missed him terribly." Her fingers shook.

With slow even stokes, Jerek absorbed the trembles. "Kind of like how he misses Suzanne, I imagine."

Her face scrunched. Little lines formed around her eyes and over the top of her nose. "Excuse me?"

"Willie. I can tell how much he misses his wife."

The adorable, crumpled lines disappeared. Her mouth gaped. "H-he does?"

He'd hit the nail on the head. April didn't know about the overpowering bond of love between a man and a woman. She'd never experience it. He'd have to help her understand love before he could put his plan in action. After a few bumps, where she'd learn to think of herself instead of her brother, she'd be ready.

Jerek took a moment to consider his options.

"It's a good thing he has you during this time of sorrow. He needs the support and care. Granted you're not the same as Suzanne, the person he wanted to spend the rest of his life with, the mother of his child."

"Huh?"

"And it's a good thing you never married otherwise you might not be able to help him so much."

April's gaze fluttered across his face for a few moments before she turned and stared over the water. She pulled her hand away.

His palm became cold and lonely. He leaned back in his chair and crossed his arms. After several minutes he said, "Yes, I think he's very lucky to have you for a big sister."

She ran her hands down her skirt. "Mr. Brinkley, would you excuse me? I think I'd like to return to my cabin now. I'll await for Willie and Susie there." Her voice was low and shaky.

He stood and held out a hand. She looked at it for a moment before laying her fingers across his palm. The pulse at the base of her wrist raced. She rose to her feet. Before letting go, he raised the hand and brushed the knuckles against his mouth. His lips lingered longer than necessary. He let her fingers slip from his, and said, "Certainly, Miss Simonson, thank you for a delightful visit."

She turned, hitched her skirt an inch or two, and took off for her room. After a stumble, she caught her footing, arched her back, and with a slower pace made it to the cabin.

When her door snapped shut, Jerek leaned back on the rail and pulled a cigarillo from his breast pocket. He lit the tip and pondered the woman. She was like a little bird that had been kept in a cage and never given a chance to spread her wings. Seduction was no different than selling expensive riverboats; his instincts said he had an interested buyer. He'd broken through her first barrier. A sharp sting bit into his fingers. The rolled tobacco had turned to ashes except for the hot stub. He flicked the butt into the water.

Pushing away from the rail, he walked over to the crates then lifted several out of the way. Passing the boiler room, he knocked on the door, "Thanks, Daniel, you can put the boxes away now."

"Right away, sir," the shipmate said as he opened the door.

****

Later that day, after her mind processed what Mr. Brinkley had said, and raw emotions were in check, April knocked on the cabin next door. A muffled response made her twist the knob. Suzie lay on the bed; her tiny chest rose and fell with the deep breathing of sleep. Willie sat in the chair, gazing out the window.

"Hi," she whispered.

He turned. Wet lines streaked his face.

"Oh, Willie," she choked. The door slipped shut as she walked across the room to wrap her arms around him.

"Sissy, some times I miss her so much, my heart feels like its on fire," he admitted.

Why hadn't she comprehended this before? She'd been so happy about seeing him. *She'd been so happy.* But never once had she really asked how he felt.

Willie's body trembled beneath her hands. Tears slipped from her eyes as she whispered, "I'm so sorry, so very sorry."

He wheezed. "I loved her so much. We were happy, really, really happy. She was a wonderful mother to Suzie, the perfect wife to me. How am I going to live without her?"

"You'll survive, you have to. Suzie needs her

daddy."

He nodded.

She knelt down, framed his face with her hands. "Do you want to go back to New Orleans? Will that help?"

"I don't know. Sometimes I think I should go someplace new, where Suzie and I could start all over." His gaze rose. "Then I look at you and remember all you did for me. I owe you so much. You gave up your life for me."

"No, I didn't. We were in it together, you worked just as hard as I did," she insisted.

"Then why haven't you ever married? Ever had a beau? Why haven't you found someone to love?" Willie asked.

What is it with men and marriage today? "It doesn't appeal to me." She patted his cheeks and rose.

"It would if you experienced it. It's the most wonderful thing—the best. I loved falling to sleep with my arms around my best friend—my reason for living." His voice faded. Moments later, he wiped the water from his face. "I'm sorry, Sis. I guess seeing the married couples on the boat brought Suzanne's death to the surface again."

She rubbed his shoulders. "What can I do to help?"

He shook his head and stood. "There's nothing anyone can do."

Willie held his hands out. She wrapped her arms around his waist.

After a few minutes, she patted his back and said, "Why don't you lie down and take a nap with your daughter? You'll feel better when you wake up."

He glanced to the bed. The corners of his mouth inched up a bit and he nodded.

She waited until he was snuggled next to Suzie before leaving the room. Pressing the back of her hand to her lips, she leaned against the door. Across the hall, the number ten sparkled on a tiny brass plate. She straightened her spine, walked over and knocked on the door.

No one answered. After a quick check to her hat, she hitched her skirt and strolled toward the hurricane deck. Mr. Brinkley made her realize how selfish she'd been toward Willie, and how egotistical she'd been to the gambler. She owed the man an apology.

A stiff breeze bent the front brim of her hat over her face as she topped the stairs. She flipped the rim up and flattened a hand over the pitter-patter tickling the inside of her chest. On the far side of the deck, a tailored suit covered a broad back that tapered into lean hips and long, straight legs. Sweat broke out on her palms, and the tickle turned into a thud. Had she ever apologized to someone before? Not really. Other than Willie, or maybe Mr. Green for some slight error, but those were rare.

He turned. His gaze landed on her, wide lips pulled into a smile. The thudding beneath her palm increased. She swallowed and lifted the hand in a slight wave.

Jerek Brinkley moved. In no time his long strides brought him across the deck. "Good afternoon, Miss Simonson."

"Hello, Mr. Brinkley." Thank goodness her voice didn't croak. The frog in her throat was the size of a pumpkin.

"Jerek, please call me Jerek, Miss Simonson," he said.

The wind blew the floppy hat in front of her eyes again. "O-only if you call me April," she stammered.

He lifted the brim. "April it is." White teeth peeked out behind his smile.

Her face grew warm.

"Come on, there's someone I'd like you to meet."

He took her elbow.

Balmy heat penetrated the material of her sleeve and spread up her arm as they strolled back to where he'd been standing. Jerek stopped next to a couple of chairs. A grizzled, old man sitting in one boasted a smile as wide as the river as withered hands whittled a knife across a block of wood.

"Jake this is April, April this is Jake Houston," Jerek said.

"Hello, Mr. Houston. Thank you for the pony you carved for my niece. She has it clutched in her hand right now while napping," April said.

The old man's face lit up.

"Hi, Miss, nice to meet you. I'm making Suzie a doll right now. See." A gnarled hand held up the wood, a tiny doll shape was taking form. "Miss Suzie was up to thank me for her pony this morning. She's a precious angel. That she is."

She took the carved wood and rolled it around in her hands. Jerek Brinkley had been nothing but kind to her family, and she'd treated him so badly. Lifting her face, she softly admitted, "I'm sorry."

A warm finger brushed against her lips, and his head shook from side to side. "There's no need for that," he said.

She handed the doll back to the old man. "You have an amazing talent, Mr. Houston. Suzie is going to have a hard time choosing between the doll and the pony."

Jake Houston stood and tucked the wood in his pocket. "Time for me to go check the boilers. Thanks for the visit Jerek. It was nice to meet you, Miss."

The old man wandered away, and April shuffled her feet. Apologizing wasn't easy.

Jerek pointed to the chairs. "Would you care to sit for a bit?"

"Yes, thank you." After arranging the folds of her skirt, she checked her hat. Blocked by the high rail, the wind no longer tugged at the edges. She folded her hands in her lap.

He sat down, put his feet up on the middle rail, and crossed his arms. "So Suzie's napping?"

"Yes."

"And you're just out for a stroll?"

"Yes. No, I um-was looking for you."

"Oh and why was that?" he asked.

"I owe you an apology, Mr. Brinkley." The pounding in her heart rose to her ears.

Chapter Four

He turned to look at her. "Jerek."

"Excuse me?"

"You agreed to call me Jerek," he reminded.

She had to get this over. "Oh, yes, well, either way, I'm sorry."

"For what?"

"For the way I've treated you. For the way I've behaved."

"Well, April, you have me at a loss. I don't remember you doing anything I found offensive, but if it will make you feel better, I accept your apology." His gaze went to the water.

She leaned back in her chair and stretched her legs out. They weren't nearly as long as his, and she couldn't brace them on the railing, but the position was comfortable. A crisp, clean feeling settled across her stomach. She crossed her arms as well.

"Thank you, it does make me feel better."

They sat in silence for several minutes, watching the river flow behind the boat. Large waves, made by the huge paddles, rolled down river until the horizon made them touch the sky. The glistening waves looked nothing like the muddy brown she'd seen when leaving New Orleans. Had that only been yesterday? It seemed much longer. She felt like a different person sitting here now. She closed her eyes, trying to decipher the variations.

"I like riding on riverboats." His voice, like the boat ride, was slow and calm.

His head was tipped back, his eyes closed. She smiled.

"You do, do you?"

"Yes, don't you?"

"I'm learning. This is only my second time. On the way down it rained a good portion of the way. I stayed in my cabin most of the time. The trip south is faster than the trip north, so I'm told."

His eyelids lifted. Not wanting to be caught staring, she snapped her lids shut.

A moment later he said, "Yes, the Mississippi has a swift current, trips down river are always much quicker."

If someone had said she'd be sitting on the deck of a ship, talking with a man before the end of her trip to New Orleans, she would've called them a bold faced liar. Yet, here she was, talking with Jerek Brinkley, and...

"What do you do?" she asked.

His chair creaked. "What do you mean?"

Opening her eyes, she met his dark ones gazing at her. "For a living, Willie told me you aren't a riverboat gambler."

His brows lifted. "Oh, so that's the reason for the apology." His smile touched the corners of his face. The tiny lines above his cheeks deepened as he chuckled.

His laughter was contagious. She giggled and admitted, "Yes, in part."

He turned back to the river. "I'm a salesman."

"A salesman?"

His head rolled along the back of his chair until their gazes met again. "Believe it or not, April, I sell riverboats."

"No. Really?"

"Yup, my uncle owns a company in Cincinnati. He builds the boats, and I sell them to owners up and down the rivers."

"Like the *Sultana*?"

"Yes and no, he mainly builds rear wheelers, the *Sultana* is a side wheeler," he clarified. "But they are both paddleboats."

"How often do you go back to Cincinnati?" she asked.

"I haven't been home in over seven years."

"Then how can you sell boats for him?"

"I fill out the bill of sale, take the down payment, and write my uncle as to where and when to deliver the boat. Some people travel to Cincinnati to pick their boats up, but usually not. In most cases they are delivered to the new owner, often in St. Louis."

She wanted to know more and hoped he wouldn't mind the questions. "Besides your uncle, do you have other family there?"

"Yes, my parents, two brothers, their wives, various cousins, you know, the whole gamut," he said.

She didn't know. She'd never had family outside of her parents, Willie, and now Suzie. "Don't you miss them?"

"Oh sure, but the company needed someone down here selling the boats. It's been good." He held one hand out. Palm up, it stopped beside her knee.

Did he want to hold her hand as he had this morning? Her stomach flip-flopped.

His fingers fluttered.

She laid her fingers in his palm.

He settled their clasped hands on the arm of her chair. "This is good, sitting here, relaxing in the sun, floating on the river. Don't you agree?"

"Yes," she agreed, "it's good. In fact, it's very nice." His touch sent new and pleasant vibrations up her arm and into the center of her chest. Since fear was the only emotion to usually reside there, her thoughts changed. "Where's the alligator?"

The pressure of his hand increased a slight degree. "He's on the far side of the deck, safely caged. There's no reason to be nervous."

He was right. There was nothing to worry about. She sighed and leaned back against the chair. "I think I shall have to take a peek at him later."

"Just let me know when, and I'll escort you over. Have you ever seen one before?"

"Heavens no," she admitted. "Have you?"

He nodded. "Yes, several. They roam the south like bears roam the north."

"Tell me about one."

They sat and visited for over an hour. Tales of his adventures held her attention and filled her with questions she asked aloud. It was a new experience. She'd never sat and conversed with anyone, outside Willie.

Her brows pulled against her forehead. Was it proper for a single girl to sit and visit with a single man on a ship? His forearm stretched across the open space between their chairs and her fingers, completely at ease, lay inside his. Was that proper? She had no idea, but wasn't about to pull them away. Proper manners, the ones she drilled into Willie, came naturally, but etiquette was something else. Believing it was the last thing she'd ever need, she never bothered to read about the proper protocol between a man and a woman. Perhaps she should.

"Jerek, does Captain Mason have any reading material on the boat?"

"Are my stories boring you?"

"Oh no, not at all. I just thought something to read would be nice."

"I'm sure he does. We can ask him if you'd like."

She nodded. "Yes, I'd like to see what he has."

Taking a deep breath, she leaned her head against the back of the chair and thought—*I will read every page, twice, if he has one on decorum and propriety.*

A little voice floated across the deck. "Auntie, lookie!"

Jerek winked at her, slipped his hand from beneath hers, and turned. The breeze hit her warm palm and chilled it to the bone. Wrapping it in the folds of her skirt, she twisted to watch Suzie run toward them. One chubby arm waved a wooden doll in the air.

Suzie's feet skidded around the chair, and with a leap she landed on April's lap. "Lookie! Doll!"

April folded her arms around the child and kissed the top of her head. "I see your doll. She's beautiful."

Willie found another chair and the four of them sat on the deck until the setting sun streaked a red, orange, and yellow rainbow over the flowing water. A tinkling bell called all aboard to the galley for the evening meal, and with great delight, she strolled across the deck between Jerek and her brother.

A masculine hand cupped her elbow as Jerek guided her down the narrow stairway. She crossed her fingers in the hope Captain Mason would have the book she needed.

April couldn't remember what she ate, but knew by the end of the meal, she didn't care if Captain Mason had a book or not. She'd never enjoyed life, not like this, and no rule on earth would keep her from Jerek Brinkley's pleasurable companionship.

****

The following day while climbing the stairs to the hurricane deck, an erratic rhythm pranced around in his chest as Jerek settled his hand in the small of April's back. The pleasure of her company outweighed any he'd known.

Sitting on the same chairs, holding hands, she

shuddered when their solitude was interrupted by an odd screech. The abnormal hissing hit Jerek like a dull knife. His neck stiffened as he perked his ears, recognizing the source of the sound.

"April, please excuse me, I'll be right back." He released her hand, stood, and forced his feet to walk across the deck. Once out of her sight, he grasped the rail, bounded down the stairs and jogged to the boiler room. Arching his back against another shiver, he skidded to a halt. "What's wrong?"

"Seems we have a boiler leaking," Mason said.

Jerek ran a hand over his head. "How bad is it?"

"We shut her down. The other three will get us into Vicksburg. We'll have her checked there." Mason gazed at the door to the boiler room.

Jerek had helped his uncle build boats for years and knew the wood was twice as thick as the other doors on the ship, a fire wall when needed. "How far is it to Vicksburg?"

"No more than ten miles."

"J.C., I want you to lay up there, draw the fires, and repair the boilers as well as any other machinery that's in need of maintenance. You can't push this boat up river with a full load and faulty equipment." Jerek checked the door, tugging on how it fit within its frame, before he continued, "If it's the cost, I'll pay for it."

"That's already my plan, Jerek, don't worry. We'll be completely repaired before leaving Vicksburg," Mason assured. "The safety of my passengers always comes first, you know that."

"I also know this damn war has changed a lot of people." Jerek shoved his hands in his pockets. He didn't want to think Mason was slipping with safety issues, but couldn't ignore his gut feelings.

"I agree with that. I'll be glad when this country can get along again. Some claim it's over slavery, but we know better, bottom line rules, it's all been over money. Brothers fighting brothers, friends against friends, all over wealth," J.C. said with a sad, slow shake of his head. He slapped Jerek on the back and turned. Before walking away from the boiler room, Mason rubbed the back of his neck, and straightened his spine.

Jerek checked his breast pocket for a cigarillo, but before he pulled one out, a sixth sense drew his attention. With quick even steps, he walked to the edge of the alleyway.

April stepped off the staircase. Trim fingers lifted white fabric out of the way of those tiny brown boots as she hurried toward him. "What's wrong?" Worry filled her bright blue eyes. "We seem to have slowed."

Willie and Suzie stopped a few feet behind her. Jerek reached forward to grasp one of her hands. "Nothing to fret about, they shut down one of the boilers until we get to Vicksburg." He gave her chilly fingers a gentle squeeze. "We'll be there in a couple hours."

Willie widened his eyes.

Jerek stepped forward, slid her hand around his elbow, and turned her around to stand in front of him. Over the top of her hat, he met Willie's questioning gaze. "I think we should take a hotel in town for the night. I'm sure April and Suzie would enjoy a real bath, instead of this dirty river water. I'll make the arrangements as soon as we get to town."

Willie had a good poker face. His smile looked genuine. "Sounds good to me, what do you think, Sis?"

"Yes, I think that would be wonderful." She twisted to look up at him. Her lashes fluttered.

His breath caught somewhere in the back of his throat. April Simonson didn't know how to flirt, her batting lashes were genuine. The woman had no idea how the subtle little actions touched his soul. He smiled into the sky blue eyes.

"Let's go back up. We won't be in Vicksburg for hours yet."

Following Willie and Suzie, they climbed the steps together. His fingers rubbed hers clutching his arm. Once he had April safely settled in a hotel, he'd find his own repairman. One who'd make damn sure this boat was safe for the queen of hearts to travel on.

An enticing vision, of her stretched out in a large brass tub surrounded by bubbles, flashed across his mind. Yesterday, when she'd sought him out, he'd been quite shocked, especially when she agreed to sit and visit. Evidently, her limited knowledge of proper etiquette didn't include the fact it was highly improper for a young, unchaperoned woman to be in the company of an older man, alone. He smiled. Someday he'd properly thank her for pulling Willie out of that poker game in New Orleans.

His steps lightened as they crossed the hurricane deck to the chairs.

****

Warm water flowed over her shoulders as April sank further into the large, brass tub in the hotel washroom. The clean, fresh water was heavenly. She squeezed the sponge over her head, letting a stream trickle across her hair and face. The sun had almost set by the time they arrived at the docks of Vicksburg. The hours it took for the *Sultana* to chug up river the last ten miles made her believe they might never arrive.

The great boat had no sooner docked than Jerek escorted her family from the gangplank, and into a waiting livery that took them to the hotel. After settling them into three of the spacious rooms, he left to run some errands, and she'd hurried to the bathing chamber.

A maid agreed to wash her white dress as well as press the other one she had with her, it was a brilliant blue, and her second favorite, namely because of the wonderful hat she'd created to wear with it. She hoped Jerek would like it.

The sponge slipped from her fingers. Never before had she cared if others considered her clothing attractive. She'd worried they found her repulsive, a poor ignorant, penniless child. Years later she'd fretted they assumed she was mean-spirited and on her way to becoming an old maid. And she was always nervous someone might see her disfigured face, but not once could she remember caring if someone liked her attire.

The gowns and hats she created were made from colors, styles, and materials she found delightful and for no other reason. Had anyone ever commented on her apparel? Maybe Willie once or twice when they were younger, certainly not Mr. Green, his vision was so poor he couldn't tell what he was wearing let alone someone else. Pondering the tracks of her mind, she lifted a wide cloth of cotton from the side table and used it to dry her body as she stepped from the tub.

A mirror above the washstand caught her reflection. Light glistened off rosy cheeks. She wrapped the towel around her hair and stepped closer, tilting her head so the beams could fade. They didn't. A cheerful, almost radiant April Simonson smiled back.

She touched the mirror and her cheek bones rose higher. One eye winked. A light, carefree giggle escaped her lips as she turned to slip into her dressing gown. After straightening the room, she hurried down the hall.

As the door to her room clicked shut, she folded her arms over her chest and began to twirl around.

The room spun, and once she became completely dizzy, she flopped onto the bed. The ceiling continued to spin as she giggled with delight.

****

Having checked several other places, it was across the street from the hotel, that Jerek found R.J. Taylor, the local boilermaker he'd been tracking since he'd booked rooms at the hotel. Pacing the street in front of the blacksmith's shop, he waited for the man to exit the building. When Taylor stepped out, he took a few minutes to confirm the man's expertise, then commissioned him to examine the problems on the *Sultana*.

"I want those boilers properly repaired, if you run into any problems, I'll be at the hotel." Jerek handed the man several bills.

"Yes, Sir, Mr. Brinkley. I'll go out there right now." R.J. tucked the money in his coal-covered overalls and mounted his horse. "I'll stop at the hotel later to let you know my findings."

"Thank you, Mr. Taylor, I appreciate it." Jerek turned to cross the road, but recognized Mason hurrying up the sidewalk. Curious, he stepped back onto the boardwalk and strode toward the man.

"I sent a local boilermaker out to the *Sultana*," Jerek said as he approached the captain.

"Oh, I sent my chief engineer into town to find one as well. I'm sure between the two of them she'll be in good hands," J.C. said then attempted to step around Jerek.

"Where are you going in such a hurry?"

J.C.'s nostril's flared. "I gotta find Colonel Hatch. It seems two other steamers, the *Olive Branch*, and the *Henry Ames* just took my promised soldiers north."

"Rueben Hatch?" Jerek asked.

"Yes."

Wide-eyed with shock, Jerek asked, "That's who

you made the deal with? Surely you know he was arrested last year for taking bribes and reselling military supplies."

"President Lincoln found him innocent of all charges. He's now the Chief Quartermaster for the Department of Mississippi."

Jerek shook his head. "He was only found innocent because his brother is the Secretary of State for Illinois besides being a personal friend and financial backer of Lincoln. You'd be better off to forget this deal you two made."

Mason removed his hat and wiped at the sweat rolling down his forehead. "I wish I could Jerek, I really do. But I told you my future depends on this load."

"Hatch has a long history of corruption. You can't expect him to keep his end of a bargain, even if he does, you'll end up with the short end of the stick." His hands curled into fists.

Mason laid his hand on Jerek's shoulder. "Right now the short end is better than no end."

"I hope you know what you're getting yourself into," Jerek said.

"I really gotta find him Jerek, but don't worry, loaded or unloaded the *Sultana* won't leave Vicksburg until she's safe for the trip." The Captain hurried down the walkway.

Jerek shook his head, and as a train whistle echoed in the background, he made his way across the street to the hotel. The train was sure to be full of Union prisoners needing a ride north. He rubbed his temple, sighed, and silently chided himself. Damn, another fine mess you got yourself smack dab in the middle of.

Minutes later, he pushed the front door of the hotel shut and walked to the stairs. A middle aged woman, dressed in evening finery, walked down the steps toward him. He tipped his hat as she passed.

Visions of an enchanting creature shattered his troubled mind. His feet skipped every other step as he raced up the rest of the stairs. What was a little boiler problem? The *Sultana* was a good, sound ship. He had nothing to worry about, except getting cleaned up to have supper with a beautiful, young woman. April Simonson had a way of making everything bright and shining.

He tapped on Willie's door and rocked on his heels, waiting for it to open. When it did he said, "I'll be ready in fifteen minutes."

"No rush," Willie said, "April just sent her dress back down to be pressed again."

A little head poked out behind Willie's legs. "Hi, Misser Bink."

Jerek smiled and touched the tip of her nose with his finger. "Hi, Suzie Q."

She giggled and retreated back into the room. Willie pulled his gaze from his daughter and said, "Make it half an hour, she should be ready by then."

Jerek nodded, made his way to his room to gather fresh clothing then jogged to the bathing chamber down the hall. A light flowery scent still floated in the air from the last occupant. His mind quickly formed an image of April lounging in the tub, and with anticipation, he prepared the fresh, available water for his own cleansing soak.

An hour later, dressed in a black suit with a sparkling white shirt, Jerek escorted a stunning woman, covered in an eye-catching blue gown, and topped with a wide-brimmed, straw hat, adorned with blue ribbons and flowers, down the stairs. His grandmother's voice floated through his mind, *"You look like a rooster the way you're strutting."* He chuckled aloud, and smiled at April's questioning look.

"What's so funny?" Her hand rose to the front of her hat.

"Just happy, that's all," he answered.

"Oh," a thoughtful look crossed her face, before she added, "me too."

The meal progressed, and the sky outside the dining room windows twinkled with tiny dots of white by the time bowls of ice cream topped with sliced peaches arrived for Suzie and April.

Jerek excused himself from the table when R.J. Taylor walked past the glass pane behind April. Meeting the man near the door, he drew the boilermaker to a private corner of the lobby. "What did you find?"

"Well, she needs some extensive repairs. A shipmate told me she'd been patched at Natchez, and here on two previous trips. Captain Mason wants to patch her again, but I said you wanted the repairs done right. Mason says she has to sail tomorrow, and I don't know if I can get it all completed by then. What do you want me to do?" R.J. asked.

Jerek scratched his head. Mason depended on this trip, but he couldn't risk April's life on a faulty boiler. "How long would it take you to fix her?"

"To be perfectly honest, she needs one new boiler, but I can repair the old patches and fix a new one. She'd be fine for the rest of this trip. But I'd really say a trip home is what the *Sultana* needs, back to the ship builder to replace one of her center boilers."

"How long will it take you to make the repairs?" Jerek asked.

R.J. shrugged his shoulders, "A day or so."

Jerek rocked on his heels. Mason or the Army could order the *Sultana* to leave whenever they chose. "If I were to pay you now, in advance, could you find a couple men to help you and work through the night? Get everything done for her to leave as scheduled tomorrow afternoon?"

"Yeah, I have a couple men working on her right now. I'm sure they wouldn't mind going all night, if the price is right," the boilermaker said.

"The price is right, but the job better be right as well. Nothing shoddy," Jerek demanded.

"It'll be done right."

Jerek pulled a pouch from his pocket, "What do I owe you, Mr. Taylor?"

****

Something fluttered in April's stomach as Jerek walked back into the room. A broad smile covered his face when their eyes met. She twisted, letting her gaze float about. It landed on the table of women he walked passed. One of them lifted a fan made of lace and rapidly fluttered it beside rosy cheeks.

Expertly fashioned curls of bright red hair were piled high on the woman's head. April closed her eyes and raised a hand to the back of her neck. Her straight, dull, blond hair could only be coiled into the thick bun needed to secure the large pin it took to hold her hat in place.

"Shall we take a stroll through town before retiring?"

She snapped her head up. Jerek stood beside their table. Her heart beat increased. "Oh, that would be lovely."

"I think Suzie and I will decline your offer, Jerek. It's well past her bedtime already," Willie said as he lifted his yawning daughter into his arms. "But you two go ahead, we'll see you in the morning."

Jerek pulled her chair from the table and placed a hand on her back as they walked through the room. She lifted her head a touch higher as they strolled passed the red-headed woman.

In the lobby, Willie said good night before he proceeded up the stairs and she and Jerek walked out the wide, front doors. The fresh evening air held a cooling breeze. Yet, heat from each of his fingers and thumb penetrated the back of her dress and sent warm waves through every vein of her body.

Illumination from lanterns, hung on the street side of the town's structures, mingled with the moonlight, and cast the area with an enchanting glow.

"It's a lovely evening," she said.

"Yes, it is," Jerek agreed, before he added, "so are you."

Something bubbled in her stomach. "Thank you," she whispered.

At the end of the boardwalk, Jerek guided her step onto the street. "They have some lovely trees in blossom at the town square. I thought you might like to see them."

April nodded. "That would be nice."

Sweet scents filled the air as they drew closer to the small grove of trees near the courthouse in the center of town. Deep croaks from nearby frogs floated on the breeze and echoed with the clip clop of a passing horse. A louder, odd sound accompanied the frogs. "What's that buzzing noise I hear?"

"Locusts," Jerek said.

"Like grasshoppers?"

"Somewhat, but much larger and noisier." His hand slipped from her back to entwine his fingers with hers. He led her along a path through a couple of the flowering trees. "There's a bench in the middle. Would you like to sit down for a moment?"

"Sure." White flowers covered the tips of the lofty tree branches and fallen petals decorated the ground. Green spikes of grass peeked through the white covering and reminded her of a spring snowfall. The trees separated and a lovely flower garden emerged. Moonlight danced among colorful blossoms.

"It's beautiful," April whispered.

"I thought you'd like it. I was here a few years

ago and hoped it hadn't been destroyed." He stopped near the bench but didn't sit down.

"Thank you for bringing me, it's the loveliest thing I've ever seen," she whispered. A moonbeam highlighted his face. He was so very handsome. She ran her free hand over the side of her skirt. Her fingertips wanted to glide along the long curve of his face to the point of his chin.

"I agree." The sound of his voice was soft, almost far away, yet his eyes bore down on her with intensity. He took both of her hands.

The twinkle in his eyes sent a delightful tingle to the tips of her toes. His fingers massaged hers before letting loose to run along her arms. The sensations made her mind fuzzy.

A slight tug on her hatpin made her hands fly to the brim. "W-what are you doing?"

"Removing your hat," he whispered.

She pulled on the brim. "Why?"

"So I can kiss you," he answered.

"You can't!"

"I can't kiss you?"

"No, yes, I ca..." she stuttered, torn between wanting his kiss, and not wanting her hat removed. "Please don't take it off."

The pin slipped back into her bun. "All right, if it means that much to you. We don't need to remove it." Hands framed her face and tilted her head to one side as he leaned closer. "I'll find another way."

Balmy lips brushed against hers. "Oh," she breathed.

"Mmm." His mouth touched hers again.

The pressure was stronger and longer this time. She leaned closer and moved her lips against his. The vibration made her head swim. Her hands fell to his shoulders to explore the broad, solid span.

One of his hands roamed over her back then settled. Her breasts touched the hardness of his chest. The delightful pressure made her step closer. His hand lowered and forced her hipbone to make contact with his thigh. A knee slipped between hers. She wrapped her arms around his shoulders to keep her balance.

The demand of his mouth increased. His tongue teased her lips before slipping inside her mouth. She never imagined this was how men and women kissed. It was so intoxicating and enjoyable.

An unexplainable need grew within her body. She used her tongue to taste him, his lips, tongue, and mouth. She slipped a hand from his shoulder to wrap below his arm and mold her body to his. Warmth pooled in the lower most area of her torso. A groan escaped her throat.

Jerek mustered up the strength to pull away from the astonishing kiss. With precision, he eased the contact one step at a time, first his tongue retreated then the pressure of his hands lessoned. His lips stilled, and he removed his knee from her skirts. Drawing a deep breath, he slowly lifted his face.

His fingers touched her chin, tilting her face so he could see into her eyes. "I was wrong," he said.

Sooty lashes lifted. "What?"

Unable to stop himself, he leaned down for another quick peck, before he answered, "We didn't need to remove your hat after all."

"Oh." Her hand flew to the brim, pulling it down on her forehead.

"Don't worry, it's still in place and looks absolutely breathtaking," he assured.

A smile touched her cheeks.

Jerek clasped her hand. He brought it to his lips and kissed the knuckles. "We best head back to the hotel."

April nodded, but neither made a move.

He chuckled, kissed the fingers again before

lacing them with his, and turned to leave. She fell into step beside him as a train whistle filled the air. After it faded and they had exited the tree path, he asked, "Do you ever take it off?"

"What?" she asked.

"Do you ever take your hat off?"

"Well of course. I can't sleep in it."

Her voice trembled. Jerek wished he could see her face. When they came to the hanging lanterns, he stopped to guide her around in front of him. "I didn't mean to hurt your feelings, April. Your hats are lovely.

Unshed tears made the blue eyes glisten. He pulled her to his chest and said, "Ah, honey, I'm sorry."

"You didn't do anything, it's me, it's all me," she whispered.

"What is it? What's wrong? Maybe I can help."

"No, there's nothing you can do. There's nothing anyone can do." April stepped out of his embrace. "I'm sorry to act so silly," she shook her head, and wiped the corner of an eye with one fingertip. "I just really like hats."

She was lying. He trailed a finger around her lips then up to brush the last of a tear away from the other eye. "You're not acting silly. I like your hats too." He let his smile linger until her face did it's best to show a slight grin. Her body shivered beneath his touch. He released her and removed his jacket. Folding it around her shoulders, he said, "I better get you back to the hotel."

She gave a little nod. He circled her shoulder with an arm as they walked up the street. When they stopped for him to open the glass front doors she said, "Thank you, Jerek, I had a wonderful evening."

"Thank you, April, mine was just as wonderful, I assure you." He gave her shoulder a squeeze that forced her side to press against him for a moment before he opened the door.

****

It was well after noon before Willie said it was time for them to re-board the *Sultana*. April grabbed her bag and led him out of the room. She hadn't seen Jerek since he'd left her at the door to her room the night before. Quite worried, she found herself despising her scar more than ever. Had she angered him by not removing her hat? Had she been too forward by letting him kiss her? Had she...

The loud sound of the train whistle penetrated the air as they stepped out of the hotel and onto the street. Suzie slapped her hands over her ears and buried her head onto Willie's shoulder.

April set her worries aside and rubbed the child's back. "This place must have a busy train station," she remarked as they walked to the rented livery.

"It's bringing prisoners to the steamboats from Andersonville and Cahaba prison camps. You really must stay in your cabin as much as possible from now on, Sis," Willie said as they settled on the wooden seats.

"I will." She arranged her skirt around her feet before grasping the side rail. "Where's the driver?"

Willie glanced to the man loading their luggage in the back of the wagon.

"Oh," she said.

He gave her an unbelievable look. "What's happened to you lately?"

"What do you mean?" Her fingers tapped the rail.

"You've become so agreeable, and nice."

She laughed. "I've always been agreeable and nice. You must have forgotten." She sent him a wide smile as the driver climbed aboard.

"I don't think so, but I like it." Willie laughed.

"So do I," she said.

The flurry at the docks was great. Large crowds of men marched toward the river. It wasn't until the wagon drew closer that she realized they were the prisoners Willie had mentioned.

"Heavens," she whispered.

"Don't stare, Sis," Willie advised.

She couldn't help it. Scores of men walked side by side. Some leaned on one another and several carried others on their backs. They were little more than walking skeletons. Ribs and collarbones could plainly be seen. Tattered garments hung from their shoulders as shirts, and torn, dirty bits and pieces of cloth circled around their waists for pants. The material stopped at the knees for most of them. Very few had shoes or coverings on their feet. An astonishing number of the men were missing limbs, either an arm, leg, or hand, and others had dirty bandages wrapped around body parts here and there.

Their features were gaunt. Eyes bulged from pale skin. She took a second glance. Was that happiness she saw? Wide smiles covered their faces and joyous sounds could be heard floating from the long line snaking from the train station atop the hill to the wharf.

Mouth agape, she scanned the men again. How could they be so happy? Except for their jubilance, it was the worst human suffering she'd ever witnessed.

Willie's voice drew her gaze from the long line of men when he said, "There's Jerek."

She glanced to the waterfront. "Where?" From bottom to top, men of all shapes and size mingled about the wide gang plank next to the *Sultana*. She pressed a hand to her chest. A tall, handsome man stood out from the rest like a beacon in fog. The happiness that made her toes twitch floated upwards to produce a wide, full smile. On impulse, she raised an arm and waved.

He waved back.

Her brother arranged Suzie's bonnet then retied the knot under her little chin. His movements were slower than cold molasses. One toe tapped against the floorboard as she glanced between her brother and Jerek walking toward the wagon.

Willie began to straighten his daughter's dress. April grabbed Suzie around the waist, lifted her off the seat and thrust the child toward her brother.

He chuckled and moved to climb down. She scooted over and clenched her fingers, afraid they might give him a hearty shove.

When Willie and Suzie were finally out of her way, she hopped to the edge of the seat and jumped from the wagon. Her feet hit the wet cobblestones. Both arms flailed while her body wobbled and the heels of her boots tap danced. Preparing to hit the ground, she thrust both hands forward.

Mid-fall, strong arms grasped her upper arms. Strength and sheer quickness prevented her from landing on the wet rocks. "Whoa, where are you going in such a rush?" Jerek asked.

"Oh, um, nowhere," she stuttered. His chest was rock hard and warm beneath her fingers. Heat pricked at her face. She pulled her hands from his shirt, pressed them to her cheeks for a split second then used them to smooth away false wrinkles from her skirt.

One of his hands tickled her chin. "Just happy to see me, uh?"

"Yes," she said. Her gaze flashed to his face. "I mean no—" the breath in her lungs flowed out. "I mean it's time for us to board the boat." Her shaky fingers rose to her hat.

His got to the rim first. He pulled the garment further down on her crown, tucked his face beneath the rim and whispered, "I missed you too."

Warm breath brushed across a cheek that was already on fire. A low moan echoed between them. Realizing it came from her throat, she closed her eyes.

He laughed.

She opened one eye. Jerek lifted her bag from the wagon then turned and cupped her elbow. His smile didn't mock, it welcomed. She tipped her head up and giggled. It felt good to be happy. Head held high, she walked beside him over the wet cobblestones and up the wooden ramp of the *Sultana.*

"Watch your step," he said as they stepped onto the main deck.

The thump, thump, thump of hammers pounding echoed around them. "What's that?" she asked.

"They're putting in some extra support beams. It seems the Captain will have a few more men boarding than he anticipated. He instructed the crew to strengthen the floor of the hurricane deck," Jerek explained.

"Is that why all those soldiers are lining the shores?"

"Yes, they can't board until the work is complete," Jerek said.

"How many men is he expecting?" Willie asked.

"It was seven hundred, but close to four hundred have already arrived from the military hospital, so now it could be over a thousand." Jerek shook his head.

April pulled her brows together. The smile on his face didn't make his eyes twinkle like usual.

His fingers wrapped around her elbow. "Don't worry, the *Sultana* is sound and can carry the load."

"But we already have a full load. The hulls have over a hundred hogshead of sugar, and ninety-five cases of wine besides the livestock, forty-five mules and twenty-seven horses."

Jerek pointed a finger at her. "How do you know all that?"

"I told you. I'm good with numbers. I counted them."

"She did." Willie gave a half nod, half shake as he began to walk toward their cabins. "The boat also has seventy-six lifebelts, eight water buckets, and two life boats. I'm sure she can tell you how many forks and spoons the galley has."

April slapped her hands on her hips. Her lips parted, but the warmth of Jerek's hand in the middle of her back, and the chuckle floating from his chest made her forget whatever she'd been ready to say to Willie. Delighted to be at his side, she giggled, and they followed Willie to their cabins.

An hour later, she poked her head out the door. With a tilt she listened. The pounding had stopped. After a quick left-right glance, she slipped out of her cabin and scurried up the walkway. Resting her hands on the rail, she leaned over the edge. A solid stream of men covered the gangplank. A uniformed man shouted and the soldiers began to march onto the boat. Bodies, grossly demonstrating malnutrition, stumbled up the wood. Yet, in contrast, they were a joyous bunch. Tunes whistled from lips covered with layers of rough, messy whiskers. Jests and jokes came from others followed by all out laughter.

Amongst the joyous crowd a few could be heard asking, "Is it true?" and "Was Lincoln really shot?"

She tapped the rail beneath her fingers. The *Sultana* had carried the news of the shooting to New Orleans, so it seemed fitting the boat was where the prisoners first heard about it as well.

War was impossible to understand. It was named the Civil War, but there was nothing civil about killing one another. The government claimed it was over the mistreatment and owning of slaves, but the scores of men in front of her, made her wonder who had fared better, the slaves or the soldiers, both from the North and the South. Slavery was an evil activity, one that needed to end, but had a war that did nothing but slaughter men and destroy families by the dozens, solve anything?

She arched her neck, counting the men as they stepped onto the plank. This war wasn't over slavery. That's what politicians wanted people to believe—these men, nor their equivalents from the South, the ones fighting and losing their lives, hadn't owned slaves. They were poor farmers. The rich men, the ones who owned and cruelly mistreated the slaves, were safely tucked away in Washington, Richmond, some other capital city, or had gone abroad.

Those were the evil ones, the ones that decided how others should think, feel, and believe. They wouldn't stop until they had their way. Until they had more money than they could possibly spend. That's what it's all about—money. Working in the bank had given her first-hand experience of how some men loved money beyond all else. She shook her head. It was all so wrong. There had to be a better way, a healthier way for people to live. War didn't solve anything.

The trail of men had no end. The herd snaked up the shore and over the hill. Every size, shape, color, and age walked up the plank. The deck above creaked and groaned, and festive sounds drifted down.

April understood their joy. They were on their way home, where mothers, fathers, wives, sons and daughters, warm beds, and food would greet them. She pressed a hand to her chest and hoped they wouldn't be disappointed. The heads continued to stroll past. How many of them would find a home that was terribly different from the one they left years ago?

As the last man boarded the boat, she wrung her hands together. Five hundred and seventy-four, add that to the three hundred and ninety-one from the hospital, plus the seventy-three passengers already on board and the eighty-two crewmembers...

"April? What are you doing?"

Chapter Five

Startled, she turned around, and smiled as a handsome face drew closer. His head dipped beneath her hat and the tip of his nose touched her temple while his lips brushed her cheek. The heart in her chest melted like butter in the sun.

A loud racket made her point to the hurricane deck. "Jerek, did you know there are one thousand, four hundred and twenty-one people on this ship? This boat was designed, and is licensed, to carry three hundred seventy-six total, including passengers and crew. We are overloaded by over a thousand...one thousand and forty-five to be exact."

He flicked her hat rim. "I take it you've been counting."

She glanced down the alley to the cabin doors, where Willie and Suzie remained inside. "Yes, I couldn't help it."

"You should be in your cabin."

Warm fingers laced between hers. "I know, but Jerek did you see those men? They look like they haven't eaten in weeks, months even."

"I'm sure some haven't. At least nothing they wanted to eat," Jerek sighed.

She turned back to the rail. "Do you know who that man is?"

"Captain George Williams. He's with the Office

in Command of Prisoner Exchange. He's making a roll of the men as they board. Why do you ask?"

"He appears to be very mean-spirited, the way he ridicules and taunts the prisoners."

"That doesn't surprise me. It's only because he was a friend of Grant's that he wasn't court-martialed for cruelty and neglect while being the Provost Marshal in Memphis a few years ago. This war has been won and lost by some cruel men, April. Stay clear of him," Jerek said.

"Oh, look, another steamer is arriving." A ship as large as the *Sultana* came around the bend in the river.

"It's the *Pauline Carroll*. Good, she can take the next trainload of prisoners. The *Lady Gray* left earlier this morning without any."

April tilted her head. "Why did she leave without any—when we have so many?"

"It's all part of the war games, they claim the war ended with Lee's surrender at Appomattox two weeks ago, but battles are still being fought and deals are still being made. And will be for some time I'm afraid." He caressed her cheek. "I'm sorry, I shouldn't have said anything. I don't want to worry you. My mind doesn't seem to work right when I stand next to you."

"It doesn't?" Her mind didn't work right when he stood next to her either. Her heart beat erratically and her stomach bubbled.

His face drew closer to hers. "No it doesn't," he whispered.

The kiss wasn't long, but it was sweet and tender, and left her with an overwhelming sense of joy. His arm slipped around her shoulders as they walked to her cabin. He left after making her promise to stay put until he returned.

Wanting to please Jerek, she did stay in her room, pondering on how silly it had been to dislike a man so wonderful. An hour later, drawn by the noises echoing through the window again, she went back to the deck railing. The wind rustled the flowers on her hat as she counted another three hundred and seventy-one soldiers, dressed in faded blue rags board the *Sultana.*

After the last pale and tattered man walked onto the ship, she stopped in her cabin for a moment before going to knock on Willie's door.

Suzie's muffled giggles filtered through the wood before her brother instructed, "Come in."

The two sat together on the floor, playing with the carved horse and doll. "I think I shall have to sew a dress for that one." April pointed to the second toy.

"Would you like a dress for your doll, Suzie?" Willie asked.

Blond curls bobbed. "Yes!"

"May I see it?" She examined the size and shape closely after Willie handed her the carved doll. "I will make one for her after supper tonight."

Suzie clapped her hands then took the offered doll. The little girl went back to playing with the toys.

April turned to Willie. "I have something for you."

His brows furrowed as he took the pouch from her outstretched hand. "What's this?"

"The money I took from you in New Orleans, your gambling winnings," she said.

He handed the bag back without opening it. "Keep it. I'm sure I owe you much more than that."

April refused to take the pouch. "You don't owe me anything. And, it wasn't right for me to take it from you." She walked over, sat in the small chair and crossed her ankles beneath the hem of her dress. "The way I treated you wasn't right either."

Willie reached over and set the pouch in her lap.

"But you were right to turn it into coin. Please sew it into your petticoat, that's the safest place for it. We don't need it for the trip. I have plenty of cash." He bounced the horse across the floor, making Suzie laugh. "So is Jerek the reason for this personality turn-around?"

Her mouth fell open.

"Don't fret. It's good. It's the you I always knew was hidden beneath all the stress and pressure. As I said earlier, I like this new April."

She fiddled with the pouch string. "Oh, Willie, I'm so sorry. I never understood why you were so taken with Suzanne, but I think I do now. I didn't know…"

"Hard to explain isn't it?"

"Yeah."

"I'm happy for you, Sis."

"Willie, do you think this is how Mama and Papa felt about each other?"

"Yeah, I suspect it was." His eyes met hers. "Papa wasn't a bad man, April. Don't you remember the good times? I think a part of him died when Mama did, and he didn't know what to do about the hole it left in his heart."

She sat silent for a moment and watched Willie play with his daughter. "Do you have a hole in your heart?"

"Yes, I do. A great, big gapping one, but don't worry. I won't let it rule me. I want you to know, Suzie and I will be fine. Just fine." He touched a finger to Suzie's nose, making her chuckle again. "So if Jerek asks you to go somewhere besides Minnesota with him, do it, don't refuse on account of us. You need him much more than you need us."

His words made her scowl. "Willie—"

"No, don't say anything right now. Just remember what I said when the time comes."

A knock on the door prevented her from making

further protest. Willie rose, opened the door and said, "Yes, she's in here."

"Thank goodness." Jerek's gaze landed on her as he walked into the small room.

"Hi, Misser Bink!" Suzie greeted.

"Hi, Suzie Q." Jerek leaned over and patted the blond curls.

"Are we ready to cast off?" Willie asked.

"I certainly hope so," Jerek said.

Willie flashed a quick glance her way before he asked, "Has Mr. Taylor left?"

Jerek cast a nervous glance as well. "Yes, everything's fine."

"Who is Mr. Taylor?" she asked.

"Just a man I know from here in Vicksburg," Jerek answered.

She folded her arms across her chest. "Did you know another three hundred seventy-one men boarded?"

"Yes, I noticed," he sighed.

"That makes almost eighteen hundred passengers on the boat," she continued.

He took a step closer. His thumb brushed against her cheek. "Actually, Dr. George Kembel, the medical director for the Department of Mississippi just boarded. I'm sure he will remove a large portion of the men." Jerek looked at Willie. "And then we'll cast off."

"How many will he remove?" she asked.

"I'll let you know so you can keep count." His slight chuckle didn't sound real.

Jerek held up the basket he had in his other hand. "I had this sent out from the hotel. Anyone ready for supper?" he asked.

After consuming the meal in Willie's cabin, the four of them took a stroll. Wounded, exhausted men filled the ship. April couldn't help but stare and wonder how some had survived this long. Jerek left her, Willie and Suzie near the rail at the end of the alleyway. His departing words were lost as she noticed what had drawn his attention—the men being escorted off the ship. She frowned and began to count.

With a hiss, the neighboring steamer backed away from shore. A loud horn mingled with the inland train whistle as the ship began to chug upstream.

When the ear-piercing sounds faded, she asked, "Did she take on any passengers?"

Willie shrugged. "I didn't see any, but maybe they loaded before we came out."

"The decks look empty," she said.

"Yeah, they do," Willie agreed before he pointed to the shoreline. "Looks like that's all the doctor is taking off."

"But only three hundred left the ship. Three hundred-one to be exact," April said. "Twenty-three went out on cots and two-hundred seventy-eight by foot."

"The wagons are pulling away," he said.

"Willie, look!" She pointed to a flock coming over the hill. If possible these men appeared worse than the ones the doctor proclaimed too sick to travel. Worn-out and fatigued solders shuffled down the hill in a haphazard marching pattern. Many had rags tied around their feet, strips of material dragged the ground behind each step. Silently she watched the crowd form a long column as the men began walking two by two onto the *Sultana*.

A familiar shape walked against the crowd, down the walkway toward shore. She continued counting, but watched the broad shoulders at the same time.

Jerek weaved through dozens of emaciated soldiers marching up the plank to where Mason stood on the bank of the swollen river, talking with several men in uniforms. Reaching dry land and the men, he asked, "J.C., what is the meaning of this?"

The other men glanced between Mason and him, their annoyed gazes settled on the Captain.

Mason grabbed his arm. With quick strides, he separated them from the men. "It's under control, Jerek."

"Like hell it is," Jerek argued. "There has to be another six hundred men loading, and why did the *Pauline Carroll* just leave with only seventeen passengers on board?"

Mason let his gaze float toward the uniformed men. "My hands are tied, Jerek. They're making me take them all. Williams was on the boat and claims there's plenty of room." A worried frown covered Mason's face. "You did double check Taylor's work? The boiler is repaired, isn't she?"

"Yes, I double checked his work. The boiler is fine. It's the weight I'm worried about." Jerek pointed to the boat. "With the hurricane deck full of men we're going to be top heavy. The river is running high, and it's only going to get worse the further north we get. If we hit any rough weather we'll topple for sure."

"I know, but my hands are tied. If I don't take the men, they'll arrest me, claiming I tried to give them a kick-back." Mason shook his head.

"You are giving a kick-back. They're the ones getting it!"

"I know, but it's two against one. Hatch had to go out of town, so Speed is calling the shots, and he's included Williams in on the deal." The Captain removed his hat and rubbed his balding head. "If you have a suggestion, I'd like to hear it. But I'm sure you know as well as I do, they are the Army. They can do whatever they want and to hell with the rest of us. I've already had Captain Kerns and Major Fidler talk to them, but Speed out ranks them. Or so he claims."

Jerek pinched the bridge of his nose. Mason was right, the Army could put as many men on the boat as they wanted, kick-back or no kick-back. "What's our total load going to be?"

"Speed's been making the roll. He has a total of eighteen hundred."

Jerek scowled. "Eighteen hundred? Is that before or after this lot?"

"After," Captain Mason said.

"I think he better recount," Jerek suggested, his gaze moving to the rail of the main deck to where a hat covered with blue flowers watched the men trek up the ramp. "I have it on good authority there are already eighteen hundred passengers on the ship."

"Neither Speed nor Williams were here when the second trainload boarded, so his numbers aren't accurate." Mason shook his head. "They went to a Pub in town to eat. We'll take our own roll, once we hit the river. I want to get out of here before I hear another train whistle."

Jerek took a deep breath. Mason was stuck between a rock and a hard spot. A solution to the situation at hand was no where in sight. Bile burned his stomach. "Then, let's get these last ones on board and pull that damn plank."

It was after nine that night when the *Sultana* backed away from the docks of Vicksburg. Jerek leaned over the rail at the bow; the boat rode low in the water. Brown, froth-tipped waves slapped at the ship. He raised his face to the full moon high in the dark sky and blew out a breath of air. The last group of marchers had totaled seven hundred and ninety-one. Every square inch of the boat held a passenger or cargo and hundreds of soldiers still searched to find a nook or cranny to rest weary bones. He'd asked around the dock, inquiring about other ships taking passengers. Word was since Lee surrendered, boat Captains refused to take on civilians, holding out to make a deal with the army. Knowing Mason was their only hope of getting home, not one passenger had left the *Sultana.*

Large, black puffs billowed out of the tower smoke stacks, and little by little the bow started to break the waves as the big side-wheeler began to move up stream. The load was heavy, but the wide, solid build of the *Sultana* could handle it. Jerek pushed away from the rail then weaved through the crowd, down the stairs, and past more bone-tired men to the passenger cabins. He knocked on April's door and pushed it open when he heard an invitation.

She sat next to the lamp fastened on the wall. A needle and thread flowed through a small piece of fabric. A smile that sent his heart into high gear rose on petal-perfect lips.

"Hi," he greeted.

"Hello." The needle and thread went to rest on her lap. "We've finally left port."

"Yeah," he sat down on the edge of her cot. "What's your final head count?"

"Two thousand, two hundred and two, including crew, passengers, and soldiers."

Jerek let out a low whistle.

"Has to be some kind of a record," April said.

"The record will be when we arrive at Cairo."

"Are you concerned we won't?" Her tone held a touch of apprehension.

The hat, still perched on her head, blocked the meager light of the lamp, leaving most of her adorable face hidden in the shadow. He'd never met any one so infatuated with headwear. Jerek touched the hat brim.

"No, I'm not concerned we won't. The *Sultana* is a good boat. She could carry twice this weight if needed. I'm more concerned about the condition of some of those men." His finger bumped the tip of her nose before pointing to her lap. "What are you making?"

She held up a piece of cloth trimmed with lace. "A dress for Suzie's doll. I'm using a handkerchief that was my mothers." Pointing to a small bit of fabric on the table she said, "I've already made the bonnet."

"Imagine that?" Jerek said with a chuckle.

Her eyes slanted his way. "Well, the poor doll can't go around bald."

"No, I guess she can't," he said. Bald? His gaze went to her hat. Could she be bald? No, surely not. Strands of yellow peeked out beneath the rim. A thick bun of twisted gold sat below the hat at the back of her neck. Could her crown be bald? He'd never heard of a woman going bald, but there had to be a reason she wouldn't be seen without a hat.

"Jerek?"

"What?" he asked.

"I asked what you're thinking so hard about."

"Oh, just how pretty Suzie Q's doll is going to look in her new dress." He jumped to his feet. "Excuse me, April, but I..." His fingers itched to pull the hat away. He shoved them in his pockets.

As if reading his mind, her fingers rose to pull the brim further down on her forehead. Her eyes grew wide.

"It's late and time for bed. I'll see you in the morning." He strode to the door. "Lock this behind me."

Slipping out the door he waited to hear the latch catch, then rubbed the crown of his head. Surely she couldn't be bald.

****

Crisp, early morning air nibbled at her cheeks, and the boards above moaned from the enormous weight of men stirring on the upper deck. Standing near the rail, April folded her arms across her chest to briskly rub at a chill as she examined the freshly-built support beams. Her thoughts went to the men. Few of the soldiers had carried possessions on board. The vast majority didn't even have a blanket to protect them from the heavier breezes.

The steady chug and splash of the big wheel pushed the *Sultana* up a river which became wider by the mile. Today the backwaters flooded inland as far as she could see. Tall Weeping Willow trees looked like some kind of water foliage as their prolonged branches swirled in the water around flooded trunks.

"April!"

She whirled around to the sound of Willie's voice and pressed a finger to her mouth, "Shh." Tiptoeing around several sleeping forms, she eased her way to where he stood outside his cabin door.

Willie grasped her hand and pulled her into his room. "You can't be out there by yourself."

"Those poor men are so exhausted they can't do anything but sleep. I was perfectly safe." She straightened the bunched up sleeve of her dress.

"What were you doing out there?"

"I wanted to see the sun come up. But I was too late. Maybe tomorrow morning," she lied. The door to Jerek's room had snapped shut while she dressed in hers. Quickly, she'd exited her room but hadn't even caught a glimpse of his tall form. He had yet to return.

"We'll watch the sun come up after the soldiers depart in Cairo, for now you'll stay in your cabin unless you are with Jerek or me." Willie gave her an ominous stare. "Do you understand?"

She walked over to the cot and sat down beside Suzie. "Yes, Willie, I understand." Pulling a tiny garment from her pocket, she said, "Good morning, Suzie. Where is your doll? I have her dress ready."

A sleepy smile covered the little girl's face. Suzie picked the doll off the bed beside her and handed it to April. Turning the toy around to slip the dress over the wood, she paused. Someone had drawn a face on the front of the doll's head. Not just a mouth, eyes, and nose, but a likeness of a woman so real she had to run a finger across it to see if it was imagined.

The three dimensional drawing gave depth and character to the block of wood. "Willie, did you do this?"

He gave a nervous nod.

"It's beautiful," she said.

"I thought it might help Suzie remember her mommy," he said.

"How? When?"

"I borrowed an ink well from the Captain so it would be permanent. I drew it last night after Suzie fell to sleep."

"When did you learn to draw so well?" The dress fit perfectly over the wood. "I know you were always scribbling away at something when you were little, but this..."

Willie sat in the chair. "Suzanne never thought I was scribbling. She thought I was creating masterpieces. She encouraged me to draw all the time. While we were in Europe she took some of my drawings to a dealer, and they bought them, as well as several others. They wanted American scenes for books and such. When we left they asked me to continue to send more whenever possible, said they would purchase any I sent."

She tied the bonnet in place. The clothes and face brought the toy to the verge of being real. Crinkling her nose with a smile, she handed the doll to Suzie. "Here, sweetie, she's beautiful, just like you."

Suzie giggled then kissed the doll before she

cradled it in her arms.

"Do you have any of your drawings with you?"

"Yes, several books full of portraits and landscapes are in our steamer trunk down in the hull. I don't really know what I'll do with them. Maybe when Suzie and I get settled I'll send them to Europe, or maybe try to sell them here in the States. I haven't decided. I don't need the money. I still have plenty left from the others I sold." His voice sounded far away.

April rubbed her arms. She'd been so dreadful about his drawings years ago. Biting her lip, she gazed at the tall, thin, blond man sitting on the chair. Even though he was her brother, she really didn't know him. She sniffled, tears in her eyes making the back of her nose sting.

"I would like to see them."

His face lit up. "Sure, when we get home, I'll show them to you. There are several of Suzanne and Suzie. A couple of them I'd like to frame."

Suzie scooted off the bed and skipped across the floor. "Look, Daddy." Her little fingers held the doll in front of him.

"She is very pretty all dressed up." Willie took the doll and wrapped his other hand around Suzie's waist. "Almost as pretty as you," he said as he nuzzled the tiny neck beneath the curls while lifting his daughter onto his lap. He kissed Suzie's forehead then kissed the doll when the little girl held it up to his lips.

April blinked several times, but the water wouldn't dissipate. She hadn't cried in years, not since she'd awakened that frightful morning. The tears trickled down her cheeks, warm and cold at the same time. The faster she wiped the water away, the quicker it fell. She pressed a hand to her chest and waited for anger to come. It didn't. Instead something in her chest opened, like a door that had been closed for a very long time.

Willie's arms wrapped around her shoulders, and she sobbed as a deep, dark mass oozed out of that locked room inside her heart. His arms tightened. She cried while the clump in her chest broke apart and like a cleansing, spring rain, her tears washed away every last morsel.

****

Lanterns cast long shadows across the Captain's face as Jerek stepped into the alleyway. Pulling the boiler room door shut he asked, "How are the troops doing?"

"Best as can be expected." J.C. rubbed blood shot eyes. "We just weren't expecting this many. It's only been one day and the food stores are already running low. With so many not even being able to walk, the crew is working hard to get them a cup of coffee and a sandwich for supper. We'll have to make a quick stop in Helena tomorrow morning to pick up more food. They've been starved for so long I can't bear not feeding them." Mason pointed to the door. "How's the boiler?"

"Fine, I don't think we'll have any more problems. I told them to be sure and keep her water levels high. We can't take a chance of any hot spots with this load," Jerek answered.

Mason laid a hand on his shoulder. "I do appreciate your aid. Knowing you've been on top of the boiler has been a great assistance."

"You can thank me when the last man walks down that plank in Cairo."

"You going that far?"

"I am now."

"Then it's a deal. I'll even buy more than the first round of drinks." Captain Mason held out his hand, pumped Jerek's then left to continue his stroll to the galley.

Jerek tucked his shirt tail into his pants, pulled

the front of his jacket straight and with a happy whistle strolled down the companionway. The boilers were fine. He'd checked every inch himself and was confident the worse was behind them. Now, he could focus a little harder on Miss April Simonson. Not that he'd been lax so far, but there was more to come—so very much more.

In Willie's room, sitting on the bed and playing with Suzie, sat the vision of his dreams. He paused, leaned back against the door, and pretended to be interested in Willie's one-sided conversation. After being caught without an answer too many times he walked across the small room and fluffed a set of gold curls. "Hi, Suzie Q."

"Hi, Misser Bink." She held up the wooden doll now covered with a frilly, white dress and sporting a matching bonnet.

"She's almost as pretty as you."

The little head bobbed.

He turned to the sound of a soft giggle. April's face shone as fresh and brilliant as a spring daisy. He touched the brim of the straw hat and asked, "How about a bit of air, after being cooped up all day?"

"I would like that." A blush of pink touched high cheeks as she handed the wooden pony to Suzie and stood.

He waited for her to adjust the hat then took her hand. When the door closed behind them, he asked, "Would you like to go for a walk?"

"Thank you, but I'm afraid we may step on a sleeping solider if we wander too far," she said.

He winked. "I know a hidden spot."

"Really?" Her fingers curled around his.

"Yes, really." He tugged on her arm. As she stepped closer, he let go of her hand and wrapped the arm around her shoulders.

They walked around sleeping forms and greeted

others who were awake and talking with comrades. He led her past the wide paddles of the side-wheeler and up to a small look-out deck near the pilothouse. The repetitious chugging and rotations of the large paddles was noisy, but the clatter settled into the background as he directed her to one of the chairs he'd carried up the steep steps earlier.

The setting sun had turned the sky a bright orange. A soft sigh flowed over her pink, slightly parted lips as she stared at it. "It's beautiful."

"Wait until the stars come out, it's almost as if you can touch them."

She sat down and arranged the blue skirt around her knees. "Where are you going?"

"Nowhere." He sat down in the other chair and reached over to take one of her hands. Their fingers laced and fell to rest on her lap.

"I don't mean right now. I mean when we get to Cairo. Willie and I will board another steamer to take us to Minnesota. Where will you go then?"

He could lie, make up some tale or another, but he didn't want to. He leaned back until the hard wood of the chair pressed against the back of his neck and admitted, "I don't know."

"What do you mean you don't know? You have to know in order to buy a passage. Where'd you buy a ticket to?"

Her eyes tracked the side of his face as he stared over the water. "I didn't. I said I wanted a ticket north, and I wanted the cabin across the hall from yours."

"You what?"

He turned. The fading rays of light highlighted her exquisite features. He leaned forward and traced a fingertip along the fine bone of her chin. "You intrigued me when you hoisted Willie out of The Golden Girl, so I followed you, hoping to get a chance to meet you. When I discovered you'd boarded the

Sultana, I checked out of the hotel and bought a ticket." He lifted her chin and tilted his head sideways. "And here I am, getting ready to kiss the most beautiful woman in the world." Velvet soft lips met his. His palm rolled to the back of her neck to increase the union.

She kissed him back, gentle and steady at first, but as he increased the pressure of his lips, the pace of his tongue, so did she. He drank the sweetness from her mouth, and it wasn't until the heat in his loins became close to unbearable that he pulled back. Leaving a trail of kisses across her cheeks and chin, he whispered, "Mmm, perfect."

Her gaze seeped through his skin to pierce his heart. It was a sweet, painless stab, filled with passion, delight, and a touch of satisfaction. He wiggled his brows, and she giggled.

Jerek laughed, and leaving one hand to massage her neck, leaned back in his chair. The wide brim of her hat made it impossible for him to pull her head onto his shoulder. She shifted in her chair, the movement gave his hand more space, and the warmth of her skin soaked into his palm.

A faint whisper left her mouth, "Really?"

"Yes, that was perfect."

"No," she giggled, "I mean you really boarded the *Sultana* just to meet me?"

"Yup, and I'm very glad I did."

"Me too." Her hand inched over and settled on his thigh.

He stretched his legs and settled his shoulders against the chair. An unexplainable peace and contentment drifted around them like a cocoon. Together they watched the orange streaks disappear behind the trees lining the mighty river, and a million, blinking lights appear in the darkened sky.

****

Close to ten the following morning, the *Sultana*

pulled into Helena, Arkansas. Thick ropes tied the boat to massive pillars, and several crewmembers debarked to pick up supplies. April stood next to Willie and Suzie watching the activity from the rail near their cabins.

A warm, familiar hand curved around her waist. "Maybe when we dock in Memphis this afternoon there'll be enough time for you to go ashore," Jerek said. "We won't be here long enough."

April smiled at him over her shoulder and shifted a hip so it would brush against a long, lean leg. "That's okay, there's nothing I need." There wasn't, with him near, she had more than she ever dreamed.

"Daddy, look, pony," Suzie said.

A painted Morgan pony pulled a stylish black buggy along the shoreline. "Yes, that's a pony like yours," Willie agreed.

The buggy stopped near the pier, and a man stepped down from the carriage seat. After looking around, he began to unload several small packages. Busy as a beaver, the man lifted contraption after contraption out of the buggy, then began to assemble the items. Before long a camera on a tripod pointed at the *Sultana,* and he slipped beneath a dark cloth hung over the back.

"He's going to take your picture, Suzie," Willie said.

Scuttle on the upper deck made joists creak and groan. April grabbed Jerek's arm when the boat tilted from the transfer of weight above.

Dark, muddy water rose up along the hull. A deeper tilt thrust them forward. She grabbed the rail with her other hand. A scream left her throat as the boat tipped closer to the brown froth. Straight below waves slapped against the boat, splashing water onto her shoes. The wide board of the rail pressed against her stomach.

Something tugged at her hips. She clasped the rail tighter.

Jerek plucked her fingers from the wood. "April! Get back!"

Both feet left the ground as he picked her up, twisted, and rushed toward the center of the boat. Her body flattened against the outside wall of the cabins, Jerek yelled over his shoulder, "Get back! Get away from the edge!"

Men scrambled in all directions. She grabbed onto the frame of a small window in front of her and tried to hug the wall as the boat continued to lean. Her feet, following the slant of the deck, started to slip.

Crew members ran past screaming, "Don't crowd the side!"

"Get to the cabin!" Jerek shouted as Willie grabbed her arm and pulled her along the wall to the alleyway.

"Jerek!" She screamed as he turned to sprint across the deck. "No!"

"Get to the cabin!" He pointed down the open hall. His feet hit the stairs and his arms flayed over his head. "Get back, you're upsetting the boat!"

"Willie, we're gonna tip!" She fought an uphill battle.

"No we aren't! Come on!" He continued to pull on her arm.

The boat unexpectedly bounced. She grasped the long hand rail bolted to the wall as she lurched forward. The ship went backwards again and then began to haphazardly rock back and forth. Loud thuds and squeals sounded as men scrambled from left to right above and below them. Like a cork plug, the *Sultana* bounced from side to side.

The uncontrolled motions jostled her body, stirring the contents of her stomach. Undigested breakfast threatened to erupt. She pressed her mouth against her sleeve and holding onto the rail, braced her body against the unsteady movements. Her knees wobbled, and her head bobbed.

"Daddy!" Suzie cried. "Stop!"

"Daddy has you. It's okay," Willie comforted his daughter as he wrapped her tighter in his arms and leaned against the wall.

The rocking grew instead of lessoned. "Willie, we're going to tip!"

"No, no, we aren't going to tip, April. Just hold on."

She squeezed her eyes shut. The river water was so brown, and muddy. She hated water, and all of the creepy, crawling things that lived in it. Fear of what might lie beneath the surface had always prevented her from joining Willie whenever he jumped in the lake near their home on hot summer days. She didn't know how to swim, and certainly didn't want to learn now. Her throat tightened as another deep slant made her feet slip.

"Willie!"

"Don't worry, it's slowing." He grabbed her hand and helped her straighten.

"No, it's not."

"Yes, it is. Just stand still."

"I am! It's the ship that's not!"

He chuckled. She opened one eye. The rolling had eased. Slowly the creaking, cracking, and shouts reduced, and after a few minutes the ship settled into a smooth sway.

"Heavens," she sighed. Tremors of panic left her arms and legs feeling rickety. She shook them, one at a time.

"Come on, let's go to the cabin," Willie said, and wrapping his free arm around her, led them into his cabin. He placed Suzie on the bed where she picked up her toys and began to bounce them across the blanket.

April buckled onto the chair. "What on earth happened?"

"I assume everyone wanted to be in the picture and crowded the port side," Willie answered. "We're tied up, so I doubt we'd have actually tipped, but it was pretty rocky there for a few minutes."

"To say the least," she agreed and checked the position of her hat. "I shall certainly be glad when this trip is over."

"Will you?" he asked.

"Yes, won't you?"

"Sure." He tickled Suzie's tummy, making her giggle with delight. His eyes came back to April, brows lifted. "What about Jerek?"

"What about him?" She pulled the sleeves of her dress down to her wrists.

"What are his plans?"

"I don't know. Why do you ask?" Her fingers rolled along a tiny lace ruffle.

"I can tell you are quite smitten with each other."

"Willie!"

His gaze went back to his daughter. "Life is too short, Sissy. I know that for a fact." He leaned over to kiss his daughter's cheek before he looked back at her. "I don't want you to keep living in the past. I want you to be happy, to experience all you've missed by raising me. And I see that happening with Jerek."

"Willie, I didn't miss anything by—"

"Yes, you did," he interrupted. "And you still are by dedicating your life to me. I want you to know, you don't have to. You have your own life, and please, I beg you, live it."

She frowned. "Are you trying to get rid of me?"

"No, I'm not trying to get rid of you. I just don't want you to make choices on account of me any longer. I told you before, and I'm saying it again. If

Jerek asks you to go with him, instead of going to Minnesota with Suzie and me, do it. Just do it. There's so much more to life than making sure you have food on the table. I've never seen your eyes light up like they do when he's around. I've never seen you smile, or laugh like you do with him. And you deserve it. You have the right to be happy, whether you believe it or not."

"Since when did you become an expert on happiness?" She did feel happy. A feeling she'd never really felt before, and one she didn't want to end. But she couldn't leave Willie and Suzie. They were her family.

"Since I experienced it," his finger twisted a curl of Suzie's hair, "and lost a large piece of it," he said. His brows furrowed. "April, haven't you looked around this boat?"

"Of course I've looked around the boat."

"No, I mean, looked at the soldiers, really looked at them, beyond their injuries, past their physical conditions, and into their faces. They're happy. They're joyous. They've already put the past behind them. They refuse to let it and the injustices of the war rule their lives."

"Well, of course, they're happy. They're Union soldiers. They won the war."

"Neither side really won. Both suffered more losses than any of us will ever realize." He put his finger to his lips, stood and opened the small window. "Listen to them. They're singing, telling jokes, and making plans for the future."

The sounds he described floated across the boat. Even now, after almost tipping, a harmonica mingled with a banjo, and laughter fused with whistling. The voices were happy. More than happy, they sounded cheerful, excited even.

"We don't have the power to change the past, Sis, but we do have the choice of making the best of the future."

"You've grown into a remarkable man, William Simonson. I am very proud of you." For the first time in her life, April sincerely felt the pride she confessed.

A quick knock sounded on the door before it pushed open. Jerek's glance bounced off Willie and Suzie before it landed on her.

"Everyone all right?" he asked.

"Yes, Jerek, everyone is just fine," she said, her heartbeat increasing in pace at the sight of him.

A perplexed look crossed his face for a brief moment. "We're casting off now."

She nodded and the smile on her face grew. Willie was right, she did deserve to be happy, and Jerek Brinkley certainly made her happy.

His gaze went to Willie. "No one was injured. Mason had warned the men not to make sudden movements, and to keep the weight evenly distributed, but in the excitement of seeing the camera they forgot." Jerek looked back at her. "It won't happen again."

"Well, you can't blame them." She folded her hands in her lap.

Willie squeezed her shoulder. The touch was light, and made her wonder if he'd never heard her say the words before. Probably not—her whole life she'd been blaming someone for something. She always looked for the problem, never the solution. Well, no more, from now on she was going to see her glass half full instead of half empty. She, April Simonson was going to *live*.

Willie's face held a bright and knowing smile. Jerek looked puzzled. She stretched a hand toward him. He took it. "I think I shall go see if any of the soldiers would like a drink of water," she said and rose from her chair.

"You're gonna what?"

Chapter Six

"Some of those men can barely move off their cots. I think I will go see if they need something. The crew can't possibly see to all of them." April patted his handsome face, glanced to Willie and said, "Would you care to join me?"

"Sure," he said and picked up his daughter. "Come on Suzie. Do you want to help Auntie April?"

Suzie nodded and wrapped her arms around his neck.

Jerek reached out an arm to stop April, but pulled it back. The rocking of the boat had been frightening. This must be her way of getting over the scare, and if that's what she needed who was he to stop it? She was an amazing creature. With a slight chuckle, he pulled the door shut and directed her to the water barrels.

Within minutes, and following her instructions, he and Willie each carried a bucket of fresh drinking water and a dipper. Walking from group to group, they offered drinks, conversed, and listened to descriptions of destination points.

Suzie's cherub face brought bright smiles as the little girl shared her precious pony and doll with soldiers. Jerek didn't know who had more fun, the little girl or her aunt. April's face beamed with delight as they wandered around the crowed decks.

Stronger breezes flowed over the hurricane deck and ruffled the flowers of her tightly pinned hat. Every once in a while she'd tug the brim low on her brows. Several strands of long blond hair fell from the bun and fluttered across her shoulders.

Never had he wanted to see beneath something so badly. Once, when he was a small child, his grandfather had come to see them. He'd brought Jerek and his brothers each a wrapped present. He couldn't remember what had been in the packages, but he could remember looking at the paper and trying to imagine what was underneath it. When his mother had given permission, his brothers had torn the paper from theirs, but he'd slowly untied the string and folded back the paper, taking time to relish the experience of revealing the prize. That's what he wanted to do now, remove the hat, inch by inch, and let a golden treasure be discovered.

She wasn't bald beneath it, he couldn't believe that, but there had to be a reason she wouldn't be seen without a hat. Maybe she had a misshapen head. A kid in school, Bob, or Bill, no, Brad, or some B name, had had a weird-shaped head. The other children had called him Blockhead, yeah, Bob the blockhead. Funny, he hadn't thought about him in years.

The steam whistle of the *Sultana* pierced the air and scattered his wayward thoughts. He stepped beside April and touched her arm. "We'll soon pull into the port of Memphis. Perhaps you'd like to return to your cabin now to freshen up. We'll go ashore for supper while the ship unloads cargo."

"Oh," April glanced at the long stream of men they hadn't visited yet. A frown tugged at the corners of her eyes. "I suppose you're right. I guess we'll have to get to the others tomorrow." Her head gave a little nod, the kind people use when they agree with themselves. She looped her arm through

110

his and beset him with a deep smile.

By the time the boat docked, their small group was ready to disembark. The ship had nosed into port due to the large fleet of various sized boats already lining the shore. Moored as such meant there was only one way on and off the ship. A long line of the stronger soldiers formed near the hulls. The men anxiously awaited the opportunity to earn a little pocket money by helping to roll the hogsheads of sugar ashore. Jerek steered April past the long line, they needed to be off the boat before the unloading started or be trapped until it ended.

Mason halted their steps. "Jerek, could I speak with you for a moment?"

Jerek held a sigh and nodded before he said to April, "I'll meet you on shore." Glancing to Willie, he added, "Please secure a carriage. I'll just be a minute."

He followed Mason beyond the crowd of men. "I was wondering if you could secure a boilermaker to check the patch we got in Vicksburg."

"Is something amiss?" Jerek asked.

"No, no, the engineer claims she's fine. But we'll be going through some rough water north of Memphis. Spring rains have the river flowing four miles wide in places, and I want her checked one more time before we leave here. If all checks out, we should set out about midnight."

"All right, I'll send a man out before we dine," Jerek agreed and took his leave of the boat.

Wet, uneven layers of cobblestones filled the hill from the river to the street level of Memphis and made Jerek slow his hurried climb. The slight mist of the evening air held a promise for stronger rains to form as night fell. Topping the ridge, he saw Willie escort April into a covered buggy. He maneuvered through the crowd and after asking the driver to make a stop at the office of a boilermaker

R.J. Taylor had recommended, climbed in to take a seat beside her.

The clops of the horse's shod feet bounced off the cobblestones as the buggy jerked forward. He leaned close and over the echoes said, "I have to run a quick errand for Captain Mason then we'll have supper and maybe do some shopping."

"There isn't anything I need to shop for, but we'll gladly accompany you," April said.

"Perhaps you'd like a new hat?"

One hand flew to the floppy white hat she'd worn in New Orleans. A worried frown covered her face.

"It looks perfect."

Her smile became wide and bright. "Thank you," she whispered before she turned to glance out the side window. "Memphis seems to be as large as New Orleans."

"It too is a thriving port city," he answered.

April nodded and began to point out sights for Suzie to look at from her own window as they traveled along. He and Willie joined in on the site seeing, and he didn't know who had more ooh's and ahh's, the little girl or her aunt.

When the wagon halted, Jerek assured, "I'll be right back." The mist wasn't as thick near the buildings, but the evening air was heavy with humidity. He pulled the lapels of his black suit together and fastened the bottom button as he walked into the building.

After setting a meeting point following the boilermaker's assessment, he left the building, directed the driver to a restaurant, then climbed back into the carriage.

April pulled the material of her white skirt aside as Jerek resettled onto the seat. Her fingers twisted in the material. Why hadn't she packed more than two dresses when she left Minnesota? Though they were two of her favorites, she'd grown tired of both the blue one, and the white one she'd once again donned.

Under her lashes, she glanced at Jerek. Maybe she should buy a store-bought dress. The petticoat beneath her skirt held plenty of coins—she could afford to part with a few. Perhaps she'd find something while shopping later, but only if it had a nice, matching hat.

The men conversed as they traveled past tall buildings. People roamed the streets, and music blared from several open doorways. Hopefully the restaurant wouldn't be filled with the bawdy men strolling in and out of the establishments. A shiver ran over her shoulders. Unshaven faces were every where. She'd yet to see a man without whiskers, other than the handsome one whose leg pressed against hers.

She tapped her knee. Her cheeks grew warm and her smile brighter than a banker's in a safe, when Jerek's warm hand merged with her drumming fingers.

The wagon traveled beyond the boisterous downtown and entered quieter streets. Small, green-leafed trees and ornamental glass lanterns lined the road. Tall, brick buildings and men with neatly dressed women on their arms promenaded down the sidewalks. The carriage slowed to a stop, and a minute later the driver opened the door. Jerek waved for Willie and Suzie to exit before he made his way down the steps and turned to take her hand. His attention made her feel like Cinderella, a story her mother often repeated, about a maid who became a queen, a fairy tale. She'd never liked fairy tales, but now, she believed in them.

He held her hand until her feet stepped on the brick walkway, and then folded her fingers around his elbow. His hand lay atop hers as he led them toward a brightly lit building.

Massive wooden doors, decorated with etched, beveled glass, had large, elegant handles painted a brilliant gold. A man, dressed completely in black, opened one of the doors then held it wide for their small party to enter the building.

April pressed a hand to her throat as they entered. A foyer two-stories tall hosted a brilliant chandelier. It held over sixty candles and hung from a center point in the ceiling. Hundreds of small, crystal pendants dangled from the brass holders on delicate chains and reflected the light. Soft rainbows of yellow and orange emanated from the crystals to nonchalantly bounce off the brightly painted walls and give the area a festive, elegant glow. *This must be what a castle looks like.*

Another man, dressed in black, greeted Jerek by name and happily escorted them into a large dining room. Tables draped with black cloths and adorned with flowers and candelabras filled the room. Sophisticated couples and groups quietly conversed as light music played in the background. A slight tug on her arm encouraged her to continue through the room.

The man led them to a table near a set of windows. Jerek pulled out a chair. She sat, smiled her thanks, and twisted to the eight-foot high, solid panes of glass. A small fountain sprayed a stream of water in an arch before it fell into a rock pond amass with flowers of every size, color, and shape. Another man dressed in black walked around lighting the small lanterns that circled the area.

April turned back to the table and sighed, "This is the most beautiful thing I've ever seen."

"I thought you said that about the garden in Vicksburg," Jerek said with a wide smile.

She wrinkled her nose at him. "No, I said that was the loveliest thing I'd ever seen. This is the most beautiful thing I've ever seen." She reached over to pat his hand as he lifted the folded napkin from the table. "There is a difference."

His gaze danced across her face, pausing for a moment here and there before he said, "I agree again, the most beautiful thing I've ever seen."

The out of control pounding in her chest might cause her heart to beat its way right up her throat and out her mouth. She'd heard of swooning, but never imagined it would happen to her. Jerek's gaze went over her shoulder, and he gave a slight nod.

A waiter, dressed as the other workers, held out a menu. Jerek let go so she could grasp the large leather bound tablet. Fancy script covered both pages. The words blurred.

"Would you like me to order for you?" he asked.

"Y-yes, please," she agreed and handed the binder back to the waiter. Not really listening to what anyone ordered, she let her gaze take in the room. It was magnificent. Black velvet drapes hung from the windows, and flocked, black flowers decorated the paper on the walls. Her eyes settled on Willie, he didn't appear to be amazed. Neither did Suzie.

Willie's brows rose, and he smiled. "I thought you'd like it when Jerek suggested it. Suzanne had a favorite place in London. It was very similar to this."

The waiter returned to pour them each a glass of wine. April started to protest, "I never—"

"Live a little, Sis," Willie interrupted as he lifted his glass. "May I propose a toast?"

Jerek raised his glass. April followed suit while Willie helped Suzie lift her water glass. "To April, eighteen sixty-five, a month we'll always remember," Willie said.

Crystal goblets clinked together over the center of the table. Jerek's glass touched hers again. "Here, here." His gaze held hers in a deep, thoughtful stare

before he said, "An April to remember."
****

April wished the night didn't have to end, but the sleeping child in her brother's arms encouraged Jerek to hail a carriage and instruct the driver to take them to the river front. After a six course meal of delectable, appetizing foods she'd never seen, nor tasted before, the four of them had strolled along the storefronts. Much to her disappointment and it appeared, Jerek's as well, the establishments had already closed for the day. Beautiful, flowing dresses decorated some of the wide windows, and she made mental notes of styles and designs she'd like to recreate.

The night sky had grown dark, not a single star could be seen through the heavy fog hanging over the water. A man waved to Jerek as he escorted her from the carriage. He excused himself, and she, Willie, and the sleeping Suzie began their descent of the cobblestone hill. The walkway was clear of other passengers, and in no time they stepped onto the gangplank.

April squinted through the mist to see Jerek still engaged in conversation at the top of the ridge. She followed her brother to their cabins, bade him a good night and entered her room. The locking bolt slid into place with a click. She let out a sigh of contentment and leaned against the door. Her hands rose to clutch together over her heart. It had been the most romantic night of her life.

She took a few moments to seal the cherished memory in her mind then stepped away from the door to light the lamp hanging on the wall. Blowing out the match, she twirled around in the small open space before she set the spent wooden stick on the metal tray. Spinning the opposite direction, she lifted her skirt with both hands, and practiced a curtsy. As she rose she stretched one hand out and cocked her wrist, emulating Abigail Hanson's movement.

She giggled and continued her game by batting her lashes, and saying aloud, "Oh, Mr. Brinkley, you spoil me so. You simply make my heart go pitter patter, and I do believe I would like to spend the rest of my life in your presence."

A knock on the door startled her enough to lose her balance. She landed on the bed with a flop that sent her hat askew. Scrambling to her feet, she rushed to the door. "Who is it?"

"Jerek."

Fretfully, she straightened the hat then ran trembling fingers down her dress before slipping the bolt out of its holder.

Jerek pushed the door open and peeked around the frame. "Who were you talking to?"

"Talking to?"

"Yes, I heard you talking to someone," he continued to look around the small area, "and giggling."

"Oh, I was-uh-thinking of something Suzie said earlier." Her face grew hot, and she turned, hiding the flush from his view. "Did you complete your business?"

"Yes, well almost," he said as the weight of his hands fell on her shoulders. With gentle pressure he turned her around. "I still have to go up to the Captain's quarters on the Texas deck, to meet with Mason, but I was afraid you'd be asleep when I came back down."

She couldn't stop her roaming gaze. It started at his dark hair, went over his brows, across eyes that met hers with intensity, down his straight nose, chiseled cheeks, past full, wide lips to a finely molded chin.

"Oh?" she sighed. Her gaze went back to the dark brown eyes. "Why should it matter if I was asleep?"

"Because then I would have to wake you."

"And why would you need to wake me?"

His finger skimmed below her chin. The slow, gentle caress sent tingles down her neck. He drew closer and said, "So I can kiss you good night."

Their lips met. Her sigh mingled with his breath. Wide, sure hands slid off her shoulders and down her back. One traveled up and down her spine then made wide circles across her shoulder blades.

Her fingers traveled over his hips, before they slid up to his waist, and over his ribcage to follow the molded lines around to his back. She kneaded at the solidness, feeling the flesh beneath his suit coat.

One of his hands stilled at the valley of her lower back, and while pressing her breasts against his chest, he took a step forward to fuse their bodies. Her fingers lowered, found a way to sneak under his jacket, and ran along the smooth material of his shirt. The heat beneath her palms was immense and stimulating. She twisted her hips and forced his thigh to press harder against her pelvis where a burning need ignited. A moan rumbled from her throat.

Jerek pulled his lips from hers. She leaned forward, trying to catch them again. As her head lifted, he ducked his and ran soft, light kisses down her chin onto her neck. He took a step back, and while one arm remained around her shoulders, the other went behind her knees.

In one swift movement, he picked her up and twisted to lay her on the bed. Her head landed on the pillow, trapping the floppy brim beneath it. Automatically she grabbed the front brim and held it over her forehead.

Jerek laughed. He settled one knee next to her hip, and leaned over her. "Don't worry, sweetheart, it's still intact." He lowered his face to search her mouth one more time. Withdrawing, he shook his head. "I need to leave before I can't."

She felt as if she were floating on a cloud. Her body throbbed from head to toe, at the same time it luxuriated in a feeling of euphoria. She ran a finger from his temple to his chin. "What?"

He laughed, pressed one last kiss on her lips, and said, "Good night, my sweet April." Seconds later, the door clicked shut.

She had no idea how long she laid there, completely unable to move. When her body began to feel somewhat normal, she rose, bolted the door, and extinguished the light. Without thought to her dress or hat, she lay back down on the bed, closed her eyes, and asked her mind to relive the last half hour.

****

Jerek stood at the railing near the end of the alleyway and let the damp night air cool his overheated body. That was as close to the point of no return as he'd ever been. He lifted his face to the sky, and shook his hips, forcing the pulsating blood to relent some of its demands. After a moment or two, he pulled a cigarillo from his pocket and struck the end of a match against the rail. The flame fought in opposition of the damp air. He quickly drew on the stogie before the fog extinguished the fire. The tip grew deep red, and he pulled it from his mouth, letting smoke mingle with his deep sigh. The stick of tobacco hung between his fingers as he draped his hand over the rail and waited for his mind to gain control of his body.

The heavy fog distorted his vision, but he heard men, a few at a time, return to the boat. Several of the stronger soldiers had ventured into town to spend the small amount of money they'd earned by unloading the sugar on a glass or two of beer. Their jesting and joyous voices drifted up as their feet clomped on the floating boards. He lifted the cigarillo to his lips, but the smoldering end had gone out. He flicked the stick outward forcing it to fall two stories to the water below before he turned to make his way up two stories to the Texas deck.

Mason stood at the top of the stairs. "The boilermaker said he talked to you," Jerek said as he climbed the final steps.

"Yes, he said she's good to go. The patch is holding, no bulges whatsoever, and the other ones look good and clean too," the Captain answered.

"What about the weight, now that the hulls are almost empty?" Jerek asked.

"I had the men transfer anything possible to the hulls, and we're going across the river to load a thousand bushels of coal. That will help too. As long as we don't hit any rough water, we should be fine. Two more days Jerek, two more days, and this trip from hell will be over."

He smiled to himself, Mason called it the trip from hell, and he considered it a gift from heaven. April's attendance made him forget the treacherous ride.

"Well, at least you don't have to worry about the boilers. They won't be giving you any problems." He glanced around the crowded deck. "The men are all doing well. They seem to be a good group."

"They are. No problems at all. We're just so heavy, and like I said earlier, the flooded waters north of Memphis are unpredictable. The river finds a way to reroute itself every spring along this stretch."

"Think this fog's gonna lift?" He rocked on his heels.

Mason let out a heavy sigh. "I hope so. Appears the storm fizzled, hopefully the fog will follow suit."

Jerek pulled two cigarillos from his pocket and handed J.C. one. "I haven't asked how the family is doing."

Mason lit the stick before replying, "Good, good, the missus still wants me to give up river boating, and after this trip, I might consider what she says a little harder."

He chuckled and encouraged Mason to converse about frivolous subjects as they sucked on the sticks of tobacco. It was close to midnight when the Captain received word that the *Sultana* was ready to deport.

Mason signaled the pilothouse to sound the whistle, and Jerek made his way down the steps. Crossing the hurricane deck, he sidestepped dozens of men trying to sleep with little or no protection against the misty air. Descending the second set of stairs, he once again heard the return of passengers scurrying up the plank before the *Sultana* pulled away.

He paused near the rail, wondering how many would be left ashore, either because time got a way from them, or by choice. The clink and clank of the plank being removed, then the slosh of the tie-downs being lifted signaled the ship was afloat. Within minutes, the *Sultana* pulled from the shores of Memphis and headed a mile across the river to load coal.

Jerek made his way into his cabin, removed his boots, and settled onto the narrow cot. Knowing April lay across the hall teased his senses. He folded his arms across his chest and relived the delightful evening they'd spent. When the boat chugged to a halt, heavy footfalls clomped down the stairs as men prepared to assist loading coal.

Two days to Cairo, then what? Would he join her and travel to Minnesota, or should he ask her to travel to Cincinnati with him? It was time for him to go home. He no longer felt animosity for his brother or Eloise. Actually, he felt happiness for them, and hoped they had found the love he'd discovered.

One hand rubbed his forehead. Had he found love? He undid the top couple of buttons on the white shirt, weaved his hands together and slipped them beneath his head. Was this love?

He liked April, and his body lusted for her. He'd need a little more time to completely figure it out—so whether it is Minnesota or Ohio, they would not separate two days from now...nor two years, or twenty. 'Til death do we part,' filtered through his mind as the corners of his mouth lifted, and his lids fluttered shut.

****

Confused, April jumped from her bed. She didn't know if the noise or the furious rocking of the boat had waken her, but either way, something was terribly wrong. Screams and moans, wood splintering and a roaring sound vibrated through the listing boat. Fighting the sways, she stumbled to the door. Pulling it open, she encountered Willie and Jerek flying from their rooms.

"What is it? What's happening?" she screamed above the roar.

"Stay here!" Jerek held his hand up before he turned and ran down the alleyway.

Flashes of light and thick smoke filled the air.

She turned to Willie. "We're on fire! The boat's on fire!"

"Get your life belt on!" Willie ran back into his cabin.

April reentered her room and grabbed the belt from the wall hook. Quickly she wrapped the stiff rope laced through several pieces of cork around her waist and tied a tight knot. What else should she grab? It would be too difficult to swim with her carpetbag. Swim? She couldn't swim! She didn't know how! She pressed her hands to her face then ran for the door.

Willie met her in the hall. Belts, identical to

hers were tied around him and Suzie, who sobbed in his arms. "We have to get to the stern, there's a lifeboat there!" April shouted and turned.

"One boat isn't going to save two thousand people!" Willie grabbed her arm. "We'll wait here until Jerek returns to tell us how bad it is. They have fire buckets, I'm sure the crew is putting the fire out as we speak."

She fought the panic rising in her chest as screams of mayhem and terror continued to grow. She clutched the hand rail on the wall and shouted, "Where is he?"

"It's only been a few minutes. Just stay calm."

"I am—"

Jerek rounded the corner.

Fear marred his face. He grabbed her arm and pulled her behind him. "A boiler blew. The force of the explosion blew the ship nearly in two. We have to get to the bow, we'll be safe there!"

"But there are two lifeboats near the stern, we have to get to one!" she insisted.

"We can't get through!" His lips continued to move, but the noise of the chaos was too great for her to hear.

As they reached the railing and began to run toward the bow, the upper deck collapsed with a great rumble. It sounded like thunder rolling across the sky. Jerek threw her to the floor then covered her body with his as splintered wood let loose and shot through the air. The noise was deafening and the heaves of the boat pitched them into others crouched low. Screams of anguish and pain sounded as men were tossed about like leaves in the wind. A lifeless body landed inches from her face; she squeezed her eyes shut against the empty gaze of the unknown man.

Jerek pulled her to her feet and pushed her forward, forcing her to run to the front of the boat.

"Willie and Suzie?" She twisted, and over his shoulder saw Willie's blond hair.

She tried to jump over broken and scalded bodies, but they littered the deck. The rumble of the boat and the way it careened, made steps falter. She screamed each time a foot landed on flesh. A familiar smell entered her nose, that of burning tissue. She began to choke and gag, tears streamed from her eyes. Her free hand covered her nose and mouth, but the smell couldn't be blocked.

They reached the bow, along with hundreds of others. The fires behind them continued to build, lighting the area as if it were daytime. The crowd pushed forward, packing them tight against one another. Men, women, and children screamed and cried at the pandemonium. Long, echoing shrieks lingered in the air as men dove off the ruins of the upper deck. From four stories up bodies sailed through the air and into the rolling water below.

The river grew with wreckage. Chunks of wood, railings, rafters, and other boat parts, floated amongst a mass of bodies, bobbing heads, arms, and legs. Fragments of still-flaming wood rolled on the high waves and crashed into other objects, often forcing whatever they encountered to sink below sharp-peaked waves.

Two men holding a large plank of wood pushed through the crowd. Once they reached the bow, they threw the wood overboard and jumped in behind it. The lumber hit the rising and falling water, slamming into the crowded river with a great splash. Men scrambled to swim and climb onto the life raft. In no time the plank, along with a handful of men, sank below the heaving waves. None of them resurfaced.

Beyond the mayhem, April searched for land, but there was only water for miles, black, mean-looking water. Tremors ripped across her body.

"What are we going to do?" she screamed and grabbed the front of Jerek's shirt. "What are we going to do?"

The havoc was too loud. She couldn't hear what he said. He crushed her tighter against his body and continued to ease them forward, through the crowd. They reached the front rail where several ropes had been thrown over the side of the boat with one end tied to the precarious railing. Like a colony of ants, one behind the other, people climbed over the banister and lowered themselves into the foamy swirls below.

Alarmed, she tried to twist from Jerek's grasp. She didn't want to be near the edge, the pressure from behind might force her over the side. Panic pulled at her skin. She couldn't breathe. Her heart raced, painfully beating against the wall of her chest. His hold was too tight and forced her into the rail. She scratched and clawed at his hands and arms.

His face was right in front of hers, his lips moved but the noises were too loud. She couldn't hear over the racket of the disaster.

She shook her head from side to side, screaming, "I can't! I can't swim!"

Something tugged on her arm. Willie let his hand fall from her sleeve as he climbed over the side, and with Suzie clutched in one arm, began to slide down the rope.

"No! Willie, no!" Her throat burned as his head disappear over the edge.

With movements so quick, she couldn't protest Jerek lifted her, climbed over the edge, and began to descend the length of the rope. She buried her face against his shoulder, and wrapped her arms around his neck. Uncontrollable sobs racked her body as they slipped closer and closer to the water.

The boat, rocking out of control, caused the rope

to swing and sway. They slammed into the side of the boat; the force almost knocked them from the lifeline.

Her arms around his neck tightened. Water boiled up to meet them. Tears blurred her vision, but not enough to block the horror below. Heads bobbed like apples in a barrel.

Arms stretched out of the water, grabbing at Jerek's feet. She felt his body being tugged down, and turned from the sight as he kicked at the hands wrapped around his boot. Waves splashed against them, and her feet lowered into ice-cold water, she pulled them upward, fearful of what they might encounter and tried to grab the rope above his head. A boot stamped at her hands. Above them a trail of people climbed down the rope.

Without warning and with a great swoosh, she fell. The bitter cold stole her breath as her head went below crashing waves. Deeper and deeper she sank into a dark abyss.

Horrified, her arms flayed and her feet lashed out, slapping and kicking at whatever might be near. Everything was black. Icy water stung her eyes and filled her nose with a force so great it penetrated her brain. Crushing pressure engulfed her chest, the useless air in her lungs burning with the need to be released.

Something clawed at her arms. She thrashed about, but it snagged her wrist and pulled. The force ripped on her shoulder and hurled her through the water. Fighting against the swift movements made air bubble out of her mouth. Seconds later, something grabbed her ribs and propelled her upward.

With unexplainable speed, she shot through the water. Gulps of air scorched aching lungs as her face broke the surface. Amongst the debris of wood, cargo and bodies, the colossal side of the *Sultana* careened.

White-capped waves boiled, threatening to drive her into the massive hull or back into the frightening abyss below. Murky water hit the back of her throat before a scream could join hundreds of others echoing through the night.

She threw her head back, choking and gasping for air as her arms flayed against the assaulting water, and kicked both feet at the force lugging her downward. Something wrapped around one hand and another strong heave wrenched her shoulder. She twisted away from the splashes trying to fill her mouth and nose. The steely grip tightened as it towed her away from the ship.

"Jerek!" Her free hand tried to latch onto the fingers wrapped around her wrist.

"I've got you!" he yelled above the roar of chaos. His other arm swiftly glided in and out of the water before it wrapped around a bobbing object. With a hard tug, he pulled her next to it. "Grab on with both hands!"

The current was too swift. Her skirt, yards of wet material, acted like a sail and tugged her away from him. The sleeve of his shirt threatened to slip from her fingers.

Jerek seized an elbow and thrust her forward. She wheezed for air as her chest slammed against the floating log.

His hands forced her arms around the cold, wet wood. "April! Don't let go! Don't you dare let go!"

She nodded and clawed until her fingernails dug into a forced crevice. Things continued to brush and tug on her legs and the heavy material of her skirt. Each touch sent a new wave of panic through her body, making her frantically kick at the unknown predator.

Jerek hefted his chest onto the other side of the log and framed her face with both hands. "Calm down! Don't panic. Listen to me!"

She shook her head and kicked her feet harder. She had to get on the piece of wood, out of the water.

His hands squeezed her face. "It's not big enough to hold you, but it will keep you afloat if you don't panic. Just relax your body and let it float on the waves."

"I can't! I can't swim! And the water is full of, all kinds of—*things!*" She wrapped her arms tighter around the wood.

"I know sweetheart, but listen to me. You're going to be fine. I won't let anything happen to you. You have a lifebelt on, it will help, just relax your legs, let them float to the top of the water and ride on the waves."

He let go of her face, and edged his way to her side of the log. His hands left the log to float under her body then lifted her legs and made them stretch out behind her.

The heaviness of her body lessened, allowing her to inch up on the log.

"That's a girl, just relax," he instructed. "Breathe, April. Take slow even breaths. You can do it. Just breathe, and let your body float."

She tried, but a mingling bout of panic hit and tension dragged her feet down. She was going to drown. Oh, God, ugly terrible things were pulling her under the water again. She dug her fingernails deeper into the wood and kicked harder.

"April!" With a sharp tug Jerek pulled her legs back up. "I'm here, I've got you."

He did have her, and knowing so lessened her fear. Sucking in a shaky breath, she willed her legs to go limp. They stretched out behind her and the sinking feeling eased. "I-I can do it, Jerek. I understand."

He floated back around the log and inched along until the wood leveled. "Good girl, you got it now. We'll just let the current carry us back to Memphis."

Over his shoulder, flames glowed against a black sky. The blaze of the fire highlighted bodies still flying from the edges to land in water that looked to full to hold another. Something floated on every square inch. The two huge smokestacks tilted at an odd angle, and she screamed as one, then the other toppled, listing the boat as they went. The side of the boat dipped beneath the surface. With an echoing crash the stacks hit the water, forcing those within range to sink beneath the massive pillars.

The flames renewed themselves and within minutes the bow of the boat, where hundreds still crowded, became engulfed with fire. People hanging on the ropes became small balls of fire as they fell to the water.

Jerek cupped her face as she screamed again. She twisted against his touch, catching glimpses of cruel scenes of death and devastation in every direction.

Wails of anguish vibrated the air near and far. Arms frantically flailed above the rolling waves then sank below with fingers still trying to grasp on to something, anything. Bodies already lifeless, floated amongst those fighting to survive. Faces were unrecognizable, nothing more than dark blobs hovering above the waves.

He flattened his palms over her ears. "April, calm down!"

She fought the pressure, trying to search the white-capped waves. "Willie and Suzie!"

Jerek leaned forward, his face inches from hers. "I saw him find a chunk of wood before you went under. I'm sure they're floating just a head of us." He touched his forehead to hers. "Honey, you have to stay calm."

Warmth from his head merged with her icy skin. "My hat, where's my hat?" Her legs began to thrash.

"April! Don't panic!" He grabbed the log. "You

don't need a hat while we're floating down the river."

Water splashed into her mouth as she gulped for air. He didn't understand! She *needed* her hat.

"April! You're making the log roll!"

Bark broke off beneath her fingernails, the log rolling out of her grasp. "Jerek!"

He pulled on her forearms, forcing her weight onto the slippery log. "Lift your legs! Don't fight the water!"

She closed her eyes and forced both legs to rise. He released the pressure on her arms as the log settled, and her feet once again floated on top of the waves.

"Good girl, I'm going to try and steer us out of the main current, we'll be safer where the water isn't flowing so hard." He began to kick with his feet.

Tall waves lifted and lowered them as Jerek angled the log away from the main stream of the river. Before long the rolling lessened and their speed slowed.

The swifter current in the center continued to carry a flow of traffic. People floated past grasping onto logs, doors, barrels, even dead horses and mules.

She started to point, but quickly returned her grasp on the log. "Jerek!"

"What?"

"It's the alligator!"

A man rode atop the crate as it floated on the faster stream a few yards away. He gave a wave and shouted, "Don't worry Ma'am, I killed it with my bayonet before I threw it over board and jumped on." He tugged on the tail protruding through two of the wooden bars to prove his story as he passed their slow moving log.

Behind him, four men struggled to hold onto a mattress. One bounded his body out of the water and crawled onto the form. Another pushed at him "Don't climb on, you'll sink us all." The words had no sooner left the man's mouth than the mattress started to sink. The men refused to let go, and soon, all four were below the waves.

April watched, but none of them resurfaced. She closed her eyes and waited until some of the sounds of carnage faded before lifting her lids again.

"Where are we?"

"The island near the boat is Hen and Chickens. It's about seven miles north of Memphis," Jerek explained.

"Seven miles?"

"I'm sure rescue boats will be along soon."

"I'm so cold. The water is so cold." Her teeth began to chatter. Each splatter of water was icier than the one before. Bitter tremors ran up and down her arms and legs.

"I know, honey, but hold on and don't think about it." Jerek ran his hands over her arms. "Just hold on, April. Hold on."

She shivered beneath his fingers. Jerek repositioned and clutched her elbows, forcing them to stay on top of the log. "When we get to Memphis, we'll get a room at a hotel, and you can climb into a bath of warm water."

She tried to smile. "I-I t-think-k... e-enough water...f-for... o-one night." Her teeth chattered so hard she could barely speak.

"How about a hot cup of tea and a warm blanket?"

"Y-yes-s," she nodded.

"Done," he said.

"T-thank y-you."

He touched her chin and looked into eyes that had begun to droop.

"Aren't.... y-... c-cold?"

"No, I'm fairly hot blooded."

"M-must... b-be...n-nice."

"I thought you'd be used to cold, coming from Minnesota."

"N-no-o." She gave a tiny shake of her head before one cheek fell to rest on the log.

Her arms grew limp. Panic rose in his chest. "April, April, honey, listen to me, you can't give in to the cold. Lift your head, look at me."

Her chin barely rose. "I-I c-can't…"

Jerek tugged on her elbows, pulling her body further up on the log. "Yes, you can! You have to!"

"I-it's s-so c-cold-d."

Jerek didn't know what to do. If he made her kick her feet, it would work against him as he tried to propel them forward and soon exhaust them both. "Think of something warm, honey," he encouraged.

"I-I'm t-tired," she whispered as her head fell to the side.

The strain of holding her on the log pulled at his muscles. He tried to pull himself up further. The wood jostled and she almost slipped from his grasp. "Don't let go! Don't you dare let go!" he screamed. Pulling and twisting, he worked until her arms were wrapped around the log again.

A whistle split the air. A faint light glistened through the mist.

"April, it's a boat! It's a rescue boat. They're coming, honey! They'll be here shortly! April do you hear me?"

Her head bobbed up and down with the log. One cheek rolled on the wet wood and water sloshed at her face. She didn't sputter, spit, or try to move away from the splashes.

"April!" He grabbed her face. "April! Can you hear me?"

"Y-yes-s."

The sound was so faint he questioned if he'd heard it.

He pumped his legs, kicking his feet vigorously,

pushing the log down stream as fast as possible. "April they're coming. They'll be here any minute. You have to stay awake so you can climb aboard!"

Her head rolled toward him, tiny, purple lips trembled with each ragged breath. "T-tell th-them...t-to h-hurry."

Chapter Seven

"They are hurrying, honey. They'll be here any minute now, stay awake, keep talking so they hear us!"

She didn't respond.

Jerek lowered his head to hers. "April?" He touched her cheek. "April!"

She was slipping away. Not from his grasp, but from responsiveness, from life. The tiny, blinking light barely touched the horizon, and land was nowhere in sight. The swollen river was over four miles wide.

He clutched her arms against the log with one hand and worked his way around until his fingers squeezed between the life belt rope and her back. Paddling with his feet, he forced the wood to make a circle. After the log repositioned to float downstream in front of them, he eased his legs beneath hers and waited as a larger wave rolled near.

Pressing her arms against the log, he took a deep breath and ducked below water. He surfaced between her arms. Her slight, limp weight settled onto his back and her head lobbed against his shoulder blade.

"April? April, can you hear me?"

"Mmm," she moaned.

He rolled his body up the log, securing her arms

over his shoulders and against the wood. "Honey, you have to wake up so you can wave to the boat. It's almost here." The light was closer, but moving slow because the boat picked up other survivors as it drew closer to the wreckage.

"April, it's coming, can you see it?" He tried to rub her arms, but the movement made the log joggle. "Don't give up on me now, honey. It'll be here in a few minutes. You can have your tea, and I'll find you a warm blanket."

He continued to talk to her, promising the sun itself in hopes of hearing the slightest mumble, until the netted rope floating beside a gunboat rolled within reach. With the help of sailors he hauled April's limp body over the rail of the *USS Tyler*.

Searching survivors for Willie and Suzie, he carried April to where others huddled beneath blankets. His chest tightened. A little blond head was nowhere amongst the wet occupants.

A sailor directed him to an empty space. Jerek sat down, wrapped a blanket around her then pulled another over his shoulders. Crewmembers continued to haul people out of the water, while others carried warm cups of coffee to dozens of shivering bodies, as he cradled April's chilled body on his lap.

Her breath was slow and shallow, but the flutter of it against his neck gave hope. He tucked the blanket tighter over the dirty brown of the once white dress, and picked small twigs and fragments of shattered wood from her hair. Afterwards he brushed the bangs away from her forehead, and pressed his lips to it as tears stung his eyes.

Never had he witnessed hell like they'd lived through tonight. It was unforgettable. The blast had ripped him from his bed with the loudest crack of thunder imaginable. Leaving April and Willie standing in the hallway, he'd made his way toward the boiler room. Flames, fueled by bodies sliding down the collapsed structure turned the center of the boat into a raging cavern of fire. Steam clouds and scalding water covered everything. Large, burning clumps of coal had landed and started additional fires sporadically across the wood.

He'd turned around to run back to April, pushing and prodding, he'd fought the crowd to get back to their cabins. Though it felt like hours it couldn't have been more than twenty minutes from the time of the blast to when the boat was completely engulfed in flames.

He forced his eyes to open, trying to rid the nasty images from his mind. But the view in front of him was no kinder. Cries and moans for mercy came from the bodies sprawled across the deck. Countless were covered with blistered and peeling skin. He could only imagine that as their bodies began to warm, the pain would become excruciating. Once again he diverted his eyes from the agony the disaster had imposed on so many.

A pale glow entered the eastern sky. Tiny fragments of light began to reflect off the bits of mist clinging in the air as the gunboat chugged closer to the remains of the *Sultana*.

An enormous hiss filled the air when the great side-wheeler gave up her struggle. A final pillar of smoke rose to the morning sky, and a great cloud of steam floated upwards as the *Sultana* fell below the rolling waves of the Mississippi. The savage hiss mingled with curses and cries for help from survivors clinging to trees on the small island as well as those still floating on debris in the water.

****

Boats of all shapes and sizes crowed the water near the docks of Memphis. Weary volunteers scrambled to unload passengers before they went back out to look for more. Wagons and carriages lined the hill, ready to haul survivors to hospitals, hotels and private homes.

From the deck of the gunboat, Jerek watched the smaller boats unloading, searching for Willie and Suzie. The morning sun chased away the fog, and his heart tore at his chest when none of those taken ashore were the right shape and size.

April still slept; the freezing water had taken its toll on her tiny body. When it was their turn to disembark, he carried her up the cobblestones and caught a ride on an overflowing wagon. It stopped near a hospital.

He separated from the crowd and walked the remaining few blocks to the first hotel. He'd hire a doctor to come visit her there. She'd become lost amongst the wounded at the small infirmary. Later, he'd move them to one of the finer establishments. Right now, he needed to be as close to the docks as possible. Willie and Suzie must be on one of the other boats.

The hotel owner met him on the front steps. "Tragic, just tragic," the man said as he held the door wide. "Right this way, we have space for as long as you and the missus need to stay."

Jerek nodded his thanks. "I need to get her warmed up."

"Yes, yes, right this way." The man pulled a key from the cubes lining the wall behind a desk and pointed. "Up the stairs, first room on the right."

Though her weight was light, Jerek's arms trembled from carrying her for so long, and he feared dropping her. He took a deep breath and started to climb the steps. The hotel owner squeezed around and bolted up the stairs. The man returned to the top of the stairs as Jerek climbed the final step.

"My name's Tim Cox. I've owned this place for almost twenty years. Never, never have we seen such a disaster. Here, let me take her." Tim Cox lifted April's body from his arms and carried her toward an open door.

Jerek slumped against the wall for a moment. His legs still trembled when he pushed away to follow.

"I'll get the missus to help you get her settled. Here you sit down." Cox pulled the chair closer to the side of the bed and guided him onto it before he left.

Jerek leaned forward and brushed long, damp hair away from April's face. The porcelain skin was chalky white and tiny lips a deep blue. He ran a hand over her cheeks; they were cold beneath his fingers. His heart skipped a beat. The chair toppled as he leaped forward, placed a hand on her chest, and positioned his face next to her mouth and nose. Relief flooded with the slow rise and fall of her chest and the faint breeze brushing his cheek.

He pressed his lips to her icy ones, and wished they'd grow warm. When they didn't respond, he raised and traced a finger over the tiny chin, around the stilled lips, across a high cheek bone, and over her brows before it moved to a faint scar that ran from temple to temple above the fine hairs. The skin was puckered, as if it had been burned, and the area was tinged pink. Was this the reason she always wore a hat? This faded injury?

"This here's the missus," Mr. Cox said from the doorway.

A little lady, well under five feet, floated into the room.

"Let's get your wife out of those wet clothes. I have a dry nightgown for her to wear." She took a bundle from the crook of her arm before turning to her husband. "You get on now Tim, go find this man some clothes to borrow."

Tim nodded and closed the door behind him. "My name's Ester." She thrust an arm forward.

"Jerek Brinkley." He shook the warm, tiny hand.

Ester's gaze went to the bed.

Jerek plucked another piece of debris from long, tangled hair. "This is April."

"All right, Mr. Brinkley, let's get her out of those wet clothes."

Fear clutched him. After leaping from a flaming ship and floating down a raging river, he shouldn't be afraid, but he was. April would be furious if she knew he removed her clothing. "Uh, Mrs. Cox..." he started. What was he going to say? He couldn't undress his wife? She wasn't his wife? Tremors shook from head to toe.

Ester Cox looked at him with sympathy and laid her bundle on the bed then took his arm. "You go downstairs. Behind the desk is a door that leads to the kitchen. There's a fresh pot of coffee on the stove. Tim will have some dry clothes for you. Tell him to show you to the water closet where you can get dried off yourself. I'll take care of April." She opened the door, gave him a gentle shove. "Don't worry. We'll take good care of both of you."

After the door clicked shut behind him, he collapsed against it.

Tim stood near the staircase. "I have clothes for you."

He pushed away from the door. "Thank you. Your wife said you might have a cup of coffee and a place I could change?"

"Yes, follow me, uh...Mister?"

"Brinkley, Jerek Brinkley." He held his hand out to greet the man before he took the proffered clothes and followed him down the stairs.

Dressed in dry clothes and warmed by the coffee, he climbed the stairs again. He met Ester as she exited the room, carrying a mass of sopping clothes.

"She's going to be fine, just needs a little more sleep. Go on in and check on her then come down and have some breakfast," she said.

"Thank you, Mrs. Cox," he said and turned the knob. Bright sunlight filled the room, glistening off the white walls. A small table, chair, and dresser occupied the area along with the bed. Above the dresser, a hanging mirror reflected the light onto April. He strode to the window and pulled the curtains together, blocking the light before stepping to the bed. He ran the backs of his fingers over her cheek. Pale skin felt warmer. Or maybe it was because he was warm now.

The knot in his stomach rolled. This shouldn't be happening. Those boilers were in good condition. He'd made sure of it. Faint breath tickled the finger running over her lips. April could have died in that explosion. With a jolt, he pulled his hand away and turned to the door. He had to find Willie and Suzie before she woke up.

Entering the kitchen of the small hotel, he pulled several damp bills from his pocket. The clothes Tim had loaned him fit except the waistband was several inches too wide, the simple act of dipping into the pocket, drew the pants down on his hip. "Mrs. Cox, April will need some clothes. Do you know of someone who could do some shopping for us?"

"Certainly, Scarlet will be up shortly, and I can send her. There's paper and pen on the desk, why don't you make a list of what you need."

"I'm not very good with sizes," he admitted.

"That's okay, Mr. Brinkley. I'll have her measure your dirty clothes," she said.

"I have to go back down to the docks, to find the rest of our family."

"Oh, dear, I'm so sorry, how many are you missing?"

"April's brother and niece. I have to find them before she wakes."

"You go along. We'll take good care of her. Don't you worry, and I'll save another room for the rest of your family." Ester reached up and patted his face. Empathy shone in her eyes.

He handed her the money. "We may need the rooms for a few days."

"They're yours for as long as you need. Don't worry about that right now." She took the money for the clothes, slipped it into her apron pocket. "I have breakfast ready. You should eat before you go out again. You need the energy."

The smell of food penetrated his senses, making his stomach growl. He nodded and said, "I'll make the list first." A few minutes later, he returned to the kitchen and handed Ester the list. "April will need a hat, a nice one with a wide brim and flowers."

"All right, you sit down now and eat."

He did as directed, but the food hit his stomach like a rock.

After checking on April one last time, he left to search the wharf. The area was a maze, buzzing with activity. Tarps had been laid out on the ground and held lines of dead bodies, some burnt beyond recognition. Scalded flesh and the smell of death was everywhere. Others had died from exposure to the cold water, their emaciated bodies couldn't withstand the chill nor had the energy to stay afloat. He hated it, but continued to search the bodies, praying he wouldn't find a little girl and her daddy.

With one oilcloth left to search, he bit his lips together and stared beyond the sting in the back of his eyes at the first body. The bright morning sun glistened off the metal buttons of J.C. Mason's jacket. The material was charred, and blisters covered the exposed skin of his face and hands.

"You one of the survivors?"

Jerek nodded to the man standing next to him. "Yeah."

141

"That was the captain?"

"Yeah."

"A couple of the men we pulled from the water said he never left the boat. They said he stood up top, ripping wood from the decks and throwing it to men in the water."

"I believe it," Jerek said. His throat burned. "He was a good man. A good captain." He pushed stiff hair off his forehead and scratched at his tingling scalp. "Do you know where they took survivors?"

"Most went to the hospitals, some went to the Soldier's Home, and others to hotels and private homes. You looking for someone particular?"

"Yes, a little girl and her father. She's three, and he's average height and build, about like us. He wasn't a soldier," Jerek explained.

"Sorry, I ain't seen any to match that description. But I've only been on shore for a bit, I brought in fifteen Union soldiers. It's strange...two weeks ago I was fighting them. This week I'm saving them. Felt a lot better to save them." The man put his hand on Jerek's shoulder. "Where are you staying? I'll send word if I see them."

"The, uh..." he shrugged. "I don't know. It's a little hotel a few blocks from one of the hospitals." Up the hill, buildings dotted the ridge. They all looked alike. "It's owned by Tim and Ester Cox."

"Sure, I know them. They're good folks. I'll send word if I hear anything."

Jerek stretched his hand to the man. "Thank you. And thank you for saving the ones you could."

The man pumped his hand, nodded, and walked away. Jerek continued his walk along the tarp. Every time he'd see a little body his heart flipped, he hadn't realized there had been so many children on the boat. He hadn't noticed any, other than Suzie. Thankfully, none of the little bodies belonged to her. But they did belong to somebody and made the tragedy all the more real. He made his way to the dock, where still another boat unloaded survivors and dead bodies.

His hunt continued throughout the day. When he thought his body was ready to give out, the innocent sound of *Hi, Misser Bink* would play in his ears, and renew his energy. The sky had grown dark, making it impossible to distinguish any differences in burnt and scalded bodies. With a heavy chest, he made his way back to the hotel.

Over seven hundred live bodies had been plucked from the wreckage and flowing water. Some had hung on tree branches all night and most of the day before being discovered in the backwaters of the river.

The hotel loomed in front of him. He sighed and rubbed his tired eyes. After checking on April, he'd go to the Soldier's Home. There was little hope of finding Willie and Suzie there, since it was a sanctuary for soldier's injured in the line of duty, but it was the only place left to look.

He lifted heavy legs up the outside stairs of the hotel, pushed the door open, and stepped into the foyer.

Ester emerged from the kitchen at the same time. "There you are! We were getting worried. I hope you don't mind, but I had Doc Robbins look at April earlier today."

His body grew stiff. "What happened?"

"Nothing happened. When Scarlet went shopping I had her go by his place and ask him to stop by. He said April will be fine. He gave her some laudanum to help her sleep." Ester took his elbow to pull him to the kitchen. "I kept supper warm for you."

"Did she wake up?" He glanced to the staircase.

"No, not really, but enough to take the medicine. Doc said she has exposure from the cold water, and he doesn't want it to turn into pneumonia. Said sleep is the best thing for her. I gave her some broth earlier." She wrapped an arm around his and pulled harder. "Come and eat now, before you collapse."

Ester towed him into the kitchen where he sat in a chair, but he wasn't hungry. Gruesome sights had filled his eyes all day. The hospitals were full of men so badly burned and injured they wouldn't survive the night. And the tarps along the banks continued to grow with lifeless forms. The images wouldn't leave.

Ester patted the top of his head. "I know you don't feel hungry, but try to eat something. Tim is filling the tub upstairs for you, and Scarlet purchased new clothes for you as well. After you've eaten you can clean up and get a good night's rest."

He shook his head. "I have to keep looking."

"You can't. You're exhausted and whether you find the rest of your family tonight or tomorrow won't make any difference."

A protest formed in his throat.

She frowned and rubbed his shoulder.

He let out a long sigh. "I suspect you're right." But he'd never be able to sleep without knowing where they were. He hadn't cared this much about others in a very long time. In less than a week, his heart had been cracked opened and all the old wounds healed. He pushed a stiff fist against his chest. And now it was broken again.

Ester sat down next to him. "Tim and I had a son. I'd bet you're about his age."

He picked up his fork. "I'm thirty."

"T. J. would have been twenty-five. He died the first year of the war. Scarlet was his wife."

He pushed the beef stew around on his plate. "I'm sorry for your loss. I'm sure he was a fine man."

"Yes, he was. Thank you. The war took a lot of fine men. I'm still trying to make sense of it all."

Ester sighed. "Doc Robbins said the wires are up again, and that yesterday they found the man who shot the President. An assassin shot him. I sure hope it is truly over. Doc Robbins also said that the boilers blew on that steamer you were on."

"Appears so," he murmured, his mind too dull to follow her jumping conversation.

"Tim and the Doc were talking. They think it was sabotaged."

That caught his attention. He laid his fork down. "Sabotaged?" Of course! Why hadn't he thought of that? Steamers had been a target since the start of the war.

"Yes, they think it was one more act of the war."

Tim walked in through the door as Ester finished her sentence. He patted Jerek on the shoulder. "Have any luck finding your folks?"

Jerek shook his head. "No."

"Maybe tomorrow." The man accepted the cup of coffee Ester handed him and sat down at the table. "There's a hot bath ready for you upstairs. The bathing room is straight across the hall from your room."

"Thank you, thank you both very much." He looked from one to the other.

"Glad we can help in whatever way possible," Tim said. "You just tell us what we can do." He raised his cup to his lips. "Tragic. Just tragic."

"We won't keep you down here any longer. You go on up, take a bath, and get a good night's sleep." Ester's tiny fingers patted the back of his hand. "Just come into the kitchen before you leave in the morning. I'll have breakfast ready for you."

Too many thoughts cluttered his mind to comment. He faced them, let loose the unused fork. With a nod, he rose and left the room.

Jerek shuffled up the stairs and into the hotel room. The lamp beside the bed cast a faint glow.

April's tiny face peeked out above the quilts. He ran a finger over her upper lip. Warm breath touched his knuckle. Moving the finger to brush over soft cheeks, he noticed the black soot and grime covering his hand. He pulled it away from her pale face then leaned down to press a kiss to her tepid forehead before leaving for the room across the hall.

Steam rose from the brass tub. He emptied the pockets of the borrowed clothes before slipping them off. The water was hot and clean. It cascaded his body in comfort. Every muscle felt sore, like he'd been beaten up—badly beaten up.

Sabotage, of course. Why hadn't he thought of that? All day his mind retraced everything the boilermakers and engineers had said, there was no reason for one of the *Sultana's* boilers to give out.

Yet, over sixty, maybe closer to one hundred, steamers had been sabotaged by boat burners during the war. If a boiler had let loose, hot embers of coal wouldn't have showered the boat. As soon as he found Willie and Suzie, he'd investigate the accident.

Jerek leaned forward, grabbed the bar of soap and scrubbed soot, silt, and grime from his skin. After donning his new underclothes and pants, he cleaned up the area, doused the light then walked across the hall.

He stopped beside the bed. Her skin was warm, but not feverish. Pleased, he sat down on the mattress. His body was tired, so was his mind. A little sleep would help. Should he ask for another room? If she woke with him lying beside her, she might be angry. Then again if she woke in the strange room without him, she might be scared.

He stood, blew out the light, slipped off the pants, and with caution, eased beneath the covers. April twisted onto her side. He slid one arm beneath her neck, placed the other around her waist and fanned his finger across her stomach. Moving closer to her back, he spooned her hips against his, snuggling against her warmth. Tomorrow night he'd ask for another room—if she wanted him to.

When he opened his eyes, filtered light decorated the room. He and April still lay in the exact position he'd created when he'd crawled into the bed hours before. Well, almost, the tightness of his groin proved, even in exhaustion, his body reacted to her soft curves.

Jerek eased out of the cocoon and slipped off the mattress. He stepped into the pants lying on the floor near his feet then retrieved the rest of his clothes from the foot of the bed. Other outfits hung on hangers beside the door, three dresses, with matching hats and another suit for him.

He stepped over and fingered the frilly garments. A yellow one, pink one, and pale green one. The dresses were fashionable, and the hats decorated with bows, flowers, lace, and feathers, just what he'd written on the list. Beneath them stood new boots, his and hers. He bent and stuck his feet in the men's pair. They slipped on with ease. Walking back to the bed, he picked up his old pair. The leather was still damp. He wiggled his toes in the dry comfort of the new ones. A moan from the bed made him turn.

April rolled onto her back. Her eyelids fluttered. Dark-tipped, curled lashes tried to lift. The edge of the bed dipped as he sat down and reached to lace his fingers through the tiny ones lying on top of the covers. With his other hand, he ran a finger beneath the lashes, along a pink cheekbone. The lids worked harder to open. He waited. The fingers laced with his folded over his knuckles.

"April?" he whispered.

Her head swayed on the pillow, tilting toward his sound. The lids fluttered again before tugging open. They blinked several times.

Sky blue spheres settled on him.

"Hi." His voice cracked.

The corners of her mouth lifted.

"Hi," she answered as the lids closed again.

He swallowed past a lump. "How do you feel?"

A low groan rumbled from her throat then her eyes popped open with more strength. Fear flashed. "Jerek, Jerek?" She glanced around the room. "Where?"

His palm flattened over her cheek. "Shh, we're in a hotel in Memphis."

"The boat, fire, water..." A shiver ran the length of her body. Her eyes closed again. A tiny tear slipped from one corner.

He wiped at the moisture. "You're safe here."

"It was awful!" she sobbed.

He continued to wipe the droplets that fell and waited for the fear to fade. "Shh." He leaned forward, and pressed his lips to her forehead.

Her free hand slapped the crown of her head. "My hat!"

Jerek tried to halt the smile that tugged at his lips. "I bought you a new one," he said. "Actually, three new ones, covered with ribbons, flowers, lace, and a feather or two."

She pulled her bangs down over her forehead before her eyes opened again. "You did?"

He nodded and pointed to the wall near the door. "You'll look stunning in each and every one of them." His hand settled back on her cheek. "How do you feel?"

"Horrible," she said with honesty.

He chuckled. "I'm going to go get Ester. She and her husband Tim own the hotel. She has some medicine the doctor left for you."

Her eyes fluttered shut again and she nodded.

He rose, but before letting go of her fingers, bent and kissed the knuckles. "I'll be right back."

He walked to the door, but as soon as it clicked shut, tore down the stairs and across the foyer. Pushing open the kitchen door, he said, "She's awake."

"I have everything ready. Just let me grab the laudanum." Ester pulled a small brown bottle from a cupboard, placed it on a tray that held a cup of tea and other food items before she scurried out of the kitchen and up the stairs ahead of him. Her tiny feet hop skipped down the hall and barely paused as he opened the door for her to enter the room.

Ester set the tray on the table beside the bed. "Good morning, April. I had a feeling you'd be waking up this morning. I have a cup of tea for you to drink."

April opened her eyes and looked at the older woman before setting sights on him. Her face scrunched with distress, and she pressed a hand to her chest.

Worried, Jerek stepped forward.

"Willie and Suzie?" she asked.

He didn't know what to say. Her pain was so apparent.

"They must have been taken to a different hotel. Jerek's going out to look for them as soon as he's had his breakfast," Ester said. "You can stay here with me. I'll take care of you while he finds your family." She patted April's hand and turned to face him. "Help her sit up a little. So she can sip her tea. It helps the medicine go down."

Jerek let his thanks show on his face. Ester had explained the situation very tactfully. He gave a smile of reassurance to April and walked around the bed. His hand slipped beneath her shoulders and gently eased her body into a sitting position against the pillows the older woman fluffed.

He brushed long hair away from her shoulders. "You drink your tea then sleep some more."

April looked at him with sad, dull eyes and droopy lids. Her small amount of renewed energy had already been used up. She sipped from the cup Ester held in front of her, but shook her head at the bread. Her face puckered with distaste at the spoonful of medicine Ester bribed her to swallow. After another sip of tea, she shook her head and let it fall against the pillow. Her fatigued body wasn't ready to wake yet.

He eased the extra pillow from behind her head and helped her lay back down. Ester tucked the covers around the tiny frame then turned to resettle the breakfast paraphernalia on the tray.

April's breathing quickly became deep and slow. Her angelic face was soft, the skin a normal temperature. He leaned over and placed his lips on her cheek then followed the older woman from the room.

As he pulled the door closed, Ester assured, "She'll be better by tonight."

He clutched the door knob. He'd find Willie and Suzie before she woke again. With renewed determination, he exhaled, nodded, and followed Ester down the steps. Half an hour later, after barely tasting the breakfast the older woman had forced him to eat, he left the hotel.

Chapter Eight

Cold water swirled around the beast tugging at her legs. It towed her beneath the surface. The force was so strong. No matter how hard she fought, it wouldn't relinquish its hold. Her heart raced. She couldn't breathe. She kicked her feet and thrashed her body about. Someone called for her, but water filled her mouth when she tried to answer.

Her eyes popped open. April gasped for air and pressed a hand against the rapid pounding in her chest. Cold sweat covered her body. She blinked and tried to focus in on the woman who stood beside the bed.

"There, there now, it was just a dream. Nothing more than a silly old dream." The woman was tiny, much shorter than she. One of her hands patted April's shoulder in comfort.

The woman looked slightly familiar? Why? How? The fog in her mind was so thick.

"Do you remember me from this morning? My name is Ester. You're in Memphis at our hotel."

She closed her eyes. "Yes, I think so. A little," she whispered. Gradually, it became easier to breathe, and the tremendous pressure on her chest lessened. She did remember the lady giving her tea, along with Jerek. Her eyes flashed around the room. "Jerek?"

"He's not back yet, but will be before long, I suspect. Are you feeling better?"

She took a moment to ponder the question. "Yes, I think so."

"Perhaps a bath would help, do you think you're up for one?"

All of a sudden her skin itched, and she could feel sand on the sheets below her. A bundle of dirty hair hung over her shoulder, falling on the white sheet covering her body. She tried to separate the dried clumps of hair. "Yes."

"Good, it will make you feel better. I already have Tim heating the water. I figured it was about time for you to be waking up." The woman had a delightful smile, one that made every feature glow. Tiny blue eyes twinkled, a button nose wrinkled, and full cheeks became wider as the woman's lips curled upwards.

April smiled back. "Thank you, Ester."

The woman rolled the covers to the foot of the bed. With a hand on one shoulder and the other on an elbow, she helped April ease her stiff frame to the edge of the mattress and sit up. "Go slow now," Ester coached.

The room swirled. She braced her hands beside her hips on the mattress. "How long have I been asleep?"

"Since he carried you in here early yesterday morning." Ester pulled the table closer to the bed. It held a tray with a glass of milk and a bowl of soup. "Here, try to eat a touch."

"Yesterday!" The last thing she could clearly recall was holding onto a log, floating on top of rolling waves. Her stomach vaulted. She pressed her palm against her lips.

Ester ran a soothing hand over her arm. "It's all right. Your tummy is empty, have a few bites of soup. It'll help, I promise."

She shook her head. The bile in the back of her throat gagged her.

The woman didn't let up. Additional coaxing convinced her to lift the spoon. It smelled wonderful. Saliva formed and sent the bile away. Several scoops later, the rumbles were gone as well, and the broth filled the emptiness.

"Which of these new dresses would you like to wear?" Ester asked from the other side of the room.

The woman held a dress in each hand, and a third hung on the wall behind her. Each one had a matching hat dangling from the wooden rack the dress was clipped to. April closed her eyes and raised a shaky hand to her disfiguring scar.

Regret pulled on her face. Jerek had seen it. When he'd kissed her forehead this morning, he'd said he'd bought her a new hat, no three new ones. Tears pricked at her eyes.

"The pink one is my favorite, but the yellow is awfully pretty, and that green one is made of the softest material I've ever felt," Ester said as she carried the pink and yellow ones closer to the bed. "That man of yours, he made a list for Scarlet, my daughter-in-law to go shopping." Ester looked at the dresser along the far wall. "The drawers in the chest have fresh, new underclothes and nightclothes in them. I washed your old ones, but I'm afraid most things couldn't be saved. I put the money you had sewn into your petticoat in a satchel. It's in the drawer as well." She laid the dresses out on the bed. "So which will it be?"

The colorful material settled onto the bed. Stylish lace and ruffles decorated each dress.

Ester walked around the bed and looked down with concern. "Does your head hurt?"

"No." She squeezed her eyes shut.

"Are you sure? The way you're holding it makes me think you have a headache," Ester put her hand on the one April used to cover the scar. "Let me see, did you get a bump?"

"No!" She pushed the hand away and tugged at her bangs.

Ester's face filled with a sad frown.

The woman must be repulsed by the massive scar. Tears burned the back of her eyes. She puckered her lips and blinked to hold them at bay.

"Sweetie, what's wrong?" Ester asked. "Do you need to lie back down?"

She lowered her head. "No, I'll wear the pink one." It really didn't matter what dress she wore, she just needed a hat. "I need a bath."

"Let me go see if Tim has it ready. I'll be right back," Ester said then scurried to the door and left it open while she peeked into the room across the hall. A bright smile filled her face again as she hopped back into the room.

"Yes, it's all ready." She looped April's arm over a tiny shoulder and wrapped an arm around her back. "Come on, I'll help you."

April didn't think she needed help, until she stood. Weak, shaky legs barely held her weight. She leaned onto the smaller woman and forced the limbs to work.

A few moments later, she settled her aching body into the tub and let the warm water wash away dirt and silt.

Ester made several trips in and out of the room, carrying in clothes, towels, scented soap and other miscellaneous items. She placed a large white pitcher on the stool beside the tub then began to roll up her sleeves. "I'll wash your hair for you. It is so pretty. I bet once we get this Mississippi sludge out of it, it'll be the color of corn silk and just as soft. I'll rinse it with cider vinegar. That will make it shine like the sun."

April lifted her hands to her hair. She could

wash it herself, but the other woman appeared to like taking care of others, and she really didn't want to hurt her feelings. Odd, she'd never thought of hurting someone's feelings before—other than Willie's.

Her heart skipped a beat. Surely Jerek must have found the hotel where he and Suzie were staying by now. She couldn't wait to see them. The poor little girl had to have been terrified in the water. That first plunge had been so frightening. It was as if the water had risen up and purposely pulled people into that terrible, cold, dark, deep hole beneath it. A shiver rippled over her skin.

"There now, you're safe," Ester said as she pulled the bangs back and included them in the suds she'd created.

Feeling exposed, she slapped a hand over the scar.

"You sure your head doesn't hurt?" Ester asked.

"No," she sighed. "It's old. I got it when I was young."

"Got what?" Ester asked.

"The scar. I fell against the stove." She closed her eyes. It almost felt good to tell someone about it.

"What scar, sweetie?"

She pulled her hand away and waited for the woman to leap away or at the least gasp for air. Ester just kept scrubbing her scalp, twisting soapy suds into her hair.

"What scar, sweetie?" the woman repeated.

She tipped her head back, and using a finger, pointed at her forehead. "That one."

Ester stopped scrubbing and looked down. Her brows pulled together.

April held her breath.

The woman picked up a cloth, dipped it in the water then wiped at the area. "Oh, I see it now." Her touch was gentle as she washed the area. "Goodness,

155

that must have hurt, but it certainly healed nicely. Just a tiny bit of puckering and pinkness, why I didn't even notice it until you pointed it out."

"You don't have to lie. I know how bad it is." She struggled to hold the tears at bay.

Ester ran the washcloth over the rest of her face. Rinsed it out and washed the area again. A moment later she said, "Here April, open your eyes."

A hand mirror lingered in front of her nose. Ester's face, positioned near her shoulder reflected, next to hers. In the mirror, the older woman's eyes went to the scar.

"See how tiny it is. It's hardly visible. Now, look at the wrinkles on this forehead." Ester pointed to her own head. "They're noticeable. But you know what? I don't care. I earned these wrinkles. I've lived." Her face brightened with a smile. "We all get a little scarred up living, sweetie. They're proof of our lives and nothing to be ashamed of."

April pulled her gaze from Ester's face to look at hers in the mirror. She squinted. That wasn't the scar she knew. What had happened to it? There was a scar there, and it ran from temple to temple, but it wasn't much more than a faint pink line. She touched it, could feel the puckered skin, but it wasn't bulging and rumpled as she remembered.

Pictures of the scars she'd seen on men on the *Sultana* floated by. Men without limbs even. For almost a dozen years, she'd sulked around, angry over a scar that was less obvious than the wrinkles on Ester's face. Shame burned her cheeks and made the back of her throat tighten.

"Ah, sweetie, don't fret. Sometimes the scars we can't see are bigger than the ones we do see," Ester whispered and pulled the mirror aside. "But in time they all heal."

A knock sounded on the door. "Mama Cox, I have fresh water for you."

"Oh, thank you, dear. Please bring it in."

She sank deeper into the water as the door opened. A beautiful, young woman, carrying two buckets of water, walked in. Her mind searched for a word she'd heard once. Exotic. Yes, the woman looked exotic. There were no scars marring the olive skin of her elegant face. Amber-colored eyes, shaped like almonds, were highlighted by the way the outside corners lifted slightly. Coal black hair hung from a center part and soft waves rested on her shoulder while others fell down her back.

"This is Scarlet, my daughter-in-law. Scarlet this is April," Ester made the introduction.

"Hello, April," Scarlet said as she shut the door.

The small room was rather crowded, and April was quite embarrassed to be naked in the tub. "H-hello."

"I'll just rinse the soap from your hair, and then we'll let the dirty water drain out of the tub, and pour in some fresh. We want to make sure we get rid of all the muck and mud." Ester forced her to tip her face forward.

She leaned down as instructed. The tub had a drain plug, just like the one at the hotel in New Orleans. She wondered where the water went once the plug was lifted. She'd forgotten to ask Willie about it.

The older woman dipped the pitcher in the water, and poured it over her hair. She closed her eyes against the soap rinsing from the tresses.

"Oh, you're going to wear the pink one," Scarlet sounded excited. "I had so much fun picking these clothes out for you. Your husband certainly has good taste."

"Who?" The water running over her face made it difficult to talk.

"Your husband. Mr. Brinkley wrote out a list for me to follow. He made it very clear what he wanted,"

Scarlet continued.

April opened her mouth to protest, but at the same time Ester dumped the pitcher over her head again, and she gulped in a great load of dirty, soapy water. Coughs tore at her throat and chest as she tried to expel the icky water, spitting against the taste of soap.

"Oh, goodness, there's the front bell again," Scarlet said. "I'll see who it is then carry the other buckets up."

The door closed as another load of water flowed over her hair. This time she kept her eyes and mouth shut, and held her breath. The apple cider vinegar mixed with this pitcher of water smelled awful and would probably taste worse than the soap had.

"There now, you pull the plug and after it drains out, we'll add the fresh water," Ester said.

After lifting the stopper, she flipped her head upright, and brushed the wet tendrils back with her hands. "Ester, Jerek, uh-Mr. Brinkley, is—"

"Is a very nice man," Ester interrupted, "who should be home soon, and will be very happy to see you up and about."

She shook her head but before she could speak, Ester pressed a finger against her mouth. It was soft and firm at the same time. "Sometimes it's easier to let people believe what they think." She pulled her hand away. "Now put the stopper back in so I can empty these buckets."

She did as requested. Why didn't the woman want her to say she and Jerek weren't married?

Scarlet reentered the room and left with the empty buckets after informing Ester she'd turned away another customer.

"We only have four rooms to let out, and they're all full," Ester explained while she dumped the warm water into the tub. She handed April the washcloth. "Here, now you scrub up while I get rid of these buckets and dirty clothes so you have room to dress."

Minutes later, April found herself being toweled dry and dressed. She wasn't allowed to do much but step in and lift an arm when told. The experience was somewhat embarrassing. But once her nakedness was covered, the help was appreciated. Weak and shaky she needed to sit down by the time the pink dress was fastened.

Ester assisted her across the hall and settled her in the chair. With a towel, she briskly rubbed the remaining water droplets from her hair before she began to brush out snarls.

Slow, smooth strokes reminded her of being a little girl, and how her mother brushed her hair every night. She tipped her head back. The bed had been made with clean sheets. Silently, the comfortable space called. She was so tired. The older woman read her thoughts and as soon as the brush ran smoothly from her crown to the tips that hung near her waist, Ester encouraged her to lie down for a nap.

She welcomed the suggestion and as a quilt nestled around her shoulders, her head sunk into the softness of the pillow. In no time her lids fell and allowed her to enter the bliss of sleep.

****

Jerek walked across the street to the little hotel. He'd found no sign of Willie and Suzie, neither at the hospitals, hotels, or on any of the barges, which continued to carry lifeless forms to the shores of Memphis. The toe of his boot sent a rock to bounce across the gravel. Hope diminished with each passing hour, and he didn't know where to start looking in the morning. There were prospects, but none were too promising.

Tiny stars decorated the sky. He pulled on the

lapels of his jacket and lifted the material off his back. The cool night air washed over skin that had been covered with sweat for most of the day. Lights glowed in the windows of the buildings surrounding the hotel. Identical structures lined the street. Each held a small barn and yard behind, necessities for the businesses they provided.

The Cox's lived on one corner and another similar hotel sat at the other end of the block. Both resembled small boarding houses rather than actual hotels. In between them were a wheelwright and a blacksmith shop. Across the street a feed store and livery took up the whole block.

He stopped in front of the Cox's. Part of him wanted to see April. The other dreaded telling her he hadn't found Willie and Suzie. He kicked at the dirt. Perhaps he should make one more pass of the docks before going in.

"Hi," Tim Cox rounded the far corner of the wooden building.

Jerek stepped into the yard. "Hi."

A hand fell on his shoulder. "Any luck today?"

He shook his head slowly. "No."

"I'm sorry, so very, very sorry." The older man pulled the hat from his head. After running a hand over the bald spot, he replaced the head covering and said, "I went to the newspaper office today, to see if they were posting lists of where survivors had been taken. Was going to add yours and the missus' name, but they said they aren't making a list." He pulled a roll of paper from his pocket. "There's a note about the accident on the back page, the guy at the paper claimed folks aren't interested in it. He says everyone wants to know what happened to the guy that shot the President."

He took the newspaper from Tim's weathered hand. Near the bottom on the inside of the back page was a small paragraph. It mentioned the *Sultana's* boilers had blown, but little more. He slapped the paper against his thigh.

"Her boilers didn't blow. She was blown up!"

"Those boat burners have been working the river since the beginning of the war. The man at the paper house said everyone's tired of hearing about it." Tim slid his hands into his pockets. "This war has hardened people. Made folks believe in, and sometimes care about, things that aren't true. Makes me wonder about the future."

Tim Cox was an average looking man. There was nothing really out of the ordinary about him. The type he'd seen all the time, in the North and South, and never really speculated on. The war had changed Tim and Ester's life forever.

"How long have you and Ester been married?" he asked.

Tim wrinkled his brow. "Well, must be going on thirty years now. We were just kids when we got married. I was seventeen and she was fifteen. And the cutest little thing you ever saw. Still is if you ask me." His face grew red as he chuckled. "Never get tired of her. No siree. But you know how that is. Your April is a fine-looking gal too."

A rush of warm blood flooded his loins. He cleared his throat. "Yes, they are beautiful, both April and Ester."

"Ester held supper for you. We best get in before she thinks neither of us are coming home." Tim put his hand on Jerek's back to propel him toward the door.

Ester came through the kitchen door as they entered the foyer. "Oh, good it's you! I was afraid it was another customer. We've had folks stopping in all day, needing a place to stay. Seems the town's full up." She waved her hand. "You two come along now. Supper's getting stiff waiting on you."

"Don't worry, Ma," Tim assured as he followed

her into the kitchen. "It'll still taste as good as always."

The door slapped Jerek's back as he jolted to a halt. April sat at the table, covered in pink muslin, and looking more breathtaking than anything he'd ever seen. Gold silk haloed her face and spilt over her shoulders. The flowing mane disappeared below the table's edge. A smile touched his lips. The tresses did look like a wheat field in July. Straight, long and that rare color God only used for his finest creations.

The corners of her mouth lifted, and her sky blue eyes sparkled as her gaze met his. The tips of her bangs caught on her lashes and... No hat balanced on her pert head. He blinked, not once but twice.

"Hi," she said, somewhat shyly.

He walked around the table, and his fingers touched the silk. He leaned down so he could press his lips against the crowning glory. Feathery tresses tickled his nose, and he took a deep breath. An enthralling, fresh flowery scent filled his senses from head to toe.

Tiny fingers brushed against his as he stroked the silky locks. Her head titled back, like she was trying to see him.

"Hi," he murmured and lifted his head to gaze on her face.

His pulse pounded so hard it echoed in his ears. Her eyes were hesitant, lacking some of the self-confidence they normally sparkled with. He touched a knuckle to the corner of one. He wanted to kiss her and leaned forward.

A hand tapped his shoulder. "Here now, sit down and eat. We women ate some time ago." Ester set a plate in front of the chair next to April.

He sat down, gathered one of the tiny hands into his. "Are you feeling better?"

"Yes." Her gaze searched his. "Did you find

them?"

He saw the moment she knew his answer. Her pert lips sucked in a small gasp of air. His hold on her hand tightened.

Ester set a cup on the table. "Now don't be getting yourself upset, April. Memphis is a big city. It's going to take a few days to find your brother. And if you get all vexed up it'll just make you ill again. Here now, be a good girl and drink your tea while Jerek eats his supper."

The muscles in his chin tightened. April wasn't going to take Ester's words kindly, though they were filled with compassion, she could be quick to anger.

"You're right Ester, it's just hard not to worry," April said.

His jaw dropped. He pulled his lips together to keep his mouth from gaping open. There wasn't a touch of sarcasm in her voice. Her fingers squeezed his, and then as prim and proper as a queen, she lifted her teacup to take a small sip. He scratched his head.

"Eat up now. It's getting late, and April needs to get back to bed." Ester pointed at Jerek as she sat down with a cup of tea.

The meal of 'stiff' potatoes, ham, and carrots satisfied hunger and the conversation, focused mainly on the spring rains Memphis had recently received, eased fears that April would snap out of her facade any moment. She was calm, tranquil, and pleasant the entire time. If he didn't know her better, he'd think her behavior was genuine. The thought scared him. Perhaps it was the medicine.

He wasted no time in escorting April from the room as soon as the meal ended. Had the accident wiped away the raw spirit he loved to see dancing in those blue eyes?

April walked into the bedroom and waited for him to shut the door. "Why did you tell them we are married?" she asked.

He shot her a baffled look. His gaze landed on her and looked deep into her soul. A slight smile touched his mouth. "I didn't. They assumed it when I carried you in, and I didn't deny it. Would you like me to go down and tell them the truth?" He turned back to the door.

"No!" She took a step forward to grab his arm. "No, I think it's okay for them to believe what they think."

"You what?" he stepped closer.

"I think it's okay for them to believe what they think." April didn't want to be alone. Not in the room, not in Memphis, not in the world. "It's of no consequence right now. And once we find Willie and Suzie, and head for home, it won't matter at all."

Jerek's fingers ran over her wrist. "Are you sure? I didn't mean to compromise you. If it upsets you, I'll go tell them."

"You're not compromising anything." She turned around. "Could you unhook me please? I would like to put on a sleeping gown."

He released the tiny hooks running down her back.

She plucked a new, white cotton garment from the foot of the bed. "I'm going to step across the hall to put this on." Her eyes met his. "You will be here when I get back, won't you?"

"No. Yes." Jerek shook his head and nodded it at the same time. His voice sounded husky. "I'll step out for a few minutes, while you change."

She sucked in a quick breath, shook her head. Was he going to leave her again?

He squeezed her hand. "Don't worry. I'm not going anywhere. I'll be right outside, in the hall." The door clicked shut before she could respond.

The pink material fell to the floor in a heap. She dropped her slip and petticoat before stepping over the pile and slipped the nightgown over her head. After buttoning the three buttons near her throat, she picked up the clothes and moved to hang them near the door. A long row of tiny fasteners ran up the back of the dress. She'd never been able to wear this type of design, because she'd never had anyone available to help her in and out of such contraptions.

She smoothed wrinkles from the material after she secured it to the wall. She stepped to the door then stopped and glanced down at her nightgown. It would be highly improper for him to see her in it. Wouldn't it? She strolled to the bed and climb beneath the covers. The flame of the lamp flickered. She leaned over but stopped short of blowing it out. Jerek would need it to prepare for bed. He could douse it.

Her heart skipped a beat and tiny tremors tickled each nerve ending. It might not be right, but a large part of her didn't care. The thought of being on her own had never frightened her before, but right now she'd sell her very soul to the devil to not have to be alone. Would Jerek mind? Would he be angry with her for being such a ninny?

She tried to conjure up justification for her feelings for several minutes before wondering if he was coming back. Was he just outside the door as he promised? Hints of fear tickled her spine. She twisted the sheet in her hands. Should she yell? Tell him it was time to come in?

A click made her gaze snap forward.

The door pushed open, he peeked around the solid wood. "Safe to enter?"

A light giggle released itself. "Yes," she answered while smoothing the covers on the bed.

He walked over, hung his jacket on the back of the chair then sat on the edge of the bed near the lamp. She scooted over, assuring he'd have enough room to lie down. He looked around the room before covering his mouth to cover a slight cough then said, "The clothes seem to fit."

She reached over to touch his arm. "Yes, they are a perfect fit, thank you." Her fingers slipped down his shirtsleeve and wrapped around his hand. "Jerek, I'm sorry, I just really don't want to be alone." She forced a sob to stay in her throat. "I'll understand if you don't want to stay with me."

He threaded his fingers between hers. "I'm not going anywhere."

"It's just...Oh, Jerek, what if we never find them?" She choked on the words.

"Shh." He leaned over, their noses, then foreheads touched. "Shh, don't get upset. We'll find them. I promise."

She couldn't talk. Unshed tears made the roof of her mouth burn, she scratched at it with her tongue. It didn't help. The tears forced themselves out and air seeped from hot lungs with a mewing sound.

"Don't cry. I promise we'll find them."

He held her while she fought the urge to break out in a full cry. When the need dissolved she sighed into his shirt. After a few stilled moments, he drew away and stood. She grasped his hand.

Feather light kisses touched her knuckles. "I'm going to blow out the light. You need to get some sleep," he said.

"W-where?"

"Shh, I'm not going anywhere. I'm going to climb into the bed beside you."

She let go of his hand and pulled the covers on the bed out of the way, opening the sheeted area for him to crawl into. The room went dark. He rustled about, removing boots and outer clothing. She scooted lower beneath the covers.

The bed creaked, and one hand slipped beneath her neck. Warm fingers cupped her shoulder, easing her closer as he settled beneath the covers.

She twisted onto her side, molded into his shape. He tucked the blanket beneath her chin as she snuggled against his shoulder. A warm and reassuring embrace held her tight. Her hand moved beneath the sheet to rest on a firm chest, feeling the even rise and fall of breathing.

"Thank you," she whispered.

"For what?" he asked, tilting to rest his chin on top of her head.

"For staying with me."

His chest rumbled with a chuckle. "You're welcome." Rough, but soft fingers roamed up and down the upper part of her arm. "Did you try on your new hats?"

"No."

"Really, why not?"

"Because I was in the house all day. I don't need to wear a hat inside." She swallowed then asked, "Do I?" Did he think the scar was worse than Ester led her to believe? Freedom from not wearing a hat was something she'd only dreamed about.

"No, you don't need to wear one inside. I don't think you need to wear one outside either."

"You don't?" She tipped her head, trying to see his eyes.

"Not if you don't want to. The only reason you need to wear a hat is to keep your head warm in the winter or cool in the summer." Warm lips brushed aside her bangs before they settled on her forehead.

She had to tell him about the scar. Wanted him to know it wasn't her fault. "It happened when I was a child."

"How?"

"I fell against the cook stove. It was hot and burnt me."

Lips moved across the area again. "It must have been painful."

She nodded.

"It's beautiful," he whispered.

"No it's not, it's hideous."

"There's nothing about you that's hideous. Believe me, it's beautiful. Just like the rest of you."

She wanted to believe him, wanted to believe he thought she was beautiful, even with her scars, inside and out. Life hadn't taught her how to react to the array of feelings his words and touches created. It seemed unfair she was so inexperienced at the things that really mattered. The sensitive skin of her cheek rubbed against the hardness of his chest.

"Jerek, do you really believe we'll find them?"

"Yes, sweetheart, we're going to find them. Now close your eyes and go to sleep. You need your rest." His voice was soft and light, yet at the same time, held conviction.

How could he be so confident? "Promise you won't leave before I wake?"

"I promise," he whispered and hugged her to his warmth. "Now stop talking, and go to sleep."

Doing as he asked was easy while he held her in such a soothing, consoling embrace. Without further thought she let a smile curve her lips, closed her eyes, and floated deep into oblivion.

Chapter Nine

The slight breeze of her breath tickled Jerek's neck as April fell into a deep sleep. A tingle that almost felt like jealousy, drifted across his chest, slumber would surely evade him. The turmoil of the past few days couldn't be blamed for it either. It was the way his body reacted to the supple, curvaceous form invitingly pressed against him.

Trying to ignore his uncontrollable reactions, he focused on making a mental list of new places to search. Before long, the satisfaction of holding the warm, lithe frame, eased the pressure in his groin, and soon contentment sent a warm glow to float through his veins like rich brandy, and his lids grew heavy.

Dreams woke him several times, the nightmarish ones that were too harsh to sleep through. But when a warm body snuggled against his movements, he fell back to sleep, gratified the frightening images had simply been visions of slumber. When the sun filtered in through the window, he wished he could stop its rise, and stay right where they were forever. His senses had never been so satisfied and fulfilled.

Silky limbs squirmed before settling again. Eyelids fluttered, and a warm cheek nuzzled his shoulder. By the time long lashes lifted, a wide smile pulled on his face.

"Good morning, sunshine," he said.

"Mmm, good morning." Sleepy, blue eyes closed, and a tiny chin nestled into the base of his neck.

He giggled at her sleepiness. When was the last time he'd giggled? That's what it was, and it felt good, better than a laugh. Genuine happiness tickled his nerves.

"Are you always this happy in the morning?" she murmured against his skin.

"I don't know. Maybe it's just the company that makes me so happy." Both arms wrapped her in a tight embrace as his body shifted to lift her onto his chest.

Silky legs followed her torso to stretch atop his frame. He pressed his hips deeper into the mattress, making warm breasts and long, pleasing curves fit into his like perfect puzzle pieces. His hands roamed her back, exploring and discovering fine, faultless features.

Her head lifted. Amusement spanned her face. "What are you doing?"

The grin on her lips encouraged him to proceed. "I'm getting ready to kiss you," he admitted.

"You are?" The grin widened and she giggled.

He tilted so his mouth was in line with hers. The tickle of her giggle ignited another to ripple up his chest. Light laughter merged as his lips brushed against soft, moist ones. Enjoyment grew as lips danced with each other. Touching, separating then moving together again.

He had to be careful, didn't want to alarm her with aggressive actions, but she was so willing, so accepting and accommodating. His hardened shaft pressed against her core and throbbed with need. Ardently, he delivered the ultimate kiss—deep, long, and more passionate than even he could comprehend. His palms framed her face as he finished it with several small pecks.

"Mmm," April moaned. Her head leaned forward and juicy lips continued to follow his as he laid his head back onto the pillow. She kissed his chin, ran small pecks down his neck.

Gently, he forced the torture to stop by holding her face still. His lips came to rest on her forehead.

"I like it when you kiss me," she admitted.

"I like kissing you."

"Will you do it again?"

"Not right now."

She frowned. "Why not?"

"Because it's time to get up," he whispered against the wrinkles that had formed on her brow.

"Oh, will you do it again later?"

"I'll kiss you as often as you'll let me."

April lifted her face and folded her arms on his chest. Her tiny nose wrinkled, and she pressed a finger into her chin. "I think I shall let you do it every day." Her head gave a dainty nod. "Yes, at least once a day, maybe more."

He took her words down a different path. "Oh, there's more, trust me, so much more."

Her fingers brushed against the whiskers on his chin. "More kisses like that?"

"Yes, and more than just kisses," he said as he tipped his head and nipped at her fingers. Two of the tiny digits caught between his lips. He brushed his tongue against the salty taste.

"There is?" she asked as her eyes fluttered shut.

"Things you aren't even going to believe," he said around her fingers.

"Like what, give me a hint."

His shaft jolted, proving her innocent teasing had driven him beyond control. "I already am, darling, I already am," he admitted as he forced her face to his for one last taste.

Ready to explode, he flipped the blankets—and

April—off his body to leap from the bed. Thankfully he had his undergarments on, for what was happening beneath the cotton at his waist might frighten her maiden mind.

Tightening the string holding his under-breeches up, he cleared his throat. "Time to get up sleeping beauty." With his back to her, he pulled his pants on before moving to the chair to retrieve his shirt.

Her arms rose above her head, and her back arched as she stretched. Full, firm mounds pressed against the thin cotton of her nightgown. He sank onto the chair. Both of her hands went to the back of her neck and lifted the long tendrils of gold. The tresses swayed back and forth before settling to cascade down her back as she sat up. She smoothed the straight strands before scooting across the bed.

He fought to breathe.

April set her feet on the floor and wiggled her toes. She felt so good. Amazing what a good night's sleep could do for a person. Using her hands to push into a stance, she smiled at the most wonderful man in the world and asked, "Where are we going to look today?"

Jerek blinked several times before he rose from the chair. The grimace on his face almost looked painful. He stepped forward and lifted a handful of hair from her shoulder. He watched the strands tumble through his fingers as if it intrigued him.

"You are not going any where. I'm going out to recheck the hospitals."

Something somersaulted in her chest. "Oh, Jerek, please don't leave me here again today." She grabbed his hand. "I'll be good, I promise. No ranting, no raving. I'll just help look."

In slow motion, he shook his head. She stepped closer and wrapped her arms around his middle. "Please. The Cox's are very nice. They've been wonderful. But I can't lie around another day. Please don't ask me to."

"Honey, it's not good out there. I don't want you to see how bad it is." His chin rested on the crown of her head.

"It's worse here, alone, without you. Not knowing." She rubbed a cheek into his shirt. "I've seen bad things before. I can handle it. And I'll be good, I promise."

He separated their bodies. With sad eyes, he shook his head again. "You'll be good by staying right here with Ester and Scarlet."

Fury rose in her chest. She couldn't let it rule her nor her behaviors. A deep breath filled her lungs and forced the anger to stay subdued.

"I can't," she admitted. With a swoosh she expelled the air and faced him with honesty. "I can't stay here. If you won't let me go with you, I'll go by myself." She turned and walked to the dresses hanging by the door. "I'd rather go with you, but if you won't let me, I'll go on my own."

She slipped the pink dress from its hook, folded it over her arm before turning around. It was time she told him the truth. "I've changed, Jerek. The April Simonson I've known all my life stayed behind in New Orleans, or sank in the Mississippi. I don't know how it happened or why it happened. But I'm no longer the same person. And I don't wish to become the old me again. However, I love my brother and niece with all my heart, and I will not sit by, doing nothing while they might be out there sick or injured. I will not rest until every stone in Memphis has been overturned in the search for them."

Tears clouded her vision. The image of Suzie and Willie falling into the brown, foamy, swirling water near the hull of the *Sultana* floated before her eyes. Blinking didn't help. Maybe if she were completely honest, he'd understand. For the first time in her life, she let the words flow from her heart.

"You're the reason I've changed. I can't explain it, and I don't know what it means for my future. I've never been so unsure of myself. But I do know I can search for them without you. I've been doing things alone my whole life." A sob leaped from her throat. She swallowed after its release and sucked in a gulp of air. "I just really, really don't want to."

The arms that wrapped around to hold her tight were strong and gentle at the same time. Their upper parts bulged with muscles, a clear vision of the strength and power they possessed, but they held her with care and tenderness. It was hard to comprehend a person could be both strong and tender at the same time. Life led her to believe you needed to be strong and demanding otherwise people would walk all over you. The strong survive—the weak perish.

Jerek proved differently. He was tough and hard, at the same time he was kind and affectionate. She'd seen it the morning they'd been blocked by cargo and sat near the railing together. His brute force had been evident in his walk and stance, yet he'd shown compassion and care in her childhood tale. He'd made her realize how poorly she'd treated Willie over his loss. How badly she'd behaved toward her brother for years. She'd been so angry when Willie married and left home. It's a miracle he'd ever even written. So filled with her own fear and anger, she'd been completely blind to his happiness and love.

If it took the rest of her life, she'd make it up to him and never again be so self-centered she didn't think of others. Staying with the Cox's was good practice with the way Ester mothered everyone. Yet, the way Jerek's gaze filled her with joy she never knew existed was all the encouragement needed to continue and become this new April. He had an uncanny ability to unconsciously persuade her to observe beauty and harmony in the smallest things.

She still had some work to do, the way Scarlet's amber eyes grew dark and sultry whenever the girl looked at Jerek had a way of making the old April leap forward. The want of smacking the other woman upside the head at the supper table last night had been extremely strong. She did forgive Scarlet. At times she too felt funny around him. A warm, tingling sensation settled in her torso, deep between her legs. That odd hunger pain was hard to explain.

The feeling was there now, as she stood encircled in brawny arms. She tilted her head back. His brown eyes shimmered, as if lined with unshed tears.

"All right," he whispered and lowered his face.

His taste was sweet and addictive. She couldn't get enough of it and stretched onto her toes, taking as much as he was willing to share.

Jerek's lips slipped away. He looked at her expectantly. That was the other uncanny ability he had, to make her forget everything around her. "What?" she asked.

"All right, you can come with me. I won't make you stay here, alone," he said.

Her mind snapped back to the situation at hand. "Oh, thank you, Jerek. I promise I'll be good."

Calluses on the tips of his fingers and the top of his palms softly scratched her skin. "Don't be too good. I like the new April, but I like the old one too." He stepped aside and one eye gave her a silly wink.

She giggled. "I'm going to run across the hall and dress. I won't be but a minute."

"I'll wait right here."

April tossed a look over her shoulder. She didn't want to doubt him, but had to see if he told the truth.

"I promise. I won't leave without you. Don't fret."

She smiled and scurried from the room.

****

Late in the afternoon, Jerek took her hand as they walked up the steps of yet another hospital. He wished there was a way to shield her from the horrors they'd already seen and would continue to see until they found Willie and Suzie. Four hospitals and still no sight of them, this one didn't give much hope either. He should go check at the dock. The coal barge that had supplied the *Sultana* with her final load of coal now floated the river each day retrieving bodies. Gently, he squeezed soft fingers. No, he wouldn't submit her to those sights. He'd go check the bodies after taking her back to the Cox's. Some kind of an excuse would form by then.

They entered the white building. Cots lined the halls, overflow from the few rooms set up to nurse the fallen. An offensive smell wafted. Blood, urine, ether, and death fused to form a distinct yet indescribable scent. He drew a handkerchief from his breast pocket and handed it to April. She blinked at the moisture in her eyes and shook her head. He understood. She didn't want to offend the ill.

Volunteers, men and women, with sweat rolling from their brows bustled to and fro in attempts to attend to each moan and groan. As hard as they worked, it would never happen. The injured were too ill, and the caring too tired to keep the pace up much longer.

He and April searched the beds for familiar faces while walking toward the sentry seated at the end of the long hall.

"Jerek, if the war is over, why do they still have army guards at all of the hospitals?" she asked.

"The Confederacy may have surrendered. But

the South hasn't given up," he said. A hoarse whisper made him take a second look at the cot to his right.

"Brinkley?" the man said again.

Jerek stopped. An unrecognizable man lay on his back; somber eyes begged him to step closer. Scalded from head to toe, skin fell from the man's flesh in layers. Bandages covered some areas, but for the most part, stale air was allowed to sting the red, blistered skin. A thin sheet hung from one side of the cot to the other and covered nothing more than the patient's hips. Empathy for the man's pain filled his soul. He walked around and knelt near the man's head. "Yes, I'm Jerek Brinkley."

"It's me, Sam Clemens," the man rasped and tried to hold his hand up.

He couldn't help the intake of breath that echoed in his ears as he recognized the engineer from the *Sultana*. Hot steam had melted the skin of Sam's face. The features left behind were like nothing he'd seen before.

He bent his knees, gently lowered the bandaged hand back to the bed and lightly rested his on top of it. "How are you doing, Sam?"

"Not so good." A tiny drop of water fell from the corner of one eye.

"Is there something I can get for you?"

The man swallowed, his Adam's apple worked to make the action happen. "Yeah, you can get the bastard that blew up our boat." His eyes glanced to the cots next to him. His other bandaged hand motioned for Jerek to lean closer.

The cots, about six inches off the floor, were nothing more than a piece of canvas stretched between wooden frames. The man fought hard to talk. Jerek leaned closer and waited for the words to come out.

"We were going into Chute Number Forty. With

the water so high we'd need a lot of steam to make the run around the island." Sam paused to take a breath. "I watched those boilers close, blew some water out, closed the valve and struck the gauge. She was good. Good to go." A slight cough emitted. "No foaming, no extra steam and plenty of water. The boilers didn't blow, the coal furnace below us did. The blast came upwards and blew steam out of the stacks and back down onto us. Go look at her. That patch never let loose." Sam's chest heaved as it tried to fill with air. A strange gurgling sound rattled with each agonizing breath. "I smelled the powder."

"Don't worry about it Sam, I know you're one of the best engineers to ever run a steamer on the river. Don't try to talk any more. You need to get some rest." Jerek tried to assure the man.

"No, pr-promise you'll find those boat burners. D-don't want people thinking she was a bad boat, or crewed by bad men."

April had maneuvered around the other side of the bed and balanced on her knees. Cautiously, she placed a hand on the man's head. "No one thinks badly of you or the ship. Don't fret so, now."

Sam Clemens looked at her.

Blonde hair framed her hatless head. It glowed in the sunlight shinning through the window behind them. A sweet smile covered her face as she leaned over the edge of the cot.

Sam licked at his dry lips, before the corners turned upwards. His eyes had a look of relief in them that changed to contentment as the lids fell shut. The uneven heaves of his chest halted, and as the final breath in his lungs expelled, his head drooped to her side of the cot.

Her eyes flashed to Jerek. He rose and walked around to kneel beside her.

"I-is he d-dead?" she asked.

"Yes, he's out of his pain," he said and pulled her close.

"Oh." She laid her head against his chest.

"Shh, you helped him."

"No, I didn't," she said.

He could hear the tears in her voice. "Yes, you did. You told him no one thinks badly of him. The one thing he needed to hear. I think he thought you were an angel sent down to take him home." He cupped her jaw with both hands and tilted her face upwards. "Maybe you were."

April looked back to Sam. She ran a hand over his singed hair. "Good-bye, Mr. Clemens."

He braided their fingers. After a few moments, he helped her rise and they continued to walk down the hallway.

"What did he mean the patch didn't give?" April asked.

The guilt he'd been bottling since they'd left New Orleans burst like a corked bottle sitting in the sun. He stopped their stroll and ran a hand over his head before he let it float down her silky locks. Stale air burnt his lungs, making remorse flare hotter. "The *Sultana* had a bulge in one of her boilers. I hired a man in Vicksburg to fix it."

April nodded. Her deep, thoughtful gaze made him wish he could read her mind. "Why did you hire someone to fix it instead of Captain Mason?"

"I wanted to make sure it was done properly. The boilermaker patched it, and before we left Memphis I hired another one to check it. He confirmed it was good and solid." She had to believe he wouldn't have kept her on an unsafe boat.

"The man must have done a good job. Mr. Clemens said it didn't give out." She patted his cheek. "You didn't do anything wrong. Why do you feel guilty about it?"

How did she know his feelings? His confused

mind couldn't come up with an answer.

April put her hands on his shoulders, and standing on her tiptoes, brushed her lips over his mouth. "I know you'd never do something that might put others in danger. Don't fret so."

Her sweet smile sent a manner of ease into his body. He leaned forward and kissed her, with a bit more intensity than her peck had held. The engaging feeling of devotion filled his senses. It was a moment before the lump in his throat dissolved.

"Let's go see if the sentry knows anything."

One arm remained around her shoulders as he turned to walk down the hall. The top of her head leaned against his shoulder and stayed there as her feet joined his slow walk forward. She straightened when they stopped in front of the guard.

He held her tight while asking, "Have there been any new patients brought in today? We're looking for a man and a little girl."

"No, sorry mister, we're full to the roof. Even with several dying, we don't have room to take no more," the young soldier answered.

It was the same story they'd heard everywhere. He had to think of new places to check. Looking for a needle in a haystack couldn't be more difficult. "Thanks," he said.

"Where you staying? If I hear of them, I'll send word," the boy said.

"At the Cox Hotel," April supplied.

"Oh, sure, I know of them. I'll remember that."

"Thank you." April turned and looked up. "Where to now?"

There was only one place left to look. Easing her around they began to walk toward the door. "It's getting late, maybe we should go back to the hotel."

She shook her head. "No, we still have several hours of daylight. Maybe we should go down to the wharf."

"April—" He should tell her *she* didn't want to go down there, but that wasn't true. "I don't want you to go down there," he said.

They approached Sam Clemens' bed. The fallen boatman remained untouched by any of the staff or volunteers. April stopped. She looked around then walked to the cot. With gentle fingers, she rearranged the tiny sheet so his nakedness was still covered, but now his deceased face was as well.

Arriving back at his side, she changed the subject. "Whom was he talking about when he said the boat burners?"

"They're a secret service agency of the Confederacy that destroyed several riverboats," he answered as they walked down the hall.

"What do you mean a secret service agency?"

He pushed the door wide. "The Confederate Congress employed a couple dozen men into the Secret Service Corp. They were authorized to destroy Union traffic on the main rivers, especially the Mississippi. The South felt it was fair because they were out numbered, out supplied, and out gunned. The North felt it was an act outside of 'civil' warfare and compiled their own agency to halt them. As an act of fairness, the South told the boat burners to never attack passenger vessels or those flying flags of surrender."

April stopped as they entered the street. "An act of fairness?"

He shrugged. "The Confederate Congress even added an amendment to their Declaration of War stating the boat burners would receive a considerable amount of money for every boat destroyed. Several men were caught and prosecuted last year. With the surrender, and the shooting of President Lincoln, the thought they're still out there escaped me."

"What do you mean?" she asked.

His head jerked, he hadn't meant for his thoughts to come out aloud. With a sigh he continued, "I should have spoken to Captain Mason about it. He would've known if they were still active." Packed full of Union Soldiers, the *Sultana* would have been a prize for a boat burner—worth a lot of money.

"What are you thinking so hard about?" she asked. "The way you're tugging at your chin, you're gonna rub your skin raw."

He had to smile. "I was trying to figure out where to go next. We aren't getting anywhere checking the hospitals again. And I left word at all the hotels and boarding houses to contact us at the Cox's if Willie and Suzie check in."

She took his hand and turned to walk in the direction of the river. "We are going to the wharf."

Jerek planted his feet. Her body jerked to a halt at the end of his arm. "I don't want you going down there."

A hint of defiance flashed in her eyes. "I'm going, with or without you." She stepped back to his side, one hand slid around his waist. The warmth of tiny fingers seeped into skin. "I'll just feel safer if it's with you."

His heart melted. How did she do it? How'd she get so deep under his skin he'd walk across a hot bed of coals if she asked him to? Of their own accord his feet fell into step beside hers.

A few minutes later they topped the levee. The coal barge had nosed up to the boat crowded wharf. *Please don't let this be the one they are on.* Please don't let her see the water swollen, disfigured bodies of her brother and niece. A painful ache tore at his chest.

"What are they unloading?" she asked.

"April—" he started.

"My God, its bodies!" Anguish filled her face.

182

He stroked silky hair as she pressed against his chest. "Shh…"

Several minutes later, she took a deep breath and stepped back. "I don't think I can look at them," she admitted.

"Let's go back to the hotel."

"No, no, I have to know if they're there. All day, I've had this feeling that I need to go to the wharf." She rubbed her nose and sniffled. "Will you look for me?"

Hot coals would be easier, but he nodded.

"I'll walk down the ridge and wait over there by that little boat." She pointed to an area several yards from the canvas sheets men were laying on the ground.

April wrapped both hands around one of his as Jerek led her down the cobblestones. For some reason, she'd expected to see rescue boats unloading joyous, live survivors. Of course the scene before them made more sense. It had been two, almost three, days since the *Sultana* blew. No one could survive the raging river for that long. It became harder to breathe the closer they drew to the water. Air became lodged in stilled lungs, burning the walls of her chest.

Jerek angled them away from the men carrying bodies and toward the overturned boat in a small area of grass. She sat down on what turned out to be only half of a boat. It had been split in two. The other half was nowhere to be seen.

He knelt before her. "It may take me a few minutes, are you sure you'll be okay?"

A passel of mosquitoes must be stinging the backs of her eyeballs. She closed her lids, hoping to relieve the pain.

Jerek wrapped her in his arms. The comfort was great and eased the pain.

With a deep breath, she pushed away and made

her body sit straight-backed. The steady beat of his heart throbbed against her palm. "I'll be all right. Please go check now. I won't move."

He stood and his palm gathered a handful of her hair. He twirled it for a moment. "I'll be as quick as I can."

She shook her head. "Don't hurry. Please know for sure before you come back."

He nodded, turned, and walked away. The urge to run and stop him was great. Blood pulsated in her temples; pressing against them didn't ease the hard thuds. Would knowing be easier than not? If their bodies were never found, she could believe they were fine, deem they'd made it ashore and into one of the smaller towns along the river. The muscles in her throat constricted and her jaw tightened. No, she had to know. Either way, she had to know.

Jerek had arrived at the tarps, and she turned, not wanting to watch him complete the task. The water was so high a bank no longer lined the river. Waves crashed onto tall grass, pushed the stalks down then pulled them back up in quick succession. The movement left puddles of foam behind. In one of the larger pools, something was caught amongst the wet leaves. It peeked above then dipped below the churning water.

Jerek still roamed through the beds of canvas. She'd promised to stay put, but whatever was in the water wanted her to see it. She bent down to remove the new boots. The wet turf would stain and possibly ruin the leather. After tucking her stockings into the boots, she stood and walked around the broken boat.

Within a few steps, the ground grew soft and mud squished between her toes. Gathering her skirt with both hands, she hitched it above her ankles. Muddy water streamed over her feet, sending a shiver up her spine. She paused, focused her strength, and then moved forward.

The water almost touched her knees and each time a blade of grass slapped her shins she jolted, imagining it was a snake or something worse. The object was close. She gathered the material of her dress into one hand, and stretched out her other arm.

A wave tugged the item further into the cluster of weeds. One more step. Her feet sunk into slippery, slimy mud. Feeling for solid ground with the tips of her toes, she eased forward. Need of grasping the object was stronger than fear of encountering the steep bank that must be somewhere beneath the growing ripples.

Extending her arm as far as she could, the tip of one finger brushed against the article, it flipped and released from the brush. The quick movement made her jolt upright. She flexed her fingers and bent to reach forward again. A rushing wave pushed the item forward. It tugged below the water then bounced up in front of her leg.

Air caught in her throat and became locked there. Eerie tremors snaked from her toes and made every limb unusable. The material of her dress slipped from shaking fingers.

Frozen, she stared at the tiny toy. It brushed against her knee and bobbed in the water. Tears streamed from her eyes.

"April!" Water splashed behind her. Firm hands grabbed her shoulders. "April what are you doing? It's not safe here. Come on." Jerek tugged on her upper arms.

She didn't move.

"April?" He stepped in front of her.

His movements made the bobbing grow and the toy floated to his leg. He bent to pick it up. Water dripped from the carved doll. The once white dress had been stained brown, and the bonnet was gone. Black, sandy silt covered the carving marks and the features of the once beautifully, hand-drawn face.

"Come on, sweetheart, you need to get out of the water," Jerek said.

She couldn't move. He handed her Suzie's doll. A sob heaved her chest as she wrapped her fingers around the toy.

Jerek lifted her into his arms, and she laid her pounding head on his shoulder as he carried her back to the overturned boat. Sobs racked her chest. He set her down, threaded her stockings on, and forced her feet into her boots.

Behind closed lids, she could see Suzie's cherub face bouncing the doll across the bed. The tears fell faster, and she sniffed at the snot trickling from her nose. She pressed the back of one hand to her nostrils and clutched the doll to her chest.

"April." Jerek put a finger beneath her chin and lifted her face. "This doesn't mean anything."

She labored to draw a deep breath. As it escaped she said, "Yes it does. They're dead Jerek."

"Oh, honey, we don't know that."

She shook her head. He was so kind. But so wrong, this time he was mistaken. "No, they're dead. Willie wanted me to know, so he sent a sign."

"April—"

She pressed a finger to his lips. "When I got burned, I was unconscious for a couple of days. During that time our father died. Willie thought I had died too. After I woke, he was scared I'd go to sleep again and he'd be alone. I swore I'd never fall to sleep before him, and until he left home, I never did. We talked a lot about dying and promised each other that whoever went first had to send a sign to the other, so we'd know they made it to heaven." Saying the story aloud offered a sense of comfort.

She bowed her head. "Oh, Jerek, I'm going to miss him. And little Suzie, she was just a baby." A fierce burn ripped at her chest. Flames licked at her heart. How would she go on without them?

Jerek sat down on the boat and created a cocoon with his arms and body. "I know, sweetheart, I know."

She smothered her face into his chest. Pain so severe it hurt to breathe engulfed her body. He rocked her back and forth, and whispered comforting, soothing sounds. His hand made wide circles over her back. Strong, tender arms held her until the well ran dry.

A white kerchief slipped between her fingers. She used it to wipe her face and blow her nose. With a heavy sigh, she drooped back against his chest.

A deep voice, thick with a rebel drawl split the air, "You Jerek Brinkley?"

Chapter Ten

April lifted her face as Jerek turned. Dressed in Union colors, a short, squat man, with a nose that took up three-fourths of his face stood on the cobblestones.

"Yes, I'm Jerek Brinkley." He stood while keeping one hand on her shoulder.

"I need you to come with me," the man said.

"What for?" Jerek glanced at her then back to the man. "Do you have news of the people we're looking for?"

"Don't know nothin' 'bout no people. Major General C. C. Washburn, Commanding Officer of Memphis wants to talk to you. I'm to bring you to his quarters henceforth. If'n you got a mind to protest, I ain't afraid to use force." The unsightly man tapped a holster hanging at his side.

"What about?" Jerek asked.

The man looked toward the crowded dock. "What do you think it's about?" he said.

"All right, but I need to take," his gaze jumped between her and the man, "my wife back to our hotel."

"Nope, can't let ya." The man nodded to another soldier a few feet behind him. "The Private'll take her back to your hotel."

Jerek took a step forward and peered down at

the stubby man. "No, I said I will escort her back to the hotel. I don't care if it's the President himself who wants to talk to me. She's experienced a great loss during this ordeal, and I will not go with you or anyone else until I know she's safely at the hotel. You and the Private can follow us. I'm sure it's on the way." His voice sounded like an angry bear growling.

The man took a step back and cleared his throat. "Well, all right, but make it quick."

Jerek glared at the man.

W-we'll follow you," the army man said as he pointed to the hill.

Jerek helped her to her feet. Her knees wobbled, and she grasped his shirt sleeve.

"Can you walk?" he asked.

"Y-yes." She gave a slight nod.

He tightened his hold around her shoulders, and they walked past the men.

The men followed. April sent a nervous glance to Jerek.

"I'm glad to hear they're starting an investigation this soon," Jerek said as they climbed to the top of the ridge.

He laid his other hand over the ones clutching Suzie's doll to her stomach. She leaned on the solid support of his shoulder as they walked the few blocks to the hotel.

The men followed them into the Cox's and stood at the bottom of the stairs while Jerek led her to their room. "I'll have Ester prepare a bath for you. I should be back in time for supper." He eased her onto the bed.

"Why would the Army want to talk to you?"

"Because I knew about the deal they made with Captain Mason, I suspect."

"What deal?"

"Mason was to be paid for each Union soldier

and officer he hauled north." His palms pressed against her cheeks. "Now don't fret about it, I'll be back before you know it."

She leaned back, away from the mouth lowering. "Is that why there were so many on the *Sultana*?"

He pulled her forward. "In part."

A loud "Brinkley!" echoed up the staircase.

"I don't have time to explain it right now. Give me a kiss goodbye, and I'll tell you about it when I return," he coaxed.

"Promise?"

"I promise," he said before his lips landed.

The touch of his mouth scattered the swirls in her mind as it focused on the juncture of warm, soft flesh.

The kiss ended too soon and as the short man bellowed his name again, Jerek said, "I'll see you in a bit." The door clicked as he shut it behind him.

If one more person told her not to fret she would scream. No, that was the old April. The new April would simply smile and nod. Her hand slapped the mattress. *Poppycock!* There had to be a happy medium between screaming and nodding. There had to be a place in the middle where the old, raging April could merge with the new, docile April. She just had to find it—soon before she went crazy.

She liked the new April, but she missed the way the old April could relieve pressure. A solid rant was good for a person. But the way Jerek coddled the new April was heavenly. He wouldn't have treated the old April that way. Would he?

A knock interrupted her self-assessment.

Ester poked her head around the frame. "Don't fret now April, Tim's carrying up the water, and I'll get the bathing chamber ready for you."

Outwardly, she smiled and nodded. Inwardly, she screamed.

****

The tiny white garment slid over the doll's head and fell into place around its wooden legs. It had taken hours to scrub the slimy silt from each carved notch, and with the aid of some of Ester's lye soap the dress had been restored a bright white. April turned the doll over. The ink had been reduced to faint lines, but if she looked really hard she could see Suzanne's portrait. The ache in her chest had been with her all night. The gallons of tears she'd shed at the loss of Willie and Suzie hadn't eased the intense pain.

After tying the miniscule ribbon around the waist, she laid the doll on the table near her bed and walked to the window.

The area bustled with people, but none were the one she longed to see. It was after ten in the morning, and Jerek had yet to return to the hotel since he'd left with the pudgy army officer yesterday afternoon. She pulled the chair closer to the window and sat down. Her elbows went to her knees and her chin into the palms of her hands.

The old April would be furious by now. She might have already gone searching for him, like she did Willie in New Orleans. The new April would calmly wait for him to arrive, whenever it happened to be. But the middle April, the one she considered being the best, did just what everyone told the other two not to do. She fretted. Worried about what had happened to him, where he was, and why he hadn't returned.

This middle April was a compromise between the other two, and she hoped Jerek would like her. He'd said he liked the new one, but had asked her not to change too much because he liked the old one as well. Maybe he'd like the middle one more than either of the other two. Maybe he'd even love her.

A knock on the door sent her mind games askew. She leaped to her feet. Her hand grabbed the knob and flung the door open. "Yes?"

"There's a man here to see you," Scarlet said. "He wanted to see Mr. Brinkley. I told him he wasn't here but you were."

"Oh, all right." She stepped out and pulled the door shut. Her feet stalled. What if it was someone with news about Willie and Suzie or their remains? She closed her eyes, took a breath, then followed the other woman down the stairs.

"Mr. Rowberry?" She recognized the man standing near the front doors as the first mate from the *Sultana*.

Scarlet proceeded into the kitchen, and April walked toward the man.

He held one hand forward. His eyes were as round as sausages. "Please forgive me, I didn't know you and Jerek were married," he said as he touched her hand with a gentle shake.

She cringed. She really needed to put a stop to this assumption.

"May I speak with you for a moment?" Mr. Rowberry asked.

"Of course."

"Perhaps we could step outside? On to the porch?"

"Certainly." She walked through the door he opened and held wide.

Once on the wide porch, he pointed to two wicker chairs near the corner. The large wooden awning blocked the morning sun, shading the area. She took a seat and waited for him to sit. "What can I do for you Mr. Rowberry?"

"Well, Mrs. Brinkley," he started.

"April," she said, "just call me April."

"And I'm Bill, well William, but I go by Bill."

He was a taller than she, but not nearly as tall as Jerek, and round shaped, not fat, more like a tree trunk, the same size from top to bottom. His face was long and kind, green eyes blinked rapidly as he looked her way.

The pounding in her chest increased with velocity. She clutched her hands together. "Did you find my brother and niece?"

"What? Oh, no, no. I didn't know they were missing." He reached over and patted her hands. "I'm so sorry."

"I fear they have perished." She wasn't yet able to admit their deaths to anyone but Jerek.

"Ma'am, the shoreline of the Mississippi is dotted with small encampments, every day word of a passenger or two being cared for at one of them wanders in. Don't give up hope."

"Thank you, that's kind of you to say." She turned to the traffic traveling past the hotel. Wagons, saddle horses, and people walking went about their business as she sat, unable to do anything but wait.

A few moments later, Bill Rowberry said, "I really need to talk to Jerek. Do you know where he is?" He pointed to the front door. "The folks inside simply said he wasn't here, but that his wife was."

"I'm afraid I don't know where he is. He left with two army men late yesterday and hasn't returned yet. They said some general wanted to talk to him." She folded her arms across her chest. "Do you know why they would want to speak with him?"

"The accident I suspect," he said.

"I know about the deal Captain Mason made with the army," April said.

His eyes opened wide to stare at her. "You do?"

She nodded. "Jerek told me."

Bill Rowberry hung his head. "The deal was for a few hundred men. They reneged and loaded over a thousand on that boat. Way more than what we expected."

"Two thousand, two hundred, and two," she said

slowly.

His face rose. "How do you know that?"

"I counted them. That's minus the sick ones the doctor had removed."

"That's close to what I had figured too," he admitted.

"Over fifteen hundred perished," she sighed.

Rowberry gave her a questioning look.

"To the best of my calculations, six hundred and eight have been taken to hospitals, hotels and private homes, leaving one thousand, five hundred, and ninety-four people either dead or missing." She wiped at the wetness seeping from the corner of her eye. "Many of those taken to one of the hospitals or the Soldier's Home have died after arrival. I figure the death toll will be close to eighteen hundred by the end of the week."

Silence was thick as he absorbed her estimate.

Letting out a deep sigh, she asked, "How'd you survive?"

He rubbed his eyes and shrugged. "I was in the pilot house. Honestly, it was a nice night. The fog was a little thick, but nothing to worry about. The boat was running smooth, chugging up the river. I could hear the snores of the men. They floated up past the wheelhouse almost like a lullaby. I know that sounds strange for me to remember, but I do."

He paused for a moment. One hand picked at the knee of his pants. "It was like nothing I'd ever imagined. One second I was at the wheel, and the next I was catapulted into the night sky. Half the pilothouse blew upwards and I went with her. It was the strangest feeling. I can't even describe it, sailing through the air like a bird. Then there were the sparks flying with me. It was like being in the middle of a fireworks explosion. Sparklers skipped and fell all around. I hit the water and kept falling. Thought I was going to drown because I didn't know which way was up. I didn't know which way to swim. Finally I surfaced. Sparks continued to land around me. Before long I found a floating plank and grabbed on."

April remained silent and waited for him to continue.

"Men dropped into the water around me like leaves falling from trees in October. Soon there were six of us clinging to the same chunk of wood. All I could do was watch as flames destroyed the boat, and the current carried us further and further away." He rubbed his forehead. "It was horrible, and something that shall haunt me until the day I die. There was nothing I could do. Nothing." Anguish filled his eyes.

She patted his arm in understanding.

He shuddered. "The other five men on my log all drowned. Some fought it, struggling to hold on, and shrieking as they lost their grip, others just silently sank below waves. They were already so worn down from the war they simply had no more fight in them. A man in a rowboat pulled me from the water. I believe it wouldn't have been much longer before I would have sank as well. He took me to the coal barge which brought me ashore the next morning." Mr. Rowberry remained silent for several minutes before asking, "How about you? How'd you survive?"

"Similar story, except we weren't blown off the boat, we climbed down a rope. I can't say I remember much about it. I remember floating on a log, and being colder than I'd ever been before. The next thing I remember is waking up here at the hotel..." she let the words float away and thought— *how did I get here?* Her hand went to her chest. "Jerek saved my life," she whispered.

Bill Rowberry nodded.

They both watched the traffic for a few minutes before he said, "The boiler didn't blow. She was a sound ship."

"Mr. Clemens swore the same."

"Sam Clemens? He's alive? Where is he?"

She shook her head. "I'm sorry. He died at the hospital yesterday afternoon. But he talked to us before he passed away."

"What did he say about the explosion? Could he tell you anything about it?" Bill Rowberry leaned forward.

"Yes, he said the patch didn't let loose and that the fire came from below."

He slapped his leg. "I knew it! It was those damned boat burners and one of their coal torpedoes that did her in."

"Coal torpedo?" she asked. "Jerek told me about the boat burners, but he didn't say anything about a torpedo."

"Jerek probably mentioned some of the ships the boat burners have destroyed, the *Ruth*, the *Allan Collier*, the *J. W. Cheesman*, the *Venus*, the *WestWind,* the *Champion*, the *Imperial*, the *Hiawatha*, the *Post Boy*, the *Forest Queen*, the *Jess K. Belle*, the *Chancelor*, the *Welcome*, the *Sam Kirkman*, the *James Wood*, the *Minnetonka*, the *Glasgow*, the *E. M. Ryland*, the *Sally Wood*, the *Catler*, the *Mussellman*, the *W.H. Sidell*, the *D.A. Taylor*, the *A.J. Sweeny*, the *Sunshine*. Oh, the list just goes on and on." He touched a different finger each time he named a boat, as if counting them. "Their tactics have varied a touch here and there, some boats were only sent out of commission for a short time, but the majority of them are at the bottom of the rivers, what didn't go up in flames that is. For the wood burners they started to hollow out logs, fill them with gun powder then plant the logs in the piles of wood lining the rivers. Boats stop along the way to load up from those piles. The torpedo, which looks just like the other logs gets thrown on board, and eventually into the fires where it explodes."

Her brows tugged into a frown. "But the *Sultana* didn't have any wood fires."

"Yeah, the coal burning ships thought they were pretty safe, until recently. Courtenay, a no good insurance salesman from St. Louis invented a coal torpedo. It's made from cast iron. They're odd shapes and sizes so they're not detected very easily. I've seen one. To the regular guy it's nothing but a lump of coal."

The door of the hotel opened, April held her question as Ester, carrying two glasses of lemonade said, "I thought you two might be getting thirsty out here in the sun."

Bill stood. "Thank you, Ma'am." He handed a glass to April before taking his. "The shade of the porch is very comfortable. It's a nice place you have here."

"Thank you, we like it." Ester waved a hand. "You two enjoy your visit."

Her question, still fresh at hand, came out as soon as Ester closed the door. "How would a coal torpedo have gotten on the *Sultana*?"

"I got some ideas. That's what I need to talk to Jerek about." He took a long drink of lemonade.

April sipped at hers. "Why do you think he would know?"

"I'm curious if he knows the whereabouts of Robert Louden."

"Who's that?" she asked.

"Only the worst boat burner of 'em all." A scowl of disgust covered his face.

"Why would Jerek know him?"

"He's one of the men who testified against Louden at his court marshal. Hours before the man was set to swing, it was detained, for reasons still unknown. Then he escaped while being transferred.

Slipped the handcuffs from his wrists and swam away from the transport boat. It's real fishy if you ask me."

"What was he court marshaled for?"

"Don't really recall now, he's been arrested for everything, mail running, espionage, boat burning, smuggling, contraband. Heck his whole family has been involved in the deepest, darkest, underground, no-good deeds since the beginning of the war, probably before then even." Rowberry shook his head with disgust.

"And you have reason to believe he would sabotage the *Sultana*?" she asked.

"Oh yeah! He and Mason go way back, they're both from St. Louis, ran into each other a time or two. But when Louden's wife Mary was exiled for war crimes—"

She widened her eyes in disbelief.

"I told you his whole family is full of criminals. Anyway, when Mary was exiled to Mississippi, it was a boat J.C. captained that carried her there. Louden got word to Mason saying he'd pay for leaving his children motherless. Hear tell his two daughters are being raised in the convent. With the *Sultana* heaped with soldiers, Louden would get three birds with one stone, burn a boat, revenge on Mason, and kill a massive amount of Union soldiers. He'd consider it the mother lode."

"And you say Jerek might know the whereabouts of this Robert Louden?" she asked.

"Don't know. Guess I hoped for some help in investigating my theory. I want to know the truth. If someone can prove the boilers blew, fine I can live with it. It's happened before. But if a no-good boat burner murdered all those helpless, homesick men, then I want him to pay for it."

The anger in his voice sent a shiver up her spine, but at the same time conviction of his righteousness filled her mind.

"I'll help," she offered.

He smiled, an unsure odd grin, the kind men offer when they are placating a woman or child. "I don't think your husband would like you getting involved."

It irritated her, the smile, and his words. "Whether Jerek likes it or not, I'm already involved. I'll be here in Memphis until I find my brother and niece. Helping you will give me something to do beside look at dead bodies."

Bill Rowberry gasped.

She flattened a hand over her cheek. She hadn't meant to say the words so callously. Sometimes the old April popped forward. As her mind searched for a more appropriate way to say what she meant, her gaze wondered to the street and landed on a tall, dark haired man.

"There's Jerek now!" She leaped from her chair, hurried across the porch, and down the steps.

Sea green material twirled around her feet and both hands landed on her hips when she came to a halt at the bottom of the porch. Jerek felt the tension from the long night ooze from his body. Quick steps brought him forward to wrap her in his arms and attack her mouth before she had a chance to mutter a word.

She tilted her head, giving him a deeper taste. Then her head tilted the other way. He caught the playful lips again as petite hands snuck inside his open jacket to roam over his chest and around to his back. She unknowingly massaged away the strain of sitting in the straight back chair for so long. Their tongues played hide and seek for several moments before he remembered they stood on a busy Memphis street corner.

Lifting his face he asked, "Miss me?"

"Yes! Where have you been?"

Her cheeks were flush, her eyes sparkling and her lips moist from his kisses. He leaned down for one more quick taste.

"Talking with the army, believe me, my sweet, I didn't leave you here alone by choice." He'd been so worried about her, concentrating on the General's questions had been extremely difficult.

"I believe you," she said. Her eyes widened, as if she just remembered something. "Oh, Jerek, Mr. Rowberry is here to see you." She turned and pointed to the hotel's porch.

The first mate raised a hand in greeting. Jerek replied with a nod. "Bill, how are you?" He took her hand to climb the steps.

"Fine," the man shrugged.

He aided April into a chair, shook Bill's hand, and then reclined against the porch railing. April handed him a glass of warm lemonade. He emptied it in one swallow.

"Thank you." He handed back the glass.

She set it on the table next to another empty one and said, "Mr. Rowberry and I were discussing the accident."

He shot the man a look of disdain. "You were?" He let his disapproval come through his voice.

Rowberry's head lowered, and his gaze fell to his boots.

"Yes, we were," April snapped.

He rubbed his forehead. How could women shame men to the bone with nothing more than a look? "I'm sorry, my dear, I'm sure it's the topic of conversations everywhere." He turned to Bill. "I'm glad you survived. How are you doing?"

"I'm good, thanks. Oh, and congratulations, I had no idea the two of you were married."

Why would she have told Rowberry that?

Her eyes now sent an apology his way.

There was no need, he really didn't mind. She

was safer if people thought she was married. He winked at her and jumped over the subject.

"Washburn has commissioned an investigation of the incident. They asked about your whereabouts, I told them I didn't know if you survived or not."

Bill asked, "Do they think it was boat burners?"

Jerek shook his head. "I'm afraid they aren't interested in why she blew up. They want to know how so many men ended up on one boat. I refused to leave until they'd sent a wire to Washington, asking for a full investigation. The best Washburn would agree to do was request an inquiry as to why so many men boarded the *Sultana* in Vicksburg when two other steamers left there empty. I hope once they start investigating it'll go deeper." Jerek sighed. He'd spent hours arguing his case with Washburn. The man refused to discuss the reason for the explosion. "I watched the transaction happen, so I know the request arrived in Washington."

"They're worried about who was making money?" Bill asked.

He huffed and nodded. "And who wasn't."

"Jerek, do you know Robert Louden?" April asked.

Jerek snapped his head from her to Bill. Rowberry shuffled his feet and his face grew red. "I know of a Robert Louden, why do you ask?"

"Mr. Rowberry believes he may have planted a coal torpedo on the *Sultana*."

"Oh, he does, does he?" Jerek drew his lips into a tight pucker as the muscles in his chin tightened. The man was addlebrained.

Bill cleared his throat. "I-uh, been researching my theory, and hoped you could help me out a touch. Since you weren't here, I guess I shared more than I ought to have."

"You guess?" Jerek growled.

"I offered to help Mr. Rowberry investigate his

theory," April said.

"You what?" God he was tired, exhausted from being up all night. Wet leather made his feet hurt and a pounding headache emerged as he listened to the two sitting in front of him.

"I offered to help him," April repeated as if he hadn't heard her the first time.

"I don't think so, my dear." He shook his head.

"What do you mean you don't think so?" Her face drew into a deep, dark scowl.

"I mean, no. You are not going to help him investigate his theory," he explained.

"Says who?" she challenged.

"Says me," he explained.

"You can't tell me what I can do!"

A little embarrassed by arguing with her in front of the other man, he gave Bill an apologetic look before he responded. "Yes, I can, and I will."

"No you can't! I can do what I want. I always have," April huffed. Even sitting, she found a way to brace her hands on her hips.

"I'm sure you have, but not any more."

"And why not?" Her toe tapped the floor.

He didn't know why. She just couldn't. Didn't she see how unsafe it would be? An answer jumped to his tongue. "Because I'm your husband and I say so."

Her look was one of the most unpleasant he'd seen her make. "Mr. Brinkley, let me assure you, you have a lot to learn as to what my husband will ever be able to tell me to do or not to do." Her smile grew uncomfortably sweet and her lashes fluttered at him. "Now do be a dear, and don't pretend to know things you don't."

He felt his cheeks growing as red as Rowberry's. "I believe it would be best if we continued this conversation in private, my dear."

Bill stood up. "I think I better make my way

202

down to army headquarters and talk to Washburn. I'll stop by to see you tomorrow." He turned to April. "If I hear anything about your brother or niece I will be sure to let you know. Thank you for the visit." Turning back to Jerek, he finished by holding out his hand in farewell and saying, "Good luck, Brinkley."

Jerek pumped his hand and waited until after the man had turned the street corner before he let his gaze fall to April. She was mad and doing a poor job of hiding it—if she was trying to hide it, he couldn't quite tell.

"April, I'm sorry. I didn't mean to hurt your feelings or tell you what to do. It wouldn't be safe for you to be out investigating boat burners." He knelt down in front of her. "Please forgive me. The thought of something happening to you scares me." He let his head bow. "It's been a long night, and I am extremely tired."

She cupped his cheeks and lifted his head. "Oh, Jerek, I'm sorry. I didn't even think about how tired you must be. Come in the hotel, you need to go to bed for awhile." She pulled on his arms, making him stand so she could rise from her chair.

Thank goodness it worked. He really didn't want to fight. Snuggling next to her on the bed in their room for a few hours would be much more revitalizing.

His hand slipped to her waist as they walked into the hotel and up the stairs to their room. Disappointment slapped him in the face when they encountered Scarlet stripping the covers from their bed.

"I'll be out of your way in a moment." She pulled the sheets from the mattress. "It's wash day. Ma Cox has lunch ready if you want to go down and eat. I should have some fresh bedding dry in an hour or so and will have your room all tidied up then."

April put her hands on his hips then turned him

back to the door. "You must be hungry as well."

"No, not really," he admitted.

"Let's have some lunch anyway and then you can take a nap," she insisted.

Chapter Eleven

Jerek stomped back down the stairs. *Thwarted at every turn.* First by the army and their little interest in the reason for the *Sultana* being blown to pieces, and now by not being able to spend a few moments alone with April. It was certainly a down on his luck day.

They entered the kitchen, and he took a deep breath in preparation of enduring an hour-long meal. His body hadn't missed nourishment nearly as much as it had missed lying next to April.

All night, while arguing his point of view with Washburn, he'd thought of her lying in the bed alone and wanted to be with her, to feel her body pressed against his and rub his hands over her succulent curves.

Ester piled the food on the table and engaged April in chatter of no particular interest. Tim joined the table and the two of them discussed the weather, simply making polite conversation that went nowhere.

The meal ended. Scarlet went to check on her drying sheets. She'd mentioned stripping the beds for the other guests, which brought up a nagging question.

Rubbing his chin, Jerek asked, "Ester why is it none of the other guests eat with you?"

"Oh, sometimes they do, but right now the men in the other rooms are helping the watch brigade so they eat with the army," Ester answered and began to carry dirty plates from the table to the sink, while Tim went to answer the bell ringing at the front desk.

"Why don't they sleep with the brigade as well?" Jerek didn't believe it. Brigade men don't rent hotel rooms.

Before she answered, Tim stuck his head back in the room and said, "Jerek, there's a man here to see you."

Jerek rose and pulled out April's chair, knowing she wouldn't remain behind. Hand in hand, they walked into the other room.

A young man fumbled with his hat as he stood near the door.

"I'm Jerek Brinkley."

"Mr. Brinkley, Ma'am," he acknowledged April by tipping his head. "I was informed you were looking for a man and a little girl."

April wheezed. Jerek ran a hand up and down her back. Feeling her stiff spine relax a touch he said, "Yes, yes we are."

The man shuffled his feet and hung his head. "I, I-uh brought in a couple bodies you might want to look at. They're down at the docks."

Jerek wrapped the arm around her. "Thank you, and yes, I'll follow you right now if you don't mind."

"W-we," April said. Her hand trembled as it settled on his chest and watery eyes looked at him. "We will follow you."

He would have liked to protest, but he couldn't. Without further ado they followed the man out the door. Entering the street, he said, "Thank you, for finding us."

A hand came toward him as they walked. He shook it and the man said, "Name's Harry

Wooldridge. My folks have a farm just above Memphis. Pa died in the war, and ma and I still have cows." He paused as a wagon rolled by. "Critters got stranded on some high spots when the river flooded. I had to take feed out to them."

Jerek nodded.

"Day before the accident, a Union gunboat came through, looking for rebels in the area. The gunboat destroyed all the skiffs, rowboats, and canoes in the Memphis area so the rebels couldn't get their hands on 'em and use 'em for no good. Ours included. They blew it to bits and pieces, left nothing for me to repair. I had to come to town to find one I could use to feed the cows. Gotta tell you, that was scary."

"What was?" he asked.

"The sentries. I was afraid they were gonna take me for a rebel. I rowed for hours through flooded fields so I could go up the back rivers to the cows trying to avoid all of 'em." He shook his head.

"I didn't realize the river is that closely guarded." He tightened his hold on April.

"Yeah, especially since the truce was called," Harry answered. "Doesn't make much sense does it?"

He shook his head.

"I finally got the cows all fed and was able to move a few closer to home. This morning whilst bringing the boat back I found...Anyway, I brought them into the docks. A feller told me to come over to the Cox's and ask for you."

"Are the backwaters starting to recede?" Jerek asked.

"Somewhat. I got enough feed to the furthest out ones. It should last until I can drive 'em home. Cows are stupid you know. They'd stand there and drown, whereas a horse, he'll start swimming."

They arrived at the top of the ridge. Harry pointed to two large tarps once again lining the ground. Men mulled about, while others unloaded another barge.

Jerek turned to April and took both of her trembling hands. "Would you like to wait up here?"

She shook her head and tightened her grasp on his hands.

He nodded to the other man and they started to walk down the cobblestones.

A few yards from the canvas sheets Harry stopped and said, "They're at the far end. I'll wait here if'n you don't mind."

Jerek pinched at the bridge of his nose. It hurt to put one foot in front of the other. Her step faltered. He grabbed her shoulder and waited while she took a deep breath and began to walk over the cobblestones again. Odors twisted in the air. Coal steam, muddy water, stale fish, and the host of others now included decaying human bodies.

He steered her around the edge of the tarp. The once white canvas was now the color of the river. At the far end they stopped.

The small frame looked out of place amongst the long, gangling ones lying next to it. Remnants of a tattered dress clung to the shape and twigs stuck amongst mud filled hair.

April let out a long sigh. "Suzie didn't own a red dress."

He folded his hand over the ones she wrung together at her waist. "Honey sometimes the water discolors things, we need to look closer."

"Go ahead, if you must, but it's not them." She turned her back to the bodies.

He did look closer, examined each feature for a touch of familiarity. It was difficult with the body already decomposing. He moved to the man lying next to the little girl. The dark hair and long face wasn't familiar.

"No, it's not them." He stood, wrapped an arm around her shoulders and pulled her into a hug.

Their deep sighs mingled. After a few moments, he steered them away from the cadavers.

Near the dock they met up with Harry. "Thank you, Mr. Wooldridge." Jerek shook his hand.

The man glanced from one to the other. "W-was it them?"

"No, it's not, but thank you for allowing us to check."

"Whew, I'm glad. Well, no I'm not glad, but, wow...this is tough." The young man tried to explain his reaction.

"Yes, it is," he agreed.

Harry glanced around the dock area. "You know, I was here when the men were unloading the sugar off the *Sultana*. That was the night I was looking for the skiff. And right over there one of the casks broke open. The men all started cheering and picking up handfuls to shove in their mouths. More men came a running to get a taste. The pile of sugar was gone in no time. The ground wiped cleaner than my ma's floor." The man shook his head. "Well, I best be headin' out now. I hope you find your family, and I hope they're alive when you find them." He tipped his hat and turned to walk the opposite direction from their route.

At the top of the hill, April stopped then turned around to look at the area below. "What are they doing with all the dead bodies?"

"They notify the next of kin of the ones they can identify. If no one can come to get them, they bury them up at the Soldier's Cemetery."

"And the ones they can't identify?"

"They track identifying markings and bury them in the same place," he answered.

"What can we do to help?" She turned to face him. "While we wait."

His mouth opened, but no words came out.

"I can't leave Memphis until I see or at least

know Willie and Suzie are put to rest." Both of her hands wrapped around his. "But in the meantime, I can't just sit and wait at the Cox's. I need to do something to stay busy."

"We could buy some material and you could sew yourself some new dresses."

She giggled, but it wasn't sincere. "No, I'm not going to sit around sewing." She turned around and tugged him away from the levee. "I think I shall go to the hospital. The one near the Cox's, they probably need more volunteers."

"Are you sure you want to see that suffering everyday?" He wasn't trying to shock or dissuade her, well maybe he was, but more than that he didn't want her out and about. There was too much mayhem on the streets of Memphis.

"I've seen suffering everyday of my life."

"Honey, that wasn't the same," he said.

"Maybe not to you," she answered.

She had him on that one. He didn't know what she'd lived through in her life. No more than she knew what he'd experienced. Without further protest he walked beside her down the street.

They stopped at the hospital and Jerek, believing her proposal would wane after a few minutes, took a chair next to the sentry while April asked about volunteering.

It was almost dark when he tried, once again, to convince her it was time to go home.

April looked at his tired eyes. "All right." She patted his face. "I can finish this first thing in the morning."

With a sigh of relief, he pulled her down the hallway. "April—" Jerek started as soon as he shut the door to the hospital behind them.

She held her hand up. "They need me here. The doctors are so short handed. You can walk me down in the morning and then come walk me home in the evening if it will make you feel better." The hospital was the perfect place to investigate Bill Rowberry's theory. If by chance she could find the monster responsible for blowing up the boat, she might feel justified. It wouldn't bring Willie and Suzie back, but it might stop those boat burners from attacking another ship.

The evening air was warm and sultry, but certainly cooler and more refreshing than the air in the hospital. The poor men were practically piled on top of one another. There was just enough room to walk between the cots. It had taken some time before one of the doctors had been able to interview her, and agreed to let her help. Then she had to wait for another volunteer to show her what needed to be done, which was silly because she could see what needed to be done. The place was in complete disarray.

Jerek yawned. "We'll talk about it in the morning. I need to get some sleep."

"I thought you took a nap at the hospital," she said.

"That is no place to sleep, my dear, if the sound doesn't keep you awake the smell will. Those poor men." He shook his head.

"Precisely why I need to help out while I can," she answered as they walked up the steps of the hotel.

He stopped. She smiled and sent a pleading look into his caring face. She didn't want to upset him, but this was something she needed to do. Something she wanted to do.

He grasped a handful of her hair. As always he watched the ends flow through his fingers. Why did it fascinate him so? It was nothing more than a nuisance. It couldn't hold a curl and forever slipped out of any ribbon tied around it.

Jerek leaned forward. A quick blast of

excitement shot across her chest. His lips touched her forehead before he turned to open the door. Disappointed, she licked her dry lips and stepped through the opening.

"I have supper ready in the kitchen," Ester said. "Oh and Jerek, there's a message for you in your key box." She pointed to a rack on the wall behind the desk before walking into the kitchen.

"I'm going out back to wash my hands," April said as Jerek walked to the desk.

"Be right there." He was already ripping open the envelope.

She wondered about the note, but not enough to keep her from using the facilities. The pain of a full bladder had been stinging for some time. The outhouses at the hospital were the filthiest things. First thing tomorrow they would have a thorough cleaning. There was so much to do to get that place in proper condition for nursing the sick. The challenge made her feet skip.

****

April fluffed the pillow then flopped back onto the sack of feathers. Where was he? After supper, Jerek had asked Ester to prepare a bath for her before they mounted the stairs.

Once they arrived in the room, he said he needed to go meet someone and would be back in an hour or so. She'd taken a bath, combed her hair, and planned how to organize the hospital. The activities had taken about an hour of the five he'd been gone. The rest of the time she'd laid here—waiting.

She needed him. Her body had this indescribable yearning only his touch could satisfy. Lying in the bed, visions of the morning before, when he'd pulled her onto his chest and kissed her, floated across her mind. Her toes curled.

It had been so surreal, and though his kiss had been satisfying, and so very pleasurable, her body had wanted more. Her skin prickled at the thought of his fingers moving over the flesh. Tingles shot across the low part of her stomach, where his groin had rubbed. The tempo of her heart increased. The deep ache grew stronger and beads of sweat broke out on her body.

She kicked the covers from her feet and flung her legs on top of them, searching for a touch of cool air. It didn't help. She flipped off the bed and walked to the window. Several grunts later, the sash lifted and a night breeze fluttered into the room.

She leaned out. The cool air stung her heated flesh. A barren street sat below, not a single person walked about. She pulled her head in, grabbed the chair, and positioned it in front of the window. Resting her elbows on the window edge, she placed her chin in her palms.

Who had the note been from? What had it said? Did the army need to talk to him again? A thousand questions ran through her mind. She didn't have the answers for any.

Flames of gas lanterns flickered in glass chimneys. Tiny insects buzzed around, drawn by the dancing blaze. The old April would have thought the bugs crazy for being foolishly enticed by something that would only harm them. The new April would feel empathy for them; sorry they would never be able to get what they were after, but the middle April could relate to them. She knows about being so captivated by something that even if it's risky, it's worth the trial. That's how she felt about Jerek.

One moment in his arms was worth the twenty-three years it took her to get there. The promise of more was enough to make her do just about anything to stay within the shelter of those arms. To look upon that handsome face everyday for the rest of her life would be pure ecstasy.

She leaned closer to the window and frowned. A

dark figure slid from the alleyway and moved up the street. It sulked near the shadows of the buildings and slithered along the boardwalk. She pulled back and let the curtains fall over the window opening. Cautiously, she peeked through the slit in the middle.

The man stopped across street from the hotel. Light bounced off the sides of his face as his gaze dashed left and right. Then like a black cat, he darted across the street and out of sight. A moment later, the faint squeak of the hotel's front door sounded. She jumped from the chair and covered the rapid pounding in her chest with a shaky hand.

She tiptoed to the door and flattened an ear against the wood. Nothing—not a creak of the stairs, nor clomp of a footfall. Then like pin pricks, one at a time, tiny hairs on the back of her neck stood. Someone was in the hall. She could feel it.

Wringing her hands, she bound toward the bed. The springs creaked, and she stalled her movements. Icy silence filled the room. Careful not to make a sound, she eased onto the bed. Had the knob turned? Was she seeing things? Time clicked by—seconds, minutes? She had no idea, her gaze glued to the door.

A key slipped into the hole from the outside. The click of the lock unlatching made her search for a weapon. The knob turned. She grabbed the lamp off the table beside the bed.

Quiet as possible, Jerek eased the door open, and entered the room. He stopped mid-step. Faint moonlight bounced off the glass lamp held above her head. "April!"

"Jerek?" Her whisper sounded as hoarse as his.

"Yes, it's me. Put the lamp down." He turned, shut the door and inserted the key in the lock. A smile tugged at his lips. The wet hen was back. Before the latch caught, hands wrapped around his

214

waist. His smile faded as tension oozed from her trembling arms. He secured the door, twisted, and folded the tiny, quaking body against his chest.

"What's wrong? Why are you so frightened?"

"There was man," she whispered.

"Where?" Nothing in the dark room moved.

"Lurking outside, but now he's here in the hotel."

He flipped an arm under wobbly knees, carried her to the bed, and sat down. Brushing long tendrils away from her face, he said, "I didn't see anyone outside, and the front door was locked. I just came through it and locked it behind me."

"He must be one of the men staying here," she continued to whisper.

He still had questions to ask Ester and Tim about the other guests at the hotel. "Tell me what you saw."

"I was looking for you out the window, and I saw a figure come from between those two buildings on the far corner. It lurked along the wall then ran across the street lickety-split. A second later, I heard the front door open. I never heard anything else, but I-I felt someone walk past our door. It felt evil." Her shoulders shivered.

He rubbed her shaking arms. "It's all right now, I'm here, and I won't let anyone hurt you."

"I know." She snuggled into his embrace.

His lips curved into a smile. She was so honest, so sincere. He'd never tire of coming home to her. Fine hair tickled his nose. He kissed the mass. April didn't frighten easy. She must have seen something. One more mystery he'd have to investigate. A yawn escaped. Tomorrow, right now another night without sleep had caught up with him.

"Here, crawl under the covers."

"Where are you going?" She clutched his sleeve.

"No where. I have to take these wet boots off.

They're killing my feet," he answered. "I'm not leaving, I promise." When her fingers slipped away he moved to the chair.

"How did your boots get wet?" she asked.

"They've been wet since yesterday." The boots slipped off before he tugged at socks that were just as damp. Wiggling toes more wrinkled than raisins, he sighed with relief.

"Oh, Jerek, I forgot. You have to be so tired." She flipped the sheet back. "Here crawl in so you can get some sleep."

Layers of clothes fluttered onto the floor as he stripped down to cotton drawers and did as she suggested.

"Come here," he whispered. One arm slipped under her neck, while he placed the other on her hip.

Soft, warm curves molded as she burrowed in. One chilly hand came to rest on his bare chest, and her head rummaged until it found a comfortable spot on the front of his shoulder. "Mmm," she sighed as the wiggles stopped.

"Mmm," he repeated and wrapped his hand around her cold fingers, massaging warmth into them.

A delightful giggle slipped from her lips. He pressed a temple to the top of her head. It wouldn't take much to encourage her to give him want he desired, but was she ready? He'd never worried about it before, had just taken sex whenever offered or encouraged. With April it was different. He wanted their lovemaking to be perfect and last a lifetime. There was time. He could wait. A deep sigh, emptying his lungs, encouraged relaxation.

She squirmed again, and her teeth nipped at his chin. The tiny, teasing bites made the muscles in his neck tighten. He tilted so their lips merged, taunted her by pulling back and pressing his mouth against hers again. She wanted more. He played with her lips until April stretched forward and forced his head deep into the pillow by consuming his mouth with a long, deep, and sensual kiss.

He fully participated. His hands journeyed over silky smoothness. Resolve began to melt as it met persistence. Her nectar was heady and the sweetness stimulated his heightened senses. Firm breasts teased his chest, silky legs wrapped around his thigh, and her core pressed against him. Sanity slipped.

While he contemplated his next move, her mouth parted to leave a trail of kisses down his neck. Her head nestled back into comfort as she sighed, "Good night, Jerek."

He closed his eyes and urged the throbs pulsating throughout heated loins to ease.

"Odd," she whispered.

"What's odd?" he choked.

"This has been the most wonderful ten days of my life while also being some of the worse."

His sexual urges eased as compassion funneled in. "Sweetheart, please don't give up hope, we could still find them." He kissed the silky hair below his nose. "We won't quit looking. You have to believe they're still alive."

"If you say so."

"I say so," he said. "Now try to get some sleep."

She nodded. He settled his chin on her golden crown. Soon the hand massaging his chest stilled, and her breathing became deep and even.

Had it only been ten days since they'd met? A little over a week since a headstrong, brassy woman had pulled Willie from the gaming table and stared down the other gamblers as if they were small children.

He closed his eyes. A lot had happened since that warm New Orleans morning, to her, to him, to the world. It was a month that would never be forgotten by many. Lee's surrender, Lincoln's death, the *Sultana* sinking, and he'd met the woman of his dreams.

His brows creased. Would he be able to keep her? The Pinkerton man he'd met tonight had confirmed Allan Pinkerton was on his way to Memphis. Would his arrival shatter their bliss?

****

Jerek woke to an empty bed. The covers landed on the floor as he fought the pile of clothes to release his pants. With one leg stuffed in his britches he hopped across the room before stuffing the other leg in and opening the door. An empty hall reflected morning light, fear sent blood to pound at every pulse point. The door across the hall opened, and April, dressed in yellow from head to toe, flashed him a smile brighter than the May sun.

"Good morning," she said.

"Why didn't you wake me?" he grumbled.

She patted his cheek before her hands slipped around his waist. "You were sleeping so good, I just couldn't."

He pulled her into a bear hug. "Don't do that again."

She rolled her eyes. "Don't worry, we aren't late yet."

"Aren't late for what?" he asked.

"For me to report to the hospital, silly." She tipped her head to the door across the hall. "I have a bath ready for you. And after breakfast you can walk me to the hospital."

He would have liked to say no, but he couldn't. Who could say no to a face too beautiful to describe, to eyes more glittery than a midnight sky, and a mouth more kissable than a new born babe? He leaned down to sample it before saying, "All right."

Her tongue licked his lips as the merger ended. "You are a very special man."

His heart somersaulted. "You are a very special woman. So very special to me," he said as his mouth took hers again. Not in overwhelming need or passion, but in simple, pure devotion. When they separated even the tips of his toes felt warm and tingly. He could only imagine the look in his eyes resembled what he saw in her blue ones—absolute worship.

"Go climb in the tub. I'll get your clothes." With flushed cheeks, April pointed to the bathing chamber.

It was a tight fit, but he lowered into the short, oblong, brass tub. His knees jutted up in front of his chest. Nonetheless the hot water was divine. April entered as he leaned his head back with a deep sigh. She giggled and went about laying his clothes out on a long bench near the wall.

"Would you like me to scrub your back?" she asked.

"Would you?"

"With pleasure," she said.

He leaned forward. Soft hands kneaded the skin and scrubbed away days of sweat. She dipped the sponge and let the water trickle down, rinsing away the suds as it flowed.

"How many other backs have you scrubbed, my dear? You seem to know what you're doing," he wondered aloud.

"None. Well, Willie's when he was little." She dropped the sponge into the water by his knees. "It must just be natural."

Mid-air, he grabbed her hand and kissed the knuckles. "I would appreciate it if mine was the only other one you ever scrub."

"Oh, you would, would you?" He could hear the smile in her words. "I'll have to consider it." Fingers ran through his hair. "Would you like me to wash your hair?"

"I live for the thought," he said.

She giggled again and dipped a pitcher into one of the extra water buckets sitting near the tub. Jerek closed his eyes as the water flowed past and sighed deeply as her tiny fingers worked the soap into a rich lather.

"Close your eyes," she warned before dumping another pitcher of water over the suds. One more rinsing flush followed before she added, "Done."

April wiped her hands on a towel then laid it on the stool she'd sat on. "I'll let you finish and meet you in our room when you're dressed."

"I hope some day I can reciprocate your aid."

"I'll take that under consideration too," she said with a laugh and slipped from the room.

Jerek finished his bath and dressed in record time. Feeling clean and happy, he rinsed the tub and hung the towel on the rack before leaving for the room across the hall. A click of a door drew his attention. The hairs on the back of his neck stood. The walkway remained empty, the doors all shut tight.

He stepped to his room and scanned the area again before turning the knob. April was perched on the bed, running a brush through her glorious mane. Leaving the door open, he said, "Are you ready, my dear."

"Yes." She settled the brush on top of the dresser, and they left the room.

His hand rested in the small of her back as they walked down the hall to the stairs. The eerie feeling remained. Maybe her idea was best. He wouldn't feel safe searching the city for Willie and Suzie, and researching further proof of the boat burners attack with her here alone. The hospital would be a better place to leave her for a few hours.

They entered the kitchen as Ester walked in from the back door. "I thought I heard you two. I'll scramble some eggs."

"Thank you." He pulled out a chair for April. "Ester, how many other guests do you have staying at the hotel?"

April's eyes grew wide at his question. He patted her shoulder and sat down.

"Just two right now." Ester cracked eggs on the edge of the pan.

"But you have three other rooms," April said.

Ester shot a nervous glance to Jerek. "When Mr. Brinkley checked in he paid for a room for your brother and niece as well. We've been saving it for them."

April closed her eyes and lowered her head. He patted her hand. "And please continue to save it for them. They will need it when we find them."

Ester nodded as she carried the coffee pot to the table.

"You said the other two guests are with the watch brigade?" He poured two cups from the pot and slid one in front of April.

"They're helping the watchmen," Ester corrected.

"What do you mean, helping the watchmen?" he asked.

"They're in town this time to help the brigades watch the river." Ester pulled biscuits from the oven and transferred them to a plate.

The more she spoke the more confused he became. "Are they Army men?"

"No, they're insurance salesmen. But they help out whenever they can." She piled eggs onto two plates and continued, "They both are good boys."

"You talk like you know them well," April said.

"Oh, we do. Charlie has been renting his room from us for almost four years now, and Abbie for the last two. Never give us any trouble at all." She carried the plates to the table. "We may not have made it through the war without their money. They pay by the year."

Jerek swallowed his mouth full of eggs. "They pay by the year?"

"Yes, they travel through quite regularly and want to make sure they always have a place to sleep."

He pushed the fluffy eggs around on his plate. "Where did you say they were from?"

"St. Louis." Turning to April she changed the subject. "I have a bucket and cleaning supplies ready for you. And I made you a lunch."

"Oh, thank you, Ester," April said.

Jerek bit into a biscuit and absently chewed. He needed to know more about the other guests. Their story held no creditability, but he couldn't alarm Ester or April by making too much of it right now. He forked eggs into his mouth and decided he'd do some checking on Charlie and Abbie from St. Louis while she was at the hospital.

Chapter Twelve

April sat down and wiped her brow. The morning had been exhausting. Sweat trickled down her back and from her underarms. She scanned the list written on the paper tablet in front of her, flipped to the second page, and made perfect check marks next to three additional chores.

Doctor Boas walked into the small workroom assigned to the volunteers. "April, my dear girl, you have worked miracles here this morning."

Her cheeks grew warm. "Thank you, Dr. Boas." The pencil tapped the list. "But we still have a lot to do."

"Don't wear yourself out on the first day," he chuckled.

At her arrival this morning, she'd taken over the volunteer assignments. At first her zeal had distressed the doctors, not clearly understanding how her actions could organize the place. She'd also had to maneuver around the charge volunteer, allowing the woman to believe she was still in charge, then plea her case to all three of the surgeons. Before long they'd agreed to allow a few changes to be made.

"I won't," she said. "As I told you this morning, people are just like numbers. Each one has its own particular purpose and order. Once that's established, more work will be accomplished in a smaller amount of time."

"I now understand what you're saying," he agreed.

April had suggested instead of volunteers running around like chickens with their heads cut off, they become organized like bees in a hive. Each one needed a specific job to focus on and complete. She created a list of duties and assigned volunteers to each one. Now, the floors were scrubbed, meals were served, bandages were changed, bedding washed, and soldiers attended to in a timely manner.

"I'm glad you approve," she said.

"I certainly do. I'm very grateful you chose our hospital to volunteer at. However, I'm afraid when word gets out how quickly you organized this place others are going to come calling."

"By the end of the week this place will be running so smoothly, I'll be able to go help another one and you won't even miss me," she said with honesty.

"I don't doubt that my dear, other than the part about us missing you. Not with the way your lovely face brightens the room." Dr. Boas picked up a rolled bandage and gave her a wink as he bent to exit the door.

The man was well over six feet tall, taller than Jerek even, and as skinny as a beanpole. He must be over sixty and had a large hump between his shoulders, which she assumed came from walking around bent over all the time. He was a jolly sort and had quickly become her first ally this morning.

Her madness did have meaning behind it. Knowing she'd never find the time to question the men from the *Sultana* about the accident with things in such disorder, she'd concluded to systematize the activities and ultimately make everything easier, both for her to gather information while assisting the injured, and for the doctors to do their jobs.

A sly smile twisted her lips as she gathered a pail, bar of lye soap, and scrub brush then left the room in search of a volunteer. The other nice thing about being the organizer was you could assign jobs to others, and she knew the perfect person for this job. Mrs. Wentworth—the snooty woman who'd been in charge of the volunteers for several months.

The pail swung in her hand as she walked down the hall. Yes, cleaning the privies behind the hospital was the perfect job for Mrs. Wentworth. It was fun to let the spiteful old April emerge now and again. A satisfied smile pinched her cheeks as she searched and found the woman bossing about the kitchen volunteers.

"Mrs. Wentworth," she said above the screech of the other's voice. The woman might be in her mid-thirties, but the constant frown of seriousness made her look much older, as did the corset, which tried to make a thirty-six inch waist into a thirty inch. What would ever encourage a woman to torture her body so? No wonder she was grumpy. "May I talk to you please?"

"Oh, April, I was just telling the ladies that lunch should have been served at noon." Mrs. Wentworth lifted her fully bustled skirt and, waddling like a duck, skittered across the room.

"I'm sure they're working as fast as they can. And since the patients didn't have breakfast until after nine, feeding them lunch a bit late won't matter." She smiled and continued, "I'm hoping you can help me out."

"Well, certainly, I have been the lead volunteer here for almost a year now," Mrs. Wentworth said with a knowing nod.

"I know, and I'm so thankful you are here." She

cupped the woman's elbow and led her out of the kitchen. "The latrines need to be cleaned, and I just can't find anyone who knows how a clean one should look."

"Excuse me?" Mrs. Wentworth pressed a hand to her chest. "You don't expect me…"

"Oh, Mrs. Wentworth, of course I wouldn't expect you to clean them. It's just that it appears no one here knows what a clean one looks like. They think those ones out back are fine. I know you know how important it is that the seats are scrubbed and well, I don't have to tell you…" She sighed. "I'm sure your home has the cleanest ones around. But without an example to show the others how to do it, I'm afraid the ones here will just never pass inspection."

"Inspection?" Mrs. Wentworth's eyes bugged from her face.

"Yes, Dr. Boas will be doing an inspection so he can inform the other area hospitals of how one should be run. And, well, I know how important this would be to your reputation, being the lead volunteer and all." The old April didn't mind telling a little white lie. Actually it was a good idea. Dr. Boas surely wouldn't mind completing an inspection sheet.

"Oh, and we could publish it in the papers, both the *Bulletin* and the *Argus*. April! What a marvelous idea. And just between you and I dear, that would make Mrs. Bernstein green with envy!" Mrs. Wentworth clapped her hands together with glee.

"Mrs. Bernstein?"

"Yes, she's a volunteer over at the north hospital."

"Oh, well, the articles won't happen until we get the outhouses cleaned, and we won't get them clean until I find someone who knows how they should look." She shrugged her shoulders.

"Good grief, that's no problem! Give me that bucket. I know how they should look and once I get them inspection perfect, I'll let you know so you can show the other volunteers." Mrs. Wentworth pulled the bucket from her hand.

"Oh, Mrs. Wentworth, thank you. I knew I could count on you."

"Well of course you can count on me." The woman twirled around and headed for the back door.

April shook her head. The woman was twitter headed. She was willing to clean the outhouses just to get her name in the paper.

"Oh, well, better her than me," she muttered and turned to go write up an inspection sheet for Dr. Boas. Walking past the rows of beds, she started counting and stopped when she came to the end of the room. There were only twenty-four beds in this room, yet it looked way too crowded.

She estimated the room size and figured square footage. A better arranged floor plan came to mind. Her fingers snapped. A drawing would help the volunteers rearrange the room tomorrow. She'd put them through enough changes already today.

Turning from the room, she bumped into someone. "Oh, excuse me."

The man reached out. She took a step back, out of range of his touch. Goosebumps exploded on her flesh. She folded her arms across her chest to rub at them.

"Sorry, I didn't mean to startle you." The man said. His voice was low, gruff, and thick with a drawl.

The stranger was of average height and size, nothing really out of the ordinary, but there was something menacing about him. A dark, bushy beard and mustache covered most of his face, and a straw hat sat low over his eyes.

Her spine stiffened. "Can I help you?"

His shoulders drooped and his head hung lower. "I hope so. I'm looking for survivors of the *Sultana*."

"Were you on the boat?" she asked.

He shook his head. "No, but my brother, his wife, and their little girl was. I've been looking everywhere for them."

She pressed a hand to her stomach. "Oh."

He didn't raise his head. "I'm beginning to think they perished. Little Lucy was only three."

Breath caught in her chest. "D-did your niece have a red dress?"

"I don't know. Why? Have you seen her? Is she here?" His head lifted but not to where she could see his face.

"No, no, I'm sorry, there are no children here."

He extended his hand. "My name is Charles Deal," he said.

She didn't raise a hand, but said, "I'm April."

"April?" he asked.

"Just April," she answered. "Mr. Deal, I'm sorry to be the one to say this, but I suggest you talk with the men at the docks. They're tracking the um-victims."

"Why, did you ask about a red dress? Did you see a little girl in a red dress, April?"

She squared her shoulders at the way he made her name sound creepy. "Yes."

"Dead or alive?" he asked.

She frowned. "Mr. Deal, I—"

"I'm sorry, I don't mean to sound so bad-tempered. I haven't slept in days."

Guilt washed over her. He'd lost his family just as she'd lost hers, and here she was unjustly judging his character. "Think nothing of it, Mr. Deal. It has been quite an ordeal."

"Were you on the boat?" he asked.

She nodded.

"Did you see them?"

"I'm sorry, I don't remember seeing your family," she answered.

"No, not my family. The boat burners?"

"Excuse me?"

"Those damned bastards that blew up the ship!" He glanced around, appearing to be embarrassed by his outburst. "Forgive me, April. It just angers me how these men keep getting away with such evil activities."

She rubbed her fingers together. Maybe he could tell her more about the boat burners. A hand fell onto her shoulder, making her jump.

"April, I didn't mean to startle you, but you have a visitor," Dr. Boas said from behind.

She glanced back to Mr. Deal and held up one finger. "Excuse me, just one minute? I'll be right back."

Mr. Deal nodded. She turned then walked beside Dr. Boas through the room and down the front hall to the entranceway. Bill Rowberry stood near the door. Dr. Boas patted her arm then walked across the hall and into another room full of patients as she stopped near the visitor.

"Hi, April," Bill said.

"Hi, Bill. What are you doing here?"

"Sorry to bother you, but I need to find Jerek. Do you know where he is?"

"No, I haven't seen him since he walked me here this morning. He said he'd be back to walk me home this afternoon. Did you check at the hotel?"

"Yeah, he wasn't there. When you see him, tell him that Washburn is going to have a hearing about his findings at headquarters day after tomorrow, and I really need to talk to him before then. He knows where to find me."

She nodded then asked, "Bill, how did you know where to find me?"

"Jerek told me last night."

"You saw him last night? Were you the one who left him the note?"

"I saw him, but don't know anything about a note." Bill shook his head. "I have to go. Please remember to ask him to get a hold of me." He turned to walk out the open door.

"I will." She wanted to ask about his investigation, but more than that she wanted to gather information from Mr. Deal. Jerek would certainly approve of her helping when she came home with solid facts. She hurried back down the hall and into the other room.

After walking around the room twice, she made a full round of the entire hospital, even the rooms on the second floor. Where had he gone? She and Bill had been at the front door, and the only other way out was the back, through the kitchen. He hadn't been there either, and the back yard had a fence all around it. It was as if he'd disappeared. The few other volunteers she questioned hadn't seen anyone with the description she gave. He seemed so full of sorrow. Poor man, a part of her hoped the little girl in the red dress wasn't his Lucy.

****

Jerek walked up the steps of the hospital. Spring in Memphis was hotter than he remembered, and the temperature would continue to rise as May arrived. A thatched rug lay in front of the entrance. It hadn't been there this morning had it? He wiped his feet and proceeded into the building.

The smell of lye soap and vinegar consumed the building. The scent was unexpected. For the past few days, his stomach had churned at the smell of blood, sweat, and stale air when he entered any of the medical buildings. Cots still lined the walls, but the men were covered with clean, white sheets and piles of dirty clothes no longer lay about.

He walked further in and peeked into the first

room. Several men sat up on their cots with trays of food balanced on their laps. Volunteers strolled up and down, or sat helping others consume their food. The area seemed calmer than it had before. He glanced about. None of the women had long blond hair. He turned and walked to the other room. April wasn't in there either.

"Ah, Mr. Brinkley," a voice said from behind.

"Hello, Dr. Boas," he greeted. The man's face held a smile, which sent relief through his body. All day he'd worried that April had taken on more than she could chew.

"Looking for April?"

"Yes, I am."

Dr. Boas pointed. "Down the hall, she converted the supply room into a volunteer check in site. First door on the left."

"Thank you."

"No, thank you. That wife of yours has done more in one day than a dozen volunteers." Dr. Boas slapped Jerek's shoulder before walking the opposite direction to disappear in a room filled with patients.

Whistling a soft tune, Jerek strolled down the hall and found her sitting at a small table. Behind her, neatly stacked shelves displayed various medical needs, sheets, blankets, bandages, and other such items.

"Hi," he said.

Her head snapped up. That adorable smile, the one that made his heart flip, covered her face.

"Hi," she said.

"How was your day?"

"Wonderful. How was yours?"

"I don't think it was as productive as yours. I hardly recognize the place." He leaned against the frame of the door.

"All it needed was a little organizing." She shrugged her shoulders and continued to write on the pad of paper.

"I didn't know you were so good at organizing things."

She laughed. "I didn't either. I just figured it's like numbers, each one has its place and purpose."

"Uh? No, never mind. I'm sure it makes perfect sense to you, and it certainly seems to have worked." He'd never understand her knack for numbers.

"It does. I'll be ready in a minute. I just want to finish this inspection list for Dr. Boas."

"Inspection list?"

"Yes, he agreed to make a walk through and check off the condition of each room before he goes home. It will tell me where the volunteers need to start first thing in the morning," April said.

Her fingers flew across the paper. He'd never seen any one write so fast. "You plan on coming back tomorrow?" he asked.

"Of course. Tomorrow I need to write an article about Dr. Boas' inspection for the newspaper." She looked up at him and rolled her eyes. "I promised Mrs. Wentworth I would."

"The pudgy little woman who can't breathe?"

She giggled and nodded. "That's her. Wait until I tell you what happened today." She laid the quill down and blew on the paper to dry the ink. "I had her clean the outhouses."

He arched his brows. "Mrs. Wentworth cleaned the outhouses?"

"Yes, and she loved it." April stacked the papers into a neat pile and rose from the chair.

"That sounds amusing. You'll have to tell me about it." His hands settled on her tiny shoulders as she stepped forward. "Right after you kiss me."

"Mmm," she murmured and rose on her toes to meet his lips halfway.

"I missed you," he said as they parted. Someday he'd have to let her know how inappropriate it was for a man and woman to kiss in public, but not today.

"I missed you too."

"Hah! From the looks of this place you didn't have time to miss me." He wrapped her hand through his arm at the elbow.

"I can be busy and still miss you," she said as her head touched his shoulder while they walked to the front door.

Molten lava rushed through his body. "So tell me about Mrs. Wentworth and the outhouses." They stepped outside and proceeded down freshly swept steps.

Animated, April talked about the stone-faced woman. He listened without really hearing. The way she skipped and circled about him while embellishing the tale was delightful. He enjoyed each movement. She pressed a hand against her tiny waist, holding in her mirth as she finished, "Those privy's are spic and span clean. Oh, that reminds me, Bill Rowberry needs to talk to you. He stopped by the hospital today."

"He did?"

"Yes, he said there'll be a hearing of the Army's investigation day after tomorrow and needs to talk to you before then." She twisted her arm back through his and their foot steps fell into sync.

"I heard that today." He hoped the Army's finding would be truthful and acceptable so he could focus more time on finding what became of Willie and Suzie. April wouldn't leave until she knew, yet he'd grown anxious to put the whole ordeal behind them and take her to Ohio. She had no reason to return to Minnesota now. He had a burning desire to take her home, show her off to his family then settle down to raise a couple kids. The notion should shock him. It hadn't been his plan a week ago. But it didn't, instead it filled him with excitement.

"May I attend it with you?" she asked.

Before his mind had a chance to clear and think about her question his mouth responded, "Yes."

"Thank you."

"You're welcome," he said and pulled open the front door of the hotel. What harm could it do for her to attend the hearing?

"Oh, good your home," Ester said as they stepped in. "I'm ready to put supper on the table."

"Your timing is perfect, Ester. How do you do it?" Jerek chuckled as they followed her energetic skip into the kitchen.

"Years of practice I suspect." She gestured to the table set with place settings.

****

Ester's wonderful food left April feeling full, satisfied, and tired. Jerek led her from the kitchen and up the steps. She sighed and rested her head against the solid muscles of his upper arm.

They stopped in front of the door for him to insert the key. She let her gaze lift. No one had ever looked at her the way he did. She couldn't explain how it made her feel. His coffee-colored eyes engulfed her and sent a balmy, extraordinary rush of blood to race through tingling veins. Giddy? Is this what it feels like?

He winked at her before turning to unlock and open the door. She sighed. Yes, this happy, excitement must be what giddy feels like. A giggle escaped as he playfully gave a slight bow and waved a hand as if she were a queen and he a footman.

Back straight, chin up, and dress hitched well past her ankles, she sashayed into the room, twirled around, and plopped onto the bed. She laughed aloud at his raised brows.

Still giggling, she leaned down to remove her boots while Jerek struck a match to light the lamp before he walked to the window. Warm air gushed in as the sash lifted.

Fanning her face with one hand, she asked, "Doesn't it cool off in the evenings here?"

"Not as much as it does up north." He leaned out the window.

"I'd still need a fire to take the chill from the house at home," she remarked and set her boots beneath the table beside the bed.

Her forehead tightened as she spied the tabletop. She reached out to touch the items on the table. The lamp sat as usual in the center of the small lace doily, the match Jerek had used lay on the small tin tray, and several others were neatly stacked with a flint stick in the small wooden box.

"Jerek?"

"Hmm?"

"Did you move Suzie's doll?"

He glanced at the table. "No, it was on the table this morn..."

"I know it was here this morning." She moved the few items around.

"It must have fallen off while Scarlet was cleaning." Jerek dropped to his knees to look beneath the solid wooden legs. "Maybe it's under the bed," he suggested and lifted the quilt edges to peek beneath. He sat back and looked up. "Did you put it in one of the drawers before we left?"

She shook her head and flattened a hand on her chest. "No, it was right there." A deep, painful sting pierced her heart.

"Maybe Scarlet did." He stood and walked across the room.

On shaky legs, she followed.

Jerek pulled open the top drawer, and April shuffled underclothes about. Her hand encountered something hard. Disappointed she lifted a lacy pouch, which held the money from her old petticoat. She dropped the bag back into the drawer. Jerek opened the next one, her fingers filtered through his undergarments.

After he closed the fourth and final drawer they both looked around the room. The bed, table, chair, and dresser, upon which a pitcher and bowl sat, completed the room's furnishings. She glanced into the top of the pitcher. It was full of crystal clear water from top to bottom.

"What could have happened to it?" She pressed the heel of her hand into one eye.

"Ah, sweetheart, don't cry, we'll find it." He pulled her close.

She laid her head into his chest and sobbed, "It's not here."

Jerek's hands held her while the tears flowed. Large palms patted and rubbed until the flood decreased, and she sucked in small gulps of air.

"You're exhausted," he said. "Come on, I'll help you across the hall where you can get ready for bed."

He retrieved her nightgown and housecoat from the hooks before opening the door and ushering her across the hall. "You get ready for bed. I'll go ask Scarlet if she knows where Suzie's doll is."

His pleading look encouraged her to agree. She nodded, entered the room, and pulled the door shut. Her trembling fingers had a hard time unhooking the tiny buttons running down the front of the yellow dress. Draping it over the stool, she turned and poured water from the white, porcelain pitcher into the matching bowl. Painted bluebells on the bottom of the bowl sparkled through the water. The tiny petals reminded her of Suzie. She sniffled, dipped a cloth into the water and pressed it to her burning face.

The cool material absorbed some of the sting, but the raw pain continued to burn stronger than it had when she found the doll floating in the weeds.

Water splashed over the top of the bowl as the

rag landed in the basin with a plop. She removed her camisole, slip, and petticoat before retrieving the cloth and running it over her chest. It helped to eradicate some of the heat but did little to relieve the blazing ache in her heart.

Noises across the hall encouraged her to dip and wring the rag again, and continue a quick sponge bath. Moments later, she pulled on her nightclothes, then gathered her discarded dress and left the room. The door across the hall stood open. Tim, Ester, Scarlet, and Jerek stood around the bed.

Scarlet rushed to the hall. "April, it was here when I made the bed this morning. I saw it lying on the table."

She couldn't answer, her head hurt, her body ached, and her heart bled. Jerek took the clothes from her hands, handed them to Scarlet, and led April to the bed.

"We don't know what could have happened to it, but we won't quit looking until we find it," Tim said as they drew near. "I've looked under the bed and behind the headboard."

"We'll look downstairs, maybe it accidentally got carried down there," Ester added, patting her shoulder.

April was afraid to speak. The pain might increase.

Jerek flipped the covers back and turned to the others. "Thank you, we appreciate your help. Now if you'll excuse us, April needs to go to bed."

"Yes, yes. You get a good night's sleep now, April. And don't fret sweetie, we'll find your little doll," Ester said as she backed out of the door.

Jerek locked the latch before he came back to the bed. He slipped the wrapper from her arms then lifted her feet onto the bed.

"Don't—" he started.

April stopped his words by pressing a finger to

his lips. "Please don't tell me not to fret, please don't say it."

He nodded and turned to blow out the lamp. The sound of clothes slipping to the floor was slight. Seconds later his arms pulled her close and held her until exhaustion overtook the encroaching pain.

Chapter Thirteen

The light of day made everything brighter. Jerek's promise to find the doll followed by taste-filled kisses, eased pain and provided hope. Even the hat on her head felt good. She'd never worn one just because she wanted to, and it did prevent the blazing sun from bearing down on her head. The day was already extremely warm as they walked the few blocks to the hospital. Halfway there he paused to lean over, one arm stretching to the ground.

She twisted, trying to see what he'd found. He straightened and handed her a black-eyed Susan. No one had ever given her a flower. Petals of yellow surrounded the dark brown center she lifted to sniff. The pleasant smell was light, almost undetectable. Jerek dipped beneath the wide brim of her hat and kissed the tip of her nose.

"Thank you," she whispered.

"You're welcome," he said as they started down the street again.

He left her at the doorway where they encountered Dr. Boas, and in no time April became completely immersed in needed tasks. By noon all of the rooms were rearranged into a more orderly fashion, and the restructuring opened additional space to move the cots from the hall into the patient rooms. Curtains hung between some of the more critical patients to allow a touch of privacy and solitude.

Satisfied with the results, she made her way down to the storage closet to write the article Mrs. Wentworth prodded for all morning. Holding the editorial over the woman's head had worked out nicely. Over-zealous want of recognition and fame made the woman work harder than any other two volunteers put together.

"Twitter brain," April muttered as she settled onto the chair.

Her sunflower lay on the table. A frown formed. She forgot a glass of water to put it in. Withered and limp, the fuzzy green stem had curled into a hook shape. Was it already too late for water? Perhaps Ester had a book she could press it in, if so she'd be able to keep the flower forever. The thought filled her with contentment. She smoothed the yellow petals with one finger then situated the flower above the tablet and began to write.

Words came quickly, and as she re-read the final draft for Mrs. Wentworth to approve, a shadow fell over the paper. Her pulse picked up a beat in the base of her neck. Expecting to see Jerek's smiling face and hoping her disappointment didn't show, April squared her shoulders as she recognized the man.

"Mr. Deal?"

"Hello, April," he said from the doorway.

"Did you find your family?" she asked.

"No. No. Not yet." He shook his head. The bill of his hat ominously covered the upper half of his face again. The bushy beard and mustache moved as he spoke, "I was wondering if you had any new patients today."

"No, I'm afraid not. I'm sorry, Mr. Deal."

Charles Deal leaned back and glanced up and down the hall before he stepped further into the room. "He's here in Memphis," he whispered.

"Who? Your brother?"

"No, the head of the boat burners."

Her heart skipped a beat. "He is? Have you seen him?" She'd have to find a way to get a hold of Bill, tell him what Mr. Deal knew.

"No, but I've heard he's out asking questions."

"Asking questions? You'd think he'd be in hiding!" April stood, slapped the table. Robert Louden must be addlebrained to be out in public.

Mr. Deal shook his head. "He's a master of disguises. And the way he's going about town, you'd think he was a victim of the crime instead of the mastermind behind it all."

"Really?" Her brows pulled together. "How do you know so much about him?"

"I've met him before." He leaned against the doorframe.

The relaxed manner allowed her to seek more information. "You have? Where? When?"

"A couple years ago, I was on another boat he blew up. He was shot, but escaped."

"Shot?"

"Yes," he touched his right shoulder, "right here. He swam through the rushes and got away. But it won't happen again. Jerek Brinkley won't get away this time. The bastard will pay for his deeds!"

She clutched the edge of the table. "W-who?" she choked.

"Jerek Brinkley," he repeated.

She shook her head. "You must be mistaken. The leader of the boat burners is Robert Louden."

He looked down his nose at her. "They, Jerek Brinkley and Robert Louden, are one and the same."

"No," she whispered and pressed a hand to her breastbone in opposition to the rapid thudding beneath.

"April, you look shocked. Do you know Jerek

Brinkley?"

How should she answer? If she said yes, he'd want to know where Jerek was. If she said no...Her eyes refused to blink. Had one of the volunteers told him she was married to Jerek?

"April?" he repeated.

Beads of sweat oozed from her forehead. "I-I um," she paused to clear her throat. "I met um-Mr. Brinkley while we were on the boat."

"Oh, I'm sure you did." A dry laugh sounded. "He couldn't possibly have passed up something as pretty as you."

"He couldn't have?"

"No, seducing women is his second greatest pastime. He's known to have a silver tongue."

Pain ripped across her chest, making breathing difficult. "Huh?"

"Yes, his trail of broken hearts is almost as long as his trail of burnt boats."

"It is?" A thick glob grew in the pit of her stomach. Bile pressed its way up.

Mr. Deal's head rose and fell ever so slowly. "Yes, it is."

Her heart broke open with each nod. She looked to the floor, almost expecting to see a pool of red. A low buzzing noise came from her inner ear, and her temples began to throb. She raised a hand to press at the pounding.

"His escapades have been very profitable. Besides getting money from the Confederate Army for blowing up the ships, he makes a commission every time he sells a new boat for the one he destroyed. He likes to play both sides of the game."

April pressed harder at her temple. The man couldn't possibly be talking about *her* Jerek. He detested the boat burners. He couldn't be one of them.

"He's a thief too," Mr. Deal continued.

"He is?"

"Yes, but he steals more than money. He likes to pilfer tiny, treasured items, from his conquests. Say a locket, jewel, or other precious memento." Charles Deal stepped into the room, placed his hands on the table. "Did he steal anything from you, April?"

"No, no, I don't have any precious jew…" the words stopped. Suzie's doll!

"Allan Pinkerton is after him too."

It was hard to hear around the buzzing noise. "Who?"

"Allan Pinkerton of the Pinkerton agency. Of course he too is using an alias, Major E. J. Allan. He has had agents working undercover in the Confederate for years…"

The man continued to mumble on about undercover agents until April found the breath to say, "Excuse me, Mr. Deal, but I do have work to do. I'm going to have to excuse myself." Rolling bile threatened to erupt. She needed air. Had to have time to digest all he'd said. It just couldn't be…could it?

"Oh, I'm sorry, I forgot you were working." He leaned further across the table. "You do look a little flushed. You will tell me if you see Brinkley, won't you, April?"

She needed air, he blocked the doorway. "Good-bye, Mr. Deal."

His gaze settled on her forehead. "Did you hit your head during the accident?" He tugged at the brim of his hat, pulling it over his eyes. "You really should have someone look at that. It looks painful." He turned and strolled from the room.

April fought, but it was a losing battle. Between the gulps of air she tried to take in, and the sobs gushing out, air became lodged in her lungs. Within seconds the buzzing in her ears stopped, and the room went black.

****

Faint sounds swirled then grew stronger. April twisted. She had to get away—away from the people asking her name, away from the wet cloth pressed against her forehead, away from the smell of sick and dying bodies. Her eyes snapped open. Dr. Boas and Julia Wentworth hovered over her.

"How are you feeling, April?" Dr. Boas asked.

"I'm fine," she murmured.

He touched her cheeks. "You fainted."

Her mind swirled, Charles Deal's words still echoed in her ears. She glanced around. The small cot was outside the closet door. Someone must have laid her on it. April swung her legs around, and sat up, ignoring the blood rushing to her brain. The cloth fell from her head, and she pulled damp bangs down over the atrocious scar. "It-it must be the heat."

Dr. Boas reached out a hand in aid.

She shook her head. "I just need to go home."

"Really, dear, you should lie back down."

She turned to Julia Wentworth. The woman's look of concern made tears threatened to burst from her eyes. She rose. "No, I just need to go home."

Slowly, April walked into the small closet to retrieve her hat and secure it to her head. The wilted sunflower sat on top of the tablet. She reached down and picked it up. There was no way Jerek could be a boat burner. He was too righteous, too honest. A hard knot formed in her chest. She cared about him too much. Mr. Deal must be so distraught over his family he was confusing things, people.

Walking back into the hall, she whispered to Mrs. Wentworth, "Your article is on the table."

"April, are you sure you're all right?" Dr. Boas' face was furrowed with worry.

The sight made her chest constrict harder. When had people started to care about her? When had she started to care about them?

"April?" Mrs. Wentworth reached out a hand.

She took a step backwards, preventing the woman from touching her. It was all too much. She shook her head and nodded it at the same time. Pressing a hand to the pain in her chest, she turned and hurried for the door.

Her mind swirled. None of it was possible. People had never cared about her. And she never cared about others. She glanced over her shoulder. Dr. Boas and Mrs. Wentworth stood on the porch, watching her cross the street.

She stumbled, almost tripped, before she caught her balance. The tiny flower fell from her fingers. Her foot landed on it before she could halt her steps. She bent down, but the petals had been separated from the stem. Her hand stilled.

She felt liked the flower looked—crushed. Mr. Deal might be confused about him being a boat burner, but Jerek did have a silver tongue. He'd completely duped her into trusting men.

The early afternoon street was busy, eyes from all directions stared, big ones, little ones, old ones, young ones. Old fears and wounds began to open. They made her head pound. Quick, uneven gulps stung going in and coming out. She lowered her head and ran the last block to the hotel. Tripping on the steps, she grabbed the rail and followed it before collapsing on one of the wicker chairs.

Covering her face with both hands she let the tears fall.

****

His feet glided over every step as Jerek flew from the hospital door and onto the street. Dr. Boas was clearly upset, and Mrs. Wentworth shed alligator tears as she explained how strange April acted when she awoke after fainting. He dodged one, then another wagon as he ran across the street and down the other side to the hotel. He should have kept a better eye on her. She'd been so distraught over the missing doll.

It would be dark soon. He hadn't meant to be so late in meeting her, but the day's work had gotten away from him. A single leap brought him to the top of the hotel steps, and he flung the door open. It hit the wall with a loud smack.

"Mr. Brinkley?" Startled, Ester looked up from behind the desk.

"Where's April?" he gasped.

"She's in the kitchen. We've been waiting supper for you."

He tore to the door. It swung open with a snap. A blond head turned at the sound. She sat at the table, laughing. His feet skid to a halt. "Are you all right?"

A glint of something he'd never really seen before flashed in her eyes. "Yes, I'm fine."

He crossed the room to lay a hand on her shoulder. The tiny frame shuddered beneath his touch. "Dr. Boas said you fainted."

"April! Why didn't you tell us? What happened? Are you all right?" Scarlet leaned over to pat her arm.

April didn't look at him, but smiled at the other woman. "I'm fine, Scarlet, and I told you it became too warm at the hospital today."

"But you didn't say you fainted," Scarlet said.

"It was of no consequence. I'm fine. And now that Mr. Brinkley has arrived, I think we should eat." April twisted her shoulder out from under his hand. Her fingers rubbed the area where his had been.

"April? Honey, what's going on?"

Her eyes peeked at him from beneath her hat. "Supper is getting cold." She turned back to the other occupants at the table.

"I'm sorry, you shouldn't have waited." Jerek sat down. "Please, go ahead and eat."

Ester pulled several dishes from the oven to pass to Scarlet who set them on hot plates and inserted spoons. He didn't care about the meal. Something was dreadfully wrong. April carried on conversations throughout the meal, but never once did she turn to face him. Not a glance or touch acknowledged he sat beside her.

When the meal ended, she allowed him to escort her from the room. Her spine stiffened beneath his touch. As the kitchen door fluttered shut behind them, he asked, "April what happened at the hospital today?"

"Nothing really." She bounded up the stairs ahead of him.

After he'd unlocked their door and walked into the room, Jerek stopped her flight across the room with both hands. He twisted her around to face him. The brim of her hat hid her face. He tugged it from her head and let it fly to the bed.

"I'm asking again. What happened at the hospital today?"

Her lips puckered and tiny brows angled down in the center. She gave a half-hearted shrug. "I fainted."

"I know that much. Why did you faint?"

"Because it is hotter than Hades in this town."

He almost grinned, recognizing her quick to anger ability. Yet there was something else. He liked her spite, had since the moment he'd met her, but this was different. "And?"

"And nothing, I fainted, so I came back to the hotel. Now if you'll please let go of me, I would like to prepare for bed." Her shoulders twisted.

Jerek let his hands fall away. His gaze followed hers to the dresser. The top drawer was slightly ajar. She crossed the room and pulled open the drawer.

He walked to the table and lit the lamp.

Her hands dug around in the top drawer. "What are you looking for?" he asked.

She slapped her hand on her hips. "As if you don't know?"

He hadn't seen that stance in several days. It tickled the corners of his mouth. Rubbing a hand over his lips, he grew serious and walked across the room. "We looked in there last night for the doll."

"It's not the doll that's missing now." She slammed the drawer shut.

"Did you find it? Where was it?"

She opened the next drawer. "No, I didn't find it. But I would like it back. Along with my money that is no longer here." Her eyes snapped at him.

"Your money? What money?" He pulled open the drawer.

"The pouch of money that was in there this morning. The money I had sewn in my petticoat while on the *Sultana*. You know the *Sultana*, don't you? The ship that blew up!"

"April, calm down." He stepped closer.

"Don't tell me to calm down! Within the last ten days I've lost everything that ever mattered. I have a right to be upset!" She wiped at the tears slipping from her eyes.

"Ah, sweetheart,"

"Don't sweetheart me either!" She flounced around him and grabbed her nightclothes from the hook. The water closet door slammed hard enough to shake the hotel.

Jerek ran a hand through his hair, scratching at his scalp. Jittery and itchy frustration swirled in every inch of his frame. It was like being caught in a whirlwind. Things coming from all directions and he couldn't dodge them.

He walked to the window, threw open the sash, and peered below. What would be the best reaction to her tantrum? April was unpredictable at times, but her behavior tonight was out of the ordinary even for her. He removed his jacket and draped it over the back of the chair. His tie and shirt soon followed. They landed atop the jacket as the night air floated into the room.

Several moths danced around the gas street lanterns and sent shadows onto the ground below. The dancing insects reminded him of April. Bright, light, and care free, yet dark, veiled, and mysterious all at the same time. The door opened behind him, he turned, pasted on a smile.

"Feel better?"

She didn't look his way nor say a word. After hanging her dress next to the others she walked to the bed.

"Hey? Talk to me. Please," he begged and took a step closer. He'd get on his hands and knees if that's what it would take.

She twirled and her mouth parted. It dropped open wider as her gaze floated across his bare chest. A tiny gasp sounded as she stared at his shoulder. "What's that?" she whispered.

He shrugged. "A scar."

"I know it's a scar, how did you get it?"

"A bullet."

"Who shot the bullet?" she asked.

"Robert Louden."

"Robert Louden shot you, or Robert Louden was shot?"

His mind swirled with confusion. Nothing made sense, least of all her questions.

April covered her eyes. Her head slowly tilted from side to side. He wanted to pull her into his arms, but she was wound tighter than a coiled rattler. And her strike would surely be as deadly.

"I need you to leave the room," she whispered.

"What?"

"Please find a different place to sleep."

"April, I don't want to leave you alone." His hands rose, but stopped before touching her. "I can't leave you alone."

Tears fell behind her hands. They trickled down to drip off a trembling chin and her voice came out in small sobs, "Please, please just leave."

Dumbfounded, he didn't move.

"Please," she sobbed.

Completely helpless and against his better judgment, he took his clothes from the back of the chair. He pulled the key from his pants pocket and laid it on the table. "I'll go sleep next door, lock the door behind me, and don't open it for anyone. Understand?"

She nodded.

"I'll be right next door if you need anything."

She nodded again.

Jerek waited for her to change her mind. Minutes ticked by. She didn't make a move, but her body shook as the tears flowed. He walked to the door and waited some more. His hand grasped the knob. The metal stung his palm. When it sank in she wasn't going to ask him not to leave, he opened the door and walked out. At a loss, he stood in the hall. The key latched the lock with a loud click, the final signal he wasn't welcome. Several minutes later he went down to the desk to get the key for the room he'd reserved for Willie and Suzie.

April waited until she heard him move away from the door before she pulled the key from the lock. Tears flowed down her face and onto the cotton nightgown.

She'd prayed all afternoon it wasn't true—hoped beyond hope that Jerek wasn't Robert Louden. But the scar proved it. She didn't want to believe it— hadn't believed it. Had even mustered up anger at the way he'd duped her into trusting him. Now...

Her back slid down the door as her sobbing body melted to the floor. She'd never felt so lost and alone in her life. The pain tearing at her chest took her breath away.

Years of isolation didn't ease the pain. It amplified it. She didn't want to be alone again. It was awful, no matter how much she denied it, her life in Minnesota had been dreadful, and she didn't want to return to it. She didn't want a life that didn't include Jerek. The tears intensified. Clutching her knees to her chest, she cried until her body became numb.

Sniffling, she rose and shuffled to the bed. The wide brimmed hat sat where it had landed. He'd lied about her scar too. It was appalling—always had been.

How had it all happened? Had she been so starved for attention she was ready to believe everything said by the first man to be kind to her? It had been so easy.

No, it had been *too* easy. She let out a long sigh. Too easy to accept she deserved to be happy.

The fear and anger she'd lived with for so many years began to bubble in her stomach. Damn that man for coming into the hospital today. And damn these three Aprils floating around in her head. The old spiteful and selfish April, who wanted to tar and feather Jerek Brinkley; the ignorant new one who wanted to forgive and forget his transgressions; and the broken hearted middle one who really wanted to find a resolution.

With shaky fingers she picked up the hat and carried it across the room. It was so unfair. Even if she wanted to return to Minnesota, she couldn't. She had no money. It had been stolen, just like Suzie's doll, and her heart.

Lifting the hat to a hook, she spied his clothes hanging there. She touched the light gray material.

This one made his dark features all the more handsome. It faintly smelled of spicy, bay rum. The material fell back against the wall. She pressed a hand to her stomach, tried to control the flutters that always happened when she thought of him.

The sensations wouldn't ebb. Her body longed for him even when he wasn't near. Closing her eyes she dug deep into her past, searched for the times in her life when men couldn't be trusted.

It was several minutes before she turned and strolled to the bed. Now that she had proof, there was only one thing to do. See him jailed for his crimes. She flipped the covers back. Maybe even hang from the gallows. A pain shot across her chest. All right, not hanged, but some time behind bars would do the low-down gambler some good. Teach him a lesson or two.

The thought made her flinch. Jerek wasn't low-down, nor was he a gambler. She squeezed her eyes shut again.

Seeing him jailed wouldn't bring back Willie or Suzie, nothing could do that. Nor would it bring back the Jerek Brinkley she'd fallen in love with, but that was because he didn't exist. Never had. Only Robert Louden existed.

Her lips puckered. Well, old Robert Louden may have met his match. The Union Army couldn't catch him, but the old, vengeful April Simonson certainly could.

She blew out the lamp, crawled onto the bed, and refused to let the caring and compassionate April surface. The battle was fierce.

Chapter Fourteen

"Good morning," April greeted as she stepped from the water closet.

A flutter lightened the heavy feeling in his chest. Jerek smiled.

"Good morning. Feeling better?"

"I feel fine, thank you," April said.

Her smile didn't quite reach her eyes. He tucked his hands in his pockets. "Are you going into the hospital today?"

"No, but I would like to go to the Army hearing with you. If that's all right?" She walked across the hall and opened her door a crack.

"Of course, if you feel up to it."

"I'm fine. What time shall we leave?" she asked with chilly politeness.

"The hearing is at noon. It's down town so we should leave a little after eleven or so."

"Fine, I'll meet you on the front porch."

Before he could say anything more April slipped into the room and shut the door. She wasn't her old self, but she was a damn sight more rational than she'd been last night. He could handle baby steps, and if that's what she needed to get through this ordeal, then that's what he'd give her.

Sleep had eluded him most of the night as he fought for reason—justification—cause—anything

253

that might help him make sense out of her behavior yesterday. Nothing had come, but it appeared something had resonated for her. A deep sigh left his chest. He'd have to ask her about it someday, years from now when there was no chance of retaliation.

His steps grew lighter as he strolled down the stairs and into the kitchen. A man with a long face, full beard, and Roman nose sat talking with Tim.

Jerek took a second look. "What are you doing here?"

Allan Pinkerton rose. "Looking for you."

"Oh yeah?"

"Yeah."

Jerek nodded. "About time."

"I was a little busy with the assassination of the President." Allan sat back down and took a swig from his coffee cup.

"How'd that happen? You stopped it once before."

Allan shook his head. "I wasn't there. But I had good, capable men there." He shrugged his shoulders in a sullen manner. "I don't know. It just happened."

"I'm sure your men did all they could. Don't beat yourself up over it." He slapped Allan's shoulder.

"Thanks," he sighed. "Sad, so sad."

"Yeah, it is. The whole war is," Jerek answered.

Allan nodded. "I'm going back out there to do some more investigating, but I got your wire and knew you wouldn't ask me to come if it wasn't serious."

Jerek looked around the room. "Where's Ester and Scarlet?"

"Morning chores," Tim replied.

The old man's ears all but twitched to hear more from the detective. Jerek turned to Allan. "I take it you've met Mr. Cox?"

"Yeah, I've been here for some time now." Allan gave one of his half chuckles, half coughs.

He tried to hide the smile that snuck onto his face. The man had a way of gaining information more rapidly than anyone else on earth. "Learn anything new?"

Allan nodded. Sparks danced in his eyes. "You aren't even going to believe it."

He knew exactly what the detective had learned. He was married, though not officially, and he had spent the night in the 'spare' room. Good thing he didn't count on gambling to make a living. His bluffs were all played out. He shook his head and pulled out a chair at the table.

****

A cramp in her big toe forced April to stop tapping her foot against the floorboard of the porch. Where was Jerek? It was well after eleven. She repositioned her seat on the wicker chair and exchanged the crossing of her knees. The sore toe relaxed while the other foot took a turn at filling the humid, mid-morning air with a drum beat.

If she knew the way to the courthouse she'd go herself. She didn't have money to rent a carriage, but she could walk, that is if Mr. Cox would let her out of his sight.

Her fingers on the table kept time with her toe. Tim Cox sat on the top step of the hotel, whittling away at a small chunk of wood like he had nothing better to do. She twisted her face forward and pulled her chin up as he turned her way. She checked the perfection of her hat, ignoring him and the way he insisted she wait for Jerek.

Men. They bonded like cows in a pasture. Always ready to follow the leader. Silly things, the leader was no smarter than the rest of them, just thought he was. Put a little bell around his neck and pretty soon there's a whole herd following his steps.

She almost smiled at her own wit, had to force the grin to remain hidden. During the long, sleepless night a plan had formed. As soon as she had enough money, she'd travel back to Minnesota and forget Jerek Brinkley ever existed.

Two matching black horses, pulling a wagon with three rows of seats, drew up in front of the hotel. The driver, sitting on the first seat set the brake, and Jerek climbed down from the second row.

The way his lean body glided to the ground made her heart skip a beat. She tore her gaze away, took a deep breath of fortitude, and stood to walk to the stairs. She had to find a way for his presence not to affect her. Gritting her teeth, she concluded it was going to be very difficult, but the old April could do it. She just had to pretend to be the new April. A deep sigh left her lungs as she walked across the porch.

"Thank you for keeping me company while waiting for Jerek, Mr. Cox." She disregarded the look of shock on Tim's face. A twinge of guilt at being so snippy with the man earlier rippled her spine. Focusing on her plan, April wrapped her arm through Jerek's, turned, and said, "I was starting to worry. It's getting late."

Jerek nodded to Mr. Cox then smiled down at her. "I didn't want you to have to walk in this heat. It took awhile to find a carriage."

"I could have walked. You shouldn't have bothered." This was harder than she thought; just walking next to him made her body melt like ice in July.

His hands cupped her hips as he guided her climb onto the wagon. She stepped out of the hold and sat down on the long seat. The leather was warm from the sun and penetrated the thin cotton of her skirt and slips. She rearranged the extra material around her legs, flaying it across the seat so it took up most of the area.

Jerek spoke to the driver before climbing up. He

pushed the folds out of the way and sat much closer than necessary.

"Ready?" he asked.

"Yes," she choked.

The driver set the horses into motion. April bit her lips together and sucked air in through her nose. She had to act like she didn't know his real identity, at least for a while. One leg brushed against her. The contact stung like a bee.

She pulled her leg away from his, cleared her throat, and said, "This is an interesting carriage. I've never seen one like it. It's quite large."

"It's a station wagon. It takes guests from the hotel to the train station and back again. It makes several trips a day and can hold up to ten people at a time on the bench seats," Jerek explained before asking, "How was your morning?"

"Fine." She wrung her hands together. Now was as good a time as any to set up her first installment. "Jerek, I did realize there are a few things I need, could we stop and do some shopping on our way back?"

"Of course, just tell me where you need to stop." A long arm slithered along the backrest of the seat.

She leaned forward. "All right, I'll know the store when I see it."

His fingers reached out to comb through her hair, the way he twirled the strands around each digit sent shivers up her spine. She couldn't squirm enough to make him let go. Frustrated, she turned her face as far from his as possible, and attempted to ignore the sensations.

His touch drove her crazy. She would protest if she didn't need his money so badly. Her lips pulled sideways, and her eyes rolled as she resolved to put up with his actions for the time being.

Traffic grew thick as they pulled next to a large, brick building. Over a dozen other wagons unloaded before the driver pulled forward and nodded for them to step down. An acre of lush, green grass dotted with huge, weeping willow trees surrounded the building. Flowers of all shapes, sizes, and colors danced in the breeze. The lavish beauty of the structure was like an oasis in a desert. So much of Memphis displayed the toll the war had taken, but not here, everything was manicured to perfection.

Jerek's hand, held up to assist, interrupted her appraisal of the property. She placed hers in it and climbed down from the wagon. His long fingers wrapped around hers, but she decided not to object as they walked along the flower lined, brick walkway to the Army Headquarters. She had to be civil to him, not let him know she knew his secrets—yet.

His voice floated above the mumbles of others. "If it gets to be too much, just let me know, and I'll escort you from the room."

"Don't fret. I'll be fine," she said as they entered through a door at least twelve feet high. People merged in before and after them.

The heavy brick allowed the interior of the building to be cooler than she expected, and the overwhelming beauty continued on the inside. Larger than life paintings decorated the long hall. Canvas filled with colorful landscapes, and stern looking, but presumably, famous people, stretched between brilliant gold frames.

The glitz of the building frazzled her. Another confirmation of how the government fared while people across the land went hungry. Frustration merged with her suppressed anger and made the muscles in her neck tighten. Greed was a terrible guide to live by.

The trail of people led them into a large room. Several men sat on huge chairs behind a long, tall, panel desk and were separated from the rest of the seats in the room by a small, wooden fence. April recognized faces from the *Sultana* as Jerek led her to their seats. Most of the hundred and ten seats were already taken. He nodded to and greeted several people. Many looked like they should still be in one of the hospitals. A chill tickled her spine. If he was Robert Louden, his actions had injured these men.

She pulled her hand from his and twisted sideways to walk down the front row of seats. Ignoring how he pointed to the first couple chairs, she took the one closest to the wall. He followed and sat down next to her. She quivered.

Bill Rowberry joined them and took a seat in their row. She smiled and nodded as the first mate greeted her before sitting down. Did the man know Jerek's real identity? Surely not or he wouldn't be on such friendly terms.

Another man entered the row of chairs. Jerek stood and shook hands with the man before he turned and introduced her, "April, this is E. J. Allan, E. J. this is April."

E. J. Allan. Why it was none other than Allan Pinkerton. He was after Robert Louden. Her gaze flashed to Jerek. How could the detective not know who he was? Or did he? She glanced between the two men. They smiled at each other as if they knew a secret. Her knees trembled.

"Happy to make your acquaintance, Ma'am," Allan Pinkerton said as he removed his hat and gave a slight bow.

The air in her lungs felt tight. Would he arrest Jerek here, today? Her lower lip quivered, she bit at it, and nodded a greeting before looking away. He couldn't be arrested. At least not until she got the money she needed. The noise in the room made it hard to think. Her hands rose to cover her ears.

Jerek touched her knee. "Are you all right? You look a little pale."

"Fine, I'm fine," she swiftly answered, pushing

his hand away.

"You look quite lovely today," he said.

She didn't comment, turned to gaze out the window instead. If only she'd sewn those coins back into her petticoat. Why had she been so foolish lately?

She took a deep breath. It wasn't as if she was destitute, she did still have her bank account, and Mr. Green would wire her money if she requested it. But that wasn't the point. Jerek stole her money, and she wanted it back.

A shudder ripped down her neck when his hand touched the skin below her chin and forced her face to turn his way.

A worried gaze scanned her face. "April, what's going on in that mind of yours?"

"Wouldn't you like to know," she huffed and pulled her chin from his touch.

"Find a seat! These proceedings are about to begin!" A man in the back of the room bellowed above the noise of the crowd.

Hurried movements filled the remaining chairs, and within moments, the room grew quiet. She tried to listen as the men in the front of the room made introductions, but the names rolled together, and she couldn't remember who was with what division of what commission. It was all too confusing. Each man mentioned people he'd talked to concerning the accident, making it impossible for her to remember all of the names. The last man explained today's hearing was only a small part of the overall investigation.

The grey haired man in the center of the long desk waved his hand and invited someone from the crowd to step forward. The thump of a wooden crutch sounded as a man limped through the gate of the small partition wall. Bandages covered his hands, and red, blistered skin made his face undistinguishable and unforgettable at the same time.

"State your name," the man in the middle said.

"Chief Engineer Wintringer," the injured man said.

"Take a seat, Mr. Wintringer."

"Thank you, General Washburn." His voice sounded raspy and his face winced as he settled onto the chair.

"Engineer Wintringer, do you know how many passengers were on board the *Sultana*?"

"No, Sir. Other than we were crowded. But I do know about her boilers, Sir."

"All right then, please tell us the condition of the boilers on the *Sultana*," the General encouraged.

"Just south of Vicksburg we discovered a small leak. We shut the fires of that one down and eased our way into port. A boilermaker, R. G. Taylor, was hired to check it out while we were in port. He put a good, strong patch on the leak, and cleaned out the entire system." The Engineer glanced toward the panel and continued, "The waters of the lower Mississippi are full of silt that can get into the flues. More than one boiler's gone down 'cause of that silt, but not the *Sultana*. She was as clean as a whistle when we pulled out of Vicksburg."

"Were the boilers checked at Memphis?" General Washburn asked.

"Yes, Sir. A boilermaker, here in Memphis, Raymond Harper, checked her out and gave her a clean bill of health before the crew even began unloading cargo. We decreased the pressure in the boilers to about one hundred pounds, banked the furnaces, and told the stokers to take a break while the soldiers and deckhands unloaded the cargo. We had sugar and cases of wine to drop."

"What time did you exit the port?"

"Must been 'bout midnight when the Captain

blew the whistle. We waited for a few stragglers to run down the hill, and then pulled the plank. We fed the fires and crossed to the Arkansas side to the coal barges. The stokers lit lanterns and torches and had to wake up several sleeping soldiers to clear the way for the loading crew. Again some of the soldiers helped the deck hands load. It took a little over a thousand bushels to fill the coal bins." Chief Engineer Wintringer pointed at Bill. "First Mate Rowberry oversaw the refueling. He can confirm what I say."

The General nodded and motioned a hand for the engineer to continue.

"Well, we must have pulled out sometime after one in the morning. We stoked up the fires and headed north. The stokers were busy getting the last loads into the bins. When the area was all settled, I headed up to the wheelhouse and told Rowberry everything was in order and then went to the Texas deck to get some sleep."

April leaned forward, waiting for the man to go on. Jerek had told her he'd hired the boilermakers. If he was Robert Louden and planned on blowing up the boat, why would he have done that?

"A short time later, an explosion like I'd never heard before knocked me out of bed. The Texas deck behind my room was gone. It had collapsed into the cabin and lower decks. Lickety-split I made my way down to the pit. Sparks and chunks of burning coal had been shot in all directions. I leaped over small fires the whole way. I yelled at the stokers to get the water buckets, but they," his head lowered, "the stokers and buckets had been blown overboard or were covered in flames before my very eyes. Ain't never seen nothin' like it."

The room grew completely silent for a few moments. Wintringer's voice shook when he continued, "There was this big, gapping hole in the middle of the boat, looked like the bowels of hell. Flames lapped at the men who slipped off the steep edges. I helped many a man scramble over the weaker and dead ones to get back to the top, and away from the fire."

April pressed a shaky hand to her mouth.

The engineer cleared his throat. "You see, the blast made the boilers blow, and steam flew across the upper decks. The water put out some of the flames started by the sparks, but not all of them. Fires licked across the boat like it was dry kindling wood." Wintringer used one bandaged hand to wipe his cheeks. "The steam splattered across the rows of men sleeping on the Hurricane deck. It melted the skin right off some of those poor guys. The lucky ones never woke. They never knew what killed them. Only a few had blankets to protect them from being scorched by the steam."

April knew the scene, and it brought tears to her eyes. She swallowed against painful memories trying to overwhelm her senses.

"They woke up to hell on earth. We tried to find the coal buckets, but by then the bins were on fire. As I said, it was what I'd imagined hell to look like. Flames jumping up to grab those too close the edge. I caught fire, and someone threw a blanket over me to smother it. The heat and fire pushed us back to where the livestock were. The horses and mules were kicking and screaming. Men jumped on their backs and forced the scared animals to jump over the side of the boat. I guess they thought they could ride as the animals swam. More men in the water would try to grab on and soon the animal and then men would disappear below the water."

April folded her arms, rubbed at prickled skin in effort to ward off the shivers.

The General let mumbles float around the room for a few minutes before he asked, "Did the patch blow?"

"No, Sir. That I can say for certain. I found my second engineer, Samuel Clemens, who'd taken over when I went up to bed. He was scalded from head to toe. I got him in one of the lifeboats. He told me he saw the furnace doors blow open. The explosion went up, and the steam came out of the back of the boilers. The patch had been made in the larboard boiler, the third sheet from the forward end and a few inches below the horizontal diameter," he said.

The row of men sitting behind the bench looked as confused as April felt. The compassion Jerek had shown at the hospital for the dying boatman swirled in her mind.

"The patch was made on the front of the boilers, not the back. It held tight," the engineer explained.

"Engineer Wintringer, would you say the boat was top heavy?" the General asked.

"Yes, Sir, we were very top heavy. She almost toppled back at Helena afore we got to Memphis. But if you're asking if we were careening before we blew, no, Sir, we were not. I would know, like I said I was in my bed on the Texas deck, and when a ship starts waving, you feel it up there." The engineer nodded to the onlookers and received agreeing comments and nods.

"It was rough water, was it not?" General Washburn asked.

"Yes, we were entering Chute Number Forty. The current was strong; we had to angle across, and needed a lot of steam to make the run. The *Sultana* was running smooth, no careening, rough water or not. Sam Clemens was a good engineer and knew what he was doing. You see, sometimes there's foaming, it can make a man think there's plenty of water in the boilers when there's not. But like I said earlier, she'd been cleaned in Vicksburg and foaming happens when there's silt plugging her. Sam said on his deathbed there was plenty of water. And no foam." He emphasized the last sentence and turned back to the audience. His gaze landed on Jerek as he added, "He also said he saw the furnace doors blow open."

A chill ran up April's spine, did the engineer think Jerek was a boat burner? Her gaze went to Jerek in time to see him give the man a slight nod. She swallowed over a thick lump.

"But if you were listing, hot spots might have occurred," the General said.

Wintringer turned back to the bench. "I said we were not listing. There was no foam. The ride was smooth. We didn't have any hot spots happening."

"Were you aware of the number of men Mason planned on hauling?" General Washburn asked.

The engineer gave the General a cold stare. "First off, Captain Mason fought for every one of those men to the very end. He ripped doors from their hinges, mattress from the beds, barrels and crates, anything he could find that would float and threw them to the drowning men in the water."

The General along with several others sitting near him, gave slight nods, accepting the Captain's valor.

"Second, the Captain didn't want all those men on his boat. He tried telling the Army folks in Vicksburg, but they wouldn't listen. They wanted those men out of there, and just kept marching them up the plank," Wintringer said.

"Thank you, Chief Engineer Wintringer, you can step down now. We will contact you if we have any further questions." The General abruptly ended the engineer's testimony.

"Next up will be First Mate Rowberry," a man standing near the row of sitting men announced.

April wrung her hands as Bill walked through the gate and up to the chair. General Washburn certainly didn't seem to be a very friendly person. She hoped he would be kind to Bill. The warmth of Jerek's hand fell atop hers. His long fingers massaged and soothed her fretful nerves.

"State your name," the General said.

"First Mate William Rowberry," Bill said.

"First Mate Rowberry, did you know about the men Captain Mason had agreed to transport?" he asked.

"Yes, I knew we were going to pick up released prisoners and take them north, sir," Bill answered.

""Did you know how many?"

"None of us did. Not the Captain or anyone else. We were just told it would be several hundred."

"And how many did it prove to be?"

"No official count was made, but a very reliable source said two thousand, two hundred and two people were on the *Sultana* when we docked in Memphis," Bill answered as he glanced to April.

She dipped her chin, agreeing with the number.

"What about when you left Memphis?" General Washburn continued.

Bill shrugged his shoulders. "Well, I know a few men departed here, and a few others went abroad for a drink or two and missed the ship. My best guess would be the total might have been less than a dozen though."

"So you figure there was still over two thousand on the ship?"

"Most definitely."

General Washburn held up a piece of paper. "Military records show a total of one thousand, two hundred and thirty-eight."

Bill shrugged his shoulders. "As I said, a very reliable source stated two thousand, two hundred and two."

She held her breath. She'd counted correctly. How could the army have been over a thousand short of her count? Her fingers rolled to link with Jerek's.

The General changed his route of questioning. "Mr. Rowberry, do you know how this transport deal came to be? Who guaranteed Captain Mason a load of prisoners to bring north?"

"Yes."

The General waited a moment before he said, "Please do tell."

"To the best of my knowledge, General Napoleon Dana, Lieutenant Colonel Reuben Hatch, Brigadier General Morgan Smith, Captain George Augustus Williams, and Captain Fredrick Speed all had a hand it in."

Murmurs echoed through the room. She couldn't distinguish words, but it was clear many of the attendees were not happy so many upper Army personnel were involved.

"Silence! Silence!" General Washburn shouted above the noise.

It was several minutes before the room quieted and the General continued questioning Bill. "Do you know the payout amounts?"

Bill scowled. "Captain Mason was promised five dollars for each solider and ten dollars for every officer. He was to provide a kick back to those involved of a dollar fifteen a head, or two thirty, accordingly."

The mumbling rose again. It settled as Bill started speaking again. "The payout was to happen in Cairo. Hatch and Speed wanted their kick back money in Vicksburg, but Captain Mason refused to pay them until he was paid. He also argued with Williams, Hatch, and Speed in Vicksburg about how many men they were boarding on the *Sultana*, but it didn't stop them from sending more up the gangplank. He implored Captain William Kerns and Major William Fidler to talk to Williams, Hatch, and

Speed about the load. They did, but the other men refused to listen to them and their concerns either. Williams was the one who was supposed to be creating the muster rolls, listing all the men boarding the ship, but he went into town."

Bill's gaze shot through the crowd before he continued, "To visit a local pub and wasn't even present when a full group loaded, nor when the doctor removed the more severely ill ones. No wonder, the numbers are off."

The rumble rose again. "I said silence!" the General reminded. "Silence or I will end this hearing!"

Bill Rowberry shouted above the crowd, "Don't rightly matter how many were on the boat. What matters is that we catch the boat burners who blew it up with one of their torpedoes!"

The room roared as men rose to shout in agreement. Fearful of the commotion, and ignoring the lingering thought that she no longer liked him, April pressed her head against Jerek's shoulder.

Her body trembled beneath his touch. Jerek pulled her closer to his chest as General Washburn continued to try and shout above the thunder of voices. A mallet slapped against the table, but the noise couldn't penetrate the bellows. The hearing bailiff walked to an open window. Jerek covered her ears as the man pulled the pistol strapped to his hip and fired it into the air.

April screamed and almost crawled onto his lap as the shot rippled the room. The noise shocked the crowd and stilled the protests. He lifted her face. Fear filled her eyes, and tears trickled down her cheeks.

He used his thumbs to wipe away the water, and assured, "It's all right, you're not in any danger."

Her bottom lip trembled, and her gaze danced about fearfully.

He loved her. The thought smacked him like a two by four. Warmth flooded his chest, and a smile grew on his face. April's eyebrows drew together, and her head titled sideways. The position was too much to resist. He lowered his face and brushed a kiss against her lips. They were soft, and sweet, so very sweet.

A slap on his back made him stop the kiss before it went any deeper. He lifted his head and realized where they were. Blood rushed to his face. Half the room stared at him. The glare he sent across the heads, forced everyone to turn back to the front of the room.

"Oh..." April muttered as she pulled the front of her hat down lower.

Jerek laid a hand on top of hers, but she pushed it away and sent him a look of disgust. He fought the urge to laugh aloud and folded his hands on his lap. He picked a hell of a time to decide he was head over heels in love.

Chapter Fifteen

"First Mate Rowberry, you can step down," General Washburn gained control of the room, dismissed Bill with a wave of his hand, and sent an expectant look at the bailiff.

The man glanced at a piece of paper in front of him and said, "Mr. J.J. Witzig, please step forward."

Jerek gave a groan of disgust. Rowberry and Witzig, who was as round as he was tall, met near the gate, Bill had to step aside so Witzig could waddle through the opening.

The man squeezed his frame into the chair and the General said, "State you name."

"J.J. Witzig, Supervising Inspector of Steamboats." The man grasped both of his lapels as his bald head bobbled like a dandelion in the wind.

General Washburn looked squarely at Jerek. "Since our audience seems so interested in the explosion of the *Sultana*," he turned to Witzig, "We will allow a professional inspector from St. Louis to repeat his finding. Go ahead, Mr. Witzig."

"Thank you, General." Witzig's fat tongue licked his lips before he started. "I rented a tug boat and followed the exact course taken by the *Sultana* from Memphis to the explosion site. It was made clear to me that diagonally crossing from the right side of the river to the left, at high flood stage, would cause significant careening of the ship. As it did for the tug." He shot a disapproving look over Jerek's shoulder, at Wintringer.

"With no cargo or freight in the hold, and with over twelve hundred passengers on board," this time the look landed on Rowberry, "it would have been impossible for the *Sultana* not to be listing—heavily listing."

Jerek pulled his lips together to keep from shouting at the pompous little man.

"The careening would pose serious danger to the boilers. Hot spots would form and an explosion would have been imminent." J.J. nodded to the General.

"Please continue, Mr. Witzig," Washburn encouraged.

"I must disagree with Engineer Wintringer about the patch as well. My findings show without doubt it gave out and caused the explosion."

Jerek leaped to his feet. "That's outrageous!"

"Mr. Brinkley, sit down!" General Washburn instructed.

Witzig's gaze flashed between Jerek and the General. Beads of sweat broke out on the man's forehead.

"General Washburn, this is a fiasco. Witzig is nothing more than an incompetent drunk. He only became an inspector because his wife's father owns an inspection business." Jerek could no longer hold his disgust of the hearing. "Ask the captain of the tug he rented. He'll tell you he fell off the boat in a drunken stupor during his so called investigation."

"Brinkley, that's enough!" Washburn slammed his mallet against the desk. "I'll have you and your wife thrown out if your outburst continues."

The word wife was like a slap in the face. Jerek's gaze flew to April. A look of shock covered a face flushed red. On his other side, Allan Pinkerton tugged at his sleeve. Jerek lowered to his chair. He twisted to April and whispered, "I'm sorry."

Her lips drew into a tight line. With a snap of her neck, she turned her face forward, and scooted as far away from him as possible.

Damn, he hadn't meant to upset her. This outlandish investigation grated his nerves. He'd hoped more of the true story would come out during the public hearing, but it was clear the army wasn't concerned about the truth.

"Thank you, Mr. Witzig, you may step down." General Washburn instructed.

"Since it appears we cannot have a civil hearing, I'm going to close this investigation based on the findings we have forthwith." He repositioned several sheets of paper in front of him, and glanced up at the room. "First, I want to remind the room that as a nation, we need to put the carnage of the war behind us and focus on rebuilding our country."

A mellow hum of agreement fluttered across the room. Jerek looked to April. Her cheek twitched as she kept her face forward.

"Secondly, I will remind the room this investigation is pertaining to the responsibility for having so many men aboard the *Sultana* when she blew, not how or why she blew. I'm sorry if you thought differently. But let me assure you, the evidence of why she blew is clear, the cause was a leaky, poorly repaired steam boiler."

The crowd grew defensive again, but with a few whacks of his mallet Washburn quickly gained control, and a tense silence followed.

The General began again, "After several days of testimony, interviews, investigation, and inquiries, this commission has discounted the crowded conditions aboard the *Sultana*. Evidence clearly shows the United States Government has transferred as many, if not more, troops on boats of no greater capacity than the *Sultana* quite frequently and safely. Therefore, this commission finds no fault in the Army for the accident. The incident, investigation, and hearing are closed, and this verdict stands." He hit the top of the desk with the mallet in conclusion.

Jerek let his head fall against the back of his chair. April still refused to look at him, so he turned to Pinkerton and said, "See what I said? They're only concerned about being found at fault."

"Yes, I'll wire Washington and insist an investigation be called against Speed, Hatch, and Williams."

The room's occupants began to stand and filter out. Jerek tried to assist April's stance, but she rose and stepped back against the wall. He could reach her, but chose not to. She was upset, and he couldn't blame her. Her gaze refused to acknowledge the elbow he thrust out for her hand to grasp. In response, he stepped forward, allowed her to step into the walkway and in silence followed behind as the mumbling crowd exited the room.

Hot, afternoon air greeted the mob outside the building. Jerek grasped April's elbow and pulled her aside. "Slow down, we've become separated from Allan."

She twisted her elbow from his fingers, "So?"

"So, the three of us and Bill are going to have lunch."

"I'd prefer to go back to the hotel," she said and took a step forward.

He snatched her elbow again. "And I'd prefer to have lunch with my friends before we do." He tightened his hold when she tried to escape.

Her glance went from his hand to his face. "You can have lunch with anyone you please. I'm going back to the hotel."

"No, you're not."

"Yes, I am."

People slowed in their exit to stare at them. He pulled her onto the grass. "Please don't argue now, April. Be a good girl, you'll enjoy lunch."

Her hands formed small fists at her sides. He could tell she tried to hold her temper and braced himself for the onslaught that was sure to spill over.

Breasts rose as she pulled air in and held it. Several unreadable emotions crossed her face before her lids fluttered shut and the air exhaled. He tried to keep his smile as unnoticeable as possible while watching every movement.

"Fine," she said.

"Fine?" he asked.

"Fine. Where are Mr. Allan and Bill? Let's go eat."

"They're right behind you," he said.

April swirled around and without waiting for him to accompany her, walked to the waiting men.

The restaurant across the street from the courthouse was a buzz with the Army's investigation and findings. She settled onto a chair held out by Mr. Pinkerton. Fury at Jerek made her blood boil.

He'd never asked if she wanted to have lunch, just told her that's what they were doing. Before that, he'd let the whole courtroom believe she was his wife. And the rogue had kissed her in public. The thought of it sent her heart racing all over again. She took another deep breath and tried to erase the event from her mind. There had to be a way for her to convince her body not to respond to him

She lifted the napkin from her place setting and folded it across her lap as a young woman approached their table. The girl couldn't have been more than fifteen or so, and the little flirt shamefully batted her eyes at Jerek the whole time they placed their order.

April almost kicked him when Jerek made some

sly remark, and the girl giggled with glee at his self-proclaimed cleverness. Across the table, Allan Pinkerton stared at her with an odd little smile on his face.

"What part of Minnesota is it you hale from?" he asked.

"A small town west of St. Paul, I'm sure you've never heard of it," she answered.

"Oh, I might surprise you. I've been to Minnesota several times."

"Whatever for?"

"Oh, this and that, business mainly," he answered.

"Really?"

He nodded then asked, "Have you been to Jerek's home yet?"

Why would the detective want to know that? "No." A sliver of pain touched her heart. She'd never see his home. Never meet his family.

"Oh, you'll like it, Ohio is beautiful. Minnesota reminds me of it, especially, along the lake."

"Mmm." She didn't know how to answer, the detective made her nervous. Was he searching for information? Her mind was searching for information too, or answers. If Jerek was a boat burner, why wasn't he happy about the army's findings? They claimed the accident happened because of a faulty boiler. That should make him happy. It would clear his name.

The waitress returned with four glasses and set them upon the table. April willed her hands to stop trembling as she drew the glass of lemonade to her lips. The room was airless and warm from the people mingling about. Several men stopped by the table to make a comment about the hearing.

"The Army really doesn't care who blew up the boat," Bill said after he took a sip of his drink.

"The Army has to tread carefully right now. It's

been proclaimed the war has ended. If their investigation had found the boat burners had anything to do with the burning of the *Sultana*, fear that the war hasn't ended might cause an uprising," Allan Pinkerton said.

"So you agree with them?" Bill's jaw dropped open.

"No, I'm not saying I agree, I'm trying to explain their outcome," the detective said.

"In other words, the whole investigation was for show," Bill said.

"I'm afraid so," Jerek added. "But Allan will see that Hatch, Speed, and Williams are investigated for overloading the boat and taking kickbacks."

Allan Pinkerton nodded. "I can't guarantee the outcome, but I'll see they are taken to court."

"But what about the truth?" Bill asked. "What about the boat burners? I swear it was a coal torpedo that blew up the *Sultana*."

April held her breath. Would the detective arrest Jerek, here at the restaurant? She glanced between the two men. They seemed to share a look of understanding with one another, and then Jerek gave a slight nod of his head.

Her gaze flew to Pinkerton as he said, "That's why I'm here. I don't have much time before I have to get back to Washington, but I'll find Robert Louden, if he's still in Memphis, before I leave."

The tart lemonade in her mouth threatened to spew out. She tried to swallow. It burned her throat. She coughed and gasped for air. Her eyes began to water.

Jerek rose at her side and patted her back. "April? April, are you all right?" He shouted across the room, "Bring a glass of water! Quick!"

She tried to shake her head. The burning in her throat wouldn't ease and her coughing continued.

Jerek pressed a glass to her lips. The cool water

did quench the fire, and she nodded her thanks before raising her napkin to wipe at the tears streaming down her cheeks. He hovered above her. She pointed for him to sit down.

"Are you all right?" he asked. His hand now rubbed her spine, back and forth, up and down.

"Yes, I'm fine." Her throat felt raw, but she continued anyway, "Sorry, it just went down the wrong hole. Please sit down I don't want to make a scene."

"Are you sure?"

"Yes." She took another sip of water.

The waitress appeared again. "Here, Ma'am, I apologize if the other one was too tart. Try this one," she said as she set a fresh glass of lemonade on the table.

The girl had a look of true concern on her face. "Thank you," April said. She couldn't admit it wasn't the drink's fault, but did attempt to send a grin to the girl and the rest of the table's occupants, minus Jerek.

To him she whispered between clinched teeth, "Sit down."

He followed her directions but continued to send questioning looks her way. She squeezed her eyes shut, hoping he wouldn't figure out it was the thought of him being arrested that almost made her choke to death.

Bill brought up the conversation as if nothing had interrupted it. "And if he's not?"

"If who's not what?" Jerek asked.

"If Louden's not in Memphis, then what?" Bill looked at Pinkerton.

"I'll know where he's at before I leave Memphis, don't worry, we'll find out how he blew up the ship, and he'll pay the price," Allan answered.

Thankfully, she'd place the water glass on the table before the detective answered. Her fingers shook so hard, she might have dropped it. What did he mean, he'd pay the price? Her stomach rolled at the thought of Jerek being hurt. None of it made sense. A throbbing pain started in her right temple.

The waitress arrived again, this time with plates piled high. The smell of food made her stomach queasy. She swallowed against rising bile.

"April? April, are you sure you're all right?" Jerek asked again.

"Yes, I'm fine. Eat your lunch." Why did she worry about him getting hurt? Robert Louden and the boat burners deserved to be punished. She didn't dare look at his face, the concern she heard in his voice was almost more than she could take. Her trembling fingers picked up her fork, and silently she vowed to eat the meal even if it killed her.

The men didn't speak much during the meal, and as soon as it ended, Jerek ushered her from the restaurant and hailed a passing carriage. She hoped the food she'd forced down her throat wouldn't erupt on the ride home. This whole day had become one frustrating, confusing incident after another.

The wheels jostled and bounced over the cobblestones. She hid her face behind her hands. Jerek's fingers massaged her shoulders. She could no longer tell if it made her feel worse, or better. Finally, the wagon came to halt, and she didn't have the energy to protest as his arms lifted her. One arm held her against his chest as the other cradled her knees. Her head fell onto his shoulder as he carried her into the hotel and up to their room.

Gentle hands removed her hat and shoes after reclining her onto the bed. She rolled onto her side and looked forward to the black void pulling her in.

Jerek dipped a cloth in the basin of water on the nightstand, and pressed it against April's forehead as he sat down on the bed. Her skin felt warm but not over heated. The day's trials must have been too

278

much. Maybe he should just take her home, away from all the fiasco.

Where was home? Minnesota or Ohio? He brushed tufts of hair from her face and ran a finger along her chin. It really didn't matter. Home for him would be where ever April was.

Pinkerton was right, the Army didn't care who blew up the *Sultana*, never would. It was useless for he and April to hang around, looking for answers that really didn't matter. Even if they proved Louden and the boat burners blew up the boat, no one would be prosecuted. It would be considered a wartime act. The Confederate Department of Trans-Mississippi had vowed to fight on, and would. Louden was a part of the Department, as well as numerous other boat burners. They'd never surrender and if caught, they'd be pardoned for their crimes since the war had officially ended. It was a losing battle, no different than the war itself.

Jerek lifted the cloth from her forehead, folded it, and laid it over the rim of the basin before moving to the window. The midday heat was sweltering, no wonder she buckled. It was too much for those not used to it. And it was only going to get worse as they moved into the summer months. He turned back to the bed. Yes, it was time to take her north, time for them both to go home.

****

Sweat crept down her back. Small drops trickled over her skin like dew on tree leaves. April rolled over, stared about the empty space. She sighed, not quite sure if she was disappointed or satisfied Jerek wasn't in the room.

Rising from the bed, she walked to the window. The Memphis heat was so strong. She couldn't wait to experience the cool evenings of home. Allan Pinkerton said Ohio was a lot like Minnesota. Her heart somersaulted. She pressed a hand against the sensation. Once she had enough money she'd go home to her lonely little house, where she'd probably die a lonely old woman, or a young woman from a broken heart. Her dream of marrying Jerek and living happily ever after had been shattered forever.

How could she love and hate someone at the same time? She did love Jerek, and she did hate him. Of its own accord her head gave a slow shake. She didn't hate him—couldn't ever hate him. She hated whoever was behind injuring all those people she'd seen in the courtroom. Deep down her soul told her it wasn't Jerek.

Somehow it just didn't seem fair. Her days of happiness could be counted on one hand, while it took years to count her days of sadness. And there were many more to come. Before she'd always had hope Willie would return to Minnesota. A dull ache settled in her chest. If anyone was a murderer it was her. She'd killed Willie and Susie. It was her fault they had been on the *Sultana*. If she'd stayed home, hadn't gone to New Orleans to drag Willie home, he and Susie would still be alive.

She turned from the window, retrieved her shoes, and sat down to put them on. If only her affair with Jerek had produced a child, then maybe she'd have had more days of happiness. She'd never be alone, and have a piece of him with her for the rest of her life. Like Willie had had with Suzie. Her fingers stilled. The thought surprised and intrigued her at the same time.

Her eyes went to the bed. She wasn't too educated on the mating of men and women, but knew enough. Maybe it wasn't too late yet. Could she do it? Should she do it? One finger ran across her chin. She'd tried. Tried with all her heart, mind, and soul to hate him, but couldn't. Not even the old April could conjure up anything but love for him. The mere thought of him sent her heart racing and radiance filled her body.

She slapped the bed. That's all there was too it, she'd have to find a way to make him take her to bed. With deft movements, she tied the shoelaces. Her head snapped up, and she jumped from the chair. She had to find Jerek before Allan Pinkerton had him arrested.

Sounds drew her to the kitchen as she stepped from the stairs.

Ester turned from the stove. "Hello, are you feeling better?"

Scarlet looked up from where she sat snapping beans. A teasing grin covered her face. "When we saw Mr. Brinkley carrying you in, we weren't sure if you were ill again, or if the two of you had made up."

April's cheeks flushed warm. "I guess the heat is just too much for me."

"It takes some getting used to, going to be a hot summer if this weather keeps up," Ester predicted. "If you live here long enough, you learn a few tricks."

"Tricks?"

Scarlet nodded. "Yes, as the heat rises, southern women strip."

"What?"

Ester laughed. "She means we forgo layers."

"Huh?"

Scarlet lifted the bottom of her skirt. Bare legs sat beneath the material. "We forgo our slips and petticoats."

"You do?"

Ester walked past and patted April's shoulder. "And corsets, of course, but also camisoles."

Wide-eyed with shock, April asked, "So, you wear nothing but your dress and pantaloons?"

Scarlet said, "Just a dress on the really hot days."

"Really?" It was scandalous. April pressed her palms to her burning cheeks.

"Yes, it's much better than carrying a vinaigrette everywhere you go," Scarlet said.

"A what?"

"A vinaigrette," Ester repeated. She walked to the sideboard, pulled open a drawer and handed a brooch to April. "That's a vinaigrette."

A delicate chain went from a painted brooch to a tiny, matching container about half an inch square. She looked up expectantly. Ester reached over and opened the clasp on the container. A dark, tiny sponge filled the area.

"You pin the brooch to your dress after soaking the sponge in vinegar or with smelling salts. When the vapors start to set in, you open the clasp and take a whiff. Southern women swear by them. But I'd rather not have the vapors set in. After awhile, one gets quite a headache from sniffing the sponge," Ester said.

April lifted the sponge to her nose. Repulsed, she snapped the container shut and handed the jewel back to Ester. The faint odor remained in her nose and made her sneeze.

"I haven't used it for ages and it still stinks. I only moisten it when we have to be dressed to go in public. And believe me the smell is much worse when the sponge is damp." Ester replaced the vinaigrette in the drawer and walked back to the stove. "You can borrow it, if you'd like."

"No, no thank you. I think it would make me more ill than the heat." She had seen woman with such pins decorating their dresses since she'd arrived in the South, but never imagined that's what they were.

"I agree," Scarlet said. "Taking off layers is much better."

April needed to leave the kitchen, before they started to share more southern women secrets. She already knew enough secrets to last a life time. "Do you know where Jerek is?" she asked.

"Yes, he and his friend, Mr. Allan, are on the front porch," Ester said.

The speed of her heart picked up a pace. "Oh." She glanced to the door.

"Go ahead, he won't mind if you join them. He's been running up those stairs to check on you every fifteen minutes or so," Ester chuckled.

A million thoughts flashed through her mind. She glanced between the two women.

"Go on, supper won't be ready for some time yet," Ester said.

April left the room and made her way to the front door, the low murmur of men's voices could be heard, but not distinct enough to understand what was being said. The screech of the screen door caused the conversation to stop. Both men looked her way.

Jerek walked across the porch. "Are you feeling better?" One hand cupped her cheek.

His touch was sincere, and caring, and so wonderfully real. Tears tried to form. She blinked them away. She would miss him so much. Swallowing the lump in her throat, she said, "Yes, thank you."

"Come sit down." Jerek wrapped a hand around her elbow and led her to the chairs on the far end of the porch.

Allan Pinkerton rose. "Hello," he smiled.

"Hello." She sat down in a chair.

Jerek pulled a third chair near her side. "Are you thirsty?"

She started to decline then pressed two fingers to her lips. If Jerek were to leave she would have a few moments to speak with Mr. Pinkerton. "Actually, something cool would be refreshing."

"I'll see what I can find for you," he said.

When the screen fluttered shut behind him, she

said, "Mr. Pinkerton, I don't have much time, so please let me say my piece without interruption."

Allan Pinkerton's eyes grew wide. "All right, uh, Mrs. Brinkley."

April shook her head. "First off, I know E. J. Allan is just one of your aliases. I'm also sure you know Jerek and I are not married. So there's no need for you to pretend. Just call me April."

The man nodded.

"Secondly, and most importantly, I know you know Jerek's real identity, and that you are here to see he is arrested for his crimes. But I beg you to give me a couple more days before doing so. There are some things I-we need to accomplish before his arrest."

"His real identity? I'm afraid I don't know what you're talking about."

"Please, don't make this more difficult than need be. I've heard of you. You're the best detective world wide."

"Thank you, M-April. But I really have no idea what you are talking about. Jerek is Jerek Brinkley." Allan Pinkerton leaned forward in his chair, looking at her like she'd lost her mind.

She pressed a hand to her forehead. She'd forgotten her hat. Out of habit her fingers fluffed her bangs, before she let out a huff and folded her hands in her lap.

The man watched her movements then asked, "Tell me, April. Who do you think Jerek really is?"

Could he really not know? "Mr. Pinkerton, Jerek Brinkley is none other than the man you came here to find."

"Huh?"

She closed her eyes for a moment, struggling for the decision to tell him or not. With a huff, she leaned forward and whispered, "Jerek is Robert Louden."

Allan Pinkerton started to cough at the same time the screen door opened. He grabbed a glass sitting on the table beside him and threw the contents over the porch rail.

Jerek stopped beside her chair. "Here you go. Ester had some apple cider cooling in the well."

"Thank you." Her fingers brushed against his and almost made her drop the glass.

"Jerek," Mr. Pinkerton said when his coughing subsided, "Would you mind getting me a refill?"

Jerek looked at the glass Pinkerton held out.

The man nodded his head.

Jerek looked between her and Mr. Pinkerton. One brow arched upwards.

Pinkerton nodded again.

"All right," Jerek said.

"And Jerek," Mr. Pinkerton said.

"Yes?"

"Take your time."

Jerek's brows furrowed together.

April held her breath.

His lingering gaze asked hers to meet it. She refused. He turned and walked into the building.

With a sigh of relief, she set her glass down and looked at Allan Pinkerton. His thumb and forefinger pinched his chin beneath the long beard.

She waited.

"April," he started, "Why do you believe Jerek is Robert Louden?"

"Because he is."

"Why do you believe he is? Did he tell you that?"

"No, someone else did."

"Who?"

"A man I met. He had been on one of the boats Robert Louden blew up." Her cheeks grew warm, but she continued, "Jerek has the bullet scar exactly as the man described. He told me several other things that are true as well. It all proves Jerek is Robert

Louden, but more importantly, you can't have him arrested for a least a couple more days."

"I assure you, I won't have anyone arrested until I know it is the right man." Allan Pinkerton leaned forward, "But you must tell me all you know. Help me make the right decision."

April glanced to the door. She didn't believe she had enough time to tell him everything. "The man at the hospital was looking for his family who perished on the *Sultana*. He knew all about the boat burners and Jerek's gambling, his pretense of working for his uncle, his, well, several other traits and of course the scar. He's looking for him too, but I have to wonder if he might kill him instead of turning him in to the authorities. So it would be safer for Jerek if you were to be the one to have him arrested." She wanted to tell him Jerek hadn't killed anyone, but knew they didn't have time to get into her reasoning.

Allan Pinkerton rubbed his fingers over his right temple. "Does this man, you met, have a name?"

She nodded.

"Could you tell me it? It might be extremely helpful to my investigation. And keep Jerek safe."

"His name is Charles Deal."

The man's head snapped upwards. "Did you say Deal, or Dale?"

"Deal."

Pinkerton nodded. "Charles Deal? And you say you saw him at the hospital where you're volunteering?"

"Yes."

"How many times have you seen, Mr. Deal?" Allan Pinkerton's finger tapped on the table.

"Twice."

"On the same day?"

"No, different days," she answered.

"Do you remember what he looked like?"

She thought for a moment. "Yes."

"Can you describe him?"

"It's kind of hard, because he has a beard and mustache. And he had a straw hat covering his eyes. He was taller than me, but not nearly as tall as Jerek, nor as broad. He's kind of skinny for a man. Oh, and he had really crooked teeth. They poked out of his mouth here and there when he talked."

Allan Pinkerton scratched his upper lip. "Thank you, April. That's a very good description. Your information will help my investigation, a lot."

"Mr. Pinkerton, about your investigation," she began.

"Yes?"

"I am missing a doll and a pouch of coins. If you find them, I would really like them back."

"Yes, Jerek has told me as much."

"He did?"

Mr. Pinkerton nodded.

A deep sigh exited her chest. "Too bad he didn't tell you where he's hid them."

Chapter Sixteen

That night, Jerek sauntered up the stairs, but his mind ran faster than a jackrabbit. April thought he was Robert Louden. No, she'd been told he was Robert Louden—by none other than Robert Louden himself. A shiver raced up his spine. He'd never imagined she'd be in such danger while working at the hospital. She wouldn't be allowed out of his sight ever again.

Charles Dale, or Deal as he now called himself, was one of Louden's many aliases. The man was extremely dangerous. And bold. No, the way he'd approached April wasn't bold. It was stupid. The man was extremely foolish if he thought he could accost Jerek Brinkley's woman.

His feet bounded up the final few stairs and paused outside the washroom door. Soft sounds echoed through the door. He turned and entered their room. The lamp was already lit, and the covers on the bed had been folded back. His eyes lingered on the sparkling white sheets.

The squeak of a hinge drew his look through the open door. April stepped out of the bathing chamber. A white dressing gown flowed from her shoulders to the tips of her toes. Straight, long blonde hair, glistened from a fresh brushing, and haloed her head like a golden cape. Since her nap that afternoon, her attitude toward him had changed again. Something still wasn't quite right, but she was no longer as mad as a hornet and ignoring him.

She smiled and his heart kicked like a shotgun. Her steps were so tiny and smooth, she practically floated into the room.

Jerek closed the door behind her. "Feel better?"

"Yes, but I feel guilty. Two baths in one day seems like a waste of water." Her giggle was light, almost nervous.

His fingers combed through the hair running over her shoulder. This must be what strands of pure silk feel like, he thought but said aloud, "It's not a waste of water in this heat."

Her eyes mirrored her smile, or was it his? Neither moved nor spoke, but they communicated by just gazing at one another. His hand snuck under her hair to grasp the back of her neck, and he lowered his head. He watched perfect features for a protest he prayed wouldn't come.

It didn't. Her lips parted. Warm sweet nectar flowed across his lips. Relief flooded his mind as excitement filled his loins. Her arm floated up to wrap around his neck. He twisted so she fit flawlessly against him and deepened the kiss.

Her hands ran down his back. With soft, slow movements she tugged his shirt from his waistband. Tiny, cool fingertips ran under the cloth and up his spine. The touch made him quiver.

He separated their lips. A smile played across hers. He had to break the news, but really didn't want to. Would she become angry again? "I, uh, I gave the other room to Allan for the night."

Her eyes twinkled. "You did?" Tiny fingers continued to massage his back.

"Yeah. I'm going to have to sleep in here tonight."

"Mmm. Does that mean you can kiss me again?"

She leaned forward. "I've missed them."

"So have I." Jerek took her invitation. The kiss didn't end until he was breathless and ready to explode at any moment. "Get dressed!" He pulled out of the embrace.

"What?" April stumbled, caught her footing.

She looked almost as confused as he felt. It was time, but he couldn't make love to her without taking this step first. "We have to go somewhere."

"Where?"

"You'll see." He pulled the yellow dress from the hook beside the door. "Here, put this one on."

"Jerek, can't it wait until morning? It's very late."

"No, it can't wait until morning." He opened a drawer, rifled through lacy white undergarments and holding up two items, asked, "What do you all need?"

She snatched them from his hands. "Turn around so I can get dressed."

He did as instructed.

A dressing gown flipped over his shoulder from behind. "What's so important it can't wait until morning?"

"You'll see," he said. His toe tapped the floor as he waited what seemed like hours.

"You can turn around now." She sat down on the edge of the bed to pull her socks and shoes on. "Please hang that up."

He took the gown from his shoulder and slipped it over the hook near the door. He held out a hand. As soon as the shoes were tied she took it. He drew her to her feet, smacked a warm kiss to her lips then led her out of the room.

Stars brightened the night sky, and the full moon, along with several street lamps, guided their way down quiet streets. Jerek tried to shorten his steps so she could keep up, but excitement made walking slow almost impossible. The church was only a few blocks from the hotel, but seemed much further. Half an hour later, he opened the gate of a picket fence surrounding a small house.

"Where are we? Who lives here?" she asked as they walked onto the front stoop.

"You'll see," he repeated for the umpteenth time.

Minutes later, a man dressed in a nightgown answered the door. "Yes?"

"Reverend Archer?" he asked.

"Yes," the man answered.

"I'm Jerek Brinkley," he held his hand out to the man. After shaking hands, he continued, "This is April Simonson."

"Miss Simonson," the Reverend greeted.

"Reverend," April replied.

"We need you to marry us," Jerek said.

"What?" April asked.

"Right now?" the Reverend asked at the same time.

His wide smile made his stomach fizz. He nodded to both of them. "Yes."

"I can't...we can't..." April stammered.

"It's awfully late," Reverend Archer said.

"Yes, we can," he said to April. Turning to the Reverend he added, "God doesn't care what time it is."

April pulled on his arm. "Jerek, what are you doing? This is ridiculous."

He looked down at the most beautiful woman he'd ever seen. His hands rose to cup her face. "April Simonson, I love you. And there is nothing on this earth I want more than to marry you, right here, right now."

"Ohhh..." a female voiced cooed.

Jerek and April turned to the doorway. A tiny woman poked her head out behind Reverend Archer. She patted the arm stretching across the doorway in front of her. "Papa go get dressed. You need to marry these young one's here. Hurry up now, I'll go light the candles in the church."

Jerek bowed his head. "Thank you, Ma'am."

She giggled and ducked below the arm. "You two come with me." Mrs. Archer waved a hand for them to follow. Her long dressing gown floated on the ground behind her and the nightcap on her head fluttered as she scurried across the lawn to the church.

April stopped before they followed the woman into the building.

"Jerek, we can't do this."

"Why not? I love you. I believe you love me." He leaned down and using his lips, brought her body to the fevered excitement he'd felt back at the hotel. Lifting his face, he asked, "You do love me, don't you, April?"

Her chest heaved in and out. She pressed a hand against one of her red cheeks, and whispered, "Yes, Jerek, I do love you."

"Then marry me," he said.

"I…we…" she shook her head.

"April, back at the hotel, I was ready to take you to bed, and you were ready to let me."

Her eyes cast down to the ground.

"It's nothing to be ashamed of. It's just that, well, I can't take you to bed unless we are married."

Her head lifted. "You can't?"

"No, I can't. Well, I can, but I won't." He ran a finger over her cheekbone. "I won't do that to you. I won't do that to us. When we go to bed together, I *want* you to be my wife."

"Come along you two. Papa will be here in a minute," Mrs. Archer shouted to them from where she stood near the altar of the small church. Double doors stood wide open. A carpet of royal blue led the way from the stoop to the candle lit place of worship.

He looked back to April. Her eyes flashed between him and the altar. She wrestled with her decision. Fear rose in his chest. He took a step into the church and praying his fingers wouldn't shake, raised a hand in front of April.

Tiny, pearl white teeth peeked out between her lips as a smile formed on her face. She laid her hand onto his and stepped forward.

"You'll marry me?" he asked.

"Yes, Jerek Brinkley, I will marry you."

He lifted her into his arms and swung her around the wide doorway several times. April wrapped her arms around his neck and held on as her feet flayed behind. Their laughter floated on the air and lingered after he covered her mouth with a long kiss before he lowered her feet to the floor. Hand in hand, side-by-side, they walked along the blue carpet to the altar.

The ceremony started shortly thereafter, and with intent, he listened to every word. Pledging his love to April meant the world to him, and he cherished each moment. Devoted he watched every flutter of her lids, every movement of her lips, and matched the smile sparkling from her face.

His mind faltered for a split second when Reverend Archer asked for a ring. Resolve came quickly. He released April's hands to pull the silk tie from his neck. It was bound with a small, gold band. The tiny, metal ring slipped onto her finger with perfection, and he kissed it before lowering her hand back down in front of them.

The kiss, bonding the finalization of their marriage, was full, deep, and only ended when the Reverend patted him on the back, forcing it to finish. After signing the documents, thanking the Archers, and making a generous donation to the church, he led April out into the cool night air.

They walked onto the street and turned toward

the hotel. He squeezed her hand. "Thank you, April."

She stopped and looked up at him. "For what?"

"For making me the happiest man on earth."

"Oh," she said. Her gaze danced across his face. "Jerek, now that I'm your wife, does that mean I can kiss you whenever I want?"

He chuckled. "Well, I suppose it does."

She stretched onto her tiptoes and brought her lips up to his. "Mmmm, I think I like that."

Her kiss was soft and sweet. "I like it too, Mrs. Brinkley. You can kiss me whenever, wherever, and however you'd like," he said. Now, very anxious to get back to the hotel, he pulled her down the street.

"Good," she said, "I got tired of waiting for you to do it all the time."

He laughed, "I apologize. I didn't know I was lacking in the kissing area."

"Oh, you aren't, not when you'd finally kiss me." She shrugged her shoulders. "You just didn't do it often enough."

"You should have said something."

She giggled.

They turned the corner and he said, "I assume you like being kissed."

"By you, yes."

"Oh, and have you been kissed by several men?"

"No, just you."

"Come along, my dear wife, I can't wait to show you what follows kissing." He lifted her into his arms and walked up the steps. To his dismay the door was locked. He had to lower his bride to the stoop and dig in his pocket for the key.

April giggled.

"Shhh, you're going to wake everyone," he teased.

She pressed a finger to her lips and slipped past as he held the door open. April waited at the bottom of the steps while he relocked the door. He pulled the key from the lock and turned. She held her hand out. He didn't know which leaped faster or harder, his feet, or his heart. Hand in hand they raced up the stairs and into their room.

****

April stretched her arms over her head and pulled heavy lids open. Sunlight flooded the room. She must have slept later than usual. It had been a long night.

"Oh!" Memories made her eyes all but pop out of her head. Had it been a dream? She lifted the sheet and peeked beneath it. Her body was stark naked. She dropped the sheet and raised her left hand.

A band of gold encircled one finger. A wide smile covered her lips. It was real. She was Mrs. Jerek Brinkley, and had spent the most magnificent night possible in his arms. A night filled with love, passion, and ecstasy she'd never deemed possible.

She lifted the sheet again. Her body didn't look any different, but it should. Jerek had made her feel and do the most incredible things. She sighed with pleasure and pressed the sheet to her bosom.

Startled, she sat up. Where was he? Had he been arrested? No, oh, please no. Tears burned the back of her eyes.

It wasn't true. He wasn't Robert Louden. She'd concluded the fact last night, as she glanced from the altar to Jerek, before she agreed to marry him. At that moment it all became clear. Nothing had added up. Mr. Deal was wrong. It was impossible for Jerek to be any one but Jerek Brinkley. She knew it with all her mind and her heart, and would spend the rest of her life, if need be, proving his innocence.

She'd been tossing the calculations around in her head since Mr. Deal had visited her at the hospital. At first she'd focused on how she felt, which had been a mistake. Numbers don't take emotions into account. But life does, and after discovering how real and strong love is, everything added up, and alas, problem solved.

The doorknob turned. She pulled the sheet up to cover her breasts.

Jerek's head peeked around the frame. "Good morning." He pushed the door open wider.

A giggle escaped; in the end her emotions had played a role in the answer. Love had found the correct answer. "Good morning." Her heart pounded with anticipation as he stepped into the room.

He carried a tray with both hands, kicked the door shut with his foot. Setting the tray on her lap, he leaned down and kissed her smile.

"Breakfast in bed for my new wife."

"Mmm, thank you, my dear husband." She muttered against his lips. "But, I'm really not very hungry."

"You aren't?"

She shook her head.

Jerek lifted the tray from her lap and set it on the side table. "Are you still tired, want to go back to sleep for a bit?"

She laced her arms around his neck as he sat down on the edge of the bed. "I think I'd like to kiss my husband."

"All right." He pushed the sheet aside.

His tutelage the night before had not been wasted. She remembered each and every stroke, act, caress, and touch he'd demonstrated and couldn't wait to experience them again. Her lips teased, tasted, and enticed Jerek to stretch out on the bed beside her.

The breakfast on the tray turned cold as his clothes fluttered to the floor, and she put her new knowledge to good use.

Later, feeling more content than humanly possible, she snuggled close to his side. "Hmmm."

His lips brushed over her forehead. "Hungry

now?"

"No, not really," she said. Her fingers ran over the hills and valleys of his chest, finding delight in the simplest touch. "You?"

"No, not really," he said.

Her fingers roamed up to his shoulder and rubbed across the bullet scar.

Before her mind had time to wonder about the injury, his hand lifted her fingers from his shoulder.

His lips brushed over her knuckles. "I think it's time we go home," he whispered.

"What do you mean?"

"I think it's time for us to go home," he repeated. "There's nothing more we can do here."

"What about..."

"We'll leave a forwarding address with the Cox's. They will notify us with any news about Willie and Suzie."

"But what about," she had to swallow hard before continuing, "Robert Louden?"

He twisted to lie above her. "What about him? Pinkerton is on his tail, but the sad truth is the Army doesn't really care. Even if he is arrested, he'll probably be pardoned, claiming it was a war crime."

Perhaps leaving Memphis would be best. They could find a place and start over. She pressed her lips to his. "When do you want to leave?"

"When ever you want," he answered.

A knock on the door brought their kiss up short. "Mr. Brinkley?" Ester said through the wood.

"Yes?" he answered.

"There's a man here to see you."

"I'll be right down." Pressing one more kiss to her lips, he said, "Sorry, my love, we'll continue this tonight."

"Promise?" She nuzzled her face against his neck.

"Oh, yeah, I promise." Jerek kissed the top of

her head, rolled to the edge of the bed and sat up.

She rose to her knees, and not wanting to be separated from him, now or ever, wrapped her arms under his. She laid her head on the warm skin of his back. "Who do you think is here to see you?"

"I really don't know, get dressed and come down with me." His hands ran over her forearms.

"It takes me much longer to get dressed than it takes you."

"I'll wait." He stood, twisted around, and ran his hands over her bare shoulders. "I'll even help."

She giggled. "No, I may never get dressed with your help."

He leaned down and kissed her in several places. "You're probably right."

"Go." She pointed to the door. "I'll be down in a few minutes."

"Sure?" His hands enticed her to rethink.

She flipped to the other side of the bed, out of his reach. "I'm sure."

Jerek chuckled and turned to retrieve discarded clothes. She watched the simple movements in awe, amazed by the contours and splendor. After he pulled the pants over his lean hips, she let out a sigh and moved to begin dressing. With undergarments in place, she flipped the yellow dress over her head.

He helped lower it over her body. She smiled as her head popped out the top. Jerek kissed the tip of her nose.

"I'll see you downstairs in a few minutes?"

She nodded and he turned to leave. His hand twisted the knob then he let go, and walked back. He leaned down and kissed her long and hard. "I love you, April."

"I love you too, Jerek," she said.

This time he did leave the room. She twisted around and sat down on the bed. His touch left her feeling like kindling wood, ready to burst into flames, but needing his friction to make it happen. She twisted the gold band on her finger.

How quickly life changes, it was unbelievable. The moment he'd asked her to marry him, was one of the happiest in her life. The love she felt for him took over and made everything else crystal clear.

She slipped her feet into her shoes, ran a brush through her hair, and left the room. April paused at the top of the stairs, pressed a hand to her forehead. She'd have to find a way to explain it all to Mr. Pinkerton. She'd have to convince the detective Jerek was not Robert Louden.

****

Jerek stepped off the bottom stair and looked around the front lobby. He wandered into the kitchen. "Ester, where's the man that's here to see me?"

She wiped her hands with her apron. "Oh, he's on the front porch waiting. I gave him some cider."

"Thank you. Do you know where Mr. Allan is?"

"No, he left early this morning."

He nodded and made his way to the front porch. A man he didn't recognize sat on one of the chairs. "I'm Jerek Brinkley."

The man rose and shook his hand. "Nice to meet you, Mr. Brinkley, I'm John Edwards."

"Mr. Edwards." He took the opposite seat. "What can I do for you?"

"I was at the hearing yesterday. I've told my story to the commission, but they weren't really interested. I thought maybe you would like to hear it," Mr. Edwards said.

Jerek rested one ankle on top of the opposite knee and leaned back in his chair. "Go on."

"I live across the river, on the Arkansas side. On the night the *Sultana* blew, I had been in Memphis, had a few beers with a friend at a pub on Beale Street. When the steamship whistle blew, I said I needed to go. You see, a gunboat had come through and destroyed all the skiffs and rowboats along the river the day before," the man paused.

"I'd heard about that, go on." Jerek rested his chin on his fist.

"They'd destroyed one of ours, but I'd been using the other one so they didn't get to it. When the river is this high, it's our only way to town. Sentries were still posted up and down the river, and I knew it would be safest to row across at the same time the steamer went. The sentries wouldn't be watching as closely then, and wouldn't hassle me."

Jerek nodded.

"I noticed another boat rowing across too. The current is swift out there, so you really have to concentrate to make it across. Well, that boat wasn't going straight; he was almost following the steamer, angling up river. There's not many of us who live along that side. I thought maybe it was someone I knew and that he might be having trouble, so I shouted to him. The guy ducked down in his boat, like he didn't want to be seen. I rowed closer and asked if he needed help."

Hopefully, the man's tale would soon lead somewhere. Jerek's mind had began to wander to the woman he'd left upstairs. Was she dressed by now? Would she soon join him? Maybe she'd decided to take a bath. If Mr. Edwards would talk a little faster, maybe he'd have time to scrub her back. His fingers tapped against his knee.

"The guy said he didn't need any help, was going home, north a ways. Like I said, there's not too many of us over there, and I didn't recognize him. He made me wary, and with all the pilfering going on, I rowed to the edge, just out of sight and watched him. He kept an eye on me as well. He waited until he thought I was gone before he began to row again."

Jerek nodded, and gave his hand a slight wave,

encouraging the man to go on.

"Well, he rowed to the edge and followed the river to the back side of the coal barge to where there's a small island. There he landed his boat and went ashore. A few minutes later he came back, carrying something. He put it in his boat and rowed back out, not to the barge, but to the backside of the *Sultana.*" Mr. Edwards took a drink of his cider.

Now the man had Jerek's attention. "Mr. Edwards, it was dark and hazy that night, and the air was full of mist. How could you see all this?"

"Yes, Sir, it was. I've lived on this river all my life. When I say I followed him, believe me, I was close enough to smell him, but he never saw me. I guarantee that."

Jerek turned to the sound of the screen door opening.

"Excuse me," he said and stood to go escort his wife from the hotel. His heart pounded. His wife, in her dress of yellow, shined brighter than the sun in the sky, and brightened his world with more brilliance than the golden globe ever had. "Hello, my love." He held out one hand.

April placed hers in his and giggled as he raised it to his lips. "Hello," she said.

He wrapped her hand through the crook of his elbow and escorted her to the chairs. "Mr. Edwards, this is my wife, Mrs. Brinkley."

John Edwards stood and gave a slight bow, "Mrs. Brinkley."

"Mr. Edwards," she greeted.

Jerek sat down next to her, wrapped his hand around hers. "My dear, Mr. Edwards was just telling me he saw someone row a boat out to the coal barges the night of the explosion."

"Please go on, Mr. Edwards," April said.

"I had this to help me see. My granddad was a sea captain, he gave it to me." John Edwards took something from his breast pocket and held it forward.

Jerek took the instrument, a high quality, three band, mahogany, banded marine telescope. It was about eight inches long. He extended the tube until it reached over two feet. The draw action was smooth and silent. It had a sun/dew hood, a swivel shutter for the eyepiece, and a brass cap for the objective glass.

"This is a remarkably fine piece, Mr. Edwards."

"I know, take a look through it."

He held it to his eye. Objects were clearly magnified. He could count the number of buttons on the shirt of a man walking up the street two blocks away.

"I'm impressed," he handed the scope to April. "Take a look my dear."

April twisted in her chair and held the telescope to her eye. "Oh my, that is amazing." She took another look before handing the instrument back.

He drew the extensions closed and gave the telescope to Mr. Edwards. "You were saying you saw the man row to the side of the *Sultana*?"

"Yes, that's right. He looped a rope near the side wheel and climbed aboard. The boat was a flurry of activity with all the men lugging on coal. I noticed he was dressed as a Union soldier, which seemed unusual, until I lost him in the crowd of soldiers on the ship. A few minutes later, he lowered himself over the edge, untied his boat, and rowed back to Memphis."

Jerek let questions filter through his mind for a few moments. "You said you told the commission all this?"

The man nodded. "But there's more," he said.

"Do tell," Jerek encouraged.

"Well, the whole scene kind of bothered me. It kept replaying in my mind. So the following afternoon, I rowed back out to the island." John furrowed his brows. "That's when I learned about the *Sultana*, boats were all over, looking for survivors. I talked with a couple men, then went onto the island and found a cave. Several crates were hid way in the back. When I opened one, I found what looked like a lump of coal. Each box held one. After further inspection, I discovered they weren't lumps of coal, but coal torpedoes."

"And," Jerek leaned forward.

"The next day, I came to town, talked with a few more folks about the accident, then went to the Court House to talk with the General. I told him about the cave, and he had me take a few men out there to see what I'd found." John shrugged his shoulders. "They took the boxes, but didn't say anything about it yesterday. I was sure they would ask me to testify. Especially since they made me swear to secrecy after showing the soldiers the torpedoes."

"How many did you find?" he asked.

"Ten," John said as he stood. Walking toward the porch steps he added, "The army took eight of them." He walked down the steps and picked up a small, wooden crate. "I had hid two others in the woods." Carrying the box up the steps, he said, "One is still there. This morning I decided to bring this one to you. Maybe it'll help you and Mr. Pinkerton find the saboteurs." John set the box on the floor at Jerek's feet.

"Thank you, Mr. Edwards. You know Mr. Pinkerton?" he asked.

"Nope, but I heard you introduce him to your wife yesterday. I know you called him E. J. Allan, but everyone knows he's really Allan Pinkerton. It was in the paper."

"It was?"

"Yeah, when he wasn't around when the

President was shot, the paper said it was because he was off doing undercover work as E. J. Allan."

Jerek scratched at his head. The freedom of the press didn't always work as well as it should.

"I just want to do what's right and thought the right thing would be to go to the Army." He shook his head. "I figured it was luck when I saw you with Pinkerton yesterday." Edwards sat back down and took a long drink from his glass.

Jerek glanced to April, her gaze flashed from the box to him. He pulled his knife from inside his boot and pried out the short nails securing the crate. After lifting the lid, he brushed loose straw aside. Settled amongst the soft bed was what looked like a large chunk of coal, it was about four inches in diameter. He lifted it from the packaging to gently roll it from hand to hand. Black soot covered his fingers. He ran a hand over the lump. The bottom had a plug. Carefully, he unscrewed the threaded cap, and tipped the object over the box. Black powder poured out.

"That was a small one," John said as several ounces of gunpowder fell onto the straw.

"Jerek, what is it?" April asked.

He set the cast back onto the straw and wiped his fingers across his knees. "It's just as Mr. Edwards said, it's a coal torpedo. They made a cast iron mold, rolled it in bee's wax, then coal dust, and filled it with black powder. When thrown into the firebox of a ship, it would explode. At the very least, the explosion would damage the boiler. If the boiler was full of steam, it would explode, throwing hot coals and flames across the ship, injuring the crew, and start a fire that would eventually cause the ship to sink." He reached over to squeeze her hand while asking Edwards, "You say this is a small one?"

"Yeah, a couple the Army men took were almost twice that size," Edwards said.

"Thank you for bringing this one to me."

"Yesterday, at the hearing, they didn't mention the fact that Captain Postal was out at the wreck. He found a piece of shell near the starboard knee. It was blistered and weighed over a pound. He was quite upset that it never came up and took the story to the newspaper today. But I thought you might be able to do more than the papers could. They haven't made much out of the accident. Not with all the surrenders and the assassination news still filling up the pages," Edwards said.

Jerek nodded and turned the subject back to the torpedo. "This man that you saw, did you get a good look at him?"

He shook his head. "Not really, it was dark, and he must have rubbed soot all over his face. But one thing I did notice was that he had awfully crooked teeth. They kind of stuck out between his lips. Odd and hard to forget."

"Oh, my," April gasped.

Chapter Seventeen

Thoughts swarmed April's head. Could the man Mr. Edwards saw be Charles Deal? What would he have been doing with a coal torpedo? He'd had family on the *Sultana*; surely he couldn't have anything to do with the explosion. Jerek and Mr. Edwards rose to their feet and walked to the stairs. They spoke, but she didn't listen. Couldn't listen, the voices in her head were too loud for outside sounds to penetrate. Confusion racked her mind and fear settled into the pit of her stomach like rotten milk.

She lifted her gaze. Dark, sultry eyes beckoned her heart to skip a beat. Remembrances of how those eyes had devoured her every movement until wee hours of the morning sent warmth through her veins to mix with the appalling sensations. The conflicting emotions made thinking all the more difficult.

Jerek walked closer, his hands stretched out in invitation. She saw the question on his face before he whispered, "April?"

Part of her wanted to fly past him, to the safety of her room, where she could concentrate, and make it all add up. The other part of her wanted to collapse into his arms, where she felt safe, and...the haze began to clear... and loved.

She bolted to her feet, her arms went past his outstretched hands to slip beneath his elbows and wrap around the solid, massive torso. Tears pricked the back of her eyes as she pressed a cheek against his chest. The solid, steady beat of his heart filled her ear as his arms molded her to him.

He didn't speak, just stood in the heat of the Tennessee spring morning and held her tight. An invisible shield shrouded her. She closed her eyes, letting the stronghold infiltrate her mind and send the doubt and fear away.

After she released a deep sigh, Jerek asked, "Do you want to talk about it?"

"Talk about what?"

His hands went to her shoulders, with gentle persuasion, their bodies separated. She kept her gaze focused on the white buttons of his shirt. His thumb forced her chin up. "My dear wife when are you going to accept how much I love you?"

"Huh?" she asked.

"Last night I vowed to the All Mighty to love, honor, cherish, and protect you the rest of my living life. And I take that vow very seriously. There is nothing, nor anyone, that I will let harm you, but you have to let me know who I'm fighting."

"I don't know what you're talking about."

"Let's sit back down."

April looked between him and the chairs behind her. She didn't want him to fight anyone. She must have misunderstood something. Maybe the heat was getting to her again.

"Shall we sit?" he asked.

She nodded. Once settled on the chairs, he leaned forward, inviting her to listen.

"I know you have met a man named Charles Deal on more than one occasion."

She gasped. How did he know about Charles Deal?

"And I know he has convinced you to believe I'm Robert Louden." A twinkle of a smile twitched at the corners of his mouth as he encouraged, "Breathe April."

She did suck in a gulp of air. It was warm and heavy, and made her cough. When she gained control of her breathing, she looked at him.

"I don't care what the man said. All I care is that you believe me and not him." His hands cradle her cheeks. "I may have teased you, and I may have tried to surprise or protect you, but I have never lied to you. I promise, as long as I live, I will never lie to you. Do you understand that?"

She nodded.

"I am not Robert Louden. I was born Jerek Bartholomew Brinkley, have always been Jerek Bartholomew Brinkley, and will always be no other than Jerek Bartholomew Brinkley."

The way he scowled each time he said Bartholomew made the corners of her mouth curve up.

"Do you believe me?" he asked.

"Yes," she admitted honestly.

"Do you want to talk about it? About how Charles Deal convinced you to believe differently?"

She nodded and leaned closer. "Yes, but first I want to kiss my husband, Jerek Bartholomew Brinkley."

He smiled at her affectionately and pulled her face to his. The kiss was gentle and lingering, not the feverish, searching kind of the night before. But it was just as nerve awakening and emotionally fulfilling. Her sigh was muffled by one more precious taste before they separated.

He looked at her expectantly. "What did I do to make you believe I was Robert Louden?" He leaned forward and pressed the end of his nose to hers. "Whatever it was, I am sorry. So very sorry."

She shook her head. "It wasn't anything you did, yet at the same time it was everything. It's just so confusing." A lump formed in her throat. Her face pulled together in frustration.

"What's so confusing?" he encouraged.

"You, me, all of it." She leaned back and sighed.

"I love you, there's nothing confusing about that, is there?"

April sought to permanently put his fears to rest, but didn't know how. She didn't know how to respond to love. He deserved so much more than she had to offer.

"Can I tell you what I think?" he asked.

She nodded.

"I think you had lived your whole life in a tiny bubble before you made the trip to New Orleans. Everything had a place and a purpose, like your numbers. You had a set belief of men, all men. In your world they had all let you down, at one point or another, every man you knew had betrayed you. So you hated the whole lot of us, good, bad or indifferent. And when you found yourself falling in love with one, you couldn't believe it, or let it happen. You had to find betrayal." He arched one brow and asked, "What do you think?"

A frown tugged on her brows. What he said made perfect sense. Why hadn't she seen it? She'd recognized changes happening and had reacted to them, first by trying to help the men on the *Sultana*, then by volunteering at the hospital. When all along, all she really needed to do was respond to Jerek, the only man that really mattered. Instead, she'd decided to help all of the others, while believing the very worst of him.

She bit on her bottom lip. "Was it that obvious?"

Jerek nodded. "To me it was, but probably because I was falling in love." He shook his head. "No, not falling—fell. I've been in love with you since you pulled Willie out of his chair by the crown of his head at GeeGee's."

Her chin dropped. "You have?" She'd been so very nasty to her brother that day. Nobody could love a woman that spiteful.

"Yes, you struck me like a bolt of lightning that morning, and I've been on fire ever since," he said.

The passion oozing from his gaze made her cheeks burn.

Jerek guffawed and pressed his lips to the top of her head. "Charles Deal must have recognized your feelings of men and used it to fill that beautiful head full of tales. It seems to me that he reeled you in like a fish on a string."

Her face snapped up. "Oh, Jerek, I am so sorry. I can't believe I even thought that you could be one of the boat burners. Can you ever forgive me?" She squeezed her eyes shut, hoping he would forgive her, but fearing the worse.

"There's nothing to forgive. You didn't do anything to offend me, he did."

"Well, I wasn't very nice. And I certainly didn't defend you. Not as a wife should her husband. I will never act in such a manner again. I promise. Please believe me."

"Of course I believe you. Don't fret now. It's over. But I would like to know what he said."

"I don't really even remember. He came to the hospital looking for his brother, sister-in-law, and niece. He said they had been passengers on the *Sultana*. He came back the next day asking if we had any new patients. Then he asked if I had been on the ship and if I'd seen the boat burners."

"And?" Jerek questioned.

"And I told him no."

Jerek's look said he wanted more. She really didn't want to repeat the story, what if she started to believe it again. Her head snapped, as if her brain was shocked by its own thoughts. That wasn't possible. She'd never doubt him again.

"Go on," he said.

"He said the leader of the boat burners was in Memphis, said he knew the man from when he'd blown up another ship. He said the man had been shot in the shoulder while he was trying to escape, and that this time," she took a deep breath before continuing, "Jerek Brinkley wouldn't get away from him."

"What did you say?"

"I said I thought the leader of the boat burners was Robert Louden."

After her pause had lasted a few seconds, he asked, "And?"

"Mr. Deal said that Jerek Brinkley is a master of disguises and that Robert Louden is just one of your many aliases."

"And you believed him?"

"Well, he gave me a few more reasons."

"Oh, like what?"

"Well, that every time you blew up a ship, you got to sell another one."

"Anything else?"

"And that you like to seduce women. That your trail of broken hearts was longer than your trail of burnt ships."

A false laugh huffed from his chest. "What else? There has to be more."

"Well, just that you like to steal stuff from the women you seduced, like trinkets and such, and since Suzie's doll had just came up missing and you were the only one with a key to our room..." Guilt made the words trail off her tongue.

He clasped her hands. "April, I didn't steal Suzie's doll."

"I know."

"Nor did I steal your money."

"I know."

"And just for the record, I don't have a trail of

broken hearts, or a trail of burnt boats behind me, and I don't have any aliases. But I'm afraid, part of what he told you is true."

She cringed as her brows pulled into a frown. "What part?"

"I have sold many boats and have a bank account to prove it, but they have all been honest, out right sales. And I was on a boat that Robert Louden blew up a while back. It was near Cairo. The *Ruth*. The torpedo he put in her boiler caused an explosion that killed twenty-six men. She was carrying a Union payload, a couple million dollars of Union greenbacks." He shook his head, as if the memory hurt. "I spotted him slipping off the ship and shouted for the watchmen." A long sigh exhaled. "And yes, he did shoot me in the shoulder, just like he said."

"Did you catch him?" she asked.

Jerek shook his head "No, he's a sly one. It's almost as if he can make himself disappear. But he was arrested later."

"Bill said you testified against Louden."

"I did, as a witness for burning the *Ruth*. He was sentenced to hang, convicted of manslaughter, but it was overturned. He then escaped Union custody while they were transferring him to Alton Prison from Gratiot Street Prison in St. Louis. He slipped out of the handcuffs and over the edge of the boat."

She frowned, once again confused. "You said he shot you."

Jerek nodded.

"Did you mean Robert Louden or Charles Deal?"

Jerek nodded.

"Which?"

"I'm afraid, my dear wife, Charles Deal, is Robert Louden."

"No," she said.

"Yes," he said.

A shiver raced up her spine. "Oh, Jerek, how could I have been so foolish?"

"Don't feel bad. He's duped many. He's very good at what he does."

She squeezed his hand. "Jerek, he knows E. J. Allan is Allan Pinkerton."

"I'm sure he does. Just as Allan knows Charles Deal is Robert Louden."

She nodded. It was all so much to take in. And confusing...the more she knew the less she knew. Her gaze went to her husband—the one stable thing amongst the whole rocky tale. "Jerek, I really am sorry. I don't know what else to say."

He patted their clutched hands. "I honestly understand how he duped you. His story was believable, especially for a woman who had no reason to ever trust a man."

"But I should have trusted you. You haven't done anything but help me. You haven't betrayed me." She rubbed her temple. "It's like I have three people in my head. The old April who wants to hate everyone, the new April who wants everyone to like her, and this middle one, who..." she paused, searching for the right words. "Who really just wants you to love her."

Jerek stood, pulling her to stand with him. "I do love her, and I love the old April, and the new April, and every other April that may ever decide to come forward." His kiss left no doubt he told the truth.

She never imagined love could have so many features, or that it could be expressed in so many ways. Suddenly, his mouth left hers and his gaze searched her face, as if a terrible thought had just occurred to him.

"What? What is it?"

"I just realized we are standing on the front porch," he said

"Yeah?"

"Yeah," he repeated.

"And so?"

"And what I have in mind is better done without an audience."

Understanding sank in; his hands had been stroking her in wonderful ways. Hopefully no one had witnessed.

"Oh." She took a step backwards.

He stopped her. "That's not the answer."

"It's not?"

"No." Jerek took her hand and led her to the door. "No, it's not."

She caught his suggestion, and with a giggle, quickened her steps to lead him up the stairs. Her heart raced as fast as her feet, but after throwing the door to their room open, her twirl into his arms stopped short when she saw Scarlet throwing fresh sheets across the mattress.

"Oh, hello, I thought you were done in here this morning." The woman glanced from the bed to the stilled actions in the doorway.

Unable to think of anything to say, April looked to Jerek for help.

His hands wrapped around her waist from behind. His voice came from above her head. "That's all right, Scarlet, we were just going to freshen up, we can do it in the water closet."

"Do you want me to heat some water?" Scarlet stepped away from the bed.

"No, that's not necessary." Jerek pulled April backwards out the door.

"But I haven't carried any warm water up yet," Scarlet said again.

"That's okay. I've shaved with cold water before." Jerek pulled the door shut, and twisted to open the washroom door.

April glanced into the small, cluttered room.

Questioningly she raised her eyes.

"Trust me," he said and towed her into the room.

She did.

Later, fully satisfied with spent passion, the rumbling of his stomach reminded Jerek neither of them had eaten since the day before. He crossed the floor of their room, where they had crept to reassemble disheveled clothing, and lifted the brush from April's hand.

With gentle, long strokes, he ran the bristles through the treasured tresses. Watching with amazement as the golden strands cascaded down her back like a waterfall. The tips almost reached the waistband of her dress. He'd never tire of admiring the crowning glory.

He turned her around and ran the brush down the short, straight hair that stopped just above her eyes. Her gaze danced at him with contentment. At one time, he'd thought she'd be shy about lovemaking. He'd been dead wrong and found her eagerness and enthusiasm made the smallest of activities all the more exhilarating, stimulating, and rewarding.

He bent and kissed the tip of her pert nose. "I love you, April Brinkley."

She kissed his chin. "I love you, Jerek Brinkley."

"Are you getting hungry?"

"Yes. Are you?"

"Yes," he admitted at the same time his stomach growled loud enough for Ester to hear in the kitchen.

She giggled, took the hairbrush from his hands, and set it on the dresser top. "Did I ever thank you for this?" Her fingers ran along the silver handle.

"I'm sure you did."

"I don't think so. You bought me everything I would need while I was sleeping that first day."

"Either way, you're welcome," he said and took her hand. They walked to the door. "After lunch we can go shopping."

"What for?" she asked while waiting for him to close the door behind them.

"Whatever you need." He wrapped his arm around her shoulders and they started for the stairs.

"I don't need anything."

"Yesterday you said there were some things you needed, but I brought you straight home after lunch. We can go today." His hand rubbed her arm.

"Oh, well, I really didn't need anything yesterday either." Her voice had a funny tone to it.

He stopped their decent half way down the stairs. "Yesterday—"

"I know what I said yesterday," she interrupted, "but I really don't need anything. Now let's feed that empty can in your stomach."

He stalled her steps again. She sounded way too odd. "Then why did you tell me you did?"

Her face made an adorable grimace.

"April?" he tried to sound serious.

Her eyebrows lifted in question. "Honestly?"

"Yes, honestly."

"I was going to try and... Well, steal some money from you so when you got arrested I wouldn't be penniless."

He was speechless. His mouth opened, but no words emitted, his mind completely blank.

Her head and shoulders crouched. "I'm sorry."

"You really don't trust men do you?" he asked. "Did you honestly think I would leave you destitute in a strange city?"

She shrugged.

"April, I'm not going to be arrested, but beyond that, I'll never leave you impoverished. Come here." He turned around and tugged on her hand to follow him back up the stairs.

Once they were in the room, he went to the dresser, pulled open the drawer, and lifted out a new petticoat. He handed it to her. "I had Scarlet buy you another one, and had her sew pockets full of money in it after your coins were stolen. I thought paper currency would be less noticeable. They're Union dollars and more than enough to get you any where you need to go and live for sometime."

She turned the garment inside out to investigate the pockets. Her eyes blinked as tiny tears slipped from the corners.

He dried the droplets with his thumbs. "I've never pledged my love before, and I never plan on doing so again. You have it all. My world is in your hands. Please don't ever doubt my love, my strength, or my ability to take care of you. I would rather die than see you ill treated or neglected."

April didn't say a word. She replaced the petticoat in the drawer, then raised her arms to wrapped around his neck. Soft fingers pressed deep into his skin, encouraging his head to dip and meet the lips that rose.

The love she stated to feel for him flowed from the petite, sweet lips like wine. He drank it in, feeling it gush to his heart where it mingled with his life's blood. As his heart beat, the potent mixture pumped from the top of his head to the tip of his toes.

Lightheaded, as if he'd drank one too many glasses of smooth, southern whiskey, he picked her feet off the floor and twirled her around until they were both breathless.

Giggles and light-heartedness floated around the room. "You have filled my life with more than I ever dreamed," she said.

"As you have mine," he admitted, lowering her feet to the floor.

She patted his stomach. "Except for food, let's go have our lunch before you are so hungry you take a bite out of me."

"Mmm, delightful thought." He nipped at her neck.

"Yes it is." She grabbed his hand and pulled him to the door. "Come on, I don't want you to become so weak you can't fulfill your duties later."

"Never fear that my dear wife," he said. Hand in hand they walked down the stairs and into the kitchen.

Allan Pinkerton sat at the table. Trails of wetness covered Ester's cheeks. Scarlet stood behind the older woman, rubbing her shoulders, and Tim paced the floor along the far wall.

"Oh, Jerek, April, it's just the worst possible news," Ester said with a sob.

April started to tremble. He guided her forward and onto a chair. "What is? What's happened?" Jerek asked.

"We've had a villain living here. Here at our house!" Tim stated with grief.

"What? Who?" Jerek asked.

"Robert Louden! He's been living here!" Ester sobbed.

April's hands tightened. "Oh, Ester, no that was my mis—"

"What's this all about?" Jerek interrupted.

Ester spoke first, "Our Charlie is actually Robert Louden." She pushed a picture lying on the table in front of him.

April gasped. "That's Charles Deal."

Ester shook her head. "No, dear, it's Dale, Charles Dale. He's rented from us all these years."

"No, that's Robert Louden," Allan Pinkerton corrected both women.

Jerek felt every muscle tense. "Louden's been living right here, with us. How could I not have known that?"

"Jerek, I just made the discovery. He's one of the best spies ever. He's eluded us all for a long time,"

Allan said.

"What about your other renter? Abbie?"

Allan nodded his head. "Absalom Grimes."

"I thought he was shot trying to escape Gratiot Street prison," Jerek said.

"He was, and seriously injured. It ended his career as a mail carrier. Because of friends of his new wife's family, he did get a pardon from Lincoln earlier this year. He married the girl, her name is Lucy Glascock, and they still live in Missouri. He hasn't been involved with Louden for some time now. Louden must have been using his name as well." Allan turned to Ester and asked, "Did you ever see this Abbie?"

Ester pulled her brows together in thought. She turned to Scarlet, then Tim. They both shook their heads. "Now that you mention it, I don't think so. None of us did. Charlie rented the room for him."

"That's what I thought. At least that's what my investigative work has shown." Pinkerton looked at Jerek. "Louden's been stalking April."

"What?" His heart hit the back of his throat. "Where is he?"

"I don't know. Yet." Allan leaned back in his chair. "But he's still in Memphis and has been following her every move for the past several days."

"Why?" April asked.

Jerek ran a shaky finger over the little wrinkles that formed in the corner of her tension filled eyes. Apologizing seemed insignificant. His gaze begged her to forgive him. The smile of assurance she sent him still held worry.

"I can't say for sure, but I'd guess it's because he still holds a grudge against Jerek for testifying against him. It was well known he held a strong one against Mason for captaining the ship that carried Mary, his wife, to exile in Mississippi. He probably blames Jerek for being the reason he was in jail while it happened. Perhaps figures he could have stopped her court-martial if he hadn't been incarcerated at the same time," Pinkerton explained his assumptions.

"We gotta find him." Jerek clenched one hand into a fist. Fear had never been this painful. Every muscle stung as they tightened.

"I know, Jerek, and I will," Allan assured.

"Today! Now!"

"Jerek, calm down. You know how it works. Be patient. Nothing good comes from going off half-cocked."

"Damn it, Pinkerton, don't tell me to calm down. You need to get some more detectives out here. The whole damn agency if that's what it takes!" Steam threatened to explode from top of his head.

"Pinkerton?" Tim questioned. "Are you with the Pinkerton agency?"

"He is the Pinkerton agency," Jerek said. "Mr. Allan Pinkerton himself."

"I thought your name was E. J. Allan," Tim said.

"That is my undercover name."

"Which is no longer undercover to anyone," Jerek said.

"Thanks to Robert Louden. He leaked it to the Memphis press after Lincoln was shot. I told you, he is a very good spy," Allan explained.

"So what do we do to catch him?" Jerek asked.

"You don't leave April's side, and I will find Louden. I'm sure he knows I'm here, so I think," Pinkerton glanced at April, "you'll be safe here." His gaze went back to Jerek. "He is a dangerous man. Cool, calculating, resourceful, and bold."

"He's nothing more than a coward who's met his match if he thinks he's going to harm a hair on my wife's head!"

April jolted in her chair as his outburst echoed across the room. Jerek wrapped one arm around her shoulders to squeeze her close to his side. He nuzzled the hair over her ear, and whispered his apology. He'd never known fear could create this all-consuming terror racking his body.

Robert Louden may never pay for blowing up the *Sultana*, but the man would pay, with his life, if April were injured in anyway. The room grew heavy with a thick, deep silence, and he had to wonder if he'd made the vow aloud.

Chapter Eighteen

Only late that night, after they'd spent hours exploring new wonders and delights in their marriage bed, did some of his pent up tension dissolve. No harm would come to her. If it meant he'd never leave her side, ever, as long as they both shall live. Jerek had never imagined love could be like this, and he told her so while pulling her naked body closer, glorifying the way her soft skin kissed his from head to toe.

"Mmm, I feel like I'm floating on a cloud," she murmured in response.

"Then float off to sleep, my love." His fears, just below the surface made themselves known as he added, "Have no worries, I'm here."

"I know," she whispered and brushed her lips against his chest. "The devil himself wouldn't dare cross you. I must be the luckiest woman in the whole world."

"Naw." His lips went to her hair. "I'm the luckiest man."

The gentle fingertips combing through the hair on his chest slowly came to a halt and her breathing grew deep and lazy as she floated into slumber. He rested the back of his head deep into his pillow. His arms continued to cradle her, while his hands stroked skin softer than a baby.

Throughout the day, he'd kept her within arm's distance, while making the hotel a fortress. He'd sent Tim to the mercantile and replaced every door lock, double bolted both outside doors, and created window locks from stout boards. Robert Louden would play hell getting near her.

Not normally a praying man, he found his late night thoughts going to the heavens, asking for the strength, wit, and courage to keep her safe in all the days to come. Confident his request had been heard, he let a bliss-filled sleep float over his mind to consume his body.

A pounding noise and swift movement on the bed jolted April awake. A hint of moonlight allowed her to see Jerek shoving his feet into his pants.

"What? Who?" She tried to make her thick tongue work.

He stood to pull the trousers over his waist. "Stay there. I'll see who it is."

The racket on the door grew louder. "Damn it, Brinkley, open the door before I tear it down!" A man's voice bellowed.

Jerek grabbed the key and a pistol from the nightstand and walked across the room. "Who is it?" he asked.

The voice outside the door was so laced with anger she couldn't understand what it said. April sat upright and pulled the sheet over her bare breasts.

"Who?" Jerek repeated with a surprised tone.

Her eyes had adjusted to the darkness enough to notice Jerek shot her a smile before he unlatched the lock and pulled the door open with hurried movements.

A lit lamp in the hall cast an eerie light through the open space. A tall, lean, shadowy figure had a fist raised high. The clenched knuckles thrust forward and connected with her husband's jaw, forcing him to fly backwards.

"Jerek!" Tugging the sheet, she scampered toward the edge of the bed.

His head hit the floor with a loud thud.

"Damn it, Brinkley! Who the hell do you think you are taking advantage of my sister this way? Get up and fight like a man!" Willie stormed into the room.

Anger at her brother's actions made her blood run hot. "Willie, what are you doing?"

Willie reached down to grab Jerek as he tried to sit up.

"Don't touch him!" April screamed. She waved one index finger at her brother like it was a loaded gun. Her lips puckered as she growled, "Don't you dare touch him!" Still clutching the sheet, she grabbed her nightgown from the metal rail at the foot of the bed. Flipping the gown over her head and with quick, precise movements, she stuck her arms through the long sleeves. Alternating her hands, she kept her pretend weapon pointed at Willie.

Her feet slipped to the floor. As the material floated over her legs, she rushed to her husband's side and knelt down to touch his face.

"Jerek? Darling, are you all right?"

Jerek's stunned look floated from her to Willie and back again. A smile covered his face. "He's alive!"

She ran a hand over his jaw. "Yes, but are yo—" Her head snapped up. "Willie? Willie! You're alive!" She looked back down at Jerek. "He's alive!"

He nodded. She leaned over, kissed his lips, and then twisted to leap into her brother's arms. "Oh, I can't believe you're alive!" Making sure he wasn't a vision of her imagination, she touched his face and patted his arms.

"Yes I'm alive," Willie stated. His voice was still lined with anger and he set her aside. "But that bastard isn't going to be for long. Get to your feet,

Brinkley."

Excitement at seeing Willie quickly faded. "Willie! Stop it!" she insisted. "Why are you so angry with Jerek?"

"Why am I so angry at him? Why aren't you? The way he's been going around town, pretending to be married to you. And you, April, where's your decency? You were naked in bed with him."

The click of a gun being cocked echoed into the room. All eyes went to the doorway. Allan Pinkerton held a pistol toward Willie. "Don't move." One eye dashed about the room, as he asked, "What's going on Jerek?"

Jerek, now on his feet, pulled April from Willie's side. His body stepped between her and Willie. "Of course she was naked in my bed. She's my wife."

"Your pretend wife you mean," Willie insisted.

Allan Pinkerton stepped up beside Willie, still holding the firearm. "Who's this?" he asked.

April peeked around Jerek's shoulder when it was clear that neither of the two men, nose to nose, was going to answer. "My brother," she said.

"Your brother? From the *Sultana*?"

She nodded.

"No, she's not my pretend wife. She is my real wife," Jerek growled.

Allan Pinkerton tapped Jerek on the shoulder. "Ah, Jerek, from what I've learned, you two really aren't married."

"Exactly!" Willie agreed.

"Yes, we are," Jerek argued. He turned to Pinkerton. "We got married."

"When?" Willie and Allan asked simultaneously.

"Last night," Jerek answered.

"Last night?" Both of the other men said in unison again.

"Well, actually now it was the night before last. But either way, we are truly married." Jerek reached around and pulled April forward.

Her grin was from ear to ear. She couldn't help it. She loved the fact that she was married to him. Cocking her wrist, as she had always wanted to do, she flashed her left hand, decorated with the necktie wedding band, before their eyes.

"Oh," Willie said as his anger deflated.

"Really?" Allan questioned.

"Yes, really. You can put your gun away." Jerek said, and his hold around her shoulders tightened. His twinkling eyes made her smile brighter. His gaze then went to Willie. "I can't believe you're alive." His voice became more serious. "Where's Suzie?"

"Yes, oh, yes, where's Suzie?" April's heart skipped a beat. She couldn't wait to see the little girl. A moment of fear brushed across her chest as Willie looked from she to Jerek.

Willie's lips parted and a laugh expelled. "She's downstairs, with the hotel owner's wife. I didn't want her to see her daddy beat up Mr. Bink."

Jerek held his hand out to Willie, who took it. His other arm slipped from her shoulder to embrace Willie. Her brother copied his actions. After they patted each other's backs several times, the two men separated, and April leaped into Willie's arms for another hug.

While April slipped into her dressing gown, Jerek introduced Willie to Allan Pinkerton then they all hurried from the room and down the stairs.

It was one of the most glorious sights. The little blond head that bobbed and turned as the kitchen door flew open. "Auntie!" Suzie squealed.

"Suzie!" She rushed to the table and lifted the child into her arms. Tiny arms wrapped around her neck, and April hugged the tiny frame in her arms.

After a few moments, Suzie twisted her head and reached her arms out to the side. "Misser Bink!"

"Hi, Suzie Q," Jerek said as he took his own turn for a hug. After crushing the little girl to his chest, he lifted her high in the air and twirled her around. "How have you been? I've missed you."

She giggled with delight. "I missed Misser Bink."

Laughter floated around the room as Jerek handed her back to April. "How about Uncle Bink?" He gave a soft kiss first to Suzie's cheek and then to April's lips.

"Unkie Bink," Suzie nodded and giggled again.

April looked to her brother. "How, where?" She didn't know where to begin asking about their survival.

Willie scooped Suzie into his arms and pointed to the chairs, encouraging everyone to take a seat as he sat down to cradle Suzie on his lap.

April scooted her chair close to Jerek's, so his arm could wrap around her shoulders, and give the support she wanted as Willie told his story. It had to be horrifying, hers was. Everyone's had been.

Suzie's thumb went into her mouth as Willie began, "As soon as we hit the water, I knew I had to get Suzie out of it. It was so cold and swift." He lifted his gaze from his daughter to April and Jerek. "I don't know if you two noticed the coffin on the Hurricane deck, but all of sudden it floated past us. Whether someone threw it overboard, or if the blast did, I really don't know, but I hoisted Suzie into it, and climbed aboard. I grabbed a board from the water and started to paddle. The current was swift and tried to pull us down stream. I fought it because I thought if I got to calmer floodwaters I'd find land sooner." He closed his eyes and took a deep breath.

"It was hard going, and I had to fight men off. But any more weight would have made the coffin sink. All I could focus on was getting Suzie to dry land. Their pleas for help were anguishing.

Something I never want to hear again. Men sank all around me. Screams, curses, and gurgles." He paused again.

April reached over and laid her hand on his knee.

"I paddled for what felt like hours before I found land. But even there the water seemed to go on forever. Then much like an oasis in the desert, a hill appeared. As we rowed closer the sun began to rise, and I saw several buildings. I rowed as close as possible then carried Suzie to the house. Mrs. Hobbs lives there, and she welcomed us in. I don't know who the soldier was whose coffin became our raft nor do I know where his body ended up, but his death saved our lives. Of that there is no doubt."

Willie ran a hand over his daughter's curls. "Suzie became very ill, and for a bit I feared I might lose her, but Mrs. Hobbs nursed her into the best of health. This afternoon, a neighbor brought us by boat to Memphis, and we began to look for you two."

Suzie pulled her thumb out to say, "Daddy, doll?"

Willie's eyes searched the table. "Where did you put it, sweetheart?"

"Oh, I think it fell to the floor when her auntie came in," Scarlet said. She scooted her chair back and bent under the table. "Here, Suzie, here's your doll." The woman knelt beside Suzie and offered a friendly smile.

"Tank you," Suzie said and clutched the toy close to her chest.

Goosebumps tickled April's skin as she recognized the doll.

"Where did you find that?" Jerek's solid grasp covered both of her shoulders.

"The man who told us where you were staying, the same one who told me you two weren't, or were married," Willie said and shook his head as if he still tried to figure out if they really were married.

Everyone had questions at the same time.

"Did he tell you his name?" April asked.

"What else did he say?" Jerek wanted to know.

"Where did you see him?" Allan Pinkerton asked.

"What did he look like?" Tim Cox questioned.

Willie held his hand up. "Whoa, one at a time." All eyes were on him, waiting for his answers. He looked at April. "No, he didn't tell me his name, but said he'd met you at the hospital."

Willie's eyes squinted at Jerek and he said, "I think we need to talk in private, I have some questions about other things he told me." His gaze wandered to Allan Pinkerton, "He was down on the wharf, rowed in a skiff while I was asking about April and Jerek."

Looking at Tim Cox, he shook his head. "Nothing about him really stands out in my mind, other than he had really crooked teeth."

"Did they kind of stick out between his lips?" April asked.

"Yeah," Willie agreed, "Like he had too many teeth for his mouth." His gaze hopped around the table. "Why so many questions about this man?"

Allan Pinkerton answered, "Because he's Robert Louden, or Charles Deal."

"Dale. Charlie Dale," Ester corrected.

"The head of the boat burners," April supplied.

"The one responsible for blowing up the *Sultana*," Jerek finished.

"Huh?" Willie's mouth dropped open. "Robert Louden? He told me you were Robert Louden."

"Yeah, I'm sure he did," Jerek gave a frustrated sigh.

April sent him a teasing smile. "It's not really a bad name, if you don't know anything about the man."

He gave her an 'I will pay you back later' scowl. "Oh, really?"

The thought of receiving his payment made her giggle with delight. "Yeah, really."

His finger touched the tip of her nose as one eyebrow formed a perfect arch. She loved those brows, and her fingers itched to run over the fine, dark hairs, and then trail down his face to...

Willie cleared his throat, breaking the silent conversation she and Jerek were having. "I think there are a lot more questions, but I have a little girl who's exhausted. Perhaps we could resume this conversation in the morning."

"I think that's a very good suggestion," Jerek said without pulling his smoldering gaze from hers.

"Oh, yes," she sighed. "Morning will be a much better time to talk."

Jerek lifted her elbow so she rose at the same time he did. He turned to the table, "Ester, do you have a room ready for Willie and Suzie?"

"Yes, I've registered them in Abbie's old room." She turned to Willie. "Scarlet will show you the way."

"Good night, then," Jerek said as he pushed the door open for April to leave the room ahead of him.

She didn't bother wishing the others a good night. It would waste time. Time she wanted to spend in her husband's arms. She hitched the skirt of her gown to her knees and flew up the steps, followed closely by Jerek's swift moving feet.

****

Light shining in through the window gave the room a red hue. Jerek slipped from the bed and pulled the curtain aside. The sun rising over the Memphis horizon was blood red and surrounded by a colorless sky.

Red in the morning, sailor take warning, red at night, sailor's delight. He recalled the old boatman's

330

weather prediction. Not surprising, the heavy, hot days of late had to be the forefront to something. The curtain flipped into place as he crept back to the bed. It was early, and the house still in slumber.

Lounging on his side, one elbow propping his head, he took a handful of fine gold hair and let it flow over his fingers. The graceful strands occupied him for sometime before he gathered a cluster and let the soft ends brush across April's nose.

She grimaced and he repeated the action.

After the ends tickled her nose, cheeks, and chin, several times, her eyes opened. A sleepy smile mumbled, "Good morning."

"Yes, it is." He continued the tickling.

"Will you leave my hair alone?" Her voice was soft and husky.

"No," he answered with honesty.

She rubbed her eyes then peeked through her fingers. "Please tell me Willie and Suzie are really here. That it wasn't a dream."

"It wasn't a dream. They're here, safe and sound," he assured.

Her hands ran down her face until they clutched together below her chin. Her cheeks took on a reddish hue. "Oh, my," she sighed.

"What?"

"The way we ran from the room and up the stairs. Do you...Do you think they know what we came up here to...to do?"

Jerek laughed. "Since they've all been married, at one time or another, I'd say...yes!"

She rolled and buried her head in his pillow. "Oh."

He leaned and blew on blond strands. "Oh what?"

"Oh, what they must think of us."

"That we are married, that we are in love, that we enjoy each other, that we..." Her face had rolled out of the pillow, and he took the chance to kiss it, a quick, short peck, and then another. "Why do you care what they think? There's nothing to be ashamed of. We are married."

She kissed him back, tiny little kisses across his lips and chin. "You're right." Her arms rose over her head, and she stretched her body from head to toe, arching her back in a most delightful way. "Do you want to know what else?"

"What?" he asked.

"The only person I care what they think is you, because you are the only one that matters."

His hand snuck below the sheet to run across her stomach. "I only have the most delightful thoughts about you, too."

"I'm being serious."

"So am I." he answered.

"Think about it. Why should I care what others think? I'm no concern to them."

Her hand ran over her forehead. Jerek understood. Years of believing the scar was a horrible disfigurement had kept her behind closed doors.

"I agree completely." He leaned forward, brushed his lips over hers.

She stroked his cheek. "I'm not even going to care about all those women who ogle when you walk by."

"I've never noticed women ogling me."

"All the time. But I'm not going to worry what they think of me, because their thoughts are full of jealousy. I have what they want." Her smug smile filled his chest with joy.

"Does that mean I need to ignore the men who stare at your backside when you walk by?"

Her brows furrowed. "Men don't stare at my backside."

"Yes, they do. It's very enticing and quite

pretty." His hand roamed up beneath round, full breasts and down to firm pelvic bones, then inched over to massage her hip. "The way you roll these hips is quite spectacular."

"I don't roll my hips," she insisted.

"Ah, yes you do." He leaned down and covered her mouth. Though he enjoyed the conversation, he was ready for their petting to go to the next level.

Later, as they lay completely content, he said, "I hear people mingling about. We probably should join them."

"Yes, you're right," she said but made no effort to move. "Jerek?"

"Hmm," he answered.

"Yesterday morning you said it was time to go home," she said.

He waited for her to continue. When she didn't, he said, "Yes, I did."

"Where is home?"

"My home is where ever you are."

Her head tilted up, and a warm smile covered her face. "Thank you, for that. But when we leave, where are we going?"

"Where do you want to go?"

"Where ever you are."

"Thank you, for that." His fingers ran through her hair again. He couldn't stop them from searching out the silkiness, nor did he want to. "But, when we leave, where do you want to go? Our home can be anywhere you want it to be."

"Then I think I would like to see Ohio. I don't think I ever want to go back to Minnesota."

"We can go to Ohio. I'll be very proud to show you off to my family. But sweetheart, the girl that left Minnesota is gone. The woman lying in my arms is April Brinkley, a beautiful, intelligent, kind, and loving woman. One I am thrilled to be able to spend the rest of my life with. When and if we ever go to

Minnesota, you'll see it all in a different light. And it'll see you in a different light."

"How do you do that?"

"Do what?"

"Know exactly what I'm thinking, and find a way to make me understand it, and also make it all so wonderful?"

He thought for a moment. "You do the same for me," he said and pressed his finger to her lips as she shook her head. "Yes, you do, whether you realize it or not. Before I met you, I always had this feeling that something was missing. You've filled that void, and made my life whole and crystal clear." He leaned forward and kissed her. "Now, we better get out of this bed, before I decide we should skip breakfast again this morning."

April slipped from his side, giving him room to crawl from the bed. As he sat up and swung his feet around she said, "That wouldn't be all bad. I didn't mind missing breakfast."

She had to be the most splendid woman on earth. He turned and held out his hands for her to grasp. April took both of them, rose to her knees and scooted to the edge of the bed.

"Promise me you will always be so welcoming to my advances," he whispered.

"As long as you promise me you will always look at me the way you do. It makes me feel like I'm the most precious thing on earth."

"You are." She was his priceless treasure and evoked overwhelming emotions he couldn't even begin to describe. His throat tingled and his eyes stung. He pressed her naked body to his. It was several minutes before he lessoned the embrace and took a step back to ask, "Ready for breakfast?"

"If you insist," she sighed.

He laughed and lifted her from the bed. "I insist."

April twisted around and pulled her nightgown from the bedrail. "I'm going to run across the hall. I'll just be a few minutes."

"I won't go down without you." He stepped into his pants and walked over to unlock the door.

She slipped the gown over her head and drew on a wrapper before she joined him at the door. Jerek stepped out, inspected the hall, and then peered in the bathing chamber. He nodded to her and couldn't resist giving her backside a gentle smack as she walked by and into the room.

Her light laugh stayed with him as he reentered their room and dressed for the day. True to her word, she was back before he'd pulled on his boots and began to dress in the pink, ruffled dress. Jerek carried the pitcher across the hall and filled it from the bucket of warm water sitting inside the door. He returned to their room and set his shaving knife out in front of the mirror above the dresser.

He tilted sideways to get a better view of the bruise that had formed on his lower, right jaw.

A saucy voiced sounded across the room. "If you don't shave, it might not be as noticeable."

The humor on her face was infectious. "I don't mind showing battle scars, especially when I received them on your behalf."

"Maybe I don't like being reminded that it's my fault you got hurt," she said.

Was she serious? Her smile had faded. April finished tying her shoe, flipped her dress down, and rose. She began to walk toward him, rolling her hips extravagantly. He laughed aloud. "You are worth any injury I may ever obtain. Don't worry, I'm tough, and can take it."

"Oh, stand up and take it like a man?" she teased, closely repeating the words Willie had used the night before.

"Yeah, it builds my stamina so I can keep up

with you."

April rolled past him and picked her brush off the dresser top. "I am quite demanding aren't I?"

He covered his face with shaving soap before agreeing, "Quite."

Their playfulness followed them out the door and down the stairs to the kitchen where they consumed breakfast with the rest of the hotel's occupants. But a frown tugged at April's brows every time Jerek's eyes wandered to Scarlet as the woman served the food and cleared the table of debris afterwards.

It wasn't the same way he looked at her, but still the behavior caused the pit of her stomach to gurgle. The maid was quite attractive, if you liked long, black hair, almond-shaped eyes, and a trim, curvaceous, body.

Jerek leaned over and whispered in her ear, "I think Scarlet has taken a liking to your brother."

"What?" she mouthed, and turned to watch the woman wait on Willie and Suzie hand and foot. When her chores were complete Scarlet spread a quilt on the floor and invited Suzie to play with her while the conversation at the table deepened and caught April's attention.

"Willie, one thing about your arrival last night confuses me," Allan Pinkerton began. "If you met Robert Louden at the levee yesterday, why was it so late when you arrived at the hotel?"

"That has me confused too," Willie said.

Chapter Nineteen

Everyone gave Willie a dumbfounded look.

"We arrived at the wharf early in the evening, and asked around a bit before speaking with Mr. Louden. He told me April and Jerek were at the Cox Hotel, but he said the hotel was a few miles north of town. He offered to give us a ride, but then seemed to disappear. So we started walking and looking for a carriage. They are hard to find in Memphis."

"The sentries have taken over most of them," Tim explained.

"We were almost to where he said the hotel was when a man asked if we wanted a ride. When I told him where we were going, he said the Cox Hotel was back here, only a few blocks from the wharf. I thought maybe Louden had the name of the hotel wrong and asked the man to please take us to where I'd been instructed to go. But when we got there, it was nothing more than an abandoned house. The man's house was on the way back to town, so we stopped there, had a late supper with him and his wife, and then he gave us a ride here. Why would Louden have sent us way out there?"

All eyes went to Pinkerton. He shrugged his shoulders. "I'm sure he had a reason. Could you show the place to me? I'd like to have a look around," Allan asked.

"Sure, it's not hard to find, right off the road. Who is this man anyway?" Willie questioned.

April, along with the others in the room, again looked to Allan Pinkerton, knowing he had the most accurate information about Robert Louden.

He rubbed his long beard for a moment and then began. "Robert Louden is a member of an association that goes by several names, the boat burners, Minute Men, The Deacon's Men, the OAK-the Order of American Knights, as well as others, but they all fall under the Confederate Secret Service. Most of the men have been hand picked by Joseph Tucker, a lawyer, Methodist Deacon, St. Louis newspaper editor, and an extreme secessionist. Tucker has worked very closely with Jefferson Davis, and a host of other Confederate leaders."

He took a swallow of his coffee and continued, "The South has really given little attention to slavery as being the cause for the War. Their foundation is succession, the right of states self-government and independence. They call it the Preservation of the American Union. Tucker has preached this from the pulpit, in his paper, and everywhere in between. His men are mail runners, spies, arsonists, murderers, and thieves. They're funded through the Confederacy and have had a focus on the waterways of the interior United States. But we also know it was his clan that set fire to the Colt Pistol and Gun factory in Hartford, Connecticut. Tucker was the man who introduced the coal torpedo, and the landmine to Jefferson Davis."

April was astonished by the extensiveness of Allan's knowledge and the complexities of the war. It was so much more than battlefields full of men with guns killing each other. Before her trip South, her awareness of the war had been little more than hearsay and a few newspaper articles she'd read.

She turned to Jerek. "Did you show him what Mr. Edwards brought over?"

He nodded while Allan Pinkerton answered aloud, "Yes, April, Jerek gave me the coal torpedo. One exactly like it was found in Jefferson Davis' office after he evacuated Richmond. Ironically enough, the Confederate Secretary of State, Judah Benjamin, burned all of the official papers of the Confederate Secret Service Agency, but left the torpedo behind, as well as several other interesting weapons and inventions."

"Oh," she said.

"The reason I was able to respond to Jerek's wire so quickly is because I was already in Tennessee. I'd been dispatched to help apprehend Davis. He fled from Richmond before its fall. The Rebel president without a capital has been on the run for several weeks now, and he's on the top of my list. That list also includes Joseph Tucker, who has now escaped to Bermuda and is untouchable for the time being. You see, Robert Louden is not the head of the boat burners, nor is Joseph Tucker."

She frowned. "Who is?"

"The true leader of the Secret Service and all their activities is Jefferson Davis. In some opinions the war has been Davis' attempt to have his own country. He's a dictator, and greedy. His greed has made him a powerful man, one who's tried to convince others they want the same as he does. He doesn't want a country that works for the best of all its citizens, he wants a country he can control. Be the king of his very own kingdom and answer to no one. Many believe he is the true origin behind this civil war."

"Jerek summoned you to help with the *Sultana* explosion?" Willie asked after the room sat in silence for a few minutes.

"Yes and no." Allan looked to Jerek.

Jerek gave a brief nod.

"Our agency has many civilians who report suspicious activities, keeping us informed at all times. Jerek has been one of our regular contacts for several years."

"You're a spy?" April asked with disbelief.

"No, I'm not a spy. I don't work for the agency. I just relay information. It's completely different." His eyes implored her to believe him.

She did. Her fingers threaded through his with a reassuring squeeze.

"Robert Louden is one of the most elusive of the boat burners. He was recruited by his partner Ab Grimes to be a mail runner, but quickly took on a higher role. Grimes specialized in carrying letters between the troops and their families, but Louden became an official mail runner. He ran official, secret orders, strategic decisions, payouts, and reports. He's been caught a couple times and jailed twice. The one time he was unable to escape before trial, his prestige within the Secret Service led to his conviction being overturned. However, his wife was convicted and exiled. Mason captained the ship that carried her out of St. Louis, and it has been a burr under Louden's saddle ever since. His love of explosives and undercover work lured him into including blowing up steamships besides his other duties."

"Oh," Ester sighed, "I could never have believed our Charlie was capable of such deeds."

"Your Charlie?" Willie looked confused.

"Louden has many aliases including Charles Deal, and Charlie Dale. He's rented a room at their hotel for several years. Giving him a place to stay whenever needed here in Memphis." Allan looked to Ester. "Please know, Mrs. Cox, you aren't the only place. Mail runners have had rooms such as yours on contract across the nation."

Tim patted his wife's shoulders.

Allan continued, "James Baker from Minnesota has become the new Provost Marshall of the Department of Missouri. He's turned the heat up on Tucker's boat burners and is unraveling the organization. Ten have already been arrested and two are talking, leading to more arrests everyday. When Jerek wired me about the *Sultana*, I thought it could be our chance to stop Louden. Robert knows the death penalty is hanging over his head if he is ever captured again."

"Will the war ever truly be over?" April asked aloud.

"I'm afraid, not for many, many years yet," Jerek answered with a sigh.

Apprehension tickled her spine, would she have to live with Robert Louden stalking her for years? She glanced at Jerek.

Jerek wished he could assure her everything would soon be over, but his own fears prevented it from happening. Louden was too smooth and had proven his abilities to elude captivity. Moving to Ohio wouldn't stop the man's pursuit. He was at a loss and very worried.

Willie again was the one to break the silence. "What can we do to help you capture him?"

"As I said, I want to see this farm he sent you to, it might be insightful," Pinkerton answered.

"If you're gonna ride out there, you better do it quick. There's a mighty storm a brewing," Tim said.

"I noticed that too," Jerek said.

"I'll go procure a couple more horses." Pinkerton stood, turned to Jerek and asked, "You riding with us?"

He was torn, he wanted to investigate the farm, but he didn't want to leave April unprotected. Tension pulled at the muscles on his face and neck. April's hand settled on his bicep.

"You should go with them," she said.

He shook his head. "I don't want to leave you here alone."

"I know but I won't be alone. Tim, Ester, Scarlet, and Suzie will be here with me."

The list of protectors didn't sound too strong.

"You've secured this building, no one can get in. If it will make you feel better, I promise to lock myself in our room and not open the door to anyone but you."

"We'll make it a quick trip, Jerek," Pinkerton said.

April looked at Willie, then back to Jerek. "Please go with them." Silently, she asked him to protect her brother.

Apprehension made his stomach roll. "Promise you won't leave this house for anything."

"Of course I won't leave the house. Don't worry, I'll be here when you return," she said with sincerity.

"I'll be back with the horses in a few minutes. Hopefully the rain will hold out for a couple of hours," Pinkerton said and slipped out the back door.

****

A clap of thunder brought April upright on the bed. Her movement caused Suzie to roll over. A tiny thumb poked into the child's mouth as she resumed her afternoon nap. Cautiously, April slipped from the bed and walked to the window.

The sky was a dark greenish hue, filled with heavy, low clouds. Large raindrops began to fall and splatter against the glass. She picked the key off the table, and exited the room. April made her way down the dim hall and stairs to the kitchen.

"Hi," Ester said.

"Are they back yet?" she asked.

"No, but they should be before long. Do you want something to drink?" Ester sat at the table. Long

342

rings of potato peels fell as she rolled a knife around the vegetable.

"No, thank you." She pulled out a chair.

"Suzie still sleeping?"

"Yes. Where are Tim and Scarlet?"

"Tim went out to close up the henhouse before the rain hits, and Scarlet just went up to her room for some lace." Ester pointed to a mound of blue material lying on the table. "She's sewing a new dress for Suzie."

April reached over and picked up the cloth. The sleeves had yet to be put on, but a wide skirt had been gathered with perfect stitches and sewn to the bodice. "This is very nice. Suzie will look adorable in it," she admitted.

"Scarlet does a wonderful job, and she has taken quite a liking to your niece." Ester let out a deep sigh. "She lost a baby a few years ago."

"Oh, I'm sorry Ester. What happened?"

Ester shook her head. "The little tyke was born too soon. He was too little to survive. Scarlet is such a good girl. I tell her she needs to find a new man, and move on, but she won't. Insists on staying here to help me and Papa."

April laid the material down as Scarlet came through the door on the far side of the kitchen.

"Hello, April. Is Suzie still sleeping?" the woman asked.

"Yes, she's in my room. She's going to love the dress you're making."

"The material was just lying around, so I thought I'd put it to good use this stormy afternoon. Have you looked outside? It's as dark as night." Scarlet had no sooner said the words than a loud crack vibrated the house and lightning lit up the room.

"I better go check on Suzie." She scurried out of the room and up the stairs. The child was still sleeping, but she didn't want to leave her, nor stay upstairs. Rain pounded on the window and echoed off the ceiling. She gathered Suzie in her arms and returned to the kitchen.

Scarlet rose from her chair and scooped the quilt from this morning off a neighboring chair. She spread it out in the corner of the room.

"Here, April, lay her down here."

April did so, and Suzie continued sleeping. The racket of the storm filled the room, making her wonder how the child could sleep through it. She turned around to see Ester peeking out the back door and moved closer.

"I don't see Tim anywhere. He should have been back in by now," Ester said.

She peered over the other woman's head. The rain pouring off the roof of the back porch was too thick to see through. The wind caught it every few seconds and sent it swirling, the gusts gave a quick glimpse of the small buildings in the back yard, a chicken coop, out house, and small barn that housed a milk cow.

"Maybe he's in the barn, waiting for the rain to slow," she suggested.

"You're probably right," Ester said and pushed the door shut. A loud thud hit the door as it snapped close. Ester pulled it open again to find a chair lying on the porch floor. "The wind must have blown it over." She stepped out. "Oh my! April, Scarlet come help me. Tim must be hurt. He's lying on the ground."

Followed closely by Scarlet, April hurried through the doorway and beyond the water falling off the roof. Tim laid face down on the ground in front of the barn door. Simultaneously, she and Scarlet bounded off the porch and sprinted across the yard to where Ester tugged on his arms.

The torrential rain soaked her dress in a matter

of seconds, water streamed down her face, and into her eyes. Blinking didn't help. Everything was a wet blur. The wind whipped the water into her mouth, making talking almost impossible.

"Help me get him in the house!" Ester screamed above the roar of the storm. Lightning flashing overhead and rumbling thunder heightened Ester's urgency. "Hurry, girls, hurry!"

The older woman had one arm wrapped around her husband's shoulder and tried to lift and pull his body toward the house. Scarlet grabbed the other arm, leaving April to wonder what she should do to help. She reached out and tried to pull on the same arm as Scarlet, but there wasn't enough room.

Over her shoulder, Scarlet shouted, "Go hold the door open."

April turned to run ahead, but something caught one foot. Mud splattered into her eyes as the wind swooshed from her lungs. Thick muck oozed beneath her dress, and she gasped for air. When the tight pain in her chest lessened, she raised her torso. The rain washed the mud from her eyes and mouth, but it hadn't let up. It was impossible to see what tripped her. Pushing with her arms, she pulled her legs forward to stand, but again, something caught one ankle and pulled her back down.

She kicked and tried again. This time it tugged and began to tow her backwards. Mud slipped between her fingers as she tried to dig them into the ground. A strong grip grabbed her other leg and stifled her frantic kicks. Her hipbones smacked the ground as she fought the hold. Raging weather carried screams away as soon as they left her throat. Through the downpour Scarlet and Ester dragged Tim further and further away.

She twisted, and tried to flay the rain from her face. An eerie shape crouched over her legs, pulling her toward the barn. Menacing eyes met hers, and a mouth bared crooked teeth as an evil smile formed on the man's face. Fear raced up her throat. She screamed, tossing her body to and fro. Bucking like a mule, her legs flipped about, but his hold couldn't be broken.

Robert Louden towed her past the barn, then grabbed the back of her dress and jerked her to her feet. Searching for air, she tore at the material crushing her windpipe. As soon as the pressure released, both of her wrists were grabbed with brutal force and twisted behind her back.

She screamed as pain ripped across her shoulders. Her feet lashed out to kick. She arched her back trying to relieve the strain. The tight hold propelled her through an open gate and into in alleyway. She dug her feet into the ground, but he just pushed harder.

She fought each step, stumbling in deep puddles of water as her torso twisted and spun. His hands painfully forced her forward. The fierce wind poured rain into her mouth and nose with each scream.

Another loud crack shook the air. The sky lit with a flash, and tiny bits of hail began to pelt down. The tiny chunks quickly turned into larger stones of ice, and slapped with enough force to make welts form beneath her clothes. She tucked her chin to her chest, trying to avoid the sharp, piercing stones of ice.

Louden twisted her arms tighter, forcing her steps to quicken. She jerked her body backwards, to upset his progress, but it held no advantage. He shoved his chest against her back, jolting her forward. The hail continued to painfully hammer down as the boat burner pushed her down the street.

Now and again overhangs from buildings would block the storm for short distances before he'd force her to turn down a different street or alley. Completely lost, unable to find anything familiar about a building or road, she dug her toes into deep mud.

Louden grabbed her waist with one hand and lifted her feet from the ground. Pain ripped up her confined arms. She kicked her feet in the air in front of them. Water filled her mouth. She spat it out and tried to scream again. Lightning flashed and thunder vibrated the air.

Her anger bubbled and made any fear she had of Robert Louden dissolve. When he let loose, she'd pull the hair right out of his head. He was nothing more than an intolerable bully, forcing her through a torrential thunderstorm, dragging her through the mud, and ruining one of her favorite dresses. The man would pay for his behavior.

Tall buildings on both sides blocked some of the downpour, and the hail slowly played itself out as he carried her past door after door.

"Help!" she yelled. "It's a boat burner!" The storm still carried the words away but she continued to scream and spat water.

He let go of her waist to slap a hand over her mouth while still holding her hands behind her back with his other one. She bit at the skin.

Louden pulled his hand away from her mouth and tightened his hold on her wrists. Painfully, he directed her to a set of steep steps with an unnecessary thrust. In reaction, she kicked backwards and connected with his right shin. His steps faltered, but not enough to break his grasp. With a mumbled curse, he drove her up the steps at an unruly speed.

At the landing, he threw the door open. She kicked, twisted, and screamed against his insistence of entering the room. His strength overrode hers. Before she knew it, he released his hold and her body flew into the room. A wood framed bed sat against the far wall.

She thrust her hands forward and stiffened her arms as her palms hit the mattress. Using the mattress as a springboard, she pushed backwards and flipped around to land on her feet.

"You insufferable fool!" She slapped her hands on her hips as the door slammed shut. "Who do you think you are? Look at my dress, it's ruined!"

Robert Louden's head snapped up. His look of shock was quick, before his eyes narrowed, and he pulled a sopping hat from his head.

"You filthy little man! You will be buying me a new one."

"What?" he said as if confused.

"My dress! It's ruined!" She held the skirt wide for him to see the damage. Mud streaked the once pristine outfit. "Completely ruined." She dropped the material and held out her forearms. "And look at that, I do have welts from the hail!"

Robert Louden stomped across the room. With one hand he pushed her bangs aside.

Her arm flew up shoving his hand aside. "What do you think you're doing?" she demanded.

"Just checking to make sure I had the right woman. I can tell by that nasty scar you're the April I was looking for."

"Mr. Louden that is a very rude thing to say."

His eyes widened. "It's quite despicable."

She took a deep breath and rolled her eyes. "It's hardly noticeable. Besides, it's mine, not yours, and I really don't care what you think about it."

"Yes, you do."

"No, I don't."

Robert Louden folded his arms across his chest. "Yes, you do!"

As quick as a snake, she shot her hand out and grabbed a handful of his hair. "No, I don't!"

"Ow!" He grabbed her wrist, but she refused to let loose the wet mass. The harder he tugged on her arm, the harder she tugged on his hair. She sidestepped, hoping to twist off his hold. He followed like a puppy chasing its tail.

Hair began to break off beneath her fingers. She repositioned the grasp and pulled on the roots. He screamed and bent his head toward the floor. With his other hand he tired to grab her body. His arms weren't quite long enough; fingertips barely brushed against her skirt as she twisted and turned, dragging him about by his hair.

With a painful wrench one of his hands caught a handful of her hair. "Ouch! You beast! Let go of my hair!" she screeched.

Deep breathing echoed the room as they stood, bent head to bent head, playing tug of war with each other's hair.

"You let go of mine first!" he growled.

"No, you let go of mine first!"

"Ow! Damn it, woman," he yelled and tried to push her forward with his head.

Determination gave her strength. Her feet dug into the floor like cat claws. She twisted the direction of her hand, forcing his neck to tilt sideways. A few scraggly whiskers hung on his chin. Glue! He must have used glue to cover his face and the rain had washed it away.

"You let go first," she screamed. Her scalp was on fire, but she'd never give in to the intolerant bully. She gave another hard jerk, hoping his scalp hurt as bad as hers did.

"Ouch!" He stomped his feet like an angry child. "All right, we'll let go at the same time. On the count of three."

"I'll do the counting."

"Fine, you do the counting," he growled.

"One..." she stretched her back, trying to find a bit more space between them just in case he leaped forward. "Two..." What was she going to do next?

"Three!" His hand fell from her head, and with one last snap to his hair, she pulled her hand from his head then jumped forward and kicked him in the kneecap.

"Ow!" he cried.

She shook her foot against the sharp pain in her big toe.

He hopped about the room on one leg until he hit the door. His back slithered down the wood as he rubbed his leg with one hand while the other massaged his head.

April took a moment to pluck strings of dark hair from between her fingers. Then she checked her own scalp, trying to feel if she still had any hair in the area he'd pulled on.

His gaze rose to her. "You know, Miss, er, April, I just kidnapped you. Don't you think you should be less concerned about your appearance, and more concerned about your safety?"

Chapter Twenty

Sitting on the floor, looking like an injured child, April had to wonder why she'd ever been afraid of the man.

"You didn't kidnap me."

"I didn't?"

"No, I'm not a 'kid'," she said. A quick surveillance of the room didn't offer a weapon of any kind. She'd have to talk her way out.

"Well then I abducted you."

"Why?" she asked.

"Huh?"

"Why? Why would you want to abduct me? I've never done anything to you. I scarcely know you."

"It's not you I'm really after. Just figured I'd settle a score while in town," he didn't make a move to rise.

"With who?"

"Jerek Brinkley!"

He said the name like it gave him a bad taste in his mouth. She gritted her teeth. "He's never done anything to you either!"

"Yes he did!"

"What? What did he do to you? Testified against you in a court of law? That was his duty as a citizen. Jerek just happened to be the one who saw you blow up the *Ruth*. You did blow up the ship, didn't you?"

His mouth opened.

"Tell the truth, you did blow up the *Ruth*, didn't you?" She slapped her hands onto her hips and tapped a toe on the floor.

"Yes."

"So it wasn't Jerek's fault that you were found guilty. You were guilty!" she snapped. "Nor can you blame Captain Mason that his ship took your poor wife into exile. That too was your fault. How could you do that to your wife? Encourage her to get mixed up with your misdeeds. That's despicable. I hope if she sees you again, she takes a willow switch to your backside. That's what I would do." The man was loathsome. "And, think of your poor little girls! That's your fault too! Trust me, Mr. Louden, being an orphan is no life for a child. You should be ashamed of yourself!"

"I had no choice!" His face instantly became red.

She took a breath and continued her rant, "What is it with you men? Blaming everything that happens on someone else? Never taking responsibility for your own actions. Life is what we make it, Mr. Louden, and you chose to ruin it for everyone around you. Even Tim and Ester. What right did you have to pull them into this mess of a war?" She took another deep breath, and squinted. "Think of your little girls. You have two of them, right?"

His shoulders slumped as he nodded.

Good thing she'd listened so closely to Rowberry and Pinkerton's information. "Where are they now?" One finger pointed at him. "Not with their mama or papa, that's for sure, Your poor wife is down in Mississippi, full of worry as to what's happened to her babies, and you're here, abducting innocent women." Pacing the floor, she shook her head. "Despicable, I tell you, absolutely appalling. And for what? What are you hoping to gain from all your misdeeds? A life in prison? Death? What? I just don't understand how you men can claim to have a brain."

Confusion covered the man's face. "Freedom," he said, but the word sounded more like a question than a statement.

"Freedom?" she screeched. "Freedom for whom? Not the slaves. You were fighting for the South!"

He slapped the floor beside him. "Freedom for the states to govern themselves!"

She couldn't let him find potency in his tutored statement. "Oh what a pile of gobbledygook! Who told you that? Ab Grimes? Joseph Tucker? No, I bet it was Jefferson Davis himself. You do know he's escaped Richmond, don't you? What a coward that man is, hiding in the woods like a polecat. Why on earth would you believe the likes of him? Has he ever put his life in danger fighting for the 'cause'? I bet not! He's the type that sits on his throne, ordering others to obey his every word. It's not freedom he wants. It's power. He wants to be the ruler of his own little country full of his own little soldiers."

He opened his mouth.

She wiggled a finger in front of his face. "And you are nothing more than one of his little toy soldiers."

He rubbed his forehead. "Will you shut up? I have to think for a minute."

"No, I won't shut up, and you should have done some serious thinking before you ever got yourself hooked up with the Confederate Secret Service."

"How do you know all this?"

"Everybody knows who you are. Robert Louden, Charles Deal, Charlie Dale, and all the other names you call yourself." Her throat had become raw from shouting. "Oh, and by the way, the rain washed the glue off your face."

His hand went to his cheeks and chin, patting

and rubbing.

"You're disguises haven't been that good. You really don't think you could go around blowing up steamers and no one would know, do you?" Another thought occurred to her. "And those nasty torpedoes! Did you know the one Jefferson Davis left in his office had your name on it?"

"What?" His face became distorted with disbelief.

"Oh, yes, that man won't take blame for anything either. And Joseph Tucker, you do know he's already in Bermuda. Oh, how the rats jump when the ship is sinking," she said with a sigh.

"Sit down and shut up!" he shouted.

"Don't yell at me!" she shouted back.

"Why not? You've been yelling at me for the last half hour. It's making my head hurt."

"I have a right to yell. You abducted me!"

He leaped to his feet. "That's right! I abducted you. And I set a trap for your Mr. Brinkley. By now he's probably been blown into smithereens."

A knife shot through her heart. She flipped around so Louden couldn't see the pain in her face. "I doubt it, he wasn't going anywhere near a steamer."

"No, but I planted landmines around an abandoned farm. And that's where he was going."

She pivoted. "Landmines?"

Louden shrugged his wet coat off and threw it on the floor. "Oh, something you don't know about? They are just like the torpedoes, but have a friction primer on the plug. I buried them a few inches under the dirt, so when someone steps on one. Boom!" His arms thrust in the air.

Fists formed at her sides. Jerek hadn't wanted to go, and she'd made him. She'd put his life in danger. A thought crossed her mind. She needed a gambling face. Couldn't let the man see her true feelings.

He rambled on, "They were very successful until Sherman started his march. The bastard ordered Confederate prisoners to march ahead of his men. After so many Southern boys were killed, Davis ordered the troops to stop using them."

She searched her mind for something to use and gain the upper ground again. "Well, of course Davis would order them out of use. He was losing soldiers a hundred at a time and couldn't afford to lose any extras. Who would fight for his cause? If all you Southern boys died, he wouldn't have any one to rule over."

"Shut up! You don't know Jefferson Davis. He went to West Point. He has the heart of a soldier."

"And the brain of a duck!" She threw her arms in the air. "His dictatorship has done nothing but prolong a war that never should have started."

Louden sneered.

She pointed a finger at him. "What has this war done for you? Destroyed your family?" Mocking his sneer, she continued, "Ruined your life? I don't even want to think how it's damaged your girls."

"You don't know what you're talking about," he huffed.

She gave him an honest look. "I was orphaned, Mr. Louden, not by the war, but orphaned nonetheless. It's not an easy life. And I still bear a grudge against my father for allowing it to happen."

"Your father?" His voice quivered. "Y-you do?"

"Yes, there is one job parents have." She stepped forward, pointing her finger at his nose. "And that is to protect their children."

He opened his mouth, but didn't speak.

She stepped back and let out a deep sigh. "I know it wasn't all his fault, but he was my Daddy and should have protected me. He should never have let it happen." She shook her head. "Just like you.

You should never have put the war before your little girls. You've gambled their lives away."

He wiped a hand across his eyes.

A deep feeling of regret entered her heart. "Up until now, all of your actions have been acts of war. But if one of your landmines," she paused to swallow, "kills someone. It will be murder. The war is over and there's no one left to protect you." She sighed. "Or your daughters from finding out their daddy is a gambler of the worst kind. A cold blooded murder."

His Adam's apple quivered in his throat. "I didn't have a choice. I was trying to protect them, keep them safe. I just wanted them to have a better life than I had."

"Yes, well, I'm afraid you may have played your last hand." She took a step closer to whisper, "And lost."

****

The storm had moved on, leaving mud, broken trees, and debris to cover the streets of Memphis. Like a bull seeing red, Jerek charged down the alley, searching for stairs that led to second floors. The abandoned farm had been a wasted trip, but it had given Louden the opportunity to get to April. His hands throbbed to tear the man apart.

Hail the size of silver dollars had pelted against the hotel when he'd ran up the steps, expecting to find the welcoming arms of his wife. The falling stones hadn't hampered his launch back out the door in search of her.

Pinkerton gave several suggestions as to where Louden may have taken her, and so far none of them had been accurate. But something told him, he'd find her in the upper room of a pub on Beale Street. Which pub, he didn't know, but he'd check every one until he found her.

A staircase loomed before him. He grabbed the

rail and bounded up the stairs, barely touching a step now and again. His pace didn't slow at the landing. He kicked the door. It flew from its hinges, and Jerek launched into the room, ready to attack.

His feet skid to halt, and he blinked in disbelief.

It was as if he'd been transported back in time, to the night he'd found Eloise and Jared in her father's barn.

His heart sank to the pit of his stomach.

April and Robert Louden stood in the middle of the room, locked in each other's arms. She didn't struggle or try to fight the embrace. Her arms were willingly wrapped around the man. He blinked, hoping the vision would change.

It didn't.

The bang of the door crashing to the floor interrupted the tryst. Startled, the couple separated and turned to gap at him.

"Jerek!" she screeched, a second later her arms wrapped around his neck with such force he stumbled.

Tiny kisses flew over his neck, chin, and cheeks. His arms automatically wrapped around her, but his mind couldn't change paths this fast, the red haze was too thick. He'd believed in her, believed in their love. He bit his molars together. This time he wasn't going to walk away. He'd fight to the death for the woman he loved. He grabbed her shoulders, set her away from him. "What the hell is going on here?" He took a step forward. "You filthy bastard!"

"S-She—" Robert Louden's eyes widened.

"Jerek!" April jumped in front of him. Her arms went around his waist again. "Jerek!"

"Don't move!" Allan Pinkerton leaped through the door. His gun drawn, pointed at Louden.

Without any form of protest, Louden bent his elbows, raising his arms in surrender.

The soft lips pressing little kisses across his chin

and down his neck could no longer be ignored. Jerek cupped her cheeks, forcing her to stop. He peered into her face.

His mind whirled. The last few weeks raced before him. This wasn't the past. It was the present. It was April staring back at him, his wife, and she believed in him. Hell she'd even married him when she'd been told he was a boat burner.

The dancing blue eyes gazing at him were full of love and excitement. Her roaming hands settled on his cheeks. The last bits of haze lifted. He'd never doubt her love.

With hunger, he bent and devoured the sweet lips. He didn't have to fight for her. He already had her. His hands ran through golden tresses, wet with rain, and across a dress clinging like a second skin. The embrace consumed him, mind, body, and soul.

Someone tapped his shoulder, Jerek shrugged off the touch, refusing to end the rendezvous. The tap came again, followed by someone talking. When the voice wouldn't stop, he pulled his head up to glare at the speaker.

Allan Pinkerton said, "There'll be time for that later."

He started to protest, but April cupped his cheek. Her gaze assured there would be time later, plenty of time.

April turned to Allan and pointed at the gun. "You can put that away, Mr. Pinkerton." She turned to Louden. "Can't he, Robert?"

The boat burner shuffled his feet and nodded. "Yes, Ma'am."

Jerek tightened his arm around her shoulders. "April?"

"It's fine, dear. Mr. Louden is tired of running and hiding." She glanced to Allan. "Mr. Pinkerton, do you think if Robert helps you catch some of the other men you're pursuing, you could assist him in getting the charges against him cleared, so he can eventually be reunited with his wife and daughters?"

"Huh?" Pinkerton's questioning gaze danced around the room's occupants. "Well... probably."

"See?" April smiled at Louden. "It'll work out. I promise." A worried frown covered her face. "Jerek, is Mr. Cox all right?"

While Jerek searched his mind for a response, from the doorway Willie answered, "Yes, he's fine. He has a bump the size of a potato, but he'll be fine."

"Oh, thank heavens! And Ester, Scarlet, and Suzie, how did they fare the storm?"

"Fine, just fine," her brother answered.

"Well, then, shall we be on our way back to the hotel?" she asked.

"I'll take Louden over to headquarters, where he can't escape," Pinkerton stepped forward.

April jumped between the detective and the boat burner. She laid a hand on Pinkerton's forearm. "That really won't be necessary. Mr. Louden can come back to the hotel with us. He won't try to escape. He's ready for the war to be over. Isn't that right, Robert?"

Louden let out a shy cough. "Yes, Ma'am."

Pinkerton gave Jerek a questioning look.

Jerek, feeling as confused as Pinkerton looked, shrugged his shoulders.

"All right, Ma'am," Allan said. He looped his arm through one of Louden's and Willie took the other. As they walked to the door, the detective pulled a set of handcuffs from his pocket.

Jerek gathered her into his arms again. "Are you all right?"

"Yes, now that you're here." She tilted her head upwards.

"What happened here?"

"I'll tell you all about it back at the hotel," she whispered as she tugged his head down to meet her lips.

****

The weather behind the storm basked the evening sky with a sunset of red and gold streaks. Fresh, clean air floated in through open windows and filled the hotel with peace and tranquility. Everyone gathered around the long table in the dining room off the foyer for the evening meal. Jerek sat in his chair listening to Tim and Willie discussing the storm damage with little interest. He nodded to Pinkerton and Louden as they entered the room. Scrubbed clean and dressed as a commoner, Robert Louden looked nothing like a notorious criminal.

Upon their arrival, Ester had lit into the boat burner like a mother hen. She'd pecked and pecked until the man was red with embarrassment and hung his head lower than a naughty schoolboy.

The 'I told you so' look his wife gave Louden had made Jerek once again wonder what had happened above that pub on Beale Street. He had yet to confront his wife about finding her in the arms of another man; there just hadn't been time. Then again, maybe he didn't need to know. She was safe and hadn't betrayed him, never would, the rest was of little concern.

The kitchen door opened, and April, dressed from head to toe in yellow, glowed brighter than a sunflower in a field of daisies as she carried serving dishes into the room. She set the bowl of mashed potatoes in front of him and ran her hand up his arm before turning to return to the other room. Over her shoulder, she gave him a saucy wink and after a quick glance, assuring no one else looked her way, extravagantly rolled her hips while walking back to the kitchen.

He laughed aloud then smiled as the other men peered at him questionably. Helping his wife shed wet clothing, bathe in warm water, and redress in the shimmering gown had been delightful to say the least. And though she'd been ready to share her adventure, he'd silenced her mouth and demonstrated how fun sharing the bathing room could be. Without an ounce of protest, she'd joined in, and then hung around to scrub his back when the time came.

The kitchen door opened again, and this time he rose to pull the chair beside his out from the table. He placed a kiss on the top of her golden tresses as she sat down. Hearty appetites consumed the meal, and it wasn't until the dessert plates had been removed that the conversation turned to Louden.

Allan leaned back in his chair, rested a hand on the back of Robert's chair. "Mr. Louden has agreed to travel with me to St. Louis. There we'll record all of the data and facts, I'll find a suitable method to settle his adverse activities of late, and assure his payment is accepted by the government. I feel I can safely declare his days of Secret Service are over. With his assistance those who are the real leaders will be caught and punished." His gaze went to April. "It's going to take some time, but I pledge within the next two years, he'll be reunited with his daughters, and hopefully his wife."

Her hand squeezed Jerek's. "Thank you, Mr. Pinkerton."

The smile she gave Louden was so sincere it made Jerek's stomach gurgle. He remained silent but gave Allan a look that said they needed to talk. Her eyes settled on the side of his face. Not willing to pretend approval of the outcome, but happy Louden had been apprehended, he brushed his lips against her cheek.

Louden's only response was to send April a gaze full of worship.

Jerek folded his arms across his chest. April

loved him, and only he, of that he was certain, but his mind still had to sort out the outcomes of the day's events.

Louden cleared his throat. "Mr. Brinkley, I'll understand if you are unwilling to accept my apologies, but, well..." The man's gaze settled on April for a moment before he turned back to say, "I am sorry for my actions. Your wife made me take a hard look at what I had become and...It's not..." He shook his head. "Nothing turned out how I first thought it would. I...I don't even know how it all happened. How it all became so out of control. But April made me realize what is important, and I pray I have an opportunity to redeem myself."

A ripple raced up his spine. Jerek stretched an arm to curve around April's shoulders. Long ago imbedded manners made him give a slight nod in acknowledgment he'd heard the man confession.

Pinkerton gave one of his sniffling chuckles. "The information Robert has already shared has put me weeks ahead in my investigation."

Jerek raised an eyebrow.

"Do you think you'll be able to catch Davis?" Tim asked.

Pinkerton replied but Jerek no longer listened. Having his wife defend one of the worst criminals of the era was irksome. The only thing keeping him from leaping to his feet in outburst was the way her hand ran over his knee and up the inside of his thigh. Her movements were sly, concealed by the table, but the effect her hand had on him was very apparent and becoming more than he could tolerate.

Suzie's wide yawn was the out he needed. "Look's like someone's ready for bed." He pointed to the little girl. "It's been a long day, and probably time for all of us to call it a night."

"Oh, you poor little angel." Scarlet patted the child's hand. "How about I take you up and read you a story. Would you like that?"

Suzie gave a bright smile and nodded.

Willie pushed his chair back, but Scarlet stopped his movements. "That's all right, you stay and visit. We'll be fine." Scarlet took Suzie's hand and helped the child climb down from her chair. The woman patted their clasped hands with her other one then talking to the child, led her to the staircase.

No one else attempted to rise, Jerek gritted his teeth.

April let out a tiny giggle before she said, "I'm quite tired myself. I think I'll go up too."

He leaped to his feet and tugged the front of his suit coat together.

After he pulled her chair out, she looked at him with a teasing glint, patted his arm and said, "You can stay and visit."

He narrowed his eyes. "No, I think I'll join you."

She batted hers. "If you must."

"Oh, I must."

She giggled then began to bid goodnight to everyone. One at a time.

Not caring what anyone thought, he put his hands on her waist and as she continued to talk, turned her around and propelled her to the stairs. Below his fingers, her hips rolled to and fro as she walked up the stairs in front of him. He nipped at her neck and she giggled.

With the door securely locked behind them, he attacked. His searching lips locked onto hers. He ran his hands over every inch of shimmering yellow material covering her breasts. His fingers clasped onto the first button, intending to remove her clothing with agonizing slowness. Repayment for the way she'd been torturing him the last couple of hours.

Before the button slipped through the hole, a knock sounded on the door. Frustrated to the point of detonation, he glared at the door and growled. "Who is it?"

"It's Allan," the voice sounded startled.

April giggled, slipped from his arms and went to the door. She turned the key he'd left in the hole and opened the door.

Wearing a sheepish grin, Allan peeked in the room. "I'm sorry to interrupt, but I'll be leaving early in the morning and would like to talk with you before I leave."

Jerek looked at the ceiling. The last thing he wanted was to get caught up in a conversation with Pinkerton. His mind searched for a resolution. He did want to talk to Allan before he left, but...

"Come in, Mr. Pinkerton," April invited.

"Perhaps Jerek would come downstairs." Allan looked at him.

"No, come on in. I'm sure April is interested in what you have to say. We have no secrets." With her in the room, Pinkerton would make the conversation quick.

Allan pushed the door shut and accepted April's invitation to sit on the only chair in the room. She sat down on the bed and patted the mattress. Jerek ran a hand through his hair, sat down, and waited for Pinkerton to begin.

"Jerek, I just want you to know, I'll still see the Army investigates the *Sultana*, and why so many men where allowed to sail on her."

A twitch pricked his cheek. "You know who I feel is behind it all," he answered.

"Yes, they'll all be investigated." Pinkerton glanced to April. "Actually, what your wife arranged with Louden is better than I'd hoped for."

"Better than you hoped for? The man is a villain. A murderer!" Jerek stood and began to pace the floor. "I can understand how he brainwashed April, but Allan, you too?"

He flinched at the way April's lips pulled together.

Allan saved him. "He didn't brain wash anyone. You know as well as I do if he were arrested for his war crimes, he'd simply be pardoned without ever having to give up his secrets."

"He has the death penalty hanging over his head." Jerek pointed toward the window. "And what about the minefield he created out at that abandoned farm? Those bombs would have killed us if you hadn't known what to look for."

"Which is why I had some of Washburn's men ride out there with us. The Army dug them up and defused them. They won't harm anyone." Allan gave him a solemn stare. "We both know the death penalty won't be enforced."

He put both hands on the open window frame and leaned toward the breeze. Allan was right. The war was over. The government would hand out pardons like candy to try and get the country united again. He arched against the tension in his neck.

Allan continued, "This way we'll be given the inside workings of the Secret Service. Information we never anticipated gaining. Louden's adamant about being reunited with his daughters, and I believe he'll tell all to make it happen."

Jerek turned and let out a deep sigh. It wasn't what he wanted, but it was better than nothing, which is exactly what the Army would give Louden.

Pinkerton tipped his head at April. "Thank you, April. Whatever you said to him... Well, it hit home."

"He was simply following orders, not the mastermind behind it all." She shrugged. "He's a war victim, no different than thousands of others." Her hand rose. Jerek stepped closer to lace the tiny fingers amongst his. Her gaze begged him to understand. "So are his daughters. They deserve the chance to know their daddy, not just what other people think of him."

He wrapped his other hand over their entwined ones. There was more to her words than Robert Louden. She'd found a way to forgive her father through it all. The old, spite-filled April was being cleansed, and he knew how important it was to her. His anger leaked out like water through a sieve.

He sat down to brush his lips against her hair. "Allan will make sure it happens, don't fret, my dear."

She rested her head on his shoulder.

"I'll keep you updated," Allan said. He ran his hands over his knees. "Well, I just wanted to know you understand my actions, Jerek. Your aid has been invaluable the past few years, and I value your friendship."

"I do understand, and though it's hard to admit, I agree it is the best outcome." He rose and held his hand out to the man. "I value your friendship too, and we'll look forward to your visits whenever you're home."

Pinkerton rose and pumped Jerek's hand. "So you two are going to Ohio?"

He glanced to his wife.

Without a pause April said, "Yes, as soon as possible."

"We plan on leaving early, so I probably won't see you until I, too, arrive home. I'll look forward to the reunion," Allan said.

Jerek followed him across the room, said a final farewell and closed the door. April's hands slipped around his waist from behind. He turned, and instantly reinstated his plan of seduction. His hands massaged her curves as his feet glided them toward the bed.

The top button of her dress was ready to slip through the hole when another knock sounded on the door. His frustrated sigh was long and deep. Not exaggerated at all.

April didn't giggle this time, but sighed in disappointment as well.

A muffled, "April? Jerek? It's Willie, could I talk to you for a minute?" came through the door.

Her head fell against his chest.

Jerek lowered her to the bed then turned to shuffle to the door. He opened it, with a hand invited Willie to take the chair before he sat down on the bed and looked at the other man expectantly.

"Sorry, but Allan just told me you two plan on leaving for Ohio soon," Willie said.

"For a detective, he sure seems to have a loose tongue," April remarked.

Jerek chuckled. "Apparently."

Willie crossed his knees, but then uncrossed them to lean toward his sister. "I just wanted to tell you, I think I'm going to stay here in Memphis for awhile." His face bunched up like he expected her to disagree or box his ears.

She gave no outward complaint.

Willie started talking again, "The storm did some damage here, and Tim is too old to fix it all himself. And then there's Mrs. Hobbs. The woman was so kind to us, I'd like to repay her. Besides, you two are newlyweds and don't need a brother and niece tagging along."

Jerek wrapped an arm around her shoulders. "Willie, you'd be welcome to travel with us. We'd never consider you a tag, but we do respect your wishes to remain here. It may prove to be very profitable. Please know you'll always be welcome to visit us in Ohio as often and for as long as you wish."

"Thank you. I'm sure we'll be making a trip up that way before long. When do you plan on leaving?"

He looked to April and said, "Within the next day or so, as soon as we can make travel arrangements."

Willie nodded and rose to his feet. He bent down and kissed April's cheek. "Then I'll see you in the morning. Good night, Sissy."

Jerek walked Willie to the door and bade him a good night.

Before he had a chance to push the door closed April stepped in front of him and slammed it shut.

He stepped back. "April..."

"We're not answering this door again." She twisted the key in the lock. After the latch clicked, she withdrew the key and threw it.

The key flew across the room and out the open window. A faint, tinkling noise floated up from the street below. He turned and cradled her face. "If leaving Willie and Suzie upsets you, we can stay here for as long as you like."

"No, it's time Willie lives his own life, and I live mine. That doesn't upset me."

"Oh, well you seem a little upset."

"I am! For over three hours I've been trying to get my husband to take me to bed and I refuse to be interrupted again." April pulled his shirt from the waistband of his pants. With precise movements, she began to unbutton it.

Jerek laced one arm behind her knees, lifted, and then carried her to the bed. "You've been trying to get me into bed?"

Infatuating, coffee-brown eyes gazed deep into hers and took her breath away, just as they had that morning in the saloon in New Orleans. They touched her core, offering love, passion, and life.

"Yes," April said, intoxicated by promises.

"I thought I was trying to get you into bed." Jerek lowered her onto the mattress and started to separate the tiny buttons of her gown. "It's been my goal since I boarded the *Sultana*."

She stopped his hands and pulled her knees beneath her body to kneel on the bed. Face to face she wrapped her arms around his neck.

"Somehow that seems so long ago."

His hands cupped her waist. "I know."

"But it wasn't. A little more than a week ago, we sat in a fancy restaurant and toasted the year."

Jerek laughed. "I didn't toast the year."

"Yes, you did—"

"No, Willie made a toast to an April to remember." His lips brushed over hers. "And that's what I toasted to, the most remarkable April I had ever met, the woman I wanted to spend the rest of my life loving."

Her mouth led his in a long, gratifying kiss. "Thank you for boarding that boat. Thank you for saving my life. Thank you for making me the happiest person on earth."

"You're welcome." He ran a finger over her bottom lip. "I love you."

"We must think alike." She pushed his shirt wide to nuzzle and nip at his chest. "Because I love you too," her lips whispered against his skin as her fingers found the waistband of his pants.

"Good thing, us thinking alike." He finished unbuttoning her dress, spread the front open, and pushed it over her shoulders.

"It's a very good thing." She wiggled so the gown would slip to her waist. As long as there was breath in her body, she'd welcome his simplest touch, his ardor, and his love.

"Oh, yes, it's a very good thing." he whispered.

A word about the author...

As a young girl I remember spending warm summer days and long winter nights with Nancy Drew and Laura Ingalls-Wilder. As the years slipped by the books evolved into romance novels by Kathleen Woodiwiss, LaVyrle Spencer and a host of others. In 2000 when my husband said I should write one, I took the challenge, and have loved every moment of the journey. To create characters from once upon a time and lead them through a life that ends in happily ever after is such fun. Of course, you have to torture them a little bit along the way, and just like real-life children you often have to clean up after them. But, just like real children, they are worth it. My husband of more than twenty-five years, and I live in Minnesota, have three grown sons and the most precious gift ever--a granddaughter, Isabelle. I work as the resource development manager for our local United Way program, am a life-long Elvis fan (yes, I've been to Graceland) and love spending Sunday afternoons watching NASCAR with family and friends.

Contact Lauri at www.laurirobinson.blogspot.com

Thank you for purchasing
this Wild Rose Press publication.
For other wonderful stories of romance,
please visit our on-line bookstore at
www.thewildrosepress.com.

For questions or more information,
contact us at info@thewildrosepress.com.

The Wild Rose Press
www.TheWildRosePress.com

With unexplainable speed, she shot through the water. Gulps of air scorched aching lungs as her face broke the surface. Amongst the debris of wood, cargo and bodies, the colossal side of the *Sultana* careened. White-capped waves boiled, threatening to drive her into the massive hull or back into the frightening abyss below. Murky water hit the back of her throat before a scream could join hundreds of others echoing through the night.

She threw her head back, choking and gasping for air as her arms flayed against the assaulting water, and kicked both feet at the force lugging her downward. Something wrapped around one hand, and another strong heave wrenched her shoulder. She twisted away from the splashes trying to fill her mouth and nose. The steely grip tightened as it towed her away from the ship.

"Jerek!" Her free hand tried to latch onto the fingers wrapped around her wrist.

"I've got you!" he yelled above the roar of chaos. His other arm swiftly glided in and out of the water before it wrapped around a bobbing object. With a hard tug, he pulled her next to it. "Grab on with both hands!"

The current was too swift. Her skirt, yards of wet material, acted like a sail and tugged her away from him. The sleeve of his shirt threatened to slip from her fingers.

Jerek seized an elbow and thrust her forward. She wheezed for air as her chest slammed against the floating log.

His hands forced her arms around the cold, wet wood. "April! Don't let go! Don't you dare let go!"

Praise for *Mail Order Husband*
by Lauri Robinson:

"This book is a great read and I was not ready for it to end. I envision this book will be a keeper for many bookshelves; I highly recommend that you read it!"
~Brenda Talley, The Romance Studio

"I would recommend reading MAIL ORDER HUSBAND by Lauri Robinson."
~Julie Kornhausl, Romance Reader at Heart

"Ms. Robinson has written a delightful and witty tale with an eastern-born hero any cowgirl is going to love. I look forward to more from Lauri Robinson."
~Carol Aloisi, LoveWesternRomances.com

"Lauri Robinson has turned the tables on mail order forever."
~Arianna, Two Lips Reviews